CLASSIC IRISH
SHORT STORIES

CLASSIC
IRISH
SHORT STORIES

Selected and Introduced by
FRANK O'CONNOR

Oxford   New York
OXFORD UNIVERSITY PRESS

To the Memory of
AUGUSTA LADY GREGORY

Oxford University Press, Walton Street, Oxford OX2 6DP

Oxford New York Toronto
Delhi Bombay Calcutta Madras Karachi
Kuala Lumpur Singapore Hong Kong Tokyo
Nairobi Dar es Salaam Cape Town
Melbourne Auckland Madrid

and associated companies in
Berlin Ibadan

Oxford is a trade mark of Oxford University Press

First published as Modern Irish Short Stories 1957
Reprinted ten times
First issued as an Oxford University Press paperback with
the title Classic Irish Short Stories 1985

British Library Cataloguing in Publication Data
Data available

ISBN 0-19-281918-6

10

Printed in Great Britain by
Clays Ltd
Bungay, Suffolk

CONTENTS

v

CONTENTS

CONTENTS

INTRODUCTION

I believe that the Irish short story is a distinct art form: that is, by shedding the limitations of its popular origin it has become susceptible to development in the same way as German song, and in its attitudes it can be distinguished from Russian and American stories which have developed in the same way. The English novel, for instance, is very obviously an art form while the English short story is not.

The point is illustrated in three stories in this collection: the story of the County Cork inquest as told to Eric Cross by Timothy Buckley, the Tailor; Somerville and Ross's 'Lisheen Races, Second-hand'; and George Moore's 'Home Sickness'. Timothy Buckley was one of the really great folk story-tellers and severely criticized some of my own stories which someone had read him for their lack of 'marvels'. There is no lack of 'marvels' in 'Lisheen Races, Second-hand'; like most good English stories—Kipling's 'Bread Upon the Waters', for instance—it is a tale rather than a story. While Buckley's story *requires* an audience, this *implies* one. It contains more talent than Moore's story and shows far more knowledge of Irish life and character. But Moore's story is a masterpiece as the other is not. Its form is dictated solely by the material and not at all by the presence of an audience, real or imaginary. The difference is that between even the finest German folk-song and some little poem by Moerike set by Wolf. It is not necessary to take sides, merely to recognize that the former is rudimentary, the latter highly organized.

What accounts for the difference is not only that Moore's model was Russian rather than English. Besides that, one must also realize that in the meantime Yeats had effected a revolution, part literary, part political, against contemporary English literature which was dominated by money and rank. His movement affected even English writers of the period, and its effects can be perceived on Lawrence's early stories. One of the most famous of these, 'Odour of Chrysanthemums', is clearly a pastiche of Synge's *Riders to the Sea*. But generally, it affected mainly poetry and the theatre. Moore's *The Untilled Field* stands alone in its generation in Ireland.

The next generation produced a change. O'Kelly, Colum, Stephens, Corkery, had one foot in Yeats's camp, one in Moore's. Joyce's work represents a revolt against Yeats's romanticism. His early work, also influenced by Russian and French models, bears a strong resemblance to the early stories in *The Untilled Field*, but whereas Moore's stories develop a disillusionment that turns into polemic, Joyce's stories, though equally disillusioned, become formally more and more intricate. This was the direction that Joyce's talent continued to take for the rest of his life and it is illustrated fully in *Dubliners*. His problem—a problem for all naturalistic writers, and even for some realists—was what you use to replace the Tailor's 'marvels'. How do you arrive at organic form? Joyce does so by the use of metaphor and symbol. This was already an old device and one that Henry James frequently adopted. Joyce's original contribution to the technique was to use metaphor in a dissociated form, to conceal and disguise it as it is disguised in dreams, so that the whole story might be read without the reader's becoming aware of it. At its most elaborate—in *Ulysses*

—we find Mr. Bloom making use of an outdoor lavatory rather than climb upstairs because Mr. Bloom represents a reincarnation of Ulysses himself and the whole chapter in which he is introduced illustrates the doctrine of the transmigration of souls by reference to the transmutation of matter. 'The Dead' represents a rudimentary form of this technique, and only the most careful reading will elicit the complicated threads of metaphor that run through it. That Gretta takes three 'mortal' hours to dress is a simple example of a device that in *Ulysses* turns into a rolling stream of puns like the 'mortgage' or Molly's dress with the 'rip' in it.

His contemporaries, as I have said, still kept one foot in Yeats's camp. Corkery, though a city man, writes mainly of country people; Stephens uses mythological material. One may sometimes regret it and feel that it injured their talent. In Stephens, for example, under all the wit and warmth is a vision of life that makes Joyce's look like *Peg's Paper*. Beside the enchanting piece of fictionalized autobiography I have used, I wish I could have had space for a story like 'Hunger' to illustrate that darker side of his nature.

It was O'Casey and the Civil War between them which finally exploded the romantic myth of Yeats. O'Casey himself, as his fascinating autobiography shows, is the last of the romantics, and his great early plays were directed not against the gunmen and politicians as critics of the day believed but at the romantic in himself which made him—a poor, uneducated, sickly Dublin navvy—give himself to every cause from the Gaelic League to the Communist Party that seemed to promise a betterment of men's lot.

After him, writers like O'Flaherty, O'Faoláin, Mary Lavin, and myself turned from the theatre and adopted fiction—mainly the short story—as our medium. There

were, of course, other reasons for this than purely
literary ones, like the difficulties O'Casey himself encountered in dealing with a moribund theatre—but
there was also, what is always to be understood in the
short story, a turning away from the public to the
private thing. This tendency of the short story can be
illustrated by a comparison between Moore's 'Home
Sickness' and O'Flaherty's 'Going into Exile'. Moore,
writing when he did, cannot ignore the fact that emi-
gration is largely caused by the sheer boredom of
religious authoritarianism; O'Flaherty ignores everything but the nature of exile itself: a state of things
like love and death that all men must in some way
endure.

O'Flaherty is one of the most exciting of story-
tellers. He flings himself on a theme with the abandon-
ment and innocence of a child, completely unaware of
any reflections that might be made on it. 'The Fairy
Goose' is an amazing example of his skill. In its mira-
culous avoidance of any of the crudities that reflection
would demand—satire, irony, farce—it stands with
'Home Sickness' as one of my two favourite stories.
He, too, would need more space than I can afford.
Some of his best stories deal with animals, and the
nearer his characters approach to animals—the child
in 'Three Lambs' for instance—the happier he is in
dealing with them.

In this, he stands at another pole from Seán
O'Faoláin who is first and foremost a man of letters,
as Gide was. As with Gide his stories and novels are a
commentary on his biographies, histories, and essays.
To take a single example: his life of Constance Mar-
cievicz, the Irish society woman who became the
friend of the labour leader, James Larkin, and fought
in the insurrection of 1916, is almost contemporary

with his first book of stories, *Midsummer Night's Madness*, in which one character sings the praises of the Anglo-Irish aristocracy.

'I tell you I'm ashamed to be called an Irishman, and in fact I'm not an Irishman. I'm a colonist—a planter—whatever you like, one of those that tried to come and do something with you people.'

His life of Daniel O'Connell shows him coming to terms with Irish democracy, and the stories in *A Purse of Coppers* are full of a sort of wry resignation to the emotional and intellectual limitations of Irish life. Once more, the life of Hugh O'Neill, Earl of Tyrone, shows him searching for a prototype, this time on a higher social plane, and this is reflected in the collection of stories called *Teresa*, from which I have chosen two. Naturally, where O'Flaherty's work remains at a constant level of performance, O'Faoláin's is incalculable, always changing with his changing thought.

Elizabeth Bowen, like L. A. G. Strong, has her place in English literature, but she also has her corner in Irish. Hers is an art of arrangement rather than construction; her characters and incidents are disposed with an apparent casualness that conceals elaborate care. Mary Lavin's on the contrary have the solidity of characters and incidents in a novel. Her great gift as a story-teller is her remarkable power of gripping a subject till she has wrung everything from it. My own experience shows as much for I hesitated for a long time over 'The Will', wondering if anyone not brought up in an Irish Catholic home could grasp all its implications. Those friends to whom I showed it found no difficulty in understanding it.

O'Faoláin, O'Flaherty, and I wrote in the period of disillusionment which followed the Civil War, though with considerable respect for the nationalism that gave rise to it. The period immediately succeeding ours does not seem to have been a favourable one for literature. In Yeats's theatre the great Gaelic sagas have been turned into pantomime enlivened by jazz; the sentimental political songs of my youth like 'Bold Robert Emmett' are sung by my juniors in the manner of 'She was pore but she was Honest'. The outstanding figure of the period is Brian O'Nolan, the brilliant columnist of the *Irish Times*. In Mr. Garrity's anthology he is represented by a story on the well-known Resistance theme of the woman who, to protect her hunted men, pretends to be a prostitute. It is probably as old as history but Mr. O'Nolan must be the first writer to have treated it as farce.

It is remarkable that the period should have produced two story-tellers as good as Bryan MacMahon and Michael McLaverty. MacMahon is a poet and a Kerryman; he delights as much as Synge did in vivid speech and characters blown up with romantic eloquence. After re-reading his two volumes of stories I was left with the delighted impression that in the rainiest country in Europe it was always sunlight. McLaverty, on the other hand, is all that Northern Irish people like to imagine themselves to be when they contrast themselves with us of the South; truthful and restrained.

Since then there is evidence of another change of temper in the younger writers. There is a new firmness and harshness in the work of James Plunkett which is obviously very deeply influenced by that of Joyce. Though he has still not solved for himself Joyce's problem of reconciling verisimilitude with artistic form, and though he spoils some of his best stories with forced symbolic contrivances, he is obviously a story-teller of high seriousness. I believe one can detect a rather similar change of temper in the work of some of the younger novelists, Benedict Kiely and Val Mulkerns, for example.

I have preferred to keep to my own idea of the short story as an art form distinct from the tale, though I realize that the distinction may be more philosophical than critical. As I understand it, the short story derives from the novel, and like the novel has attempted successfully to combine artistic and scientific truth. The latter is not an artistic standard—critics who disapprove of it are right in this—but it is its application to artistic ends that has made fiction the greatest of the modern arts.

FRANK O'CONNOR

Home Sickness

GEORGE MOORE

(1852–1933)

HE told the doctor he was due in the bar-room at eight
o'clock in the morning; the bar-room was in a slum in
the Bowery; and he had only been able to keep himself in health by getting up at five o'clock and going
for long walks in the Central Park.

'A sea voyage is what you want,' said the doctor.
'Why not go to Ireland for two or three months? You
will come back a new man.'

'I'd like to see Ireland again.'

And he began to wonder how the people at home
were getting on. The doctor was right. He thanked
him, and three weeks afterwards he landed in Cork.

As he sat in the railway carriage he recalled his
native village—he could see it and its lake, and then
the fields one by one, and the roads. He could see a
large piece of rocky land—some three or four hundred
acres of headland stretching out into the winding lake.
Upon this headland the peasantry had been given permission to build their cabins by former owners of the
Georgian house standing on the pleasant green hill.
The present owners considered the village a disgrace,
but the villagers paid high rents for their plots of
ground, and all the manual labour that the Big House
required came from the village: the gardeners, the
stable helpers, the house and the kitchen maids.

Bryden had been thirteen years in America, and

1

when the train stopped at his station, he looked round to see if there were any changes in it. It was just the same blue limestone station-house as it was thirteen years ago. The platform and the sheds were the same, and there were five miles of road from the station to Duncannon. The sea voyage had done him good, but five miles were too far for him today; the last time he had walked the road, he had walked it in an hour and a half, carrying a heavy bundle on a stick.

He was sorry he did not feel strong enough for the walk, the evening was fine, and he would meet many people coming home from the fair, some of whom he had known in his youth, and they would tell him where he could get a clean lodging. But the carman would be able to tell him that; he called the car that was waiting at the station, and soon he was answering questions about America. But he wanted to hear of those who were still living in the old country, and after hearing the stories of many people he had forgotten, he heard that Mike Scully, who had been away in a situation for many years as a coachman in the King's County, had come back and built a fine house with a concrete floor. Now there was a good loft in Mike Scully's house, and Mike would be pleased to take in a lodger.

Bryden remembered that Mike had been in a situation at the Big House; he had intended to be a jockey, but had suddenly shot up into a fine tall man, and had had to become a coachman instead. Bryden tried to recall the face, but he could only remember a straight nose, and a somewhat dusky complexion. Mike was one of the heroes of his childhood, and now his youth floated before him, and he caught glimpses of himself, something that was more than a phantom and less than a reality. Suddenly his reverie was broken: the carman pointed with his whip, and Bryden saw a tall, finely built, middle-aged man coming through the gates, and the driver said:

'There's Mike Scully.'

Mike had forgotten Bryden even more completely than Bryden had forgotten him, and many aunts and uncles were mentioned before he began to understand.

'You've grown into a fine man, James,' he said, looking at Bryden's great width of chest. 'But you are thin in the cheeks, and you're very sallow in the cheeks too.'

'I haven't been very well lately—that is one of the reasons I have come back; but I want to see you all again.'

Bryden paid the carman, wished him 'God-speed', and he and Mike divided the luggage between them, Mike carrying the bag and Bryden the bundle, and they walked round the lake, for the townland was at the back of the demesne; and while they walked, James proposed to pay Mike ten shillings a week for his board and lodging.

He remembered the woods thick and well-forested; now they were windworn, the drains were choked, and the bridge leading across the lake inlet was falling away. Their way led between long fields where herds of cattle were grazing; the road was broken—Bryden wondered how the villagers drove their carts over it, and Mike told him that the landlord could not keep it in repair, and he would not allow it to be kept in repair out of the rates, for then it would be a public road, and he did not think there should be a public road through his property.

At the end of many fields they came to the village, and it looked a desolate place, even on this fine evening, and Bryden remarked that the county did not seem to be as much lived in as it used to be. It was at

3

once strange and familiar to see the chickens in the kitchen; and, wishing to re-knit himself to the old habits, he begged of Mrs. Scully not to drive them out, saying he did not mind them. Mike told his wife that Bryden was born in Duncannon, and when she heard Bryden's name she gave him her hand, after wiping it in her apron, saying he was heartily welcome, only she was afraid he would not care to sleep in a loft.

'Why wouldn't I sleep in a loft, a dry loft! You're thinking a good deal of America over here,' said he, 'but I reckon it isn't all you think it. Here you work when you like and you sit down when you like; but when you have had a touch of blood-poisoning as I had, and when you have seen young people walking with a stick, you think that there is something to be said for old Ireland.'

'Now won't you be taking a sup of milk? You'll be wanting a drink after travelling,' said Mrs. Scully.

And when he had drunk the milk Mike asked him if he would like to go inside or if he would like to go for a walk.

'Maybe it is sitting down you would like to be.'

And they went into the cabin, and started to talk about the wages a man could get in America, and the long hours of work.

And after Bryden had told Mike everything about America that he thought of interest, he asked Mike about Ireland. But Mike did not seem to be able to tell him much that was of interest. They were all very poor —poorer, perhaps, than when he left them.

'I don't think anyone except myself has a five pound note to his name.'

Bryden hoped he felt sufficiently sorry for Mike. But after all Mike's life and prospects mattered little to him. He had come back in search of health; and he felt better already; the milk had done him good, and the bacon and cabbage in the pot sent forth a savoury odour. The Scullys were very kind, they pressed him to make a good meal; a few weeks of country air and food, they said, would give him back the health he had lost in the Bowery; and when Bryden said he was longing for a smoke, Mike said there was no better sign than that. During his long illness he had never wanted to smoke, and he was a confirmed smoker.

It was comfortable to sit by the mild peat fire watching the smoke of their pipes drifting up the chimney, and all Bryden wanted was to be let alone; he did not want to hear of anyone's misfortunes, but about nine o'clock a number of villagers came in, and their appearance was depressing. Bryden remembered one or two of them—he used to know them very well when he was a boy; their talk was as depressing as their appearance, and he could feel no interest whatever in them. He was not moved when he heard that Higgins the stone-mason was dead; he was not affected when he heard that Mary Kelly, who used to go to do the laundry at the Big House, had married; he was only interested when he heard she had gone to America. No, he had not met her there; America is a big place. Then one of the peasants asked him if he remembered Patsy Carabine, who used to do the gardening at the Big House. Yes, he remembered Patsy well. Patsy was in the poor-house. He had not been able to do any work on account of his arm; his house had fallen in; he had given up his holding and gone into the poor-house. All this was very sad, and to avoid hearing any further unpleasantness, Bryden began to tell them about America. And they sat round listening to him; but all the talking was on his side; he wearied of it; and looking round the group he recognized a ragged hunchback with grey hair; twenty years ago he was a young hunchback, and, turning to him, Bryden asked him if he were doing well with his five acres.

'Ah, not much. This has been a bad season. The potatoes failed; they were watery—there is no diet in them.'

These peasants were all agreed that they could make nothing out of their farms. Their regret was that they had not gone to America when they were young; and after striving to take an interest in the fact that O'Connor had lost a mare and foal worth forty pounds Bryden began to wish himself back in the slum. When they left the house he wondered if every evening would be like the present one. Mike piled fresh sods on the fire, and he hoped it would show enough light in the loft for Bryden to undress himself by.

The cackling of some geese in the road kept him awake, and the loneliness of the country seemed to penetrate to his bones, and to freeze the marrow in them. There was a bat in the loft—a dog howled in the distance—and then he drew the clothes over his head. Never had he been so unhappy, and the sound of Mike breathing by his wife's side in the kitchen added to his nervous terror. Then he dozed a little; and lying on his back he dreamed he was awake, and the men he had seen sitting round the fireside that evening seemed to him like spectres come out of some unknown region of morass and reedy tarn. He stretched out his hands for his clothes, determined to fly from this house, but remembering the lonely road that led to the station he fell back on his pillow. The geese still cackled, but he was too tired to be kept awake any longer. He seemed to have been asleep only a few minutes when he heard Mike calling him. Mike had come half-way up the ladder and was telling him that breakfast was ready.

6

'What kind of breakfast will he give me?' Bryden asked himself as he pulled on his clothes. There were tea and hot griddle cakes for breakfast, and there were fresh eggs; there was sunlight in the kitchen, and he liked to hear Mike tell of the work he was going to do in the fields. Mike rented a farm of about fifteen acres, at least ten of it was grass; he grew an acre of potatoes and some corn, and some turnips for his sheep. He had a nice bit of meadow, and he took down his scythe, and as he put the whetstone in his belt Bryden noticed a second scythe, and he asked Mike if he should go down with him and help him to finish the field.

'You haven't done any mowing this many a year; I don't think you'd be of much help. You'd better go for a walk by the lake, but you may come in the afternoon if you like and help to turn the grass over.'

Bryden was afraid he would find the lake shore very lonely, but the magic of returning health is sufficient distraction for the convalescent, and the morning passed agreeably. The weather was still and sunny. He could hear the ducks in the reeds. The days dreamed themselves away, and it became his habit to go to the lake every morning. One morning he met the landlord, and they walked together, talking of the country, of what it had been, and the ruin it was slipping into. James Bryden told him that ill health had brought him back to Ireland; and the landlord lent him his boat, and Bryden rowed about the islands, and resting upon his oars he looked at the old castles, and remembered the prehistoric raiders that the landlord had told him about. He came across the stones to which the lake dwellers had tied their boats, and these signs of ancient Ireland were pleasing to Bryden in his present mood.

As well as the great lake there was a smaller lake in

7

the bog where the villagers cut their turf. This lake was famous for its pike, and the landlord allowed Bryden to fish there, and one evening when he was looking for a frog with which to bait his line he met Margaret Dirken driving home the cows for the milking. Margaret was the herdsman's daughter, and she lived in a cottage near the Big House; but she came up to the village whenever there was a dance, and Bryden had found himself opposite to her in the reels. But until this evening he had had little opportunity of speaking to her, and he was glad to speak to someone, for the evening was lonely, and they stood talking together.

'You're getting your health again,' she said. 'You'll soon be leaving us.'

'I'm in no hurry.'

'You're grand people over there; I hear a man is paid four dollars a day for his work.'

'And how much,' said James, 'has he to pay for his food and for his clothes?'

Her cheeks were bright and her teeth small, white, and beautifully even; and a woman's soul looked at Bryden out of her soft Irish eyes. He was troubled and turned aside, and catching sight of a frog looking at him out of a tuft of grass he said—

'I have been looking for a frog to put upon my pike line.'

The frog jumped right and left, and nearly escaped in some bushes, but he caught it and returned with it in his hand.

'It is just the kind of frog a pike will like,' he said. 'Look at its great white belly and its bright yellow back.'

And without more ado he pushed the wire to which the hook was fastened through the frog's fresh body,

8

and dragging it through the mouth he passed the hooks through the hind legs and tied the line to the end of the wire.

'I think,' said Margaret, 'I must be looking after my cows; it's time I got them home.'

'Won't you come down to the lake while I set my line?'

She thought for a moment and said:

'No, I'll see you from here.'

He went down to the reedy tarn, and at his approach several snipe got up, and they flew above his head uttering sharp cries. His fishing-rod was a long hazel stick, and he threw the frog as far as he could into the lake. In doing this he roused some wild ducks; a mallard and two ducks got up, and they flew toward the larger lake. Margaret watched them; they flew in a line with an old castle; and they had not disappeared from view when Bryden came toward her, and he and she drove the cows home together that evening.

They had not met very often when she said, 'James, you had better not come here so often calling to me.'

'Don't you wish me to come?'

'Yes, I wish you to come well enough, but keeping company is not the custom of the country, and I don't want to be talked about.'

'Are you afraid the priest would speak against us from the altar?'

'He has spoken against keeping company, but it is not so much what the priest says, for there is no harm in talking.'

'But if you are going to be married there is no harm in walking out together.'

'Well, not so much, but marriages are made differently in these parts; there is not much courting here.'

And next day it was known in the village that James was going to marry Margaret Dirken.

His desire to excel the boys in dancing had caused a stir of gaiety in the parish, and for some time past there had been dancing in every house where there was a floor fit to dance upon; and if the cottager had no money to pay for a barrel of beer, James Bryden, who had money, sent him a barrel, so that Margaret might get her dance. She told him that they sometimes crossed over into another parish where the priest was not so averse to dancing, and James wondered. And next morning at Mass he wondered at their simple fervour. Some of them held their hands above their head as they prayed, and all this was very new and very old to James Bryden. But the obedience of these people to their priest surprised him. When he was a lad they had not been so obedient, or he had forgotten their obedience; and he listened in mixed anger and wonderment to the priest, who was scolding his parishioners, speaking to them by name, saying that he had heard there was dancing going on in their homes. Worse than that, he said he had seen boys and girls loitering about the roads, and the talk that went on was of one kind—love. He said that newspapers containing love stories were finding their way into the people's houses, stories about love, in which there was nothing elevating or ennobling. The people listened, accepting the priest's opinion without question. And their submission was pathetic. It was the submission of a primitive people clinging to religious authority, and Bryden contrasted the weakness and incompetence of the people about him with the modern restlessness and cold energy of the people he had left behind him.

One evening, as they were dancing, a knock came

to the door, and the piper stopped playing, and the dancers whispered:

'Someone has told on us; it is the priest.'

And the awe-stricken villagers crowded round the cottage fire, afraid to open the door. But the priest said that if they did not open the door he would put his shoulder to it and force it open. Bryden went towards the door, saying he would allow no one to threaten him, priest or no priest, but Margaret caught his arm and told him that if he said anything to the priest, the priest would speak against them from the altar, and they would be shunned by the neighbours. It was Mike Scully who went to the door and let the priest in, and he came in saying they were dancing their souls into hell.

'I've heard of your goings on,' he said—'of your beer-drinking and dancing. I will not have it in my parish. If you want that sort of thing you had better go to America.'

'If that is intended for me, sir, I will go back to-morrow. Margaret can follow.'

'It isn't the dancing, it's the drinking I'm opposed to,' said the priest, turning to Bryden.

'Well, no one has drunk too much, sir,' said Bryden.

'But you'll sit here drinking all night,' and the priest's eyes went toward the corner where the women had gathered, and Bryden felt that the priest looked on the women as more dangerous than the porter. 'It's after midnight,' he said, taking out his watch.

By Bryden's watch it was only half-past eleven, and while they were arguing about the time Mrs. Scully offered Bryden's umbrella to the priest, for in his hurry to stop the dancing the priest had gone out without his; and, as if to show Bryden that he bore him no ill will, the priest accepted the loan of the umbrella, for

11

he was thinking of the big marriage fee that Bryden would pay him.

'I shall be badly off for the umbrella tomorrow,' Bryden said, as soon as the priest was out of the house. He was going with his father-in-law to a fair. His father-in-law was learning him how to buy and sell cattle. And his father-in-law was saying that the country was mending, and that a man might become rich in Ireland if he only had a little capital. Bryden had the capital, and Margaret had an uncle on the other side of the lake who would leave her all he had, that would be fifty pounds, and never in the village of Duncannon had a young couple begun life with so much prospect of success as would James Bryden and Margaret Dirken.

Some time after Christmas was spoken of as the best time for the marriage; James Bryden said that he would not be able to get his money out of America before the spring. The delay seemed to vex him, and he seemed anxious to be married, until one day he received a letter from America, from a man who had served in the bar with him. This friend wrote to ask Bryden if he were coming back. The letter was no more than a passing wish to see Bryden again. Yet Bryden stood looking at it, and everyone wondered what could be in the letter. It seemed momentous, and they hardly believed him when he said it was from a friend who wanted to know if his health were better. He tried to forget the letter, and he looked at the worn fields, divided by walls of loose stones, and a great longing came upon him.

The smell of the Bowery slum had come across the Atlantic, and had found him out in this western headland; and one night he awoke from a dream in which he was hurling some drunken customer through the

12

open doors into the darkness. He had seen his friend
in his white duck jacket throwing drink from glass into
glass amid the din of voices and strange accents; he
had heard the clang of money as it was swept into the
till, and his sense sickened for the bar-room. But how
should he tell Margaret Dirken that he could not marry
her? She had built her life upon this marriage. He
could not tell her that he would not marry her . . . yet
he must go. He felt as if he were being hunted; the
thought that he must tell Margaret that he could not
marry her hunted him day after day as a weasel hunts
a rabbit. Again and again he went to meet her with the
intention of telling her that he did not love her, that
their lives were not for one another, that it had all
been a mistake, and that happily he had found out it
was a mistake soon enough. But Margaret, as if she
guessed what he was about to speak of, threw her
arms about him and begged him to say he loved her,
and that they would be married at once. He agreed
that he loved her, and that they would be married at
once. But he had not left her many minutes before the
feeling came upon him that he could not marry her—
that he must go away. The smell of the bar-room
hunted him down. Was it for the sake of the money
that he might make there that he wished to go back?
No, it was not the money. What then? His eyes fell on
the bleak country, on the little fields divided by bleak
walls; he remembered the pathetic ignorance of the
people, and it was these things that he could not endure. It was the priest who came to forbid the dancing.
Yes, it was the priest. As he stood looking at the line of
the hills the bar-room seemed by him. He heard the
politicians, and the excitement of politics was in his
blood again. He must go away from this place—he
must get back to the bar-room. Looking up, he saw the

scanty orchard, and he hated the spare road that led to the village, and he hated the little hill at the top of which the village began, and he hated more than all other places the house where he was to live with Margaret Dirken—if he married her. He could see it from where he stood—by the edge of the lake, with twenty acres of pasture land about it, for the landlord had given up part of his demesne land to them.

He caught sight of Margaret, and he called her to come through the stile.

'I have just had a letter from America.'

'About the money?' she said.

'Yes, about the money. But I shall have to go over there.'

He stood looking at her, seeking for words; and she guessed from his embarrassment that he would say to her that he must go to America before they were married.

'Do you mean, James, you will have to go at once?'

'Yes,' he said, 'at once. But I shall come back in time to be married in August. It will only mean delaying our marriage a month.'

They walked on a little way talking, and every step he took James felt that he was a step nearer the Bowery slum. And when they came to the gate Bryden said:

'I must hasten or I shall miss the train.'

'But,' she said, 'you are not going now—you are not going today?'

'Yes, this morning. It is seven miles. I shall have to hurry not to miss the train.'

And then she asked him if he would ever come back.

'Yes,' he said, 'I am coming back.'

'If you are coming back, James, why not let me go with you?'

14

'You could not walk fast enough. We should miss the train.'

'One moment, James. Don't make me suffer; tell me the truth. You are not coming back. Your clothes— where shall I send them?'

He hurried away, hoping he would come back. He tried to think that he liked the country he was leaving, that it would be better to have a farmhouse and live there with Margaret Dirken than to serve drinks behind a counter in the Bowery. He did not think he was telling her a lie when he said he was coming back. Her offer to forward his clothes touched his heart, and at the end of the road he stood and asked himself if he should go back to her. He would miss the train if he waited another minute, and he ran on. And he would have missed the train if he had not met a car. Once he was on the car he felt himself safe—the country was already behind him. The train and the boat at Cork were mere formulae; he was already in America.

The moment he landed he felt the thrill of home that he had not found in his native village, and he wondered how it was that the smell of the bar seemed more natural than the smell of fields, and the roar of crowds more welcome than the silence of the lake's edge. He offered up a thanksgiving for his escape, and entered into negotiations for the purchase of the barroom.

·　·　·　·　·

He took a wife, she bore him sons and daughters, the bar-room prospered, property came and went; he grew old, his wife died, he retired from business, and reached the age when a man begins to feel there are not many years in front of him, and that all he has had to do in life has been done. His children married, lonesomeness began to creep about him in the evening and when he looked into the fire-light, a vague, tender reverie floated up, and Margaret's soft eyes and name vivified the dusk. His wife and children passed out of mind, and it seemed to him that a memory was the only real thing he possessed, and the desire to see Margaret again grew intense. But she was an old woman, she had married, maybe she was dead. Well, he would like to be buried in the village where he was born.

There is an unchanging, silent life within every man that none knows but himself, and his unchanging, silent life was his memory of Margaret Dirken. The bar-room was forgotten and all that concerned it and the things he saw most clearly were the green hill-side, and the bog lake and the rushes about it, and the greater lake in the distance, and behind it the blue line of wandering hills.

Lisheen Races, Second-hand

E. Œ. SOMERVILLE *and* MARTIN ROSS
(1858–1949)   (1862–1915)

IT may or may not be agreeable to have attained the age of thirty-eight, but, judging from old photographs, the privilege of being nineteen has also its drawbacks. I turned over page after page of an ancient book in which were enshrined portraits of the friends of my youth, singly, in David and Jonathan couples, and in groups in which I, as it seemed to my mature and possibly jaundiced perception, always contrived to look the most immeasurable young bounder of the lot. Our faces were fat, and yet I cannot remember ever having

16

been considered fat in my life; we indulged in low-necked shirts, in 'Jemima' ties with diagonal stripes; we wore coats that seemed three sizes too small, and trousers that were three sizes too big; we also wore small whiskers.

I stopped at last at one of the David and Jonathan memorial portraits. Yes, here was the object of my researches; this stout and earnestly romantic youth was Leigh Kelway, and that fatuous and chubby young person seated on the arm of his chair was myself. Leigh Kelway was a young man ardently believed in by a large circle of admirers, headed by himself and seconded by me, and for some time after I had left Magdalen for Sandhurst, I maintained a correspondence with him on large and abstract subjects. This phase of our friendship did not survive; I went soldiering to India, and Leigh Kelway took honours and moved suitably on into politics, as is the duty of an earnest young Radical with useful family connexions and an independent income. Since then I had at intervals seen in the papers the name of the Honourable Basil Leigh Kelway mentioned as a speaker at elections, as a writer of thoughtful articles in the reviews, but we had never met, and nothing could have been less expected by me than the letter, written from Mrs. Raverty's Hotel, Skebawn, in which he told me he was making a tour in Ireland with Lord Waterbury, to whom he was private secretary. Lord Waterbury was at present having a few days' fishing near Killarney, and he himself, not being a fisherman, was collecting statistics for his chief on various points connected with the Liquor Question in Ireland. He had heard that I was in the neighbourhood, and was kind enough to add that it would give him much pleasure to meet me again.

With a stir of the old enthusiasm I wrote begging

17

him to be my guest for as long as it suited him, and the following afternoon he arrived at Shreelane. The stout young friend of my youth had changed considerably. His important nose and slightly prominent teeth remained, but his wavy hair had withdrawn intellectually from his temples; his eyes had acquired a statesmanlike absence of expression, and his neck had grown long and bird-like. It was his first visit to Ireland, as he lost no time in telling me, and he and his chief had already collected much valuable information on the subject to which they had dedicated the Easter recess. He further informed me that he thought of popularizing the subject in a novel, and therefore intended to, as he put it, 'master the brogue' before his return.

During the next few days I did my best for Leigh Kelway. I turned him loose on Father Scanlan; I showed him Mohona, our champion village, that boasts fifteen public-houses out of twenty buildings of sorts and a railway station; I took him to hear the prosecution of a publican for selling drink on a Sunday, which gave him an opportunity of studying perjury as a fine art, and of hearing a lady, on whom police suspicion justly rested, profoundly summed up by the sergeant as 'a woman who had th' appairance of having knocked at a back door'.

The net result of these experiences has not yet been given to the world by Leigh Kelway. For my own part, I had at the end of three days arrived at the conclusion that his society, when combined with a notebook and a thirst for statistics, was not what I used to find it at Oxford. I therefore welcomed a suggestion from Mr. Flurry Knox that we should accompany him to some typical country races, got up by the farmers at a place called Lisheen, some twelve miles away. It was the worst road in the district, the races of the most grossly unorthodox character; in fact, it was the very place for Leigh Kelway to collect impressions of Irish life, and in any case it was a blessed opportunity of disposing of him for the day.

In my guest's attire next morning I discerned an unbending from the role of cabinet minister towards that of sportsman; the outlines of the notebook might be traced in his breast pocket, but traversing it was the strap of a pair of field-glasses, and his light grey suit was smart enough for Goodwood.

Flurry was to drive us to the races at one o'clock, and we walked to Tory Cottage by the short cut over the hill, in the sunny beauty of an April morning. Up to the present the weather had kept me in a more or less apologetic condition; anyone who has entertained a guest in the country knows the unjust weight of responsibility that rests on the shoulders of the host in the matter of climate, and Leigh Kelway, after two drenchings, had become sarcastically resigned to what I felt he regarded as my mismanagement.

Flurry took us into the house for a drink and a biscuit, to keep us going, as he said, till 'we lifted some luncheon out of the Castle Knox people at the races', and it was while we were thus engaged that the first disaster of the day occurred. The dining-room door was open, so also was the window of the little staircase just outside it, and through the window travelled sounds that told of the close proximity of the stable-yard; the clattering of hoofs on cobble-stones, and voices uplifted in loud conversation. Suddenly from this region there arose a screech of the laughter peculiar to kitchen flirtation, followed by the clank of a bucket, the plunging of a horse, and then an uproar of wheels and galloping hoofs. An instant afterwards Flurry's chestnut cob, in a dogcart, dashed at full gallop into view, with the reins streaming behind him, and two men in hot pursuit. Almost before I had time to realize what had happened, Flurry jumped through the half-opened window of the dining-room like a clown at a pantomime, and joined in the chase; but the cob was resolved to make the most of his chance, and went away down the drive and out of sight at a pace that distanced everyone save the kennel terrier, who sped in shrieking ecstasy beside him.

'Oh merciful hour!' exclaimed a female voice behind me. Leigh Kelway and I were by this time watching the progress of events from the gravel, in company with the remainder of Flurry's household. 'The horse is desthroyed! Wasn't that the quare start he took! And all in the world I done was to slap a bucket of wather at Michael out the windy, and 'twas himself got it in place of Michael!'

'Ye'll never ate another bit, Bridgie Dunnigan,' replied the cook, with the exulting pessimism of her kind. 'The Master'll have your life!'

Both speakers shouted at the top of their voices, probably because in spirit they still followed afar the flight of the cob.

Leigh Kelway looked serious as we walked on down the drive. I almost dared to hope that a note on the degrading oppression of Irish retainers was shaping itself. Before we reached the bend of the drive the rescue party was returning with the fugitive, all, with the exception of the kennel terrier, looking extremely gloomy. The cob had been confronted by a wooden gate, which he had unhesitatingly taken in his stride, landing on his head on the farther side with the gate and the cart on top of him, and had arisen with a lame foreleg, a cut on his nose, and several other minor wounds.

'You'd think the brute had been fighting the cats, with all the scratches and scrapes he has on him!' said Flurry, casting a vengeful eye at Michael, 'and one shaft's broken and so is the dashboard. I haven't another horse in the place; they're all out at grass, and so there's an end of the races!'

We all three stood blankly on the hall-door steps and watched the wreck of the trap being trundled up the avenue.

'I'm very sorry you're done out of your sport,' said Flurry to Leigh Kelway, in tones of deplorable sincerity; 'perhaps, as there's nothing else to do, you'd like to see the hounds—?'

I felt for Flurry, but of the two I felt more for Leigh Kelway as he accepted this alleviation. He disliked dogs, and held the newest views on sanitation, and I knew what Flurry's kennels could smell like. I was lighting a precautionary cigarette, when we caught sight of an old man riding up the drive. Flurry stopped short.

'Hold on a minute,' he said; 'here's an old chap that often brings me horses for the kennels; I must see what he wants.'

The man dismounted and approached Mr. Knox, hat in hand, towing after him a gaunt and ancient black mare with a big knee.

'Well, Barrett,' began Flurry, surveying the mare with his hands in his pockets, 'I'm not giving the hounds meat this month, or only very little.'

'Ah, Master Flurry,' answered Barrett, 'it's you that's pleasant! Is it give the like o' this one for the dogs to ate! She's a vallyble strong young mare, no more than shixteen years of age, and ye'd sooner be lookin' at her goin' under a side-car than eatin' your dinner.'

'There isn't as much meat on her as 'd fatten a jackdaw,' said Flurry, clinking the silver in his pockets as he searched for a matchbox. 'What are you asking for her?'

The old man drew cautiously up to him.

'Master Flurry,' he said solemnly, 'I'll sell her to *your* honour for five pounds, and she'll be worth ten after you give her a month's grass.'

Flurry lit his cigarette; then he said imperturbably, 'I'll give you seven shillings for her.'

Old Barrett put on his hat in silence, and in silence buttoned his coat and took hold of the stirrup leather. Flurry remained immovable.

'Master Flurry,' said old Barrett suddenly, with tears in his voice, 'you must make it eight, sir!'

'Michael!' called out Flurry with apparent irrelevance, 'run up to your father's and ask him would he lend me a loan of his side-car.'

Half an hour later we were, improbable as it may seem, on our way to Lisheen races. We were seated upon an outside-car of immemorial age, whose joints seemed to open and close again as it swung in and out of the ruts, whose tattered cushions stank of rats and mildew, whose wheels staggered and rocked like the legs of a drunken man. Between the shafts jogged the latest addition to the kennel larder, the eight-shilling mare. Flurry sat on one side, and kept her going at a rate of not less than four miles an hour; Leigh Kelway and I held on to the other.

'She'll get us as far as Lynch's anyway,' said Flurry, abandoning his first contention that she could do the whole distance, as he pulled her on to her legs after her fifteenth stumble, 'and he'll lend us some sort of a horse, if it was only a mule.'

'Do you notice that these cushions are very

22

damp?' said Leigh Kelway to me, in a hollow undertone.

'Small blame to them if they are!' replied Flurry. 'I've no doubt but they were out under the rain all day yesterday at Mrs. Hurly's funeral.'

Leigh Kelway made no reply, but he took his notebook out of his pocket and sat on it.

We arrived at Lynch's at a little past three, and were there confronted by the next disappointment of this disastrous day. The door of Lynch's farmhouse was locked, and nothing replied to our knocking except a puppy, who barked hysterically from within.

'All gone to the races,' said Flurry philosophically, picking his way round the manure heap. 'No matter, here's the filly in the shed here. I know he's had her under a car.'

An agitating ten minutes ensued, during which Leigh Kelway and I got the eight-shilling mare out of the shafts and the harness, and Flurry, with our inefficient help, crammed the young mare into them. As Flurry had stated that she had been driven before, I was bound to believe him, but the difficulty of getting the bit into her mouth was remarkable, and so also was the crab-like manner in which she sidled out of the yard, with Flurry and myself at her head, and Leigh Kelway hanging on to the back of the car to keep it from jamming in the gateway.

'Sit up on the car now,' said Flurry when we got out on to the road; 'I'll lead her on a bit. She's been ploughed anyway; one side of her mouth's as tough as a gad!'

Leigh Kelway threw away the wisp of grass with which he had been cleaning his hands, and mopped his intellectual forehead; he was very silent. We both mounted the car, and Flurry, with the reins in his hand, walked beside the filly, who, with her tail clasped in, moved onward in a succession of short jerks.

'Oh, she's all right!' said Flurry, beginning to run, and dragging the filly into a trot; 'once she gets started—' Here the filly spied a pig in a neighbouring field, and despite the fact that she had probably eaten out of the same trough with it, she gave a violent side spring, and broke into a gallop.

'Now we're off!' shouted Flurry, making a jump at the car and clambering on; 'if the traces hold we'll do!'

The English language is powerless to suggest the view-halloo with which Mr. Knox ended his speech, or to do more than indicate the rigid anxiety of Leigh Kelway's face as he regained his balance after the preliminary jerk, and clutched the back rail. It must be said for Lynch's filly that she did not kick; she merely fled, like a dog with a kettle tied to its tail, from the pursuing rattle and jingle behind her, with the shafts buffeting her dusty sides as the car swung to and fro. Whenever she showed any signs of slackening, Flurry loosed another yell at her that renewed her panic, and thus we precariously covered another two or three miles of our journey.

Had it not been for a large stone lying on the road, and had the filly not chosen to swerve so as to bring the wheel on top of it, I dare say we might have got to the races; but by an unfortunate coincidence both these things occurred, and when we recovered from the consequent shock, the tire of one of the wheels had come off, and was trundling with cumbrous gaiety into the ditch.

Flurry stopped the filly and began to laugh; Leigh Kelway said something startlingly unparliamentary under his breath.

'Well, it might be worse,' Flurry said consolingly as he lifted the tire on to the car; 'we're not half a mile from a forge.'

We walked that half-mile in funereal procession behind the car; the glory had departed from the weather, and an ugly wall of cloud was rising up out of the west to meet the sun; the hills had darkened and lost colour, and the white bog cotton shivered in a cold wind that smelt of rain.

By a miracle the smith was not at the races, owing, as he explained, to his having 'the tooth-aches', the two facts combined producing in him a morosity only equalled by that of Leigh Kelway. The smith's sole comment on the situation was to unharness the filly, and drag her into the forge, where he tied her up. He then proceeded to whistle viciously on his fingers in the direction of a cottage, and to command, in tones of thunder, some unseen creature to bring over a couple of baskets of turf. The turf arrived in process of time, on a woman's back, and was arranged in a circle in a yard at the back of the forge. The tire was bedded in it, and the turf was with difficulty kindled at different points.

'Ye'll not get to the races this day,' said the smith, yielding to a sardonic satisfaction; 'the turf's wet, and I haven't one to do a hand's turn for me.' He laid the wheel on the ground and lit his pipe.

Leigh Kelway looked pallidly about him over the spacious empty landscape of brown mountain slopes patched with golden furze and seamed with grey walls; I wondered if he were as hungry as I. We sat on stones opposite the smouldering ring of turf and smoked, and Flurry beguiled the smith into grim and calumnious confidences about every horse in the country. After about an hour, during which the turf went out three times, and the weather became more

25

and more threatening, a girl with a red petticoat over her head appeared at the gate of the yard, and said to the smith:

'The horse is gone away from ye.'

'Where?' exclaimed Flurry, springing to his feet.

'I met him walking wesht the road there below, and when I thought to turn him he commenced to gallop.'

'Pulled her head out of the headstall,' said Flurry, after a rapid survey of the forge. 'She's near home by now.'

It was at this moment that the rain began; the situation could scarcely have been better stage-managed. After reviewing the position, Flurry and I decided that the only thing to do was to walk to a public-house a couple of miles farther on, feed there if possible, hire a car, and go home.

It was an uphill walk, with mild generous rain-drops striking thicker and thicker on our faces; no one talked, and the grey clouds crowded up from behind the hills like billows of steam. Leigh Kelway bore it all with egregious resignation. I cannot pretend that I was at heart sympathetic, but by virtue of being his host I felt responsible for the breakdown, for his light suit, for everything, and divined his sentiment of horror at the first sight of the public-house.

It was a long, low cottage, with a line of dripping elm-trees overshadowing it; empty cars and carts round its door, and a babel from within made it evident that the racegoers were pursuing a gradual homeward route. The shop was crammed with steaming countrymen, whose loud brawling voices, all talking together, roused my English friend to his first remark since we had left the forge.

'Surely, Yeates, we are not going into that place?' he said severely; 'those men are all drunk.'

26

'Ah, nothing to signify!' said Flurry, plunging in and driving his way through the throng like a plough. 'Here, Mary Kate!' he called to the girl behind the counter, 'tell your mother we want some tea and bread and butter in the room inside.'

The smell of bad tobacco and spilt porter was choking; we worked our way through it after him towards the end of the shop, intersecting at every hand discussions about the races.

'Tom was very nice. He spared his horse all along, and then he put into him—' 'Well, at Goggin's corner the third horse was before the second, but he was goin' wake in himself.' 'I tell ye the mare had the hind leg fasht in the fore.' 'Clancy was dipping in the saddle.' ''Twas a dam nice race whatever—'

We gained the inner room at last, a cheerless apartment, adorned with sacred pictures, a sewing-machine, and an array of supplementary tumblers and wine-glasses; but, at all events, we had it so far to ourselves. At intervals during the next half-hour Mary Kate burst in with cups and plates, cast them on the table and disappeared, but of food there was no sign. After a further period of starvation and of listening to the noise in the shop, Flurry made a sortie, and, after lengthy and unknown adventures, reappeared carrying a huge brown teapot, and driving before him Mary Kate with the remainder of the repast. The bread tasted of mice, the butter of turf-smoke, the tea of brown paper, but we had got past the critical stage. I had entered upon my third round of bread and butter when the door was flung open, and my valued acquaintance, Slipper, slightly advanced in liquor, presented himself to our gaze. His bandy legs sprawled consequentially, his nose was redder than a coal of fire, his prominent eyes rolled crookedly upon us, and his left hand swept behind him the attempt of Mary Kate to frustrate his entrance.

'Good-evening to my vinerable friend, Mr. Flurry Knox!' he began, in the voice of a town crier, 'and to the Honourable Major Yeates, and the English gintleman!'

This impressive opening immediately attracted an audience from the shop, and the doorway filled with grinning faces as Slipper advanced farther into the room.

'Why weren't ye at the races, Mr. Flurry?' he went on, his roving eye taking a grip of us all at the same time; 'sure the Miss Bennetts and all the ladies was asking where were ye.'

'It'd take some time to tell them that,' said Flurry, with his mouth full; 'but what about the races, Slipper? Had you good sport?'

'Sport is it? Divil so pleasant an afternoon ever you seen,' replied Slipper. He leaned against a side table, and all the glasses on it jingled. 'Does your honour know O'Driscoll?' he went on irrelevantly. 'Sure you do. He was in your honour's stable. It's what we were all sayin'; it was a great pity your honour was not there, for the likin' you had to Driscoll.'

'That's thrue,' said a voice at the door.

'There wasn't one in the Barony but was gethered in it, through and fro,' continued Slipper, with a quelling glance at the interrupter; 'and there was tints for sellin' porther, and whisky as pliable as new milk, and boys goin' round the tints outside, feeling for heads with the big ends of their blackthorns, and all kinds of recreations, and the Sons of Liberty's piffler and dhrum band from Skebawn; though faith! there was more of thim runnin' to look at the races than what was playin' in it; not to mintion different occasions that the bandmasther was atin' his lunch within in the whisky tint.'

'But what about Driscoll?' said Flurry.

'Sure it's about him I'm tellin' ye,' replied Slipper, with the practised orator's watchful eye on his growing audience. "'Twas within in the same whisky tint meself was, with the bandmasther and a few of the lads, an' we buyin' a ha'porth o' crackers, when I seen me brave Driscoll landin' into the tint, and a pair o' thim long boots on him; him that hadn't a shoe nor a stocking to his foot when your honour had him picking grass out o' the stones behind in your yard. "Well," says I to meself, "we'll knock some spoort out of Driscoll!"

'"Come here to me, acushla!" says I to him; "I suppose it's some way wake in the legs y'are," says I, "an' the docthor put them on ye the way the people wouldn't thrample ye!"

'"May the divil choke ye!" says he, pleasant enough, but I knew by the blush he had he was vexed.

'"Then I suppose 'tis a left-tenant colonel y'are," says I; "yer mother must be proud out o' ye!" says I, "an' maybe ye'll lend her a loan o' thim waders when she's rinsin' yer bauneen in the river!" says I.

'"There'll be work out o' this!" says he, lookin' at me both sour and bitther.

'"Well indeed, I was thinkin' you were blue moulded for want of a batin'," says I. He was for fightin' us then, but afther we had him pacificated with about a quarther of a naggin o' sperrits, he told us he was goin' ridin' in a race.

'"An' what'll ye ride?" says I.

'"Owld Bocock's mare," says he.

'"Knipes!' says I, sayin' a great curse; "is it that little staggeen from the mountains; sure she's somethin' about the one age with meself," says I. "Many's the time Jamesy Geoghegan and meself used to be dhrivin' her to Macroom with pigs an' all soorts," says I; "an' is it leppin' stone walls ye want her to go now?"

'"Faith, there's walls and every vari'ty of obstackle in it," says he.

'"It'll be the best o' your play, so," says I, "to leg it away home out o' this."

'"An' who'll ride her, so?" says he.

'"Let the divil ride her," says I.'

Leigh Kelway, who had been leaning back seemingly half asleep, obeyed the hypnotism of Slipper's gaze, and opened his eyes.

'That was now all the conversation that passed between himself and meself,' resumed Slipper, 'and there was no great delay afther that till they said there was a race startin' and the dickens a one at all was goin' to ride only two, Driscoll, and one Clancy. With that then I seen Mr. Kinahane, the Petty Sessions clerk, goin' round clearin' the coorse, an' I gethered a few o' the neighbours, an' we walked the fields hither and over till we seen the most of th' obstackles.

'"Stand aisy now by the plantation," says I; "if they get to come as far as this, believe me ye'll see spoort," says I, "an' 'twill be a convanient spot to encourage the mare if she's anyway wake in herself," says I, cuttin' somethin' about five foot of an ash sapling out o' the plantation.

'"That's yer sort!" says owld Bocock, that was thravellin' the racecoorse, peggin' a bit o' paper down with a thorn in front of every lep, the way Driscoll 'd know the handiest place to face her at it.

'Well, I hadn't barely thrimmed the ash plant—'

'Have you any jam, Mary Kate?' interrupted Flurry, whose meal had been in no way interfered with by

30

either the story or the highly-scented crowd who had come to listen to it.

'We have no jam, only thraycle, sir,' replied the invisible Mary Kate.

'I hadn't the switch barely thrimmed,' repeated Slipper firmly, 'when I heard the people screechin', an' I seen Driscoll an' Clancy comin' on, leppin' all before them, an' owld Bocock's mare bellusin' an' powdherin' along, an' bedad! whatever obstackle wouldn't throw *her* down, faith, she'd throw *it* down, an' there's the thraffic they had in it.

'"I declare to me sowl," says I, "if they continue on this way there's a great chance some one o' thim 'll win," says I.

'"Ye lie!" says the bandmasther, bein' a thrifle fulsome after his luncheon.

'"I do not," says I, "in regard of seein' how soople them two boys is. Ye might observe," says I, "that if they have no convanient way to sit on the saddle, they'll ride the neck o' the horse till such time as they gets an occasion to lave it," says I.

'"Arrah, shut yer mouth!" says the bandmasther; "they're puckin' out this way now, an' may the divil admire me!" says he, "but Clancy has the other bet out, and the divil such leatherin' and beltin' of owld Bocock's mare ever you seen as what's in it!" says he.

'Well, when I seen them comin' to me, and Driscoll about the length of the plantation behind Clancy, I let a couple of bawls.

'"Skelp her, ye big brute!" says I. "What good's in ye that ye aren't able to skelp her?"'

The yell and the histrionic flourish of his stick with which Slipper delivered this incident brought down the house. Leigh Kelway was sufficiently moved to ask me in an undertone if 'skelp' was a local term.

31

'Well, Mr. Flurry, and gintlemen,' recommenced Slipper, 'I declare to ye when owld Bocock's mare heard thim roars she sthretched out her neck like a gandher, and when she passed me out she give a couple of grunts, and looked at me as ugly as a Christian.

'"Hah!" says I, givin' her a couple o' dhraws o' th' ash plant across the butt o' the tail, the way I wouldn't blind her; "I'll make ye grunt!" says I, "I'll nourish ye!"

'I knew well she was very frightful of th' ash plant since the winter Tommeen Sullivan had her under a side-car. But now, in place of havin' any obligations to me, ye'd be surprised if ye heard the blaspheemious expressions of that young boy that was ridin' her; and whether it was over-anxious he was, turnin' around the way I'd hear him cursin', or whether it was some slither or slide came to owld Bocock's mare, I dunno, but she was bet up agin the last obstackle but two, and before ye could say "Schnipes", she was standin' on her two ears beyond in th' other field! I declare to ye, on the vartue of me oath, she stood that way till she reconnoithered what side would Driscoll fall, an' she turned about then and rolled on him as cosy as if he was meadow grass!'

Slipper stopped short; the people in the doorway groaned appreciatively; Mary Kate murmured, 'The Lord save us!'

'The blood was dhruv out through his nose and ears,' continued Slipper, with a voice that indicated the cream of the narration, 'and you'd hear his bones crackin' on the ground! You'd have pitied the poor boy.'

'Good heavens!' said Leigh Kelway, sitting up very straight in his chair.

'Was he hurt, Slipper?' asked Flurry casually.

'Hurt is it?' echoed Slipper in high scorn; 'killed on the spot!' He paused to relish the effect of the denouement on Leigh Kelway. 'Oh, divil so pleasant an afthernoon ever you seen; and indeed, Mr. Flurry, it's what we were all sayin', it was a great pity your honour was not there for the likin' you had for Driscoll.'

As he spoke the last word there was an outburst of singing and cheering from a car-load of people who had just pulled up at the door. Flurry listened, leaned back in his chair, and began to laugh.

'It scarcely strikes one as a comic incident,' said Leigh Kelway, very coldly to me; 'in fact, it seems to me that the police ought—'

'Show me Slipper!' bawled a voice in the shop; 'show me that dirty little undherlooper till I have his blood! Hadn't I the race won only for he souring the mare on me! What's that you say? I tell ye he did! He left seven slaps on her with the handle of a hay-rake—'

There was in the room in which we were sitting a second door, leading to the back yard, a door consecrated to the unobtrusive visits of so-called 'Sunday travellers'. Through it Slipper faded away like a dream, and, simultaneously, a tall young man, with a face like a red-hot potato tied up in a bandage, squeezed his way from the shop into the room.

'Well, Driscoll,' said Flurry, 'since it wasn't the teeth of the rake he left on the mare, you needn't be talking!'

Leigh Kelway looked from one to the other with a wilder expression in his eye than I had thought it capable of. I read in it a resolve to abandon Ireland to her fate.

At eight o'clock we were still waiting for the car that we had been assured should be ours directly it returned from the races. At half-past eight we had adopted the only possible course that remained, and had accepted the offers of lifts on the laden cars that were returning to Skebawn, and I presently was gratified by the spectacle of my friend Leigh Kelway wedged between a roulette table and its proprietor on one side of a car, with Driscoll and Slipper, mysteriously reconciled and excessively drunk, seated, locked in each other's arms, on the other. Flurry and I, somewhat similarly placed, followed on two other cars. I was scarcely surprised when I was informed that the melancholy white animal in the shafts of the leading car was Owld Bocock's much-enduring steeplechaser.

The night was very dark and stormy, and it is almost superfluous to say that no one carried lamps; the rain poured upon us, and through wind and wet Owld Bocock's mare set the pace at a rate that showed she knew from bitter experience what was expected from her by gentlemen who had spent the evening in a public-house; behind her the other two tired horses followed closely, incited to emulation by shouting, singing, and a liberal allowance of whip. We were a good ten miles from Skebawn, and never had the road seemed so long. For mile after mile the half-seen low walls slid past us, with occasional plunges into caverns of darkness under trees. Sometimes from a wayside cabin a dog would dash out to bark at us as we rattled by; sometimes our cavalcade swung aside to pass, with yells and counter-yells, crawling carts filled with other belated race-goers.

I was nearly wet through, even though I received considerable shelter from a Skebawn publican, who slept heavily and irrepressibly on my shoulder. Driscoll, on the leading car, had struck up an approximation to the 'Wearing of the Green', when a wavering star appeared on the road ahead of us. It grew momently larger; it came towards us apace. Flurry, on the car behind me, shouted suddenly—

'That's the mail car, with one of the lamps out! Tell those fellows ahead to look out!'

But the warning fell on deaf ears.

> When laws can change the blades of grass
> From growing as they grow—

howled five discordant voices, oblivious of the towering proximity of the star.

A Bianconi mail car is nearly three times the size of an ordinary outside car, and when on a dark night it advances, Cyclops-like, with but one eye, it is difficult for even a sober driver to calculate its bulk. Above the sounds of melody there arose the thunder of heavy wheels, the splashing trample of three big horses, then a crash and a turmoil of shouts. Our cars pulled up just in time, and I tore myself from the embrace of my publican to go to Leigh Kelway's assistance.

The wing of the Bianconi had caught the wing of the smaller car, flinging Owld Bocock's mare on her side and throwing her freight headlong on top of her, the heap being surmounted by the roulette table. The driver of the mail car unshipped his solitary lamp and turned it on the disaster. I saw that Flurry had already got hold of Leigh Kelway by the heels, and was dragging him from under the others. He struggled up hatless, muddy, and gasping, with Driscoll hanging on by his neck, still singing the 'Wearing of the Green'.

A voice from the mail car said incredulously, '*Leigh Kelway!*' A spectacled face glared down upon him from under the dripping spikes of an umbrella.

It was the Right Honourable the Earl of Waterbury,

Leigh Kelway's chief, returning from his fishing excursion.

Meanwhile Slipper, in the ditch, did not cease to announce that 'Divil so pleasant an afthernoon ever ye seen as what was in it!'

The Awakening

DANIEL CORKERY
(1878–1964)

I

IVOR O'DONOVAN knew it was Ted Driscoll had called him: raising himself above the edge of the bunk he was just in time to see him manœuvring that bear-like body of his through the narrow little hatchway, to see the splintery shutter slap to behind him. At the same moment he heard the Captain clearing his throat. The bunk opposite was his, and now Ivor saw him, all limbs, mounting awkwardly yet carefully over the edge of it. What between the sprawling limbs, the ungainly body and the hovering shadows above them, the place was narrowed to the size of a packing-case. The timber-work of the cabin had become so dark with the smoke of the stove that neither shadows nor limbs seemed to stir except when their movements were sudden and jerky. Ivor soon heard the Captain gathering his oil-cloths from the floor with one hand while with the other he dragged at the bunk where the cabin-boy was sleeping; this Ivor knew, for as he sat up he caught the familiar words:

'Come on, come on; rouse up; they'll be waiting.'

The Captain he then saw disappear through the toy-like hatchway.

Ivor O'Donovan himself with a stifled groan descended lifelessly from the bunk to the floor. He drew on his sea boots—they had been his father's—drew his oil-cloths about him and in turn thrust his hand into the warm pile of old coats and sacking in which the sleeping boy was buried. He shook him vigorously: 'Come on, come on; they'll be waiting,' he said, and then hurried aloft into the drizzling darkness and took his place with the others.

The tightness that he felt on his brain from the moment Ted Driscoll had roused him seemed natural, not unexpected; nevertheless he groaned to recollect the cause of it. Now, however, as he settled down to his night's work, planted in the darkness there at the gunwale, braced against it, facing the Captain, the dripping fish-laden incoming net between them, he noticed that the tightness had somehow slackened, was still loosening its grip of him, so much so that he had some fear that it would again suddenly pounce on him with its first heat and violence.

Ted Driscoll and Tom Mescall were forward at the windlass; beyond them the boy, bending down, was coiling the rope they passed to him.

It was very dark. Everything was huge and shapeless. Anchored as she was, tethered besides, clumsy with the weight of dripping fish-spangled net coming in over the gunwale, the nobby was tossed and slapped about with a violence that surprised him; flakes of wet brightness were being flung everywhere from the one lamp bound firmly to the mast. Yet the night was almost windless, the sea apparently sluggish: there must be, he thought, a stiff swell beneath them. What most surprised him, however, was to find himself thinking about it. That evening coming down the harbour, he would not have noticed it. The whole way out, his back to the sea, he had stood upright, his feet set wide apart, his hands in his belt, glum, silent, gazing at the cabin-boy who, sprawled upon the deck, was intent upon the baited line he had flung over the stern. But as far as Ivor was concerned that patch of deck might have been free to the sun: his own anger, his passion, was between him and the world. That afternoon he had waited for Chrissie Collins for two hours. At the very start he knew, he *knew*, so at least he had told himself, she would not come. For all that he had gone hot and cold, again and again, while waiting for her. He had broken from the spot impulsively: a moment later he had trailed back again, giving her one more quarter of an hour to make good in. Then when his rage was at the peak, hurrying down to the jetty, he had suddenly caught sight of her, all brightness, stepping briskly up the hill-side, the schoolmaster walking beside her, as eager as herself. Her head was bent, her eyes were fixed on her dainty toe-caps, and she was listening complacently to the schoolmaster's blather. Only that he should have to tear through the village and it filled with the gathering crews, he'd have told her what he thought of her.

With his eyes downwards on the sprawling limbs of the boy, he had indulged, as if it were the only thing for a man to do, the heat of the passion that that one glimpse of her had aroused in him.

Now, ten hours later, braced against the timbers, swaying and balancing, freeing the net, freeing the rope, grabbing at the odd dog-fish, the odd blob of seaweed, the tangle of seawrack, flinging them all, as they came, far out, clear of the rising meshes—he was puzzled to contrast his present indifference with his stifling anger of the afternoon. Yet he was not pleased with himself. This calming down of his seemed like a

38

loss of manhood. His mind could not, it appeared, stay
fixed on the one thought. He found himself noticing
what he had never noticed before—how the mackerel,
entangled in the meshes, would catch the light of the
worried lamp and appear just like a flight of shining
steel-bright daggers hurtling by him from gunwale to
hold. Never to have noticed so striking a thing before,
how curious! But had the Captain ever noticed it?
He glanced shyly at the aged face opposite him and
started, for the Captain, he saw, had had his eyes
fixed on him, all the time, perhaps! And Ivor recalled,
reddening slightly, that also that afternoon while lost
in his own passionate thoughts he had caught him
observing him with the selfsame silent gravity. Why
should he do it? He was Captain. But the boat was
his, Ivor's; and one day when he was somewhat older,
and when his mother was willing to trust him, he
would sail it. But this was unfair, he felt, for the
Captain, this Larry Keohane, had been ever and always his father's dearest friend and shipmate, had
sailed with him till he was drowned, had indeed been
with him that very night; and afterwards he it was
who had undertaken the management of the boat for
them; and in such a way that not a penny of the fish
money had ever gone astray on them. Later on, now
two years ago, he had taken Ivor on board as one of
the crew, and taught him whatever he now knew of
sailoring and deep sea fishing. There was surely plenty
of time yet for thinking of playing the Captain. Besides, the selling of the fish was trickier work than the
catching of it. His eyes fell on the claw-like hands of
the Captain, they were twisted with rheumatism, and
a flood of kindly feeling for this grave and faithful
friend suddenly swept over him with such power that
he found his own hands fumbling at the net without

either skill or strength in them. To glance again at the Captain's face he did not dare.

'Up, boys, up!' he impulsively cried to the windlass men as if to encourage them. In the clinging darkness, although the drizzle was becoming lighter and lighter, he could make out only the shapeless bulk of themselves and the windlass: two awkward lumps of manhood rising and falling alternately, their sou'westers and oil-cloths catching some of the flakes of the wet brightness that were flying around everywhere. 'Twas curious work, this fishing. Like a family they were, confined in a tiny space, as far almost from the other boats as they were from the houses on the hills where the real families were now huddled together in sleep. The real families—each of them was different from the others. Tom Mescall's was the most good-for-nothing in the whole place. Others had quite nice houses, clean and well-kept. But most strange of all was it to have him, Ivor, thinking of such things, his head calm and cool (and he thereupon grabbed a huge dog-fish from the passing net and with a gesture deliberately sweeping sent it far out into the splashing darkness).

II

The work went on and on and Ivor could not help all kinds of thoughts from crossing his brain, nor help noticing the onward rush of them. The dragging of the net was done in silence, no one speaking until they each and all were sure that they had had a fairly good catch, and that all the nets were heavy. Ivor then was aware that some dull and lifeless conversation was passing to and fro between the men at the windlass. He was hailed suddenly by one of them, Ted Driscoll: 'Look where Leary is, east.'

Far off, east, Ivor saw a tiny light. As he watched it the other voice came through the darkness, half speaking, half calling:

''aith then he wouldn't be long swinging on to the Galley in there.'

'Is it Leary, do you think?' Ivor asked the Captain, and he was answered:

''Tis like the place he'd be.'

Ivor then sent his gaze ranging the sea noting the disposition of the boats. They were far off, nearly all of them. Some were miles beyond Galley Head. Others were away towards the west. Here and there a pair of lights seemed to ride close together, only seemed, however, while an odd one, like Leary's, played the hermit in unaccustomed waters. Far to the west the great light of the Fastnet every few moments threw a startling beam on the waters and, quenching suddenly, would leave a huge blackness suspended before their very eyes, blinding them. He noticed how, little by little, the timid lamps of the fishing fleet would in time manage again to glimmer through that darkness. He bent himself once more on the work, thinking over and over again what a curious way they had of making a living. On the land at this time of night every one of the houses was a nest of sleep—chilly walls and warm bedding. After all Chrissie Collins was a farmer's daughter, a small hill-side farmer, a 'sky' farmer. Farm houses had ways of their own. Fishermen also had ways of their own. The next time he met her he would hold his head as high as hers.

The dragging went on and on. The unending clanking of the windlass, the wet mass of the net, the grip of his feet on the narrow way between gunwale and hold while the boat tossed and tugged, the sudden flashes of the lamp, the long silences of them all, the far-off lonely-looking lights of the other anchored nobbies and ketches, the bold startling blaze of the Fastnet, and above all the stream of shining daggers sweeping by—for the first time in his life he reckoned up the features of the fisherman's calling, and felt some sort of pleasant excitement in doing so, as if he had heard some good news or come upon some unexpected treasure. He could not understand it.

When the last of the nets was in they tidied the decks, pitching the seawrack into the sea. He heard the Captain say to Driscoll, whose head was bent down on the confused mass of fish and net in the hold: 'Good, and a fair size too. I'm very glad.'

'I'm very glad,' repeated Ivor in his mind, wonderingly, yet feeling that the words fitted in. He noticed Driscoll and Mescall, their arms hanging heavily after their night's work, their sea boots lumping noisily along the deck, going aft to the little cabin, making down the hatchway without a word. The boy had gone down previously. The waft of the smell of boiling fish, of boiling potatoes, that came from the smoke pipe told of his toil below. To Ivor it was very welcome. He was hungry; and besides they would presently all meet together round the little stove. 'I'm very glad,' he whispered, not knowing why. And the smoke, he saw, was like a lighted plume rising from the top of the iron pipe.

The Captain drew closer to him. He took the fragment of pipe from his mouth and, smothering the glowing bowl in his fist, pointed sou-west:

''Tis Casey that's going in.'

'Is it?' Ivor said, also picking out the one craft in all the far-scattered fleet that had got under weigh that— very slowly, for there was scarcely a breath of wind— was making for the land.

'Maybe 'tisn't,' the Captain then said.

'I'm sure 'tis him all right,' Ivor said, though he was not sure at all.

They stood side by side following with their eyes the distant slow-moving light. There was scarcely a morning that some boat or other did not hoist sail the moment their catch was made and hasten in. There was always some special reason for it. And the other craft, every one of them, would make guesses at the boat, as also at the cause of her lifting anchor in such haste. The others were content to make the pier any time before the buyers had received from other fishing ports and from Dublin itself their morning telegrams fixing the day's prices. Ivor thought how it was nearly always something having to do with the real house-hold, with the real family, that brought a fisherman to break that way from the fishing grounds before the others. Sickness, or the necessity for some early journey, or the emigrating of a son or daughter. 'I remember your father, one time we were out, and far out too, south the Galley, ten mile it might be, how he called out and we not ready at all: "That'll do, boys, we'll make in."'

The Captain's quiet husky voice stopped, and Ivor wondered if that was all he had to say; but the tale was taken up again:

'That was twenty-two years ago this month.'

Ivor was once more astray, he could not find reason in the words.

'Yes,' he said, quietly.

'That night he expected a son to be born to him; and he wasn't disappointed.'

Ivor knew that he himself was the child that on that night came into the world; but what kept him silent was the Captain's gravity. Such matter among them

had always been a cause for laughter. Ivor was nevertheless glad that the Captain had spoken seriously;
for all that, fearing to betray his own state of mind, he
answered:

'That's not what's taking Casey in anyhow.'

The Captain did not seem to hear.

'All night long,' he said, 'I'm thinking of things that
I saw happen out here on these waters for the last
fifty-four years.'

Ivor raised his head in astonishment. Why should
such recollections have set the Captain examining him
the whole night long?

'Strange things,' the Captain resumed, 'strange
voices, sad things too, very sad, things that should not
happen.'

After all, the Captain was in the humour for spinning a yarn, that was all. But, instead of the yarn, the
Captain, scanning the sky, merely said:

''Tis going south; the day will be fine, very fine.'

Ivor, too, felt a slight stir in the air, and from the
hatchway Driscoll called them down.

'With God's help 'twill be a fine day,' the Captain
said once more, throwing the words over his shoulder
as they moved aft, one behind the other, sauntering
along in their heavy sea boots.

III

The air in the cabin was reeking with the smell of
fish and potatoes, and so thick with fire smoke and
tobacco smoke that one could hardly make things out.
There was hardly room for the five of them there. The
boxes they sat on were very low and the men's knees,
on which they held the plates, seemed to fill the whole
space. One felt the warmth against one's face like a

cushion. Yet Ivor welcomed it all—the heat, the smell of the good food, the close companionship—not alone for the comfort it all wrapped him round with but for the memory it raised in him of those many other nights on which he had experienced it, his body as cold as ice and his fingers unable to move themselves. The others were already eating lustily and noisily.

'Not too bad, not too bad,' he cried out cheerily, planting himself between Driscoll and Mescall, just because they were head to head and nose to nose in earnest argument. They took no notice of him, continuing it still across his very face. Driscoll, who was the simplest of them, was showing how Mrs. O'Connor, the shopkeeper who supplied them with all and sundry, had done him out of two and elevenpence, and Mescall, who, in spite of his harum-scarum wife and family, was their merrymaker, was explaining how she had tried the same trick with him and how he had laid a trap for her and caught her—a trap so clever that Driscoll had no idea how it worked or how by using it he could recover his two and elevenpence. The boy was heard plunging vessels in a bucket of water. All the time the Captain held his peace, and Ivor, noticing it, glanced at him, wondering if he were still recalling what he had seen happen on the fishing grounds during his long lifetime upon them.

Leisurely yet ravenously the meal went on, and when they thought of it, or at least so it seemed, first Mescall and then Driscoll, who had had no sleep till then, threw off their sea boots and disappeared into the darkness of the bunks. In the same haphazard way Ivor, the Captain, and the boy returned to the deck.

IV

At last they had her moving: her sails were flapping, coming suddenly between their eyes and the dazzling flood of light outwelling from sea and sky. When they filled, when she settled down, Ivor heard the Captain say in a voice that sounded unusual:

'I suppose I may as well go aft.'

Unable to account for the words Ivor answered in mere confusion of mind:

''Tis better, I suppose,' as if the matter was not quite clear.

Silently the Captain went aft to the tiller, and Ivor, as was his custom, threw himself on the pile of rope in the bow: there was no more to be done. He felt the streaming sun, into which a benign warmth was beginning to steal, bathing his body from his hair down. After the work of the night, after the food, a pleasant lassitude, as thick as his thick clothing, clung to him. The cabin-boy was already fast asleep on the deck, cuddled up like a dog, his face buried in his arms. Ivor felt sleepy too, yet before he yielded to it, he recalled the memory of the handful of them, cut off from all other company, working silently in the drizzling darkness, the tossing lamp momentarily flashing in their eyes and lighting up their dripping hands. He recollected, too, the rise and fall of the awkward bodies of the two men at the windlass, the clanking of the axle, and the uncompanioned boy beyond them working away in almost total darkness. Clearer than all he recalled the flight of glittering spear-heads sweeping by between himself and the Captain. Then also the group in the smoky cabin, the hearty faces, the blue and white plates, the boy plunging the vessels in the water. How different from what was now before his eyes!

46

The sea was wide, wide; the air brisk, the seagulls
screaming, quarrelling, gathering in schools, dashing
at the transparent crests of the waves or sweeping in
great curves to the east, the west, everywhere, their
high-pitched cries filling the air with a rapture that
opened the heart and at the same time alarmed it.
Yes, very different, yet his pictures of the night time—
the groups silently working in the darkness, the gathering in the little cabin—these were dearer to him just
now than the bright freshness of the morning. He recalled the unexpected words of the Captain—'I'm
very glad.'

At last the drowsiness that he would keep from him
overpowered him.

He awoke to find the boy's hand timidly unclutching
his shoulder:

'Himself wants you.'

Rising up he caught the Captain's eyes resting upon
him with a calmness that surprised him, that disturbed
him. He went aft.

'You're wanting me?'

'Sit down there, Ivor, there's a thing I have to say
to you.'

Fearing some reference to Chrissie Collins, some
questioning, some good advice, Ivor sat down without
a word. The Captain blurted out:

'Ivor, boy, 'tis time for you to sail what belongs to
you.'

As he spoke his hand lifted from the tiller—an in-
stinctive giving up of office. Instantly, however, it fell
upon it again. Ivor perceived the action with his eyes,
not with his mind, for the words had sent a thrill of
delight through his whole body. Everything he had
been noticing that night of nights was in that over-
whelming sensation—the darkness, the clanking wind-

47

lass, the shining fish, the cabin, the seagulls, everything—but he caught hold of himself and said:

'But, Lar, why that? Why that?'

'Because 'tis time for you.'

'But why so? 'Tisn't how you're going from us;
what's after happening?'

'Nothing. Nothing. Only all the night I'm thinking
of it. 'Tis the right thing. Herself is at me too. If there's
a touch of wind in the night, she don't sleep a wink.'

'Oh! If the boat goes we all go.'

'You can't talk to them like that. Anyway 'tis right.
'Tis your due. We got on well, Ivor. Them that's gone,
they deserved as much. We done our best, all of us.'

'Lar, 'tis better wait till my mother hears of it.'

'If you wouldn't mind I'd give you Pat to be in my
place. He'd be better for you than a stranger.'

Again that thrill of delight went through him. He
thought at once if the Captain had not offered his son,
a stranger would have to be brought into the boat, one
of those unlucky creatures perhaps who had given the
best of their lives sailoring the wide world over,
creatures who were not trustworthy, who had bitter,
reckless tongues, who destroyed the spirit of goodwill
in any boat they ever got footing in. That danger the
Captain had put aside. There was therefore a clear
way before him, and a boat's crew after his own heart.

'I'm thankful, Lar, and herself will be thankful; but
what will you be doing with yourself?'

A little smile grew upon the Captain's face, and
both of them raised their eyes to scan the hill-sides
they were approaching. In the sun which now lay
thick upon their brown-green flanks, nestling in the
zigzag ravines they saw the little groups of houses
where the fishermen lived. Some of the cottages, snow-
white, faced full in the eyes of the morning, sunning

48

themselves. Others were turned aside, still asleep in the shadows, catching a bright ray only on chimney-head or gable.

'Wouldn't I want to sit in the sun and smoke my pipe as well as another? That will do, Ivor. Ted's coming up. He's after smelling the land. In the evening I'll fix up with your mother.'

V

It was a Saturday morning. That night and the next they would all sleep in their own houses, not in the boats.

In the evening the Captain went to Ivor's house, and, as he said himself, fixed things up with his mother. Then he shook hands with them all, with Mrs. O'Donovan, Ivor, his two sisters, and his young brother, who was only a boy. He then set off up the hill for his home.

Afterwards, standing up before the bit of glass nailed against the wall, Ivor stood shaving himself. His heart was blazing within him, his cheeks burning, for the Captain had been speaking his praises, and all his people had been staring at him.

It had been a day of uninterrupted sunshine, and now a bright heaven, slow to darken itself, although the sun had been a long time sunken, darkened to blackness every ridge, bush, tree clump, roof and gable that stood against it. On the roads and fields it still threw down a persistent glow; and Ivor went in and out the doorway praying for the dusk to thicken. In the midst of the Captain's praise of him he had felt a burning desire to see his boat once again with his own eyes, to be sure it was still there at the pier, where, with scores of others, it was fastened. He wanted to feel the tiller beneath his right hand—that above all. And yet he would not care to have any of his neighbours see him doing so. Nightfall was never so slow in coming. At last, however, with a yearning look at the still livid sky he set off down the path towards the roadway. He could gambol, he could sing, only that at the same time he had thoughts of the heavy responsibility that in future would rest upon him. He strove to calm himself, to walk with the appearance of one who had no other business than to breathe the cool air of the evening. He knew there would be groups of men still in the public-houses as well as along the sea wall; and these he wished to escape.

Before entering the village he vaulted over the wall, descended the rocks, and made along by the edge of the waters. At a point beyond the farthest house he climbed on to the road again, and, more assured, made towards the deserted pier. At its extreme end, almost, his *Wildwood* was moored. The pier itself, the debris on it, the fish boxes, the ranks of barrels—as well as all the conglomeration of boats along its sheltered side— the whole had become one black mass sharply cut out against the livid waters of the harbour. On a standard at its very end a solitary oil lamp, as warm in colour as the waters were cold, was burning away in loneliness. Towards it, and as quietly, almost as stealthily as if on a guilty errand, he steered his way. He was glad when the piles of barrels so obstructed the view that no one could spy him from the road. Doubtless the news was already abroad; by now the men were surely all speaking about it; as for himself, it was very strange coming at the time it did, coming, without expectation, at the tail-end of the night when for the first time he knew what it was to be a true fisherman. He was glad Chrissie Collins had her schoolmaster. It left himself as free as air. And thinking the thought he breathed in the pleasant coolness of the night, yet could not, it seemed, gulp down enough of it. Glad of the darkness, of the loneliness, he suddenly threw out his two arms wide apart, stretching them from him, and drew the keen air slowly and deliciously through his nostrils. And breathing still in the self-same manner went forward a few steps. Then suddenly, he saw a figure, outlined against the tide, seated on some fish boxes, gazing silently at the nobby for which he himself was making! He knew it was the Captain. His arms fell and he stood quite still.

'Oh!' he said, in a sudden stoppage of thought. He turned stealthily and retraced his steps, fearful of hearing his name cried out. But nothing was to be heard except his own careful footfall; and before he reached the road again he had recovered himself. It surely was a sad thing for Larry Keohane to have his life drawing to an end. Why was it that nothing can happen to fill one person with happiness without bringing sadness and pain to somebody else? Yet the Captain, he remembered, that evening in his mother's house had been quite cheerful, had told them how glad he was that they had made quite a good catch on his last night, and what a peaceful night it had been! And what a fine boat the *Wildwood* was; and how happy he was to be leaving her in hands that would not treat her foully; indeed he could well say that he was flinging all responsibility from his shoulders; and that was a thing he had been looking forward to for a long time. And saying that, he had gone from them cheerily and brightly. Yes, yes, but here surely was the real captain, this seaman staring at his boat.

Ivor waited, sitting on the wall in the darkness, for a long time. At last he heard the slow steps of the old man approaching, saw him pass by—saw him very indistinctly for the darkness, yet knew that he had his hand covering his pipe in his mouth and his head on one side, a way he had when he was thinking to himself. He waited until the footsteps had died away up the hill-side; then he rose to resume his own quest towards the nobby. He found he could not bring himself to do so. He did not want to do so.

With slow lingering steps, with stoppings and turnings, at last he too began to make towards his home. His head was flung up, almost flung back. More than once he told himself that he didn't ever remember the sky to have been so full of stars. Somehow he felt like raising his hand towards them.

The Dead

JAMES JOYCE
(1882–1941)

LILY, the caretaker's daughter, was literally run off her feet. Hardly had she brought one gentleman into the little pantry behind the office on the ground floor and helped him off with his overcoat, than the wheezy hall-door bell clanged again and she had to scamper along the bare hallway to let in another guest. It was well for her she had not to attend to the ladies also. But Miss Kate and Miss Julia had thought of that and had converted the bathroom upstairs into a ladies' dressing-room. Miss Kate and Miss Julia were there, gossiping and laughing and fussing, walking after each other to the head of the stairs, peering down over the banisters and calling down to Lily to ask her who had come.

It was always a great affair, the Misses Morkan's annual dance. Everybody who knew them came to it, members of the family, old friends of the family, the members of Julia's choir, any of Kate's pupils that were grown up enough, and even some of Mary Jane's pupils too. Never once had it fallen flat. For years and years it had gone off in splendid style, as long as anyone could remember: ever since Kate and Julia, after the death of their brother Pat, had left the house in Stoney Batter and taken Mary Jane, their only niece, to live with them in the dark, gaunt house on Usher's Island, the upper part of which they had rented from Mr. Fulham, the corn-factor on the ground floor. That was a good thirty years ago if it was a day. Mary Jane, who was then a little girl in short clothes, was now the main prop of the household, for she had the organ in Haddington Road. She had been through the Academy and gave a pupils' concert every year in the upper room of the Antient Concert Rooms. Many of her pupils belonged to the better-class families on the Kingstown and Dalkey line. Old as they were, her aunts also did their share. Julia, though she was quite grey, was still the leading soprano in Adam and Eve's, and Kate, being too feeble to go about much, gave music lessons to beginners on the old square piano in the back room. Lily, the caretaker's daughter, did housemaid's work for them. Though their life was modest, they believed in eating well; the best of everything: diamond-bone sirloins, three-shilling tea, and the best bottled stout. But Lily seldom made a mistake in the orders, so that she got on well with her three mistresses. They were fussy, that was all. But the only thing they would not stand was back answers.

Of course, they had good reason to be fussy on such a night. And then it was long after ten o'clock and yet there was no sign of Gabriel and his wife. Besides they were dreadfully afraid that Freddy Malins might turn up screwed. They would not wish for worlds that any of Mary Jane's pupils should see him under the influence; and when he was like that it was sometimes very hard to manage him. Freddy Malins always came late, but they wondered what could be keeping Gabriel: and that was what brought them every two minutes to the banisters to ask Lily had Gabriel or Freddy come.

'O, Mr. Conroy,' said Lily to Gabriel when she opened the door for him, 'Miss Kate and Miss Julia thought you were never coming. Good night, Mrs. Conroy.'

'I'll engage they did,' said Gabriel, 'but they forget that my wife here takes three mortal hours to dress herself.'

He stood on the mat, scraping the snow from his goloshes, while Lily led his wife to the foot of the stairs and called out:

'Miss Kate, here's Mrs. Conroy.'

Kate and Julia came toddling down the dark stairs at once. Both of them kissed Gabriel's wife, said she must be perished alive, and asked was Gabriel with her.

'Here I am as right as the mail, Aunt Kate! Go on up. I'll follow,' called out Gabriel from the dark.

He continued scraping his feet vigorously while the three women went upstairs, laughing, to the ladies' dressing-room. A light fringe of snow lay like a cape on the shoulders of his overcoat and like toecaps on the toes of his goloshes; and, as the buttons of his overcoat slipped with a squeaking noise through the snow-stiffened frieze, a cold, fragrant air from out-of-doors escaped from crevices and folds.

'Is it snowing again, Mr. Conroy?' asked Lily.

She had preceded him into the pantry to help him off with his overcoat. Gabriel smiled at the three syllables she had given his surname and glanced at her. She was a slim, growing girl, pale in complexion and with hay-coloured hair. The gas in the pantry made her look still paler. Gabriel had known her when she was a child and used to sit on the lowest step nursing a rag doll.

'Yes, Lily,' he answered, 'and I think we're in for a night of it.'

He looked up at the pantry ceiling, which was shaking with the stamping and shuffling of feet on the floor above, listened for a moment to the piano and then glanced at the girl, who was folding his overcoat carefully at the end of a shelf.

'Tell me, Lily,' he said in a friendly tone, 'do you still go to school?'

'O no, sir,' she answered. 'I'm done schooling this year and more.'

'O, then,' said Gabriel gaily, 'I suppose we'll be going to your wedding one of these fine days with your young man, eh?'

The girl glanced back at him over her shoulder and said with great bitterness:

'The men that is now is only all palaver and what they can get out of you.'

Gabriel coloured, as if he felt he had made a mistake and, without looking at her, kicked off his goloshes and flicked actively with his muffler at his patent-leather shoes.

He was a stout, tallish young man. The high colour of his cheeks pushed upwards even to his forehead, where it scattered itself in a few formless patches of pale red; and on his hairless face there scintillated restlessly the polished lenses and the bright gilt rims of the glasses which screened his delicate and restless eyes. His glossy black hair was parted in the middle and brushed in a long curve behind his ears where it curled slightly beneath the groove left by his hat.

When he had flicked lustre into his shoes he stood up and pulled his waistcoat down more tightly on his plump body. Then he took a coin rapidly from his pocket.

'O Lily,' he said, thrusting it into her hands, 'it's Christmas-time, isn't it? Just . . . here's a little. . . .'

He walked rapidly towards the door.

'O no, sir!' cried the girl, following him. 'Really, sir, I wouldn't take it.'

'Christmas-time! Christmas-time!' said Gabriel, almost trotting to the stairs and waving his hand to her in deprecation.

The girl, seeing that he had gained the stairs, called out after him:

'Well, thank you, sir.'

He waited outside the drawing-room door until the waltz should finish, listening to the skirts that swept against it and to the shuffling of feet. He was still discomposed by the girl's bitter and sudden retort. It had cast a gloom over him which he tried to dispel by arranging his cuffs and the bows of his tie. He then took from his waistcoat pocket a little paper and glanced at the headings he had made for his speech. He was undecided about the lines from Robert Browning, for he feared they would be above the heads of his hearers. Some quotation that they would recognize from Shakespeare or from the Melodies would be better. The indelicate clacking of the men's heels and the shuffling of their soles reminded him that their grade of culture differed from his. He would only make himself ridiculous by quoting poetry to them which they could not understand. They would think that he was airing his superior education. He would fail with them just as he had failed with the girl in the pantry. He had taken up a wrong tone. His whole speech was a mistake from first to last, an utter failure.

Just then his aunts and his wife came out of the ladies' dressing-room. His aunts were two small, plainly dressed old women. Aunt Julia was an inch or so the taller. Her hair, drawn low over the tops of her ears, was grey; and grey also, with darker shadows, was her large flaccid face. Though she was stout in build and stood erect, her slow eyes and parted lips gave her the appearance of a woman who did not know where she was or where she was going. Aunt Kate was more vivacious. Her face, healthier than her sister's, was all puckers and creases, like a shrivelled red apple, and her hair, braided in the same old-fashioned way, had not lost its ripe nut colour.

They both kissed Gabriel frankly. He was their favourite nephew, the son of their dead elder sister, Ellen, who had married T. J. Conroy of the Port and Docks.

'Gretta tells me you're not going to take a cab back to Monkstown tonight, Gabriel,' said Aunt Kate.

'No,' said Gabriel, turning to his wife, 'we had quite enough of that last year, hadn't we? Don't you remember, Aunt Kate, what a cold Gretta got out of it? Cab windows rattling all the way, and the east wind blowing in after we passed Merrion. Very jolly it was. Gretta caught a dreadful cold.'

Aunt Kate frowned severely and nodded her head at every word.

'Quite right, Gabriel, quite right,' she said. 'You can't be too careful.'

'But as for Gretta there,' said Gabriel, 'she'd walk home in the snow if she were let.'

Mrs. Conroy laughed.

'Don't mind him, Aunt Kate,' she said. 'He's really an awful bother, what with green shades for Tom's eyes at night and making him do the dumb-bells, and forcing Eva to eat the stirabout. The poor child! And she simply hates the sight of it! ... O, but you'll never guess what he makes me wear now!'

She broke out into a peal of laughter and glanced at her husband, whose admiring and happy eyes had been wandering from her dress to her face and hair. The two aunts laughed heartily, too, for Gabriel's solicitude was a standing joke with them.

'Goloshes!' said Mrs. Conroy. 'That's the latest. Whenever it's wet underfoot I must put on my goloshes. Tonight even, he wanted me to put them on, but I wouldn't. The next thing he'll buy me will be a diving suit.'

Gabriel laughed nervously and patted his tie reassuringly, while Aunt Kate nearly doubled herself, so heartily did she enjoy the joke. The smile soon faded from Aunt Julia's face and her mirthless eyes were directed towards her nephew's face. After a pause she asked:

'And what are goloshes, Gabriel?'

'Goloshes, Julia!' exclaimed her sister. 'Goodness me, don't you know what goloshes are? You wear them over your . . . over your boots, Gretta, isn't it?'

'Yes,' said Mrs. Conroy. 'Gutta-percha things. We both have a pair now. Gabriel says everyone wears them on the Continent.'

'O, on the Continent,' murmured Aunt Julia, nodding her head slowly.

Gabriel knitted his brows and said, as if he were slightly angered:

'It's nothing very wonderful, but Gretta thinks it very funny, because she says the word reminds her of Christy Minstrels.'

'But tell me, Gabriel,' said Aunt Kate, with brisk tact. 'Of course, you've seen about the room. Gretta was saying . . .'

'O, the room is all right,' replied Gabriel. 'I've taken one in the Gresham.'

'To be sure,' said Aunt Kate, 'by far the best thing to do. And the children, Gretta, you're not anxious about them?'

'O, for one night,' said Mrs. Conroy. 'Besides, Bessie will look after them.'

'To be sure,' said Aunt Kate again. 'What a comfort it is to have a girl like that, one you can depend on! There's that Lily, I'm sure I don't know what has come over her lately. She's not the girl she was at all.'

Gabriel was about to ask his aunt some questions on this point, but she broke off suddenly to gaze after her sister, who had wandered down the stairs and was craning her neck over the banisters.

'Now, I ask you,' she said almost testily, 'where is Julia going? Julia! Julia! Where are you going?'

Julia, who had gone half-way down one flight, came back and announced blandly:

'Here's Freddy.'

At the same moment a clapping of hands and a final flourish of the pianist told that the waltz had ended. The drawing-room door was opened from within and some couples came out. Aunt Kate drew Gabriel aside hurriedly and whispered into his ear:

'Slip down, Gabriel, like a good fellow and see if

he's all right, and don't let him up if he's screwed. I'm sure he's screwed. I'm sure he is.'

Gabriel went to the stairs and listened over the banisters. He could hear two persons talking in the pantry. Then he recognized Freddy Malins's laugh. He went down the stairs noisily.

'It's such a relief,' said Aunt Kate to Mrs. Conroy, 'that Gabriel is here. I always feel easier in my mind when he's here. . . . Julia, there's Miss Daly and Miss Power will take some refreshment. Thanks for your beautiful waltz, Miss Daly. It made lovely time.'

A tall wizen-faced man, with a stiff grizzled moustache and swarthy skin, who was passing out with his partner, said:

'And may we have some refreshment, too, Miss Morkan?'

'Julia,' said Aunt Kate summarily, 'and here's Mr. Browne and Miss Furlong. Take them in, Julia, with Miss Daly and Miss Power.'

'I'm the man for the ladies,' said Mr. Browne, pursing his lips until his moustache bristled and smiling in all his wrinkles. 'You know, Miss Morkan, the reason they are so fond of me is—'

He did not finish his sentence, but, seeing that Aunt Kate was out of earshot, at once led the three young ladies into the back room. The middle of the room was occupied by two square tables placed end to end, and on these Aunt Julia and the caretaker were straightening and smoothing a large cloth. On the sideboard were arrayed dishes and plates, and glasses and bundles of knives and forks and spoons. The top of the closed square piano served also as a sideboard for viands and sweets. At a smaller sideboard in one corner two young men were standing, drinking hop-bitters.

Mr. Browne led his charges thither and invited them all, in jest, to some ladies' punch, hot, strong, and sweet. As they said they never took anything strong, he opened three bottles of lemonade for them. Then he asked one of the young men to move aside, and, taking hold of the decanter, filled out for himself a goodly measure of whisky. The young men eyed him respectfully while he took a trial sip.

'God help me,' he said, smiling, 'it's the doctor's orders.'

His wizened face broke into a broader smile, and the three young ladies laughed in musical echo to his pleasantry, swaying their bodies to and fro, with nervous jerks of their shoulders. The boldest said:

'O, now, Mr. Browne, I'm sure the doctor never ordered anything of the kind.'

Mr. Browne took another sip of his whisky and said, with sidling mimicry:

'Well, you see, I'm like the famous Mrs. Cassidy, who is reported to have said: "Now, Mary Grimes, if I don't take it, make me take it, for I feel I want it."'

His hot face had leaned forward a little too confidentially and he had assumed a very low Dublin accent, so that the young ladies, with one instinct, received his speech in silence. Miss Furlong, who was one of Mary Jane's pupils, asked Miss Daly what was the name of the pretty waltz she had played; and Mr. Browne, seeing that he was ignored, turned promptly to the two young men, who were more appreciative.

A red-faced young woman, dressed in pansy, came into the room, excitedly clapping her hands and crying:

'Quadrilles! Quadrilles!'

Close on her heels came Aunt Kate, crying:

'Two gentlemen and three ladies, Mary Jane!'

'O, here's Mr. Bergin and Mr. Kerrigan,' said Mary Jane. 'Mr. Kerrigan, will you take Miss Power? Miss Furlong, may I get you a partner, Mr. Bergin. O, that'll just do now.'

'Three ladies, Mary Jane,' said Aunt Kate.

The two young gentlemen asked the ladies if they might have the pleasure, and Mary Jane turned to Miss Daly.

'O, Miss Daly, you're really awful good, after playing for the last two dances, but really we're so short of ladies tonight.'

'I don't mind in the least, Miss Morkan.'

'But I've a nice partner for you, Mr. Bartell D'Arcy, the tenor. I'll get him to sing later on. All Dublin is raving about him.'

'Lovely voice, lovely voice!' said Aunt Kate.

As the piano had twice begun the prelude to the first figure Mary Jane led her recruits quickly from the room. They had hardly gone when Aunt Julia wandered slowly into the room, looking behind her at something.

'What is the matter, Julia?' asked Aunt Kate anxiously. 'Who is it?'

Julia, who was carrying in a column of table-napkins, turned to her sister and said, simply, as if the question had surprised her:

'It's only Freddy, Kate, and Gabriel with him.'

In fact, right behind her Gabriel could be seen piloting Freddy Malins across the landing. The latter, a young man of about forty, was of Gabriel's size and build, with very round shoulders. His face was fleshy and pallid, touched with colour only at the thick hanging lobes of his ears and at the wide wings of his nose. He had coarse features, a blunt nose, a convex and receding brow, tumid and protruded lips. His heavy-lidded eyes and the disorder of his scanty hair made him look sleepy. He was laughing heartily in a high key at a story which he had been telling Gabriel on the stairs and at the same time rubbing the knuckles of his left fist backwards and forwards into his left eye.

'Good evening, Freddy,' said Aunt Julia.

Freddy Malins bade the Misses Morkan good-evening in what seemed an offhand fashion by reason of the habitual catch in his voice and then, seeing that Mr. Browne was grinning at him from the sideboard, crossed the room on rather shaky legs and began to repeat in an undertone the story he had just told to Gabriel.

'He's not so bad, is he?' said Aunt Kate to Gabriel.

Gabriel's brows were dark, but he raised them quickly and answered:

'O, no, hardly noticeable.'

'Now, isn't he a terrible fellow!' she said. 'And his poor mother made him take the pledge on New Year's Eve. But come on, Gabriel, into the drawing-room.'

Before leaving the room with Gabriel she signalled to Mr. Browne by frowning and shaking her forefinger in warning to and fro. Mr. Browne nodded in answer and, when she had gone, said to Freddy Malins:

'Now, then, Teddy, I'm going to fill you out a good glass of lemonade just to buck you up.'

Freddy Malins, who was nearing the climax of his story, waved the offer aside impatiently, but Mr. Browne, having first called Freddy Malins's attention to a disarray in his dress, filled out and handed him a full glass of lemonade. Freddy Malins's left hand accepted the glass mechanically, his right hand being engaged in the mechanical readjustment of his dress. Mr. Browne, whose face was once more wrinkling with mirth, poured out for himself a glass of whiskey while

Freddy Malins exploded, before he had well reached the climax of his story, in a kink of high-pitched bronchitic laughter and, setting down his untasted and overflowing glass, began to rub the knuckles of his left fist backwards and forwards into his left eye, repeating words of his last phrase as well as his fit of laughter would allow him.

.   .   .   .   .

Gabriel could not listen while Mary Jane was playing her Academy piece, full of runs and difficult passages, to the hushed drawing-room. He liked music, but the piece she was playing had no melody for him and he doubted whether it had any melody for the other listeners, though they had begged Mary Jane to play something. Four young men, who had come from the refreshment-room to stand in the doorway at the sound of the piano, had gone away quietly in couples after a few minutes. The only persons who seemed to follow the music were Mary Jane herself, her hands racing along the keyboard or lifted from it at the pauses like those of a priestess in momentary imprecation, and Aunt Kate standing at her elbow to turn the page.

Gabriel's eyes, irritated by the floor, which glittered with beeswax under the heavy chandelier, wandered to the wall above the piano. A picture of the balcony scene in *Romeo and Juliet* hung there and beside it was a picture of the two murdered princes in the Tower which Aunt Julia had worked in red, blue, and brown wools when she was a girl. Probably in the school they had gone to as girls that kind of work had been taught for one year. His mother had worked for him as a birthday present a waistcoat of purple tabinet, with little foxes' heads upon it, lined with brown satin

and having round mulberry buttons. It was strange
that his mother had had no musical talent, though
Aunt Kate used to call her the brains carrier of the
Morkan family. Both she and Julia had always seemed
a little proud of their serious and matronly sister. Her
photograph stood before the pier-glass. She held an
open book on her knees and was pointing out something in it to Constantine who, dressed in a man-o'-
war suit, lay at her feet. It was she who had chosen the
names of her sons, for she was very sensible of the
dignity of family life. Thanks to her, Constantine was
now senior curate in Balbriggan and, thanks to her,
Gabriel himself had taken his degree in the Royal University. A shadow passed over his face as he remembered her sullen opposition to his marriage. Some
slighting phrases she had used still rankled in his
memory; she had once spoken of Gretta as being
country cute and that was not true of Gretta at all. It
was Gretta who had nursed her during all her last long
illness in their house at Monkstown.

He knew that Mary Jane must be near the end of
her piece, for she was playing again the opening
melody with runs of scales after every bar, and while
he waited for the end the resentment died down in his
heart. The piece ended with a trill of octaves in the
treble and a final deep octave in the bass. Great applause greeted Mary Jane as, blushing and rolling up
her music nervously, she escaped from the room. The
most vigorous clapping came from the four young men
in the doorway who had gone away to the refreshment-
room at the beginning of the piece but had come back
when the piano had stopped.

Lancers were arranged. Gabriel found himself part-
nered with Miss Ivors. She was a frank-mannered,
talkative young lady, with a freckled face and promi-

nent brown eyes. She did not wear a low-cut bodice, and the large brooch which was fixed in the front of her collar bore on it an Irish device and motto.

When they had taken their places she said abruptly:

'I have a crow to pluck with you.'

'With me?' said Gabriel.

She nodded her head gravely.

'What is it?' asked Gabriel, smiling at her solemn manner.

'Who is G. C.?' answered Miss Ivors, turning her eyes upon him.

Gabriel coloured and was about to knit his brows, as if he did not understand, when she said bluntly:

'O, innocent Amy! I have found out that you write for the *Daily Express*. Now, aren't you ashamed of yourself?'

'Why should I be ashamed of myself?' asked Gabriel, blinking his eyes and trying to smile.

'Well, I'm ashamed of you,' said Miss Ivors frankly. 'To say you'd write for a paper like that. I didn't think you were a West Briton.'

A look of perplexity appeared on Gabriel's face. It was true that he wrote a literary column every Wednesday in the *Daily Express*, for which he was paid fifteen shillings. But that did not make him a West Briton surely. The books he received for review were almost more welcome than the paltry cheque. He loved to feel the covers and turn over the pages of newly printed books. Nearly every day when his teaching in the college was ended he used to wander down the quays to the second-hand booksellers, to Hickey's on Bachelor's Walk, to Webb's or Massey's on Aston's Quay, or to O'Clohissey's in the by-street. He did not know how to meet her charge. He wanted to say that literature was above politics. But they were friends of many years' standing and their careers had been parallel, first at the University and then as teachers: he could not risk a grandiose phrase with her. He continued blinking his eyes and trying to smile and murmured lamely that he saw nothing political in writing reviews of books.

When their turn to cross had come he was still perplexed and inattentive. Miss Ivors promptly took his hand in a warm grasp and said in a soft friendly tone:

'Of course, I was only joking. Come, we cross now.

When they were together again she spoke of the University question and Gabriel felt more at ease. A friend of hers had shown her his review of Browning's poems. That was how she had found out the secret: but she liked the review immensely. Then she said suddenly:

'O, Mr. Conroy, will you come for an excursion to the Aran Isles this summer? We're going to stay there a whole month. It will be splendid out in the Atlantic. You ought to come. Mr. Clancy is coming, and Mr. Kilkelly and Kathleen Kearney. It would be splendid for Gretta too if she'd come. She's from Connacht, isn't she?'

'Her people are,' said Gabriel shortly.

'But you will come, won't you?' said Miss Ivors, laying her warm hand eagerly on his arm.

'The fact is,' said Gabriel, 'I have just arranged to go—'

'Go where?' asked Miss Ivors.

'Well, you know, every year I go for a cycling tour with some fellows and so—'

'But where?' asked Miss Ivors.

'Well, we usually go to France or Belgium or perhaps Germany,' said Gabriel awkwardly.

'And why do you go to France and Belgium,' said Miss Ivors, 'instead of visiting your own land?'

'Well,' said Gabriel, 'it's partly to keep in touch with the languages and partly for a change.'

'And haven't you your own language to keep in touch with—Irish?' asked Miss Ivors.

'Well,' said Gabriel, 'if it comes to that, you know, Irish is not my language.'

Their neighbours had turned to listen to the cross-examination. Gabriel glanced right and left nervously and tried to keep his good humour under the ordeal, which was making a blush invade his forehead.

'And haven't you your own land to visit,' continued Miss Ivors, 'that you know nothing of, your own people, and your own country?'

'O, to tell you the truth,' retorted Gabriel suddenly, 'I'm sick of my own country, sick of it!'

'Why?' asked Miss Ivors.

Gabriel did not answer, for his retort had heated him.

'Why?' repeated Miss Ivors.

They had to go visiting together and, as he had not answered her, Miss Ivors said warmly:

'Of course, you've no answer.'

Gabriel tried to cover his agitation by taking part in the dance with great energy. He avoided her eyes, for he had seen a sour expression on her face. But when they met in the long chain he was surprised to feel his hand firmly pressed. She looked at him from under her brows for a moment quizzically until he smiled. Then, just as the chain was about to start again, she stood on tiptoe and whispered into his ear:

'West Briton!'

When the lancers were over Gabriel went away to

a remote corner of the room where Freddy Malins's mother was sitting. She was a stout, feeble old woman with white hair. Her voice had a catch in it like her son's and she stuttered slightly. She had been told that Freddy had come and that he was nearly all right. Gabriel asked her whether she had had a good crossing. She lived with her married daughter in Glasgow and came to Dublin on a visit once a year. She answered placidly that she had had a beautiful crossing and that the captain had been most attentive to her. She spoke also of the beautiful house her daughter kept in Glasgow, and of all the friends they had there. While her tongue rambled on Gabriel tried to banish from his mind all memory of the unpleasant incident with Miss Ivors. Of course the girl, or woman, or whatever she was, was an enthusiast, but there was a time for all things. Perhaps he ought not to have answered her like that. But she had no right to call him a West Briton before people, even in joke. She had tried to make him ridiculous before people, heckling him and staring at him with her rabbit's eyes.

He saw his wife making her way towards him through the waltzing couples. When she reached him she said into his ear:

'Gabriel, Aunt Kate wants to know won't you carve the goose as usual. Miss Daly will carve the ham and I'll do the pudding.'

'All right,' said Gabriel.

'She's sending in the younger ones first as soon as this waltz is over so that we'll have the table to ourselves.'

'Were you dancing?' asked Gabriel.

'Of course I was. Didn't you see me? What row had you with Molly Ivors?'

'No row. Why? Did she say so?'

'Something like that. I'm trying to get that Mr. D'Arcy to sing. He's full of conceit, I think.'

'There was no row,' said Gabriel moodily, 'only she wanted me to go for a trip to the west of Ireland and I said I wouldn't.'

His wife clasped her hands excitedly and gave a little jump.

'O, do go, Gabriel,' she cried. 'I'd love to see Galway again.'

'You can go if you like,' said Gabriel coldly.

She looked at him for a moment, then turned to Mrs. Malins and said:

'There's a nice husband for you, Mrs. Malins.'

While she was threading her way back across the room Mrs. Malins, without adverting to the interruption, went on to tell Gabriel what beautiful places there were in Scotland and beautiful scenery. Her son-in-law brought them every year to the lakes and they used to go fishing. Her son-in-law was a splendid fisher. One day he caught a beautiful big fish and the man in the hotel cooked it for their dinner.

Gabriel hardly heard what she said. Now that supper was coming near he began to think again about his speech and about the quotation. When he saw Freddy Malins coming across the room to visit his mother Gabriel left the chair free for him and retired into the embrasure of the window. The room had already cleared and from the back room came the clatter of plates and knives. Those who still remained in the drawing-room seemed tired of dancing and were conversing quietly in little groups. Gabriel's warm, trembling fingers tapped the cold pane of the window. How cool it must be outside! How pleasant it would be to walk out alone, first along by the river and then through the park! The snow would be lying on the branches of the trees and forming a bright cap on the top of the Wellington Monument. How much more pleasant it would be there than at the supper-table!

He ran over the headings of his speech: Irish hospitality, sad memories, the Three Graces, Paris, the quotation from Browning. He repeated to himself a phrase he had written in his review: 'One feels that one is listening to a thought-tormented music.' Miss Ivors had praised the review. Was she sincere? Had she really any life of her own behind all her propagandism? There had never been any ill-feeling between them until that night. It unnerved him to think that she would be at the supper-table, looking up at him while he spoke with her critical quizzing eyes. Perhaps she would not be sorry to see him fail in his speech. An idea came into his mind and gave him courage. He would say, alluding to Aunt Kate and Aunt Julia: 'Ladies and Gentlemen, the generation which is now on the wane among us may have had its faults, but for my part I think it had certain qualities of hospitality, of humour, of humanity, which the new and very serious and hypereducated generation that is growing up around us seems to me to lack.' Very good: that was one for Miss Ivors. What did he care that his aunts were only two ignorant old women?

A murmur in the room attracted his attention. Mr. Browne was advancing from the door, gallantly escorting Aunt Julia, who leaned upon his arm, smiling and hanging her head. An irregular musketry of applause escorted her also as far as the piano and then, as Mary Jane seated herself on the stool, and Aunt Julia, no longer smiling, half turned so as to pitch her voice fairly into the room, gradually ceased. Gabriel recognized the prelude. It was that of an old song of Aunt Julia's—*Arrayed for the Bridal*. Her voice, strong and clear in tone, attacked with great spirit the runs which embellish the air, and though she sang very rapidly she did not miss even the smallest of the grace notes. To follow the voice, without looking at the singer's face, was to feel and share the excitement of swift and secure flight. Gabriel applauded loudly with all the others at the close of the song, and loud applause was borne in from the invisible supper-table. It sounded so genuine that a little colour struggled into Aunt Julia's face as she bent to replace in the music-stand the old leather-bound song-book that had her initials on the cover. Freddy Malins, who had listened with his head perched sideways to hear her better, was still applauding when everyone else had ceased, and talking animatedly to his mother, who nodded her head gravely and slowly in acquiescence. At last, when he could clap no more, he stood up suddenly and hurried across the room to Aunt Julia whose hand he seized and held in both his hands, shaking it when words failed him or the catch in his voice proved too much for him.

'I was just telling my mother,' he said, 'I never heard you sing so well, never. No, I never heard your voice so good as it is tonight. Now! Would you believe that now? That's the truth. Upon my word and honour that's the truth. I never heard your voice sound so fresh and so . . . so clear and fresh, never.'

Aunt Julia smiled broadly and murmured something about compliments as she released her hand from his grasp. Mr. Browne extended his open hand towards her and said to those who were near him in the manner of a showman introducing a prodigy to an audience:

'Miss Julia Morkan, my latest discovery!'

He was laughing very heartily at this himself when Freddy Malins turned to him and said:

'Well, Browne, if you're serious you might make a

worse discovery. All I can say is I never heard her sing half so well as long as I am coming here. And that's the honest truth.'

'Neither did I,' said Mr. Browne. 'I think her voice has greatly improved.'

Aunt Julia shrugged her shoulders and said with meek pride:

'Thirty years ago I hadn't a bad voice as voices go.'

'I often told Julia,' said Aunt Kate emphatically, 'that she was simply thrown away in that choir. But she never would be said by me.'

She turned as if to appeal to the good sense of the others against a refractory child, while Aunt Julia gazed in front of her, a vague smile of reminiscence playing on her face.

'No,' continued Aunt Kate, 'she wouldn't be said or led by anyone, slaving there in that choir night and day, night and day. Six o'clock on Christmas morning! And all for what?'

'Well, isn't it for the honour of God, Aunt Kate?' asked Mary Jane, twisting round on the piano-stool and smiling.

Aunt Kate turned fiercely on her niece and said:

'I know all about the honour of God, Mary Jane, but I think it's not at all honourable for the pope to turn out the women out of the choirs that have slaved there all their lives and put little whipper-snappers of boys over their heads. I suppose it is for the good of the Church, if the pope does it. But it's not just, Mary Jane, and it's not right.'

She had worked herself into a passion and would have continued in defence of her sister, for it was a sore subject with her, but Mary Jane, seeing that all the dancers had come back, intervened pacifically.

'Now, Aunt Kate, you're giving scandal to Mr. Browne, who is of the other persuasion.'

Aunt Kate turned to Mr. Browne, who was grinning at this allusion to his religion, and said hastily:

'O, I don't question the pope's being right. I'm only a stupid old woman and I wouldn't presume to do such a thing. But there's such a thing as common everyday politeness and gratitude. And if I were in Julia's place I'd tell that Father Healey straight up to his face . . .'

'And besides, Aunt Kate,' said Mary Jane, 'we really are all hungry and when we are hungry we are all very quarrelsome.'

'And when we are thirsty we are also quarrelsome,' added Mr. Browne.

'So that we had better go to supper,' said Mary Jane, 'and finish the discussion afterwards.'

On the landing outside the drawing-room Gabriel found his wife and Mary Jane trying to persuade Miss Ivors to stay for supper. But Miss Ivors, who had put on her hat and was buttoning her cloak, would not stay. She did not feel in the least hungry and she had already overstayed her time.

'But only for ten minutes, Molly,' said Mrs. Conroy. 'That won't delay you.'

'To take a pick itself,' said Mary Jane, 'after all your dancing.'

'I really couldn't,' said Miss Ivors.

'I am afraid you didn't enjoy yourself at all,' said Mary Jane hopelessly.

'Ever so much, I assure you,' said Miss Ivors, 'but you really must let me run off now.'

'But how can you get home?' asked Mrs. Conroy.

'O, it's only two steps up the quay.'

Gabriel hesitated a moment and said:

'If you will allow me, Miss Ivors, I'll see you home if you are really obliged to go.'

But Miss Ivors broke away from them.

'I won't hear of it,' she cried. 'For goodness' sake go in to your suppers and don't mind me. I'm quite well able to take care of myself.'

'Well, you're the comical girl, Molly,' said Mrs. Conroy frankly.

'*Beannacht libh*,' cried Miss Ivors, with a laugh, as she ran down the staircase.

Mary Jane gazed after her, a moody puzzled expression on her face, while Mrs. Conroy leaned over the banisters to listen for the hall-door. Gabriel asked himself was he the cause of her abrupt departure. But she did not seem to be in ill humour—she had gone away laughing. He stared blankly down the staircase.

At the moment Aunt Kate came toddling out of the supper-room, almost wringing her hands in despair.

'Where is Gabriel?' she cried. 'Where on earth is Gabriel? There's everyone waiting in there, stage to let, and nobody to carve the goose!'

'Here I am, Aunt Kate!' cried Gabriel, with sudden animation, 'ready to carve a flock of geese, if necessary.'

A fat brown goose lay at one end of the table, and at the other end, on a bed of creased paper strewn with sprigs of parsley, lay a great ham, stripped of its outer skin and peppered over with crust crumbs, a neat paper frill round its shin, and beside this was a round of spiced beef. Between these rival ends ran parallel lines of side-dishes: two little minsters of jelly, red and yellow; a shallow dish full of blocks of blancmange and red jam, a large green leaf-shaped dish with a stalk-shaped handle, on which lay bunches of purple raisins and peeled almonds, a companion dish on which lay a solid rectangle of Smyrna figs, a dish of custard topped with grated nutmeg, a small bowl full of chocolates and sweets wrapped in gold and silver papers, and a glass vase in which stood some tall celery stalks. In the centre of the table there stood, as sentries to a fruit-stand which upheld a pyramid of oranges and American apples, two squat old-fashioned decanters of cut glass, one containing port and the other dark sherry. On the closed square piano a pudding in a huge yellow dish lay in waiting, and behind it were three squads of bottles of stout and ale and minerals, drawn up according to the colours of their uniforms, the first two black, with brown and red labels, the third and smallest squad white, with transverse green sashes.

Gabriel took his seat boldly at the head of the table and, having looked to the edge of the carver, plunged his fork firmly into the goose. He felt quite at ease now, for he was an expert carver and liked nothing better than to find himself at the head of a well-laden table.

'Miss Furlong, what shall I send you?' he asked. 'A wing or a slice of the breast?'

'Just a small slice of the breast.'

'Miss Higgins, what for you?'

'O, anything at all, Mr. Conroy.'

While Gabriel and Miss Daly exchanged plates of goose and plates of ham and spiced beef, Lily went from guest to guest with a dish of hot floury potatoes wrapped in a white napkin. This was Mary Jane's idea and she had also suggested apple sauce for the goose, but Aunt Kate had said that plain roast goose without any apple sauce had always been good enough for her and she hoped she might never eat worse. Mary Jane waited on her pupils and saw that they got the best

76

slices, and Aunt Kate and Aunt Julia opened and carried across from the piano bottles of stout and ale for the gentlemen and bottles of minerals for the ladies. There was a great deal of confusion and laughter and noise, the noise of orders and counter-orders, of knives and forks, of corks and glass-stoppers. Gabriel began to carve second helpings as soon as he had finished the first round without serving himself. Everyone protested loudly, so that he compromised by taking a long draught of stout, for he had found the carving hot work. Mary Jane settled down quietly to her supper, but Aunt Kate and Aunt Julia were still toddling round the table, walking on each other's heels, getting in each other's way and giving each other unheeded orders. Mr. Browne begged of them to sit down and eat their suppers and so did Gabriel, but they said there was time enough, so that, at last Freddy Malins stood up and, capturing Aunt Kate, plumped her down on her chair amid general laughter.

When everyone had been well served Gabriel said, smiling:

'Now, if anyone wants a little more of what vulgar people call stuffing let him or her speak.'

A chorus of voices invited him to begin his own supper, and Lily came forward with three potatoes which she had reserved for him.

'Very well,' said Gabriel amiably, as he took another preparatory draught, 'kindly forget my existence, ladies and gentlemen, for a few minutes.'

He set to his supper and took no part in the conversation with which the table covered Lily's removal of the plates. The subject of talk was the opera company which was then at the Theatre Royal. Mr. Bartell D'Arcy, the tenor, a dark-complexioned young man with a smart moustache, praised very highly the leading contralto of the company, but Miss Furlong thought she had a rather vulgar style of production. Freddy Malins said there was a negro chieftain singing in the second part of the Gaiety pantomime who had one of the finest tenor voices he had ever heard.

'Have you heard him?' he asked Mr. Bartell D'Arcy across the table.

'No,' answered Mr. Bartell D'Arcy carelessly.

'Because,' Freddy Malins explained, 'now I'd be curious to hear your opinion of him. I think he has a grand voice.'

'It takes Teddy to find out the really good things,' said Mr. Browne familiarly to the table.

'And why couldn't he have a voice too?' asked Freddy Malins sharply. 'Is it because he's only a black?'

Nobody answered this question and Mary Jane led the table back to the legitimate opera. One of her pupils had given her a pass for *Mignon.* Of course it was very fine, she said, but it made her think of poor Georgina Burns. Mr. Browne could go back farther still, to the old Italian companies that used to come to Dublin—Tietjens, Ilma de Murzka, Campanini, the great Trebelli, Giuglini, Ravelli, Aramburo. Those were the days, he said, when there was something like singing to be heard in Dublin. He told too of how the top gallery of the old Royal used to be packed night after night, of how one night an Italian tenor had sung five encores to *Let me like a Soldier fall,* introducing a high C every time, and of how the gallery boys would sometimes in their enthusiasm unyoke the horses from the carriage of some great *prima donna* and pull her themselves through the streets to her hotel. 'Why did they never play the grand old operas now,' he asked, '*Dinorah, Lucrezia Borgia?* Because they could not get the voices to sing them: that was why.'

'O, well,' said Mr. Bartell D'Arcy, 'I presume there are as good singers today as there were then.'

'Where are they?' asked Mr. Browne defiantly.

'In London, Paris, Milan,' said Mr. Bartell D'Arcy warmly. 'I suppose Caruso, for example, is quite as good, if not better than any of the men you have mentioned.'

'Maybe so,' said Mr. Browne. 'But I may tell you I doubt it strongly.'

'O, I'd give anything to hear Caruso sing,' said Mary Jane.

'For me,' said Aunt Kate, who had been picking a bone, 'there was only one tenor. To please me, I mean. But I suppose none of you ever heard of him.'

'Who was he, Miss Morkan?' asked Mr. Bartell D'Arcy politely.

'His name,' said Aunt Kate, 'was Parkinson. I heard him when he was in his prime and I think he had then the purest tenor voice that was ever put into a man's throat.'

'Strange,' said Mr. Bartell D'Arcy. 'I never even heard of him.'

'Yes, yes, Miss Morkan is right,' said Mr. Browne. 'I remember hearing of old Parkinson, but he's too far back for me.'

'A beautiful, pure, sweet, mellow English tenor,' said Aunt Kate with enthusiasm.

Gabriel having finished, the huge pudding was transferred to the table. The clatter of forks and spoons began again. Gabriel's wife served out spoonfuls of the pudding and passed the plates down the table. Midway down they were held up by Mary Jane, who replenished them with raspberry or orange jelly or with blancmange and jam. The pudding was of Aunt Julia's making, and she received praises for it from all quarters. She herself said that it was not quite brown enough.

'Well, I hope, Miss Morkan,' said Mr. Browne, 'that I'm brown enough for you because, you know, I'm all brown.'

All the gentlemen, except Gabriel, ate some of the pudding out of compliment to Aunt Julia. As Gabriel never ate sweets the celery had been left for him. Freddy Malins also took a stalk of celery and ate it with his pudding. He had been told that celery was a capital thing for the blood and he was just then under doctor's care. Mrs. Malins, who had been silent all through the supper, said that her son was going down to Mount Melleray in a week or so. The table then spoke of Mount Melleray, how bracing the air was down there, how hospitable the monks were and how they never asked for a penny-piece from their guests.

'And do you mean to say,' asked Mr. Browne incredulously, 'that a chap can go down there and put up there as if it were a hotel and live on the fat of the land and then come away without paying anything?'

'O, most people give some donation to the monastery when they leave,' said Mary Jane.

'I wish we had an institution like that in our Church,' said Mr. Browne candidly.

He was astonished to hear that the monks never spoke, got up at two in the morning and slept in their coffins. He asked what they did it for.

'That's the rule of the order,' said Aunt Kate firmly.

'Yes, but why?' asked Mr. Browne.

Aunt Kate repeated that it was the rule, that was all. Mr. Browne still seemed not to understand. Freddy

Malins explained to him, as best he could, that the monks were trying to make up for the sins committed by all the sinners in the outside world. The explanation was not very clear, for Mr. Browne grinned and said:

'I like that idea very much, but wouldn't a comfortable spring bed do them as well as a coffin?'

'The coffin,' said Mary Jane, 'is to remind them of their last end.'

As the subject had grown lugubrious it was buried in a silence of the table, during which Mrs. Malins could be heard saying to her neighbour in an indistinct undertone:

'They are very good men, the monks, very pious men.'

The raisins and almonds and figs and apples and oranges and chocolates and sweets were now passed about the table, and Aunt Julia invited all the guests to have either port or sherry. At first Mr. Bartell D'Arcy refused to take either, but one of his neighbours nudged him and whispered something to him, upon which he allowed his glass to be filled. Gradually as the last glasses were being filled the conversation ceased. A pause followed, broken only by the noise of the wine and by unsettlings of chairs. The Misses Morkan, all three, looked down at the tablecloth. Someone coughed once or twice, and then a few gentlemen patted the table gently as a signal for silence. The silence came and Gabriel pushed back his chair and stood up.

The patting at once grew louder in encouragement and then ceased altogether. Gabriel leaned his ten trembling fingers on the tablecloth and smiled nervously at the company. Meeting a row of upturned faces he raised his eyes to the chandelier. The piano was playing a waltz tune and he could hear the skirts sweeping against the drawing-room door. People, perhaps, were standing in the snow on the quay outside, gazing up at the lighted windows and listening to the waltz music. The air was pure there. In the distance lay the park, where the trees were weighted with snow. The Wellington Monument wore a gleaming cap of snow that flashed westward over the white field of Fifteen Acres.

He began:

'Ladies and Gentlemen,

'It has fallen to my lot this evening, as in years past, to perform a very pleasing task, but a task for which I am afraid my poor powers as a speaker are all too inadequate.'

'No, no!' said Mr. Browne.

'But, however that may be, I can only ask you tonight to take the will for the deed, and to lend me your attention for a few moments while I endeavour to express to you in words what my feelings are on this occasion.

'Ladies and Gentlemen, it is not the first time that we have gathered together under this hospitable roof, around this hospitable board. It is not the first time that we have been the recipients—or perhaps, I had better say, the victims—of the hospitality of certain good ladies.'

He made a circle in the air with his arm and paused. Everyone laughed or smiled at Aunt Kate and Aunt Julia and Mary Jane, who all turned crimson with pleasure. Gabriel went on more boldly:

'I feel more strongly with every recurring year that our country has no tradition which does it so much honour and which it should guard so jealously as that of its hospitality. It is a tradition that is unique as far as my experience goes (and I have visited not a few places abroad) among the modern nations. Some would say, perhaps, that with us it is rather a failing than anything to be boasted of. But granted even that, it is, to my mind, a princely failing, and one that I trust will long be cultivated among us. Of one thing, at least, I am sure. As long as this one roof shelters the good ladies aforesaid—and I wish from my heart it may do so for many and many a long year to come—the tradition of genuine warm-hearted courteous Irish hospitality, which our forefathers have handed down to us and which we in turn must hand down to our descendants, is still alive among us.'

A hearty murmur of assent ran round the table. It shot through Gabriel's mind that Miss Ivors was not there and that she had gone away discourteously: and he said with confidence in himself:

'Ladies and Gentlemen,

'A new generation is growing up in our midst, a generation actuated by new ideas and new principles. It is serious and enthusiastic for these new ideas and its enthusiasm, even when it is misdirected, is, I believe, in the main sincere. But we are living in a sceptical and, if I may use the phrase, a thought-tormented age: and sometimes I fear that this new generation, educated or hypereducated as it is, will lack those qualities of humanity, of hospitality, of kindly humour which belonged to an older day. Listening tonight to the names of all those great singers of the past it seemed to me, I must confess, that we were living in a less spacious age. Those days might, without exaggeration, be called spacious days: and if they are gone beyond recall, let us hope, at least, that in gatherings such as this we shall still speak of them with pride and affection, still cherish in our hearts the memory of

those dead and gone great ones whose fame the world
will not willingly let die.'

'Hear, hear!' said Mr. Browne loudly.

'But yet,' continued Gabriel, his voice falling into a
softer inflexion, 'there are always in gatherings such
as this sadder thoughts that will recur to our minds:
thoughts of the past, of youth, of changes, of absent
faces that we miss here tonight. Our path through life
is strewn with many such sad memories: and were we
to brood upon them always we could not find the heart
to go on bravely with our work among the living.
We have all of us living duties and living affections
which claim, and rightly claim, our strenuous en-
deavours.

'Therefore, I will not linger on the past. I will not
let any gloomy moralizing intrude upon us here tonight. Here we are gathered together for a brief
moment from the bustle and rush of our everyday
routine. We are met here as friends, in the spirit of
good-fellowship, as colleagues, also, to a certain extent,
in the true spirit of *camaraderie*, and as the guests of
—what shall I call them?—the Three Graces of the
Dublin musical world.'

The table burst into applause and laughter at this
allusion. Aunt Julia vainly asked each of her neighbours in turn to tell her what Gabriel had said.

'He says we are the Three Graces, Aunt Julia,' said
Mary Jane.

Aunt Julia did not understand, but she looked up,
smiling, at Gabriel, who continued in the same vein:

'Ladies and Gentlemen,

'I will not attempt to play tonight the part that Paris
played on another occasion. I will not attempt to
choose between them. The task would be an invidious
one and one beyond my poor powers. For when I view

them in turn, whether it be our chief hostess herself, whose good heart, whose too good heart, has become a byword with all who know her; or her sister, who seems to be gifted with perennial youth and whose singing must have been a surprise and a revelation to us all tonight; or, last but not least, when I consider our youngest hostess, talented, cheerful, hard-working and the best of nieces, I confess, Ladies and Gentlemen, that I do not know to which of them I should award the prize.'

Gabriel glanced down at his aunts and, seeing the large smile on Aunt Julia's face and the tears which had risen to Aunt Kate's eyes, hastened to his close. He raised his glass of port gallantly, while every member of the company fingered a glass expectantly, and said loudly:

'Let us toast them all three together. Let us drink to their health, wealth, long life, happiness and prosperity, and may they long continue to hold the proud and self-won position which they hold in their profession and the position of honour and affection which they hold in our hearts.'

All the guests stood up, glass in hand, and turning towards the three seated ladies, sang in unison, with Mr. Browne as leader:

> For they are jolly gay fellows,
> For they are jolly gay fellows,
> For they are jolly gay fellows,
> Which nobody can deny.

Aunt Kate was making frank use of her handkerchief and even Aunt Julia seemed moved. Freddy Malins beat time with his pudding-fork and the singers turned towards one another, as if in melodious conference, while they sang with emphasis:

Unless he tells a lie,
Unless he tells a lie,

Then, turning once more towards their hostesses, they sang:

For they are jolly gay fellows,
For they are jolly gay fellows,
For they are jolly gay fellows,
Which nobody can deny.

The acclamation which followed was taken up beyond the door of the supper room by many of the other guests and renewed time after time, Freddy Malins acting as officer with his fork on high.

· · · · · ·

The piercing morning air came into the hall where they were standing so that Aunt Kate said:

'Close the door, somebody. Mrs. Malins will get her death of cold.'

'Browne is out there, Aunt Kate,' said Mary Jane.

'Browne is everywhere,' said Aunt Kate, lowering her voice.

Mary Jane laughed at her tone.

'Really,' she·said archly, 'he is very attentive.'

'He has been laid on here like the gas,' said Aunt Kate in the same tone, 'all during the Christmas.'

She laughed herself this time good-humouredly and then added quickly:

'But tell him to come in, Mary Jane, and close the door. I hope to goodness he didn't hear me.'

At that moment the hall-door was opened and Mr. Browne came in from the doorstep, laughing as if his heart would break. He was dressed in a long green overcoat with mock astrakhan cuffs and collar and wore on his head an oval fur cap. He pointed down the snow-covered quay from where the sound of shrill prolonged whistling was borne in.

'Teddy will have all the cabs in Dublin out,' he said.

Gabriel advanced from the little pantry behind the office, struggling into his overcoat and, looking round the hall, said,

'Gretta not down yet?'

'She's getting on her things, Gabriel,' said Aunt Kate.

'Who's playing up there?' asked Gabriel.

'Nobody. They're all gone.'

'O no, Aunt Kate,' said Mary Jane. 'Bartell D'Arcy and Miss O'Callaghan aren't gone yet.'

'Someone is fooling at the piano anyhow,' said Gabriel.

Mary Jane glanced at Gabriel and Mr. Browne and said with a shiver:

'It makes me feel cold to look at you two gentlemen muffled up like that. I wouldn't like to face your journey home at this hour.'

'I'd like nothing better this minute,' said Mr. Browne stoutly, 'than a rattling fine walk in the country or a fast drive with a good spanking goer between the shafts.'

'We used to have a very good horse and trap at home,' said Aunt Julia, sadly.

'The never-to-be-forgotten Johnny,' said Mary Jane, laughing.

Aunt Kate and Gabriel laughed too.

'Why, what was wonderful about Johnny?' asked Mr. Browne.

'The late lamented Patrick Morkan, our grandfather, that is,' explained Gabriel, 'commonly known in his later years as the old gentleman, was a glue-boiler.'

'O, now, Gabriel,' said Aunt Kate, laughing, 'he had a starch mill.'

'Well, glue or starch,' said Gabriel, 'the old gentleman had a horse by the name of Johnny. And Johnny used to work in the old gentleman's mill, walking round and round in order to drive the mill. That was all very well; but now comes the tragic part about Johnny. One fine day the old gentleman thought he'd like to drive out with the quality to a military review in the park.'

'The Lord have mercy on his soul,' said Aunt Kate compassionately.

'Amen,' said Gabriel. 'So the old gentleman, as I said, harnessed Johnny and put on his very best tall hat and his very best stock collar and drove out in grand style from his ancestral mansion somewhere near Back Lane, I think.'

Everyone laughed, even Mrs. Mallins, at Gabriel's manner, and Aunt Kate said:

'O, now, Gabriel, he didn't live in Back Lane, really. Only the mill was there.'

'Out from the mansion of his forefathers,' continued Gabriel, 'he drove with Johnny. And everything went on beautifully until Johnny came in sight of King Billy's statue: and whether he fell in love with the horse King Billy sits on or whether he thought he was back again in the mill, anyhow he began to walk round the statue.'

Gabriel paced in a circle round the hall in his goloshes amid the laughter of the others.

'Round and round he went,' said Gabriel, 'and the old gentleman, who was a very pompous old gentleman, was highly indignant. "Go on, sir! What do you mean, sir? Johnny! Johnny! Most extraordinary conduct! Can't understand the horse!"'

The peals of laughter which followed Gabriel's imitation of the incident was interrupted by a resounding knock at the hall door. Mary Jane ran to open it and let in Freddy Malins. Freddy Malins, with his hat well back on his head and his shoulders humped with cold, was puffing and steaming after his exertions.

'I could only get one cab,' he said.

'O, we'll find another along the quay,' said Gabriel.

'Yes,' said Aunt Kate. 'Better not keep Mrs. Malins standing in the draught.'

Mrs. Malins was helped down the front steps by her son and Mr. Browne and, after many manœuvres, hoisted into the cab. Freddy Malins clambered in after her and spent a long time settling her on the seat, Mr. Browne helping him with advice. At last she was settled comfortably and Freddy Malins invited Mr. Browne into the cab. There was a good deal of confused talk, and then Mr. Browne got into the cab. The cabman settled his rug over his knees, and bent down for the address. The confusion grew greater and the cabman was directed differently by Freddy Malins and Mr. Browne, each of whom had his head out through a window of the cab. The difficulty was to know where to drop Mr. Browne along the route, and Aunt Kate, Aunt Julia, and Mary Jane helped the discussion from the doorstep with cross-directions and contradictions and abundance of laughter. As for Freddy Malins he was speechless with laughter. He popped his head in and out of the window every moment to the great danger of his hat, and told his mother how the discussion was progressing, till at last Mr. Browne shouted to the bewildered cabman above the din of everybody's laughter:

'Do you know Trinity College?'

'Yes, sir,' said the cabman.

'Well, drive bang up against Trinity College gates,' said Mr. Browne, 'and then we'll tell you where to go. You understand now?'

'Yes, sir,' said the cabman.

'Make like a bird for Trinity College.'

'Right, sir,' said the cabman.

The horse was whipped up and the cab rattled off along the quay amid a chorus of laughter and adieus.

Gabriel had not gone to the door with the others. He was in a dark part of the hall gazing up the staircase. A woman was standing near the top of the first flight, in the shadow also. He could not see her face but he could see the terra-cotta and salmon-pink panels of her skirt which the shadow made appear black and white. It was his wife. She was leaning on the banisters, listening to something. Gabriel was surprised at her stillness and strained his ear to listen also. But he could hear little save the noise of laughter and dispute on the front steps, a few chords struck on the piano and a few notes of a man's voice singing.

He stood still in the gloom of the hall, trying to catch the air that the voice was singing and gazing up at his wife. There was grace and mystery in her attitude as if she were a symbol of something. He asked himself what is a woman standing on the stairs in the shadow, listening to distant music, a symbol of. If he were a painter he would paint her in that attitude. Her blue felt hat would show off the bronze of her hair against the darkness and the dark panels of her skirt would show off the light ones. *Distant Music* he would call the picture if he were a painter.

The hall-door was closed, and Aunt Kate, Aunt Julia, and Mary Jane came down the hall, still laughing.

'Well, isn't Freddy terrible?' said Mary Jane. 'He's really terrible.'

Gabriel said nothing, but pointed up the stairs towards where his wife was standing. Now that the hall-door was closed the voice and the piano could be heard more clearly. Gabriel held up his hand for them to be silent. The song seemed to be in the old Irish tonality and the singer seemed uncertain both of his words and of his voice. The voice, made plaintive by distance and by the singer's hoarseness, faintly illuminated the cadence of the air with words expressing grief:

> O, the rain falls on my heavy locks
> And the dew wets my skin,
> My babe lies cold . . .

'O,' exclaimed Mary Jane. 'It's Bartell D'Arcy singing, and he wouldn't sing all the night. O, I'll get him to sing a song before he goes.'

'O, do, Mary Jane,' said Aunt Kate.

Mary Jane brushed past the others and ran to the staircase, but before she reached it the singing stopped and the piano was closed abruptly.

'O, what a pity!' she cried. 'Is he coming down, Gretta?'

Gabriel heard his wife answer yes and saw her come down towards them. A few steps behind her were Mr. Bartell D'Arcy and Miss O'Callaghan.

'O, Mr. D'Arcy,' cried Mary Jane, 'it's downright mean of you to break off like that when we were all in raptures listening to you.'

'I have been at him all the evening,' said Miss O'Callaghan, 'and Mrs. Conroy, too, and he told us he had a dreadful cold and couldn't sing.'

'O, Mr. D'Arcy,' said Aunt Kate, 'now that was a great fib to tell.'

'Can't you see that I'm as hoarse as a crow?' said Mr. D'Arcy roughly.

He went into the pantry hastily and put on his overcoat. The others, taken back by his rude speech, could find nothing to say. Aunt Kate wrinkled her brows and made signs to the others to drop the subject. Mr. D'Arcy stood swathing his neck carefully and frowning.

'It's the weather,' said Aunt Julia, after a pause.

'Yes, everybody has colds,' said Aunt Kate readily, 'everybody.'

'They say,' said Mary Jane, 'we haven't had snow like it for thirty years, and I read this morning in the newspapers that the snow is general all over Ireland.'

'I love the look of snow,' said Aunt Julia sadly.

'So do I,' said Miss O'Callaghan. 'I think Christmas is never really Christmas unless we have the snow on the ground.'

'But poor Mr. D'Arcy doesn't like the snow,' said Aunt Kate, smiling.

Mr. D'Arcy came from the pantry, fully swathed and buttoned, and in a repentant tone told them the history of his cold. Everyone gave him advice and said it was a great pity and urged him to be very careful of his throat in the night air. Gabriel watched his wife, who did not join in the conversation. She was standing right under the dusty fanlight and the flame of the gas lit up the rich bronze of her hair, which he had seen her drying at the fire a few days before. She was in the same attitude and seemed unaware of the talk about her. At last she turned towards them and Gabriel saw that there was colour on her cheeks and that her eyes were shining. A sudden tide of joy went leaping out of his heart.

'Mr. D'Arcy,' she said, 'what is the name of that song you were singing?'

'It's called *The Lass of Aughrim*,' said Mr. D'Arcy, 'but I couldn't remember it properly. Why? Do you know it?'

'*The Lass of Aughrim*,' she repeated. 'I couldn't think of the name.'

'It's a very nice air,' said Mary Jane. 'I'm sorry you were not in voice tonight.'

'Now, Mary Jane,' said Aunt Kate, 'don't annoy Mr. D'Arcy. I won't have him annoyed.'

Seeing that all were ready to start she shepherded them to the door, where good night was said:

'Well, good night, Aunt Kate, and thanks for the pleasant evening.'

'Good night, Gabriel. Good night, Gretta!'

'Good night, Aunt Kate, and thanks ever so much. Good night, Aunt Julia.'

'O, good night, Gretta, I didn't see you.'

'Good night, Mr. D'Arcy. Good night, Miss O'Callaghan.'

'Good night, Miss Morkan.'

'Good night, again.'

'Good night, all. Safe home.'

'Good night. Good night.'

The morning was still dark. A dull, yellow light brooded over the houses and the river; and the sky seemed to be descending. It was slushy underfoot, and only streaks and patches of snow lay on the roofs, on the parapets of the quay and on the area railings. The lamps were still burning redly in the murky air and, across the river, the palace of the Four Courts stood out menacingly against the heavy sky.

She was walking on before him with Mr. Bartell D'Arcy, her shoes in a brown parcel tucked under one arm and her hands holding her skirt up from the slush. She had no longer any grace of attitude, but Gabriel's eyes were still bright with happiness. The blood went bounding along his veins and the thoughts went rioting through his brain, proud, joyful, tender, valorous.

She was walking on before him so lightly and so erect that he longed to run after her noiselessly, catch her by the shoulders and say something foolish and affectionate into her ear. She seemed to him so frail that he longed to defend her against something and then to be alone with her. Moments of their secret life together burst like stars upon his memory. A heliotrope envelope was lying beside his breakfast-cup and he was caressing it with his hand. Birds were twittering in the ivy and the sunny web of the curtain was shimmering along the floor: he could not eat for happiness. They were standing on the crowded platform and he was placing a ticket inside the warm palm of her glove. He was standing with her in the cold, looking in through a grated window at a man making bottles in a roaring furnace. It was very cold. Her face, fragrant in the cold air, was quite close to his, and suddenly he called out to the man at the furnace:

'Is the fire hot, sir?'

But the man could not hear with the noise of the furnace. It was just as well. He might have answered rudely.

A wave of yet more tender joy escaped from his heart and went coursing in warm flood along his arteries. Like the tender fire of stars, moments of their life together, that no one knew of or would ever know of, broke upon and illumined his memory. He longed to recall to her those moments, to make her forget the years of their dull existence together and remember only their moments of ecstasy. For the years, he felt,

had not quenched his soul or hers. Their children, his
writing, her household cares had not quenched all
their souls' tender fire. In one letter that he had written
to her then he had said: 'Why is it that words like these
seem to me so dull and cold? Is it because there is no
word tender enough to be your name?'

Like distant music these words that he had written
years before were borne towards him from the past.
He longed to be alone with her. When the others had
gone away, when he and she were in the room in the
hotel, then they would be alone together. He would
call her softly:

'Gretta!'

Perhaps she would not hear at once: she would be
undressing. Then something in his voice would strike
her. She would turn and look at him. . . .

At the corner of Winetavern Street they met a cab.
He was glad of its rattling noise as it saved him from
conversation. She was looking out of the window and
seemed tired. The others spoke only a few words,
pointing out some building or street. The horse galloped along wearily under the murky morning sky,
dragging his old rattling box after his heels, and
Gabriel was again in a cab with her, galloping to catch
the boat, galloping to their honeymoon.

As the cab drove across O'Connell Bridge Miss
O'Callaghan said:

'They say you never cross O'Connell Bridge without
seeing a white horse.'

'I see a white man this time,' said Gabriel.

'Where?' asked Mr. Bartell D'Arcy.

Gabriel pointed to the statue, on which lay patches
of snow. Then he nodded familiarly to it and waved
his hand.

'Good night, Dan,' he said gaily.

When the cab drew up before the hotel, Gabriel jumped out and, in spite of Mr. Bartell D'Arcy's protest, paid the driver. He gave the man a shilling over his fare. The man saluted and said:

'A prosperous New Year to you, sir.'

'The same to you,' said Gabriel cordially.

She leaned for a moment on his arm in getting out of the cab and while standing at the curbstone, bidding the others good night. She leaned lightly on his arm, as lightly as when she had danced with him a few hours before. He had felt proud and happy then, happy that she was his, proud of her grace and wifely carriage. But now, after the kindling again of so many memories, the first touch of her body, musical and strange and perfumed, sent through him a keen pang of lust. Under cover of her silence he pressed her arm closely to his side, and, as they stood at the hotel door, he felt that they had escaped from their lives and duties, escaped from home and friends and run away together with wild and radiant hearts to a new adventure.

An old man was dozing in a great hooded chair in the hall. He lit a candle in the office and went before them to the stairs. They followed him in silence, their feet falling in soft thuds on the thickly carpeted stairs. She mounted the stairs behind the porter, her head bowed in the ascent, her frail shoulders curved as with a burden, her skirt girt tightly about her. He could have flung his arms about her hips and held her still, for his arms were trembling with desire to seize her and only the stress of his nails against the palms of his hands held the wild impulse of his body in check. The porter halted on the stairs to settle his guttering candle. They halted, too, on the steps below him. In the silence Gabriel could hear the falling of the molten wax into the tray and the thumping of his own heart against his ribs.

The porter led them along a corridor and opened a door. Then he set his unstable candle down on a toilet-table and asked at what hour they were to be called in the morning.

'Eight,' said Gabriel.

The porter pointed to the tap of the electric-light and began a muttered apology, but Gabriel cut him short.

'We don't want any light. We have light enough from the street. And I say,' he added, pointing to the candle, 'you might remove that handsome article, like a good man.'

The porter took up his candle again, but slowly, for he was surprised by such a novel idea. Then he mumbled good night and went out. Gabriel shot the lock to.

A ghastly light from the street lamp lay in a long shaft from one window to the door. Gabriel threw his overcoat and hat on a couch and crossed the room towards the window. He looked down into the street in order that his emotion might calm a little. Then he turned and leaned against a chest of drawers with his back to the light. She had taken off her hat and cloak and was standing before a large swinging mirror, un-hooking her waist. Gabriel paused for a few moments, watching her, and then said:

'Gretta!'

She turned away from the mirror slowly and walked along the shaft of light towards him. Her face looked so serious and weary that the words would not pass Gabriel's lips. No, it was not the moment yet.

'You look tired,' he said.

'I am a little,' she answered.

'You don't feel ill or weak?'

'No, tired: that's all.'

She went on to the window and stood there, looking out. Gabriel waited again and then, fearing that diffidence was about to conquer him, he said abruptly:

'By the way, Gretta!'

'What is it?'

'You know that poor fellow Malins?' he said quickly.

'Yes. What about him?'

'Well, poor fellow, he's a decent sort of chap, after all,' continued Gabriel in a false voice. 'He gave me back that sovereign I lent him, and I didn't expect it, really. It's a pity he wouldn't keep away from that Browne, because he's not a bad fellow, really.'

He was trembling now with annoyance. Why did she seem so abstracted? He did not know how he could begin. Was she annoyed, too, about something? If she would only turn to him or come to him of her own accord! To take her as she was would be brutal. No, he must see some ardour in her eyes first. He longed to be master of her strange mood.

'When did you lend him the pound?' she asked, after a pause.

Gabriel strove to restrain himself from breaking out into brutal language about the sottish Malins and his pound. He longed to cry to her from his soul, to crush her body against his, to overmaster her. But he said:

'O, at Christmas, when he opened that little Christmas-card shop, in Henry Street.'

He was in such a fever of rage and desire that he did not hear her come from the window. She stood before him for an instant, looking at him strangely. Then, suddenly raising herself on tiptoe and resting her hands lightly on his shoulders, she kissed him.

'You are a very generous person, Gabriel,' she said.

Gabriel, trembling with delight at her sudden kiss and at the quaintness of her phrase, put his hands on her hair and began smoothing it back, scarcely touching it with his fingers. The washing had made it fine and brilliant. His heart was brimming over with happiness. Just when he was wishing for it she had come to him of her own accord. Perhaps her thoughts had been running with his. Perhaps she had felt the impetuous desire that was in him, and then, the yielding mood had come upon her. Now that she had fallen to him so easily, he wondered why he had been so diffident.

He stood, holding her head between his hands. Then, slipping one arm swiftly about her body and drawing her towards him, he said softly:

'Gretta, dear, what are you thinking about?'

She did not answer nor yield wholly to his arm. He said again, softly:

'Tell me what it is, Gretta. I think I know what is the matter. Do I know?'

She did not answer at once. Then she said in an outburst of tears:

'O, I am thinking about that song, *The Lass of Aughrim*.'

She broke loose from him and ran to the bed and, throwing her arms across the bed-rail, hid her face. Gabriel stood stock-still for a moment in astonishment and then followed her. As he passed in the way of the cheval-glass he caught sight of himself in full length, his broad, well-filled shirt-front, the face whose expression always puzzled him when he saw it in a mirror, and his glimmering gilt-rimmed eye-glasses. He halted a few paces from her and said:

'What about the song? Why does that make you cry?'

She raised her head from her arms and dried her eyes with the back of her hand like a child. A kinder note than he had intended went into his voice.

'Why, Gretta?' he asked.

'I am thinking about a person long ago who used to sing that song.'

'And who was the person long ago?' asked Gabriel, smiling.

'It was a person I used to know in Galway when I was living with my grandmother,' she said.

The smile passed away from Gabriel's face. A dull anger began to gather again at the back of his mind and the dull fires of his lust began to glow angrily in his veins.

'Someone you were in love with?' he asked ironically.

'It was a young boy I used to know,' she answered, 'named Michael Furey. He used to sing that song, *The Lass of Aughrim*. He was very delicate.'

Gabriel was silent. He did not wish her to think that he was interested in this delicate boy.

'I can see him so plainly,' she said, after a moment. 'Such eyes as he had: big, dark eyes! And such an expression in them—an expression!'

'O, then, you are in love with him?' said Gabriel.

'I used to go out walking with him,' she said, 'when I was in Galway.'

A thought flew across Gabriel's mind.

'Perhaps that was why you wanted to go to Galway with that Ivors girl?' he said coldly.

She looked at him and asked in surprise:

'What for?'

Her eyes made Gabriel feel awkward. He shrugged his shoulders and said:

'How do I know? To see him, perhaps.'

She looked away from him along the shaft of light towards the window in silence.

'He is dead,' she said at length. 'He died when he was only seventeen. Isn't it a terrible thing to die so young as that?'

'What was he?' asked Gabriel, still ironically.

'He was in the gasworks,' she said.

Gabriel felt humiliated by the failure of his irony and by the evocation of this figure from the dead, a boy in the gasworks. While he had been full of memories of their secret life together, full of tenderness and joy and desire, she had been comparing him in her mind with another. A shameful consciousness of his own person assailed him. He saw himself as a ludicrous figure, acting as a pennyboy for his aunts, a nervous, well-meaning sentimentalist, orating to vulgarians and idealizing his own clownish lusts, the pitiable fatuous fellow he had caught a glimpse of in the mirror. Instinctively he turned his back more to the light lest she might see the shame that burned upon his forehead.

He tried to keep up his tone of cold interrogation, but his voice when he spoke was humble and indifferent.

'I suppose you were in love with this Michael Furey, Gretta,' he said.

'I was great with him at that time,' she said.

Her voice was veiled and sad. Gabriel, feeling now how vain it would be to try to lead her whither he had purposed, caressed one of her hands and said, also sadly:

'And what did he die of so young, Gretta? Consumption, was it?'

'I think he died for me,' she answered.

A vague terror seized Gabriel at this answer, as if,

at that hour when he had hoped to triumph, some impalpable and vindictive being was coming against him, gathering forces against him in its vague world. But he shook himself free of it with an effort of reason and continued to caress her hand. He did not question her again, for he felt that she would tell him of herself. Her hand was warm and moist: it did not respond to his touch, but he continued to caress it just as he had caressed her first letter to him that spring morning.

'It was in the winter,' she said, 'about the beginning of the winter when I was going to leave my grandmother's and come up here to the convent. And he was ill at the time in his lodgings in Galway and wouldn't be let out, and his people in Oughterard were written to. He was in decline, they said, or something like that. I never knew rightly.'

She paused for a moment and sighed.

'Poor fellow,' she said. 'He was very fond of me and he was such a gentle boy. We used to go out together, walking, you know, Gabriel, like the way they do in the country. He was going to study singing only for his health. He had a very good voice, poor Michael Furey.'

'Well; and then?' asked Gabriel.

'And then when it came to the time for me to leave Galway and come up to the convent he was much worse and I wouldn't be let see him, so I wrote him a letter saying I was going up to Dublin and would be back in the summer, and hoping he would be better then.'

She paused for a moment to get her voice under control, and then went on:

'Then the night before I left, I was in my grandmother's house in Nuns' Island, packing up, and I heard gravel thrown up against the window. The window was so wet I couldn't see, so I ran downstairs as I was and slipped out the back into the garden and there was the poor fellow at the end of the garden, shivering.'

'And did you not tell him to go back?' asked Gabriel.

'I implored of him to go home at once and told him he would get his death in the rain. But he said he did not want to live. I can see his eyes as well as well! He was standing at the end of the wall where there was a tree.'

'And did he go home?' asked Gabriel.

'Yes, he went home. And when I was only a week in the convent he died and he was buried in Oughterard, where his people came from. O, the day I heard that, that he was dead!'

She stopped, choking with sobs, and, overcome by emotion, flung herself face downward on the bed, sobbing in the quilt. Gabriel held her hand for a moment longer, irresolutely, and then, shy of intruding on her grief, let it fall gently and walked quietly to the window.

She was fast asleep.

Gabriel, leaning on his elbow, looked for a few moments unresentfully on her tangled hair and half-open mouth, listening to her deep-drawn breath. So she had had that romance in her life: a man had died for her sake. It hardly pained him now to think how poor a part he, her husband, had played in her life. He watched her while she slept, as though he and she had never lived together as man and wife. His curious eyes rested long upon her face and on her hair: and, as he thought of what she must have been then, in that time of her first girlish beauty, a strange, friendly pity for her entered his soul. He did not like to say even to himself that her face was no longer beautiful, but he knew that it was no longer the face for which Michael Furey had braved death.

Perhaps she had not told him all the story. His eyes moved to the chair over which she had thrown some of her clothes. A petticoat string dangled to the floor. One boot stood upright, its limp upper fallen down: the fellow of it lay upon its side. He wondered at his riot of emotions of an hour before. From what had it proceeded? From his aunt's supper, from his own foolish speech, from the wine and dancing, the merrymaking when saying good night in the hall, the pleasure of the walk along the river in the snow. Poor Aunt Julia! She, too, would soon be a shade with the shade of Patrick Morkan and his horse. He had caught that haggard look upon her face for a moment when she was singing *Arrayed for the Bridal*. Soon, perhaps, he would be sitting in that same drawing-room, dressed in black, his silk hat on his knees. The blinds would be drawn down and Aunt Kate would be sitting beside him, crying and blowing her nose and telling him how Julia had died. He would cast about in his mind for some words that might console her, and would find only lame and useless ones. Yes, yes: that would happen very soon.

The air of the room chilled his shoulders. He stretched himself cautiously along under the sheets and lay down beside his wife. One by one, they were all becoming shades. Better pass boldly into that other world, in the full glory of some passion, than fade and wither dismally with age. He thought of how she who lay beside him had locked in her heart for so many years that image of her lover's eyes when he had told her that he did not wish to live.

Generous tears filled Gabriel's eyes. He had never

felt like that himself towards any woman, but he knew that such a feeling must be love. The tears gathered more thickly in his eyes and in the partial darkness he imagined he saw the form of a young man standing under a dripping tree. Other forms were near. His soul had approached that region where dwell the vast hosts of the dead. He was conscious of, but could not apprehend, their wayward and flickering existence. His own identity was fading out into a grey impalpable world: the solid world itself, which these dead had one time reared and lived in, was dissolving and dwindling.

A few light taps upon the pane made him turn to the window. It had begun to snow again. He watched sleepily the flakes, silver and dark, falling obliquely against the lamp-light. The time had come for him to set out on his journey westward. Yes, the newspapers were right: snow was general all over Ireland. It was falling on every part of the dark central plain, on the treeless hills, falling softly upon the Bog of Allen and, farther westward, softly falling into the dark mutinous Shannon waves. It was falling, too, upon every part of the lonely churchyard on the hill where Michael Furey lay buried. It lay thickly drifted on the crooked crosses and headstones, on the spears of the little gate, on the barren thorns. His soul swooned slowly as he heard the snow falling faintly through the universe and faintly falling, like the descent of their last end, upon all the living and the dead.

A Rhinoceros, Some Ladies, and a Horse

JAMES STEPHENS

(1882–1950)

ONE day, in my first job, a lady fell in love with me. It was quite unreasonable, of course, for I wasn't wonderful: I was small and thin, and I weighed much the same as a largish duck-egg. I didn't fall in love with her, or anything like that. I got under the table, and stayed there until she had to go wherever she had to go to.

I had seen an advertisement—'Smart boy wanted', it said. My legs were the smartest things about me, so I went there on the run. I got the job.

At that time there was nothing on God's earth that I could do, except run. I had no brains, and I had no memory. When I was told to do anything I got into such an enthusiasm about it that I couldn't remember anything else about it. I just ran as hard as I could, and then I ran back, proud and panting. And when they asked me for the whatever-it-was that I had run for, I started, right on the instant, and ran some more.

The place I was working at was, amongst other things, a theatrical agency. I used to be sitting in a corner of the office floor, waiting to be told to run somewhere and back. A lady would come in—a music-hall lady that is—and, in about five minutes, howls of joy would start coming from the inner office. Then, peacefully enough, the lady and my two bosses would come out, and the lady always said, 'Splits! I can do splits like no one.' And one of my bosses would say,

'I'm keeping your splits in mind.' And the other would add, gallantly—'No one who ever saw your splits could ever forget 'em.'

One of my bosses was thin, and the other one was fat. My fat boss was composed entirely of stomachs. He had three baby-stomachs under his chin: then he had three more descending in even larger englobings nearly to the ground: but, just before reaching the ground, the final stomach bifurcated into a pair of boots. He was very light on these and could bounce about in the neatest way.

He was the fattest thing I had ever seen, except a rhinoceros that I had met in the Zoo the Sunday before I got the job. That rhino was *very* fat, and it had a smell like twenty-five pigs. I was standing outside its palisade, wondering what it could possibly feel like to be a rhinoceros, when two larger boys passed by. Suddenly they caught hold of me, and pushed me through the bars of the palisade. I was very skinny, and in about two seconds I was right inside, and the rhinoceros was looking at me.

It was very fat, but it wasn't fat like stomachs, it was fat like barrels of cement, and when it moved it creaked a lot, like a woman I used to know who creaked like an old bedstead. The rhinoceros swaggled over to me with a bunch of cabbage sticking out of its mouth. It wasn't angry, or anything like that, it just wanted to see who I was. Rhinos are blindish: they mainly see by smelling, and they smell in snorts. This one started at my left shoe, and snorted right up that side of me to my ear. He smelt that very carefully: then he switched over to my right ear, and snorted right down that side of me to my right shoe: then he fell in love with my shoes and began to lick them. I, naturally, wriggled my feet at that, and the big chap was so astonished that he did the strangest step-dance backwards to his pile of cabbages, and began to eat them.

I squeezed myself out of his cage and walked away. In a couple of minutes I saw the two boys. They were very frightened, and they asked me what I had done to the rhinoceros. I answered, a bit grandly, perhaps, that I had seized it in both hands, ripped it limb from limb, and tossed its carcase to the crows. But when they began shouting to people that I had just murdered a rhinoceros I took to my heels, for I didn't want to be arrested and hanged for a murder that I hadn't committed.

Still, a man can't be as fat as a rhinoceros, but my boss was as fat as a man can be. One day a great lady of the halls came in, and was received on the knee. She was very great. Her name was Maudie Darling, or thereabouts. My bosses called her nothing but 'Darling', and she called them the same. When the time came for her to arrive the whole building got palpitations of the heart. After waiting a while my thin boss got angry, and said—'Who does the woman think she is? If she isn't here in two twos I'll go down to the entry, and when she does come I'll boot her out.' The fat boss said—'She's only two hours late, she'll be here before the week's out.'

Within a few minutes there came great clamours from the courtyard. Patriotic cheers, such as Parnell himself never got, were thundering. My bosses ran instantly to the inner office. Then the door opened, and the lady appeared.

She was very wide, and deep, and magnificent. She was dressed in camels and zebras and goats: she had two peacocks in her hat and a rabbit muff in her hand, and she strode among these with prancings.

But when she got right into the room and saw herself being looked at by three men and a boy she became adorably shy: one could see that she had never been looked at before.

'O,' said she, with a smile that made three and a half hearts beat like one, 'O,' said she, very modestly, 'is Mr. Which-of-'em-is-it really in? Please tell him that Little-Miss-Me would be so glad to see and to be—'

Then the inner door opened, and the large lady was surrounded by my fat boss and my thin boss. She crooned to them—'O, you dear boys, you'll never know how much I've thought of you and longed to see you.'

That remark left me stupefied. The first day I got to the office I heard that it was the fat boss's birthday, and that he was thirty years of age: and the thin boss didn't look a day younger than the fat one. How the lady could mistake these old men for boys seemed to me the strangest fact that had ever come my way. My own bet was that they'd both die of old age in about a month.

After a while they all came out again. The lady was helpless with laughter: she had to be supported by my two bosses—'O,' she cried, 'you boys will kill me.' And the bosses laughed and laughed, and the fat one said —'Darling, you're a scream,' and the thin one said— 'Darling, you're a riot.'

And then . . . she saw me! I saw her seeing me the very way I had seen the rhinoceros seeing me: I wondered for an instant would she smell me down one leg and up the other. She swept my two bosses right away from her, and she became a kind of queen, very glorious to behold: but sad, startled. She stretched a long, slow arm out and out and out and then she unfolded a long, slow finger, and pointed it at me—

'Who is THAT??' she whispered in a strange whisper that could be heard two miles off.

My fat boss was an awful liar—'The cat brought that in,' said he.

But the thin boss rebuked him: 'No,' he said, 'it was not the cat. Let me introduce you; darling, this is James. James, this is the darling of the gods.'

'And of the pit,' said she, sternly.

She looked at me again. Then she sank to her knees and spread out both arms to me—

'Come to my Boozalum, angel,' said she in a tender kind of way.

I knew what she meant, and I knew that she didn't know how to pronounce that word. I took a rapid glance at the area indicated. The lady had a boozalum you could graze a cow on. I didn't wait one second, but slid, in one swift, silent slide, under the table. Then she came forward and said a whole lot of poems to me under the table, imploring me, among a lot of odd things, to 'come forth, and gild the morning with my eyes', but at last she was reduced to whistling at me with two fingers in her mouth, the way you whistle for a cab.

I learned after she had gone that most of the things she said to me were written by a poet fellow named Spokeshave. They were very complimentary, but I couldn't love a woman who mistook my old bosses for boys, and had a boozalum that it would take an Arab chieftain a week to trot across on a camel.

The thin boss pulled me from under the table by my leg, and said that my way was the proper way to treat a rip, but my fat boss said, very gravely—'James, when a lady invites a gentleman to her boozalum a real gentleman hops there as pronto as possible, and I'll have none but real gentlemen in this office.'

'Tell me,' he went on, 'what made that wad of Turkish Delight fall in love with you?'

'She didn't love me at all, sir,' I answered.

'No?' he inquired.

'She was making fun of me,' I explained.

'There's something in that,' said he seriously, and went back to his office.

I had been expecting to be sacked that day. I was sacked the next day, but that was about a horse.

I had been given three letters to post, and told to run or they'd be too late. So I ran to the post office and round it and back, with, naturally, the three letters in my pocket. As I came to our door a nice, solid, red-faced man rode up on a horse. He thrust the reins into my hand—

'Hold the horse for a minute,' said he.

'I can't,' I replied, 'my boss is waiting for me.

'I'll only be a minute,' said he angrily, and he walked off.

Well, there was I, saddled, as it were, with a horse. I looked at it, and it looked at me. Then it blew a pint of soap-suds out of its nose and took another look at me, and then the horse fell in love with me as if he had just found his long-lost foal. He started to lean against me and to woo me with small whinneys, and I responded and replied as best I could—

'Don't move a toe,' said I to the horse, 'I'll be back in a minute.'

He understood exactly what I said, and the only move he made was to swing his head and watch me as I darted up the street. I was less than half a minute away anyhow, and never out of his sight.

Up the street there was a man, and sometimes a woman, with a barrow, thick-piled with cabbages and oranges and apples. As I raced round the barrow I pinched an apple off it at full speed, and in ten seconds I was back at the horse. The good nag had watched every move I made, and when I got back his eyes were wide open, his mouth was wide open, and he had his legs all splayed out so that he couldn't possibly slip. I broke the apple in halves and popped one half into his mouth. He ate it in slow crunches, and then he looked diligently at the other half. I gave him the other half, and, as he ate it, he gurgled with cidery gargles of pure joy. He then swung his head round from me and pointed his nose up the street, right at the apple-barrow.

I raced up the street again, and was back within the half-minute with another apple. The horse had nigh finished the first half of it when a man who had come up said, thoughtfully—

'He seems to like apples, bedad!'

'He loves them,' said I.

And then, exactly at the speed of lightning, the man became angry, and invented bristles all over himself like a porcupine—

'What the hell do you mean,' he hissed, and then he bawled, 'by stealing my apples?'

I retreated a bit into the horse—

'I didn't steal your apples,' I said.

'You didn't!' he roared, and then he hissed, 'I saw you,' he hissed.

'I didn't steal them,' I explained, 'I pinched them.'

'Tell me that one again,' said he.

'If,' said I patiently, 'if I took the apples for myself that would be stealing.'

'So it would,' he agreed.

'But as I took them for the horse that's pinching.'

'Be dam, but!' said he. ''Tis a real argument,' he

went on, staring at the sky. 'Answer me that one,' he demanded of himself, and he in a very stupor of intellection. 'I give it up,' he roared, 'you give me back my apples.'

I placed the half apple that was left into his hand, and he looked at it as if it was a dead frog—

'What'll I do with that?' he asked earnestly.

'Give it to the horse,' said I.

The horse was now prancing at him, and mincing at him, and making love at him. He pushed the half apple into the horse's mouth, and the horse mumbled it and watched him, and chewed it and watched him, and gurgled it and watched him—

'He does like his bit of apple,' said the man.

'He likes you too,' said I. 'I think he loves you.'

'It looks like it,' he agreed, for the horse was yearning at him, and its eyes were soulful.

'Let's get him another apple,' said I, and, without another word, we both pounded back to his barrow and each of us pinched an apple off it. We got one apple into the horse, and were breaking the second one when a woman said gently—

'Nice, kind, Christian gentlemen, feeding dumb animals—with my apples,' she yelled suddenly.

The man with me jumped as if he had been hit by a train—

'Mary,' said he humbly.

'Joseph,' said she in a completely unloving voice.

But the woman transformed herself into nothing else but woman—

'What about my apples?' said she. 'How many have we lost?'

'Three,' said Joseph.

'Four,' said I, 'I pinched three and you pinched one.'

'That's true,' said he. 'That's exact, Mary. I only pinched one of our apples.'

'You only,' she squealed—

And I, hoping to be useful, broke in—

'Joseph,' said I, 'is the nice lady your boss?'

He halted for a dreadful second, and made up his mind—

'You bet she's my boss,' said he, 'and she's better than that, for she's the very wife of my bosum.'

She turned to me—

'Child of Grace—' said she—

Now, when I was a child, and did something that a woman didn't like she always expostulated in the same way. If I tramped on her foot, or jabbed her in the stomach—the way women have mulitudes of feet and stomachs is always astonishing to a child—the remark such a woman made was always the same. She would grab her toe or her stomach, and say—'Childagrace, what the hell are you doing?' After a while I worked it out that Childagrace was one word, and was my name. When any woman in agony yelled Childagrace I ran right up prepared to be punished, and the woman always said tenderly, 'What are you yowling about, Childagrace.'

'Childagrace,' said Mary earnestly, 'how's my family to live if you steal our apples? You take my livelihood away from me! Very good, but will you feed and clothe and educate my children in,' she continued proudly, 'the condition to which they are accustomed?'

I answered that question cautiously—

'How many kids have you, ma'am?' said I.

'We'll leave that alone for a while,' she went on. 'You owe me two and six for the apples.'

'Mary!' said Joseph, in a pained voice.

'And you,' she snarled at him, 'owe me three shillings. I'll take it out of you in pints.' She turned to me—

'What do you do with all the money you get from the office here?'

'I give it to my landlady.'

'Does she stick to the lot of it?'

'Oh, no,' I answered, 'she always gives me back threepence.'

'Well, you come and live with me and I'll give you back fourpence.'

'All right,' said I.

'By gum,' said Joseph, enthusiastically, 'that'll be fine. We'll go out every night and we won't steal a thing. We'll just pinch legs of beef, and pig's feet, and barrels of beer—'

'Wait now,' said Mary. 'You stick to your own landlady. I've trouble enough of my own. You needn't pay me the two and six.'

'Good for you,' said Joseph heartily, and then, to me—

'You just get a wife of your bosum half as kind as the wife of my bosum and you'll be set up for life. Mary,' he cried joyfully, 'let's go and have a pint on the strength of it.'

'You shut up,' said she.

'Joseph,' I interrupted, 'knows how to pronounce that word properly.'

'What word?'

'The one he used when he said you were the wife of his what-you-may-call-it.'

'I'm not the wife of any man's what-you-may-call-it,' said she, indignantly—'Oh, I see what you mean! So he pronounced it well, did he?'

'Yes, ma'am.'

115

She looked at me very sternly—

'How does it come you know about all these kinds of words?'

'Yes,' said Joseph, and he was even sterner than she was, 'when I was your age I didn't know any bad words.'

'You shut up,' said she, and continued, 'what made you say that to me?'

'A woman came into our office yesterday, and she mispronounced it.'

'What did she say now?'

'Oh, she said it all wrong.'

'Do you tell me so? We're all friends here: what way did she say it, son?'

'Well, ma'am, she called it boozalum.'

'She said it wrong all right,' said Joseph, 'but 'tis a good, round, fat kind of a word all the same.'

'You shut up,' said Mary. 'Who did she say the word to?'

'She said it to me, ma'am.'

'She must have been a rip,' said Joseph.

'Was she a rip, now?'

'I don't know, ma'am. I never met a rip.'

'You're too young yet,' said Joseph, 'but you'll meet them later on. I never met a rip myself until I got married—I mean,' he added hastily, 'that they were all rips except the wife of my what-do-you-call-ems, and that's why I married her.'

'I expect you've got a barrel-full of rips in your past,' said she bleakly, 'you must tell me about some of them tonight.' And then, to me, 'tell us about the woman,' said she.

So I told them all about her, and how she held out her arms to me, and said, 'Come to my boozalum, angel.'

'What did you do when she shoved out the old arms at you?' said Joseph.

'I got under the table,' I answered.

'That's not a bad place at all, but,' he continued earnestly, 'never get under the bed when there's an old girl chasing you, for that's the worst spot you could pick on. What was the strap's name?'

'Maudie Darling, she called herself.'

'You're a blooming lunatic,' said Joseph, 'she's the loveliest thing in the world, barring,' he added hastily, 'the wife of my blast-the-bloody-word.'

'We saw her last night,' said Mary, 'at Dan Lowrey's Theatre, and she's just lovely.'

'She isn't as nice as you, ma'am,' I asserted.

'Do you tell me that now?' said she.

'You are twice as nice as she is, and twenty times nicer.'

'There you are,' said Joseph, 'the very words I said to you last night.'

'You shut up,' said Mary scornfully, 'you were trying to knock a pint out of me! Listen, son,' she went on, 'we'll take all that back about your landlady. You come and live with me, and I'll give you back sixpence a week out of your wages.'

'All right, ma'am,' I crowed in a perfectly monstrous joy.

'Mary,' said Joseph, in a reluctant voice—

'You shut up,' said she.

'He can't come to live with us,' said Joseph. 'He's a bloody Prodestan,' he added sadly.

'Why—' she began—

'He'd keep me and the childer up all night, pinching apples for horses and asses, and reading the Bible, and up to every kind of devilment.'

Mary made up her mind quickly—

'You stick to your own landlady,' said she, 'tell her that I said she was to give you sixpence.' She whirled about, 'There won't be a thing left on that barrow,' said she to Joseph.

'Damn the scrap,' said Joseph violently.

'Listen,' said Mary to me very earnestly, 'am I nicer than Maudie Darling?'

'You are, ma'am,' said I.

Mary went down on the road on her knees: she stretched out both arms to me, and said—

'Come to my boozalum, angel.'

I looked at her, and I looked at Joseph, and I looked at the horse. Then I turned from them all and ran into the building and into the office. My fat boss met me—

'Here's your five bob,' said he. 'Get to hell out of here,' said he.

And I ran out.

I went to the horse, and leaned my head against the thick end of his neck, and the horse leaned as much of himself against me as he could manage. Then the man who owned the horse came up and climbed into his saddle. He fumbled in his pocket—

'You were too long,' said I. 'I've been sacked for minding your horse.'

'That's too bad,' said he: 'that's too damn bad,' and he tossed me a penny.

I caught it, and lobbed it back into his lap, and I strode down the street the most outraged human being then living in the world.

The Fairy Goose

LIAM O'FLAHERTY
(1897–1984)

AN old woman named Mary Wiggins got three goose
eggs from a neighbour in order to hatch a clutch of
goslings. She put an old clucking hen over the eggs in
a wooden box with a straw bed. The hen proved to be
a bad sitter. She was continually deserting the eggs,
possibly because they were too big. The old woman
then kept her shut up in the box. Either through
weariness, want of air, or simply through pure devilment, the hen died on the eggs, two days before it
was time for the shells to break.

The old woman shed tears of rage, both at the loss
of her hen, of which she was particularly fond, and
through fear of losing her goslings. She put the eggs
near the fire in the kitchen, wrapped up in straw and
old clothes. Two days afterwards, one of the eggs
broke and a tiny gosling put out its beak. The other
eggs proved not to be fertile. They were thrown away.

The little gosling was a scraggy thing, so small and
so delicate that the old woman, out of pity for it,
wanted to kill it. But her husband said: 'Kill nothing
that is born in your house, woman alive. It's against
the law of God.' 'It's a true saying, my honest fellow,'
said the old woman. 'What comes into the world is
sent by God. Praised be He.'

For a long time it seemed certain that the gosling
was on the point of death. It spent all the day on the
hearth in the kitchen nestling among the peat ashes,

119

either sleeping or making little tweaky noises. When it was offered food, it stretched out its beak and pecked without rising off its stomach. Gradually, however, it became hardier and went out of doors to sit in the sun, on a flat rock. When it was three months old it was still a yellowish colour with soft down, even though other goslings of that age in the village were already going to the pond with the flock and able to flap their wings and join in the cackle at evening time, when the setting sun was being saluted. The little gosling was not aware of the other geese, even though it saw them rise on windy days and fly with a great noise from their houses to the pond. It made no effort to become a goose, and at four months it still could not stand on one leg.

The old woman came to believe it was a fairy. The village women agreed with her after some dispute. It was decided to tie pink and red ribbons around the gosling's neck and to sprinkle holy water on its wing feathers.

That was done, and then the gosling became sacred in the village. No boy dare throw a stone at it, or pull a feather from its wing, as they were in the habit of doing with geese, in order to get masts for the pieces of cork they floated in the pond as ships. When it began to move about every house gave it dainty things. All the human beings in the village paid more respect to it than they did to one another. The little gosling had contracted a great affection for Mary Wiggins and followed her around everywhere, so that Mary Wiggins also came to have the reputation of being a woman of wisdom. Dreams were brought to her for unravelling. She was asked to set the spell of the Big Periwinkle and to tie the Knot of the Snakes on the sides of sick cows. And when children were ill, the gosling was brought secretly at night and led three times around the house on a thin halter of horse-hair.

When the gosling was a year old it had not yet become a goose. Its down was still slightly yellowish. It did not cackle, but made curious tweaky noises. Instead of stretching out its neck and hissing at strangers, after the manner of a proper goose, it put its head to one side and made funny noises like a duck. It meditated like a hen, was afraid of water and cleansed itself by rolling on the grass. It fed on bread, fish, and potatoes. It drank milk and tea. It amused itself by collecting pieces of cloth, nails, small fish-bones, and the limpet shells that are thrown in a heap beside dunghills. These pieces of refuse it placed in a pile to the left of Mary Wiggins's door. And when the pile was tall, it made a sort of nest in the middle of it and lay in the nest.

Old Mrs. Wiggins had by now realized that the goose was worth money to her. So she became firmly convinced that the goose was gifted with supernatural powers. She accepted, in return for setting spells, a yard of white frieze cloth for unravelling dreams, a pound of sugar for setting the spell of the Big Periwinkle, and half a donkey's load of potatoes for tying the Knot of the Snakes on a sick cow's sides. Hitherto a kindly, humorous woman, she took to wearing her shawl in a triangular fashion, with the tip of it reaching to her heels. She talked to herself or to her goose as she went along the road. She took long steps like a goose and rolled her eyes occasionally. When she cast a spell she went into an ecstasy during which she made inarticulate sounds, like: 'boum, roum, toum, kroum.'

Soon it became known all over the countryside that there was a woman of wisdom and a fairy goose in the

village, and pilgrims came secretly from afar, at the
dead of night, on the first night of the new moon, or
when the spring tide had begun to wane.

The men soon began to raise their hats passing old
Mary Wiggins's house, for it was understood, owing to
the cure of Dara Foddy's cow, that the goose was indeed a good fairy and not a malicious one. Such was
the excitement in the village and all over the countryside, that what was kept secret so long at last reached
the ears of the parish priest.

The story was brought to him by an old woman
from a neighbouring village to that in which the goose
lived. Before the arrival of the goose, the other old
woman had herself cast spells, not through her own
merits but through those of her dead mother, who had
a long time ago been the woman of wisdom in the
district. The priest mounted his horse as soon as he
heard the news and galloped at a breakneck speed towards Mary Wiggins's house, carrying his breviary
and his stole. When he arrived in the village, he dismounted at a distance from the house, gave his horse
to a boy, and put his stole around his neck.

A number of the villagers gathered and some tried
to warn Mary Wiggins by whistling at a distance, but
conscious that they had all taken part in something
forbidden by the sacred laws of orthodox religion they
were afraid to run ahead of the priest into the house.
Mary Wiggins and her husband were within, making
little ropes of brown horse-hair, which they sold as
charms.

Outside the door, perched on her high nest, the little
goose was sitting. There were pink and red ribbons
around her neck and around her legs there were bands
of black tape. She was quite small, a little more than
half the size of a normal, healthy goose. But she had

an elegant charm of manner, an air of civilization and a consciousness of great dignity, which had grown out of the respect and love of the villagers.

When she saw the priest approach she began to cackle gently, making the tweaky noise that was peculiar to her. She descended from her perch and waddled towards him, expecting some dainty gift. For everybody who approached her gave her a dainty gift. But instead of stretching out his hand to offer her something and saying, 'Beadai, beadai, come here,' as was customary, the priest halted and muttered something in a harsh, frightened voice. He became red in the face and he took off his hat.

Then for the first time in her life, the little goose became terrified. She opened her beak, spread her wings, and lowered her head. She began to hiss violently. Turning around, she waddled back to her nest, flapping her wings and raising a loud cackle, just like a goose, although she had never been heard to cackle loudly like a goose before. Clambering up to her high nest, she lay there, quite flat, trembling violently.

The bird, never having known fear of human beings, never having been treated with discourtesy, was so violently moved by the extraordinary phenomenon of a man wearing black clothes, scowling at her and muttering, that her animal nature was roused and showed itself with disgusting violence.

The people, watching this scene, were astounded. Some took off their caps and crossed themselves. For some reason, it was made manifest to them that the goose was an evil spirit and not the good fairy which they had supposed her to be. Terrified of the priest's stole and breviary and of his scowling countenance, they were only too eager to attribute the goose's strange hissing and her still stranger cackle to supernatural forces of an evil nature. Some present even caught a faint rumble of thunder in the east and although it was not noticed at the time, an old woman later asserted that she heard a great cackle of strange geese afar off, raised in answer to the little fairy goose's cackle. 'It was', said the old woman, 'certainly the whole army of devils offering her help to kill the holy priest.'

The priest turned to the people and cried, raising his right hand in a threatening manner,

'I wonder the ground doesn't open up and swallow you all. Idolators!'

'O father, blessed by the hand of God,' cried an old woman, the one who later asserted she had heard the devilish cackle afar off. She threw herself on her knees in the road. 'Spare us, father.'

Old Mrs. Wiggins, having heard the strange noises, rushed out into the yard with her triangular shawl trailing and her black hair loose. She began to make vague, mystic movements with her hands, as had recently become a habit with her. Lost in some sort of ecstasy, she did not see the priest at first. She began to chant something.

'You hag,' cried the priest, rushing up the yard towards her, menacingly.

The old woman caught sight of him and screamed. But she faced him boldly.

'Come no farther!' she cried, still in an ecstasy, either affected, or the result of a firm belief in her own mystic powers.

Indeed it is difficult to believe that she was not in earnest, for she used to be a kind, gentle woman.

Her husband rushed out, crying aloud. Seeing the priest, he dropped a piece of rope he had in his hand and fled around the corner of the house.

'Leave my way, you hag!' cried the priest, raising his hand to strike her.

'Stand back!' she cried. 'Don't lay a hand on my goose.'

'Leave my way,' yelled the priest, 'or I'll curse you.'

'Curse then,' cried the unfortunate woman, 'curse.'

Instead the priest gave her a blow under the ear, which felled her smartly. Then he strode up to the goose's nest and seized the goose. The goose, paralysed with terror, was just able to open her beak and hiss at him. He stripped the ribbons off her neck and tore the tape off her feet. Then he threw her out of the nest. Seizing a spade that stood by the wall, he began to scatter the refuse of which the nest was composed.

The old woman, lying prostrate in the yard, raised her head and began to chant in the traditional fashion, used by women of wisdom.

'I'll call on the winds of the east and of the west, I'll raise the waves of the sea. The lightning will flash in the sky and there'll be great sounds of giants warring in the heavens. Blight will fall on the earth and calves with fishes' tails will be born of cows. . . .'

The little goose, making tweaky noises, waddled over to the old woman and tried to hide herself under the long shawl. The people murmured at this, seeing in it fresh signs of devilry.

Then the priest threw down the spade and hauled the old woman to her feet, kicking aside the goose. The old woman, exhausted by her ecstasy and possibly seeking to gain popular support, either went into a faint or feigned one. Her hands and her feet hung limply. Again the people murmured. The priest, becoming embarrassed, put her sitting against the wall. Then he didn't know what to do, for his anger had exhausted his reason. He either became ashamed of

125

having beaten an old woman, or he felt the situation was altogether ridiculous. So he raised his hand and addressed the people in a sorrowful voice.

'Let this be a warning,' he said sadly. 'This poor woman and . . . all of you, led astray by . . . foolish and. . . . Avarice is at the back of this,' he cried suddenly in an angry voice, shaking his fist. 'This woman had been preying on your credulity, in order to extort money from you by her pretended sorcery. That's all it is. Money is at the back of it. But I give you warning. If I hear another word about this, I'll. . . .'

He paused uncertainly, wondering what to threaten the poor people with. Then he added:

'I'll report it to the archbishop of the diocese.'

The people raised a loud murmur, asking forgiveness.

'Fear God,' he added finally, 'and love your neighbours.'

Then, throwing a stone angrily at the goose, he strode out of the yard and left the village.

It was then that the people began to curse violently and threaten to burn the old woman's house. The responsible people among them, however, chiefly those who had hitherto paid no respect to the superstition concerning the goose, restrained their violence. Finally, the people went home and Mary Wiggins's husband, who had been hiding in a barn, came and brought his wife indoors. The little goose, uttering cries of amazement, began to collect the rubbish once more, piling it in a heap in order to rebuild her nest.

That night, just after the moon had risen, a band of young men collected, approached Mary Wiggins's house, and enticed the goose from her nest, by calling 'Beadai, beadai, come here, come here.'

The little goose, delighted that people were again

kind and respectful to her, waddled down to the gate, making happy noises.

The youths stoned her to death.

And the little goose never uttered a sound, so terrified and amazed was she at this treatment from people who had formerly loved her and whom she had never injured.

Next morning, when Mary Wiggins discovered the dead carcass of the goose, she went into a fit, during which she cursed the village, the priest, and all mankind.

And indeed it appeared that her blasphemous prayer took some effect at least. Although giants did not war in the heavens, and although cows did not give birth to fishes, it is certain that from that day the natives of that village are quarrelsome drunkards, who fear God but do not love one another. And the old woman is again collecting followers from among the wives of the drunkards. These women maintain that the only time in the history of their generation that there was peace and harmony in the village was during the time when the fairy goose was loved by the people.

Three Lambs

LIAM O'FLAHERTY

(*b.* 1897)

LITTLE Michael rose before dawn. He tried to make as little noise as possible. He ate two slices of bread and butter and drank a cup of milk, although he hated cold milk with bread and butter in the morning. But

127

on an occasion like this, what did it matter what a boy ate? He was going out to watch the black sheep having a lamb. His father had mentioned the night before that the black sheep was sure to lamb that morning, and of course there was a prize, three pancakes, for the first one who saw the lamb.

He lifted the latch gently and stole out. It was best not to let his brother John know he was going. He would be sure to want to come too. As he ran down the lane, his sleeves, brushing against the evergreen bushes, were wetted by the dew, and the tip of his cap was just visible above the hedge, bobbing up and down as he ran. He was in too great a hurry to open the gate and tore a little hole in the breast of his blue jersey climbing over it. But he didn't mind that. He would get another one on his thirteenth birthday.

He turned to the left from the main road, up a lane that led to the field where his father, the magistrate, kept his prize sheep. It was only a quarter of a mile, that lane, but he thought that it would never end and he kept tripping among the stones that strewed the road. It was so awkward to run on the stones wearing shoes, and it was too early in the year yet to be allowed to go barefooted. He envied Little Jimmy, the son of the farm labourer, who was allowed to go barefooted all the year round, even in the depths of winter, and who always had such wonderful cuts on his big toes, the envy of all the little boys in the village school.

He climbed over the fence leading into the fields and, clapping his hands together, said 'Oh, you devil,' a swear word he had learned from Little Jimmy and of which he was very proud. He took off his shoes and stockings and hid them in a hole in the fence. Then he ran jumping, his bare heels looking like round brown spots as he tossed them up behind him. The grass was wet and the ground was hard, but he persuaded himself that it was great fun.

Going through a gap into the next field, he saw a rabbit nibbling grass. He halted suddenly, his heart beating loudly. Pity he hadn't a dog. The rabbit stopped eating. He cocked up his ears. He stood on his tail, with his neck craned up and his forefeet hanging limp. Then he came down again. He thrust his ears forward. Then he lay flat with his ears buried in his back and lay still. With a great yell Little Michael darted forward imitating a dog barking and the rabbit scurried away in short sharp leaps. Only his white tail was visible in the grey light.

Little Michael went into the next field, but the sheep were nowhere to be seen. He stood on a hillock and called out 'Chowin, chowin,' three times. Then he heard 'Mah-m-m-m' in the next field and ran on. The sheep were in the last two fields, two oblong little fields, running in a hollow between two crags, surrounded by high thick fences, the walls of an old fort. In the nearest of the two fields he found ten of the sheep, standing side by side, looking at him, with their fifteen lambs in front of them also looking at him curiously. He counted them out loud and then he saw that the black sheep was not there. He panted with excitement. Perhaps she already had a lamb in the next field. He hurried to the gap leading into the next field, walking stealthily, avoiding the spots where the grass was high, so as to make less noise. It was bad to disturb a sheep that was lambing. He peered through a hole in the fence and could see nothing. Then he crawled to the gap and peered around the corner. The black sheep was just inside standing with her forefeet on a little mound.

Her belly was swollen out until it ended on each

side in a sharp point and her legs appeared to be incapable of supporting her body. She turned her head
sharply and listened. Little Michael held his breath,
afraid to make a noise. It was of vital importance not
to disturb the sheep. Straining back to lie down he
burst a button on his trousers and he knew his braces
were undone. He said, 'Oh, you devil,' again and
decided to ask his mother to let him wear a belt instead of a braces, same as Little Jimmy wore. Then he
crawled farther back from the gap and taking off his
braces altogether made it into a belt. It hurt his hips,
but he felt far better and manly.

Then he came back again to the gap and looked.
The black sheep was still in the same place. She was
scratching the earth with her forefeet and going
around in a circle, as if she wanted to lie down but
was afraid to lie down. Sometimes she ground her
teeth and made an awful noise, baring her jaws and
turning her head around sideways. Little Michael felt
a pain in his heart in pity for her, and he wondered
why the other sheep didn't come to keep her company.
Then he wondered whether his mother had felt the
same pain when she had Ethna the autumn before.
She must have, because the doctor was there.

Suddenly the black sheep went on her knees. She
stayed a few seconds on her knees and then she
moaned and sank to the ground and stretched herself
out with her neck on the little hillock and her hind
quarters falling down the little slope. Little Michael
forgot about the pain now. His heart thumped with
excitement. He forgot to breathe, looking intently.
'Ah,' he said. The sheep stretched again and struggled
to her feet and circled around once stamping and
grinding her teeth. Little Michael moved up to her
slowly. She looked at him anxiously, but she was too

sick to move away. He broke the bladder and he saw two little feet sticking out. He seized them carefully and pulled. The sheep moaned again and pressed with all her might. The lamb dropped on the grass.

Little Michael sighed with delight and began to rub its body with his finger nails furiously. The sheep turned around and smelt it, making a funny happy noise in its throat. The lamb, its white body covered with yellow slime, began to move, and presently it tried to stand up, but it fell again and Little Michael kept rubbing it, sticking his fingers into its ears and nostrils to clear them. He was so intent on this work that he did not notice the sheep had moved away again, and it was only when the lamb was able to stand up and he wanted to give it suck, that he noticed the sheep was lying again giving birth to another lamb. 'Oh, you devil,' gasped Little Michael, 'six pancakes.'

The second lamb was white like the first but with a black spot on its right ear. Little Michael rubbed it vigorously, pausing now and again to help the first lamb to its feet as it tried to stagger about. The sheep circled around making low noises in her throat, putting her nostrils to each lamb in turn, stopping nowhere, as giddy as a young schoolgirl, while the hard pellets of earth that stuck to her belly jingled like beads when she moved. Little Michael then took the first lamb and tried to put it to suck, but it refused to take the teat, stupidly sticking its mouth into the wool. Then he put his finger in its mouth and gradually got the teat in with his other hand. Then he pressed the teat and the hot milk squirted into the lamb's mouth. The lamb shook its tail, shrugged its body, made a little drive with its head, and began to suck.

Little Michael was just going to give the second lamb suck, when the sheep moaned and moved away

again. He said 'chowin, chowin, poor chowin,' and put
the lamb to her head, but she turned away moaning
and grinding her teeth and stamping. 'Oh, you devil,'
said Little Michael, 'she is going to have another
lamb.'

The sheep lay down again, with her foreleg stretched
out in front of her and, straining her neck backwards,
gave birth to a third lamb, a black lamb.

Then she rose smartly to her feet, her two sides
hollow now. She shrugged herself violently and, without noticing the lambs, started to eat grass fiercely,
just pausing now and again to say 'mah-m-m-m.'

Little Michael, in an ecstasy of delight, rubbed the
black lamb until it was able to stand. Then he put all
the lambs to suck, the sheep eating around her in a
circle, without changing her feet, smelling a lamb now
and again. 'Oh, you devil,' Little Michael kept saying,
thinking he would be quite famous now, and talked
about for a whole week. It was not every day that a
sheep had three lambs.

He brought them to a sheltered spot under the
fence. He wiped the birth slime from his hands with
some grass. He opened his penknife and cut the dirty
wool from the sheep's udder, lest the lambs might
swallow some and die. Then he gave a final look at
them, said, 'Chowin, chowin,' tenderly, and turned
to go.

He was already at the gap when he stopped with a
start. He raced back to the lambs and examined each
of them. 'Three she lambs,' he gasped. 'Oh, you devil,
that never happened before. Maybe father will give
me half-a-crown.'

And as he raced homeward, he barked like a dog in
his delight.

Going Into Exile

LIAM O'FLAHERTY

(b. 1897)

PATRICK FEENEY's cabin was crowded with people. In the large kitchen men, women, and children lined the walls, three deep in places, sitting on forms, chairs, stools, and on one another's knees. On the cement floor three couples were dancing a jig and raising a quantity of dust, which was, however, soon sucked up the chimney by the huge turf fire that blazed on the hearth. The only clear space in the kitchen was the corner to the left of the fireplace, where Pat Mullaney sat on a yellow chair, with his right ankle resting on his left knee, a spotted red handkerchief on his head that reeked with perspiration, and his red face contorting as he played a tattered old accordion. One door was shut and the tins hanging on it gleamed in the firelight. The opposite door was open and over the heads of the small boys that crowded in it and outside it, peering in at the dancing couples in the kitchen, a starry June sky was visible and, beneath the sky, shadowy grey crags and misty, whitish fields lay motionless, still, and sombre. There was a deep, calm silence outside the cabin and within the cabin, in spite of the music and dancing in the kitchen and the singing in the little room to the left, where Patrick Feeney's eldest son Michael sat on the bed with three other young men, there was a haunting melancholy in the air.

The people were dancing, laughing, and singing

133

with a certain forced and boisterous gaiety that failed to hide from them the real cause of their being there, dancing, singing, and laughing. For the dance was on account of Patrick Feeney's two children, Mary and Michael, who were going to the United States on the following morning.

Feeney himself, a black-bearded, red-faced, middle-aged peasant, with white ivory buttons on his blue frieze shirt and his hands stuck in his leather waist belt, wandered restlessly about the kitchen, urging the people to sing and dance, while his mind was in agony all the time, thinking that on the following day he would lose his two eldest children, never to see them again perhaps. He kept talking to everybody about amusing things, shouted at the dancers, and behaved in a boisterous and abandoned manner. But every now and then he had to leave the kitchen, under the pretence of going to the pigsty to look at a young pig that was supposed to be ill. He would stand, however, upright against his gable and look gloomily at some star or other, while his mind struggled with vague and peculiar ideas that wandered about in it. He could make nothing at all of his thoughts, but a lump always came up his throat, and he shivered, although the night was warm.

Then he would sigh and say with a contraction of his neck: 'Oh, it's a queer world this and no doubt about it. So it is.' Then he would go back to the cabin again and begin to urge on the dance, laughing, shouting, and stamping on the floor.

Towards dawn, when the floor was crowded with couples, arranged in fours, stamping on the floor and going to and fro, dancing the 'Walls of Limerick', Feeney was going out to the gable when his son Michael followed him out. The two of them walked side by side about the yard over the grey sea pebbles that had been strewn there the previous day. They walked in silence and yawned without need, pretending to be taking the air. But each of them was very excited. Michael was taller than his father and not so thickly built, but the shabby blue serge suit that he had bought for going to America was too narrow for his broad shoulders and the coat was too wide around the waist. He moved clumsily in it and his hands appeared altogether too bony and big and red, and he didn't know what to do with them. During his twenty-one years of life he had never worn anything other than the homespun clothes of Inverara, and the shop-made clothes appeared as strange to him and as uncomfortable as a dress suit worn by a man working in a sewer. His face was flushed a bright red and his blue eyes shone with excitement. Now and again he wiped the perspiration from his forehead with the lining of his grey tweed cap.

At last Patrick Feeney reached his usual position at the gable end. He halted, balanced himself on his heels with his hands in his waist belt, coughed, and said, 'It's going to be a warm day.' The son came up beside him, folded his arms, and leaned his right shoulder against the gable.

'It was kind of Uncle Ned to lend the money for the dance, father,' he said. 'I'd hate to think that we'd have to go without something or other, just the same as everybody else has. I'll send you that money the very first money I earn, father . . . even before I pay Aunt Mary for my passage money. I should have all that money paid off in four months, and then I'll have some more money to send you by Christmas.'

And Michael felt very strong and manly recounting what he was going to do when he got to Boston,

Massachusetts. He told himself that with his great strength he would earn a great deal of money. Conscious of his youth and his strength and lusting for adventurous life, for the moment he forgot the ache in his heart that the thought of leaving his father inspired in him.

The father was silent for some time. He was looking at the sky with his lower lip hanging, thinking of nothing. At last he sighed as a memory struck him.

'What is it?' said the son. 'Don't weaken, for God's sake. You will only make it hard for me.'

'Fooh!' said the father suddenly with pretended gruffness. 'Who is weakening? I'm afraid that your new clothes make you impudent.' Then he was silent for a moment and continued in a low voice:

'I was thinking of that potato field you sowed alone last spring the time I had the influenza. I never set eyes on the man that could do it better. It's a cruel world that takes you away from the land that God made you for.'

'Oh, what are you talking about, father?' said Michael irritably. 'Sure what did anybody ever get out of the land but poverty and hard work and potatoes and salt?'

'Ah yes,' said the father with a sigh, 'but it's your own, the land, and over there'—he waved his hand at the western sky—'you'll be giving your sweat to some other man's land, or what's equal to it.'

'Indeed,' muttered Michael, looking at the ground with a melancholy expression in his eyes, 'it's poor encouragement you are giving me.'

They stood in silence fully five minutes. Each hungered to embrace the other, to cry, to beat the air, to scream with excess of sorrow. But they stood

silent and sombre, like nature about them, hugging
their woe. Then they went back to the cabin. Michael
went into the little room to the left of the kitchen, to
the three young men who fished in the same curragh
with him and were his bosom friends. The father
walked into the large bedroom to the right of the
kitchen.

The large bedroom was also crowded with people.
A large table was laid for tea in the centre of the room
and about a dozen young men were sitting at it, drinking tea and eating buttered raisin cake. Mrs. Feeney
was bustling about the table, serving the food and
urging them to eat. She was assisted by her two
younger daughters and by another woman, a relative
of her own. Her eldest daughter Mary, who was going
to the United States that day, was sitting on the edge
of the bed with several other young women. The bed
was a large four-poster bed with a deal canopy over
it, painted red, and the young women were huddled
together on it. So that there must have been about a
dozen of them there. They were Mary Feeney's particular friends, and they stayed with her in that uncomfortable position just to show how much they liked
her. It was a custom.

Mary herself sat on the edge of the bed with her
legs dangling. She was a pretty, dark-haired girl of
nineteen, with dimpled, plump, red cheeks and rumi-
native brown eyes that seemed to cause little wrinkles
to come and go in her little low forehead. Her nose
was soft and small and rounded. Her mouth was small
and the lips were red and open. Beneath her white
blouse that was frilled at the neck and her navy blue
skirt that outlined her limbs as she sat on the edge of
the bed, her body was plump, soft, well-moulded, and
in some manner exuded a feeling of freshness and

innocence. So that she seemed to have been born to be fondled and admired in luxurious surroundings instead of having been born a peasant's daughter, who had to go to the United States that day to work as a servant or maybe in a factory.

And as she sat on the edge of the bed crushing her little handkerchief between her palms, she kept thinking feverishly of the United States, at one moment with fear and loathing, at the next with desire and longing. Unlike her brother she did not think of the work she was going to do or the money that she was going to earn. Other things troubled her, things of which she was half ashamed, half afraid, thoughts of love and of foreign men and of clothes and of houses where there were more than three rooms and where people ate meat every day. She was fond of life, and several young men among the local gentry had admired her in Inverara. But. . . .

She happened to look up and she caught her father's eyes as he stood silently by the window with his hands stuck in his waist belt. His eyes rested on hers for a moment and then he dropped them without smiling, and with his lips compressed he walked down into the kitchen. She shuddered slightly. She was a little afraid of her father, although she knew that he loved her very much and he was very kind to her. But the winter before he had whipped her with a dried willow rod, when he caught her one evening behind Tim Hernon's cabin after nightfall, with Tim Hernon's son Bartly's arms around her waist and he kissing her. Ever since, she always shivered slightly when her father touched her or spoke to her.

'Oho!' said an old peasant who sat at the table with a saucer full of tea in his hand and his grey flannel shirt open at his thin, hairy, wrinkled neck. 'Oho!

indeed, but it's a disgrace to the island of Inverara to let such a beautiful woman as your daughter go away, Mrs. Feeney. If I were a young man, I'll be flayed alive if I'd let her go.'

There was a laugh and some of the women on the bed said: 'Bad cess to you, Patsy Coyne, if you haven't too much impudence, it's a caution.' But the laugh soon died. The young men sitting at the table felt embarrassed and kept looking at one another sheepishly, as if each tried to find out if the others were in love with Mary Feeney.

'Oh, well, God is good,' said Mrs. Feeney, as she wiped her lips with the tip of her bright, clean, check apron. 'What will be must be, and sure there is hope from the sea, but there is no hope from the grave. It is sad and the poor have to suffer, but. . . .' Mrs. Feeney stopped suddenly, aware that all these platitudes meant nothing whatsoever. Like her husband she was unable to think intelligibly about her two children going away. Whenever the reality of their going away, maybe for ever, three thousand miles into a vast unknown world, came before her mind, it seemed that a thin bar of some hard metal thrust itself forward from her brain and rested behind the wall of her forehead. So that almost immediately she became stupidly conscious of the pain caused by the imaginary bar of metal and she forgot the dread prospect of her children going away. But her mind grappled with the things about her busily and efficiently, with the preparation of food, with the entertaining of her guests, with the numerous little things that have to be done in a house where there is a party and which only a woman can do properly. These little things, in a manner, saved her, for the moment at least, from bursting into tears whenever she looked at her daughter and whenever she thought of her son, whom she loved most of all her children, because perhaps she nearly died giving birth to him and he had been very delicate until he was twelve years old. So she laughed down in her breast a funny laugh she had that made her heave, where her check apron rose out from the waist-band in a deep curve. 'A person begins to talk,' she said with a shrug of her shoulders sideways, 'and then a person says foolish things.'

'That's true,' said the old peasant, noisily pouring more tea from his cup to his saucer.

But Mary knew by her mother laughing that way that she was very near being hysterical. She always laughed that way before she had one of her fits of hysterics. And Mary's heart stopped beating suddenly and then began again at an awful rate as her eyes became acutely conscious of her mother's body, the rotund, short body with the wonderful mass of fair hair growing grey at the temples and the fair face with the soft liquid brown eyes, that grew hard and piercing for a moment as they looked at a thing and then grew soft and liquid again, and the thin-lipped small mouth with the beautiful white teeth and the deep perpendicular grooves in the upper lip and the tremor that always came in the corner of the mouth, with love, when she looked at her children. Mary became acutely conscious of all these little points, as well as of the little black spot that was on her left breast below the nipple and the swelling that came now and again in her legs and caused her to have hysterics and would one day cause her death. And she was stricken with horror at the thought of leaving her mother and at the selfishness of her thoughts. She had never been prone to thinking of anything important, but now, somehow for a moment, she had a glimpse of her mother's life that made her shiver and hate herself as a cruel, heartless, lazy, selfish wretch. Her mother's life loomed up before her eyes, a life of continual misery and suffering, hard work, birth pangs, sickness, and again hard work and hunger and anxiety. It loomed up and then it fled again, a little mist came before her eyes and she jumped down from the bed, with the jaunty twirl of her head that was her habit when she set her body in motion.

'Sit down for a while, mother,' she whispered, toying with one of the black ivory buttons on her mother's brown bodice. 'I'll look after the table.'

'No, no,' murmured the mother with a shake of her whole body, 'I'm not a bit tired. Sit down, my treasure. You have a long way to travel today.'

And Mary sighed and went back to the bed again.

At last somebody said: 'It's broad daylight.' And immediately everybody looked out and said: 'So it is, and may God be praised.' The change from the starry night to the grey, sharp dawn was hard to notice until it had arrived. People looked out and saw the morning light sneaking over the crags silently, along the ground, pushing the mist banks upwards. The stars were growing dim. A long way off invisible sparrows were chirping in their ivied perch in some distant hill or other. Another day had arrived and even as the people looked at it, yawned and began to search for their hats, caps, and shawls preparing to go home, the day grew and spread its light and made things move and give voice. Cocks crew, blackbirds carolled, a dog let loose from a cabin by an early riser chased madly after an imaginary robber, barking as if his tail were on fire. The people said good-bye and began to stream forth from Feeney's cabin. They were going to their homes to see to the morning's work before going to

Kilmurrage to see the emigrants off on the steamer to the mainland. Soon the cabin was empty except for the family.

All the family gathered into the kitchen and stood about for some minutes talking sleepily of the dance and of the people who had been present. Mrs. Feeney tried to persuade everybody to go to bed, but everybody refused. It was four o'clock and Michael and Mary would have to set out for Kilmurrage at nine. So tea was made and they all sat about for an hour drinking it and eating raisin cake and talking. They only talked of the dance and of the people who had been present.

There were eight of them there, the father and mother and six children. The youngest child was Thomas, a thin boy of twelve, whose lungs made a singing sound every time he breathed. The next was Bridget, a girl of fourteen, with dancing eyes and a habit of shaking her short golden curls every now and then for no apparent reason. Then there were the twins, Julia and Margaret, quiet, rather stupid, flat-faced girls of sixteen. Both their upper front teeth protruded slightly and they were both great workers and very obedient to their mother. They were all sitting at the table, having just finished a third large pot of tea, when suddenly the mother hastily gulped down the remainder of the tea in her cup, dropped the cup with a clatter to her saucer, and sobbed once through her nose.

'Now mother,' said Michael sternly, 'what's the good of this work?'

'No, you are right, my pulse,' she replied quietly. 'Only I was just thinking how nice it is to sit here surrounded by all my children, all my little birds in my nest, and then two of them going to fly away made me sad.' And she laughed, pretending to treat it as a foolish joke.

'Oh, that be damned for a story,' said the father, wiping his mouth on his sleeve; 'there's work to be done. You Julia, go and get the horse. Margaret, you milk the cow and see that you give enough milk to the calf this morning.' And he ordered everybody about as if it were an ordinary day of work.

But Michael and Mary had nothing to do and they sat about miserably conscious that they had cut adrift from the routine of their home life. They no longer had any place in it. In a few hours they would be homeless wanderers. Now that they were cut adrift from it, the poverty and sordidness of their home life appeared to them under the aspect of comfort and plenty.

So the morning passed until breakfast time at seven o'clock. The morning's work was finished and the family was gathered together again. The meal passed in a dead silence. Drowsy after the sleepless night and conscious that the parting would come in a few hours, nobody wanted to talk. Everybody had an egg for breakfast in honour of the occasion. Mrs. Feeney, after her usual habit, tried to give her egg first to Michael, then to Mary, and as each refused it, she ate a little herself and gave the remainder to little Thomas who had the singing in his chest. Then the breakfast was cleared away. The father went to put the creels on the mare so as to take the luggage into Kilmurrage. Michael and Mary got the luggage ready and began to get dressed. The mother and the other children tidied up the house. People from the village began to come into the kitchen, as was customary, in order to accompany the emigrants from their home to Kilmurrage.

At last everything was ready. Mrs. Feeney had

exhausted all excuses for moving about, engaged on trivial tasks. She had to go into the big bedroom where Mary was putting on her new hat. The mother sat on a chair by the window, her face contorting on account of the flood of tears she was keeping back. Michael moved about the room uneasily, his two hands knotting a big red handkerchief behind his back. Mary twisted about in front of the mirror that hung over the black wooden mantelpiece. She was spending a long time with the hat. It was the first one she had ever worn, but it fitted her beautifully, and it was in excellent taste. It was given to her by the schoolmistress, who was very fond of her, and she herself had taken it in a little. She had an instinct for beauty in dress and deportment.

But the mother, looking at how well her daughter wore the cheap navy blue costume and the white frilled blouse, and the little round black hat with a fat, fluffy, glossy curl covering each ear, and the black silk stockings with blue clocks in them, and the little black shoes that had laces of three colours in them, got suddenly enraged with. . . . She didn't know with what she got enraged. But for the moment she hated her daughter's beauty, and she remembered all the anguish of giving birth to her and nursing her and toiling for her, for no other purpose than to lose her now and let her go away, maybe to be ravished wantonly because of her beauty and her love of gaiety. A cloud of mad jealousy and hatred against this impersonal beauty that she saw in her daughter almost suffocated the mother, and she stretched out her hands in front of her unconsciously and then just as suddenly her anger vanished like a puff of smoke, and she burst into wild tears, wailing: 'My children, oh, my children, far over the sea you will be carried from me, your mother.' And she began to rock herself and she threw her apron over her head.

Immediately the cabin was full of the sound of bitter wailing. A dismal cry rose from the women gathered in the kitchen. 'Far over the sea they will be carried', began woman after woman, and they all rocked themselves and hid their heads in their aprons. Michael's mongrel dog began to howl on the hearth. Little Thomas sat down on the hearth beside the dog and, putting his arms around him, he began to cry, although he didn't know exactly why he was crying, but he felt melancholy on account of the dog howling and so many people being about.

In the bedroom the son and daughter, on their knees, clung to their mother, who held their heads between her hands and rained kisses on both heads ravenously. After the first wave of tears she had stopped weeping. The tears still ran down her cheeks, but her eyes gleamed and they were dry. There was a fierce look in them as she searched all over the heads of her two children with them, with her brows contracted, searching with a fierce terror-stricken expression, as if by the intensity of her stare she hoped to keep a living photograph of them before her mind. With her quivering lips she made a queer sound like 'im-m-m-m' and she kept kissing. Her right hand clutched at Mary's left shoulder and with her left she fondled the back of Michael's neck. The two children were sobbing freely. They must have stayed that way a quarter of an hour.

Then the father came into the room, dressed in his best clothes. He wore a new frieze waistcoat, with a grey and black front and a white back. He held his soft black felt hat in one hand and in the other hand he had a bottle of holy water. He coughed and said in

145

a weak gentle voice that was strange to him, as he touched his son: 'Come now, it is time.'

Mary and Michael got to their feet. The father sprinkled them with holy water and they crossed themselves. Then, without looking at their mother, who lay in the chair with her hands clasped on her lap, looking at the ground in a silent tearless stupor, they left the room. Each hurriedly kissed little Thomas, who was not going to Kilmurrage, and then, hand in hand, they left the house. As Michael was going out the door he picked a piece of loose whitewash from the wall and put it in his pocket. The people filed out after them, down the yard and on to the road, like a funeral procession. The mother was left in the house with little Thomas and two old peasant women from the village. Nobody spoke in the cabin for a long time.

Then the mother rose and came into the kitchen. She looked at the two women, at her little son, and at the hearth, as if she were looking for something she had lost. Then she threw her hands into the air and ran out into the yard.

'Come back,' she screamed; 'come back to me.'

She looked wildly down the road with dilated nostrils, her bosom heaving. But there was nobody in sight. Nobody replied. There was a crooked stretch of limestone road, surrounded by grey crags that were scorched by the sun. The road ended in a hill and then dropped out of sight. The hot June day was silent. Listening foolishly for an answering cry, the mother imagined she could hear the crags simmering under the hot rays of the sun. It was something in her head that was singing.

The two old women led her back into the kitchen. 'There is nothing that time will not cure,' said one. 'Yes. Time and patience,' said the other.

Prongs

L. A. G. STRONG

(1896–1958)

'Ay, Johnny! C'm' home. D'ye hear me tellin' ye? C'm' on home out o' that.'

But Johnny paid no attention. Crouching over the rock pool, with ragged little trousers showing, in more than one place, the bare skin underneath, he continued to gaze intently into the water, his small round face red with stooping and excitement.

His coat was many sizes too big for him. The sleeves had been cut off half-way down, and were so wide that, when he had rolled one up, his thin arm was bare to the shoulder. On the rock ledge beside him four or five prawns moved convulsively: and, reaching precariously far, with his whole arm under water, he was patiently stalking another. Slowly his red cold hand would creep towards its prey: would be just upon it: then, with a sudden flirt of its tail, the prawn would shoot off backwards into another place, necessitating a change of position and a fresh pursuit. It was a cunning and elusive prawn: but the pool was not large. Even an eight-year-old could reach most parts of it, and when the prawn took refuge anywhere that was inaccessible, it could be dislodged with a piece of stick. Johnny had been chasing it for quite twenty minutes now, and was determined to have it in the end.

So he paid no heed to the impatient voice of Dan,

147

his elder brother, a boy some twelve years old, sulkily
handsome despite his rags and the dirt on his face,
who sat on the sea wall a few yards off, swinging his
bare legs.

For a little while there was silence, broken only by
the rapt snuffles of Johnny; then Dan spoke again,
more sharply:

'Johnny! Don't ye hear what I'm sayin' to ye? It's
time we were gone. C'm' on home, or ye'll be gettin'
me belted!'

It was no joke, sometimes, being sent out in charge of
Johnny, he reflected sourly, eyeing his small brother's
behind and the soles of his feet—all of him that could
be seen. Johnny was good company, and affectionate:
but he resented being put in Dan's charge, and would
often refuse to take his orders from him. This meant
an undignified squabble. Johnny, who was very strong
for his age, would lie on the ground and howl, attract-
ing the attention and sympathy of passers-by. If they
were late in reaching home, it was he, Dan, who got
the blame; and, despite much experience, Johnny
never seemed to realize this. He would be sorry
enough afterwards, for he was a warmhearted little
soul, and fond of Dan, but he never could seem to
grasp beforehand that his obstinacy would get his
brother into trouble. Bad trouble it was, too, if their
father happened to be at home. If Jem Foster had had
a drop too much, or was bad-tempered for the want
of drink, he became more than ever convinced of the
value of discipline in the home. As he was usually in
one condition or the other, and his sole disciplinary
measure was the belt, his family were at pains to give
him little occasion to use it.

For there was this much in his favour—that, unlike
most of his kind, he rarely laid his hand upon them

unless they gave him a pretext for doing so. When there was trouble, Dan, as the elder, had to bear the brunt of it. He hated his father, and, once his own fierce temper was roused, he could not conceal his hatred: wherefore his sufferings were worse than they might have been.

And here they were, the two of them, late for dinner already, and Johnny making no move to come, groping there in the pool after his blasted prawns. Prawns! He'd be belted for no prawns.

'Johnny! D'ye hear me? C'm' on out o' that. We'll be late.'

The little face, scarlet with excitement, looked suddenly round at him, sideways.

'Ah, Dan, can't we wait, only just a minyit! There's but one o' them left, only the one.'

'C'm' on, I tell ye. Ye'll be gettin' me belted again.'

'Only the one.'

And he bent again over the pool. Furious, Dan jumped down from the wall and ran over to him.

'C'm' on out o' that. I'll wait no more. Ye'll be gettin' me belted, I'm tellin' ye.'

He shook Johnny by the back of his trousers, nearly upsetting him into the pool. 'C'm' on home.'

Johnny uttered a wail of disappointment. 'You're after frightenin' him on me. I just had him. Ah, me lovely big prong—a grand big lad!'

'You and your "prongs"!' mimicked Dan scornfully. Johnny always called them 'prongs'. 'C'm' on home, do ye hear?'

'Ah, Danny, sure, can't ye wait just one minyit— one little minyit? Sure it's early yet. Sure—'

'C'm' on.'

Out of patience, Dan jerked the small boy to his feet, and began to drag him off towards the wall.

'Me prongs! Me prongs!'

Struggling desperately, Johnny broke free, leaving a piece of tattered trouser in his brother's hand, and stooped to collect his captures. Galvanized into sudden activity, they leaped hither and thither on their sides as the small red hands groped and grabbed for them. Gathering them up, Johnny pressed the mass against his breast, and suffered himself to be led over the uneven rocks to the wall. When they reached it, Dan jumped up first, and caught at his arm to help him up. There was a scream of protest, but too late: Johnny's arm was pulled away from his chest, and several of the prawns fell upon the rocks below.

'Ah, Danny, looka, you're after making me drop them.' He put down the survivors on the wall, at a safe distance from the edge, and prepared to retrieve the others. But Danny, his patience at an end, held him fast, and began dragging him in the direction of home.

'Me prongs! I must get me prongs!'

Wailing, the small boy pulled and struggled. He was strong: he writhed and ducked and twisted, till Dan in exasperation caught him by the hair and by one of his wrists, and haled him for several yards by main force. But it was no use. Johnny flung himself on the ground. Dan grabbed at him, and smacked his head hard; whereupon Johnny caught hold of his hand, and bit it with all his might.

A few yards off three men were talking, lounging by the wall, and spitting at frequent intervals upon it: local nondescripts, usually out of a job, and well content to remain so. Although the fight was going on close beside them, they took no notice of it, and did not even look round as Dan, white with rage, kneeled on the recumbent Johnny and set about him in good earnest. Heedless of all else, the brothers fought and cursed, till an extra hard whack made Johnny give up the battle and cover his face with his hands, screaming. Dan stood up, and looked down at him.

'Now maybe ye'll come on home when I bid ye!' he said breathlessly.

But Johnny would not rise. He lay and kicked and screamed. Dan caught hold of him in some consternation, and tried to heave him upon his feet. The only response was an even shriller scream.

Then one of the men looked round. He said nothing, but, taking his pipe from his mouth, he walked quietly over, and with the full swing of his foot kicked Dan off the edge of the wall on to the rocks below. Without even looking to see the result, he replaced his pipe, walked back to his companions, and went on talking to them as if nothing had happened.

But he was soon interrupted again: this time by a furious assault from behind, by little fists beating at his thighs and a shrill voice calling filthy curses. He looked round, to find Johnny, in an ecstasy of rage, squaring up to him, dancing up and down before him like a fury.

'C'm' on. C'm' on, ye big bully, ye!' screamed the little boy. 'I'll larn ye, ye big bully, ye!'

The man's jaw dropped in surprise and amusement. All three stared at the raving child, slow grins forming on their faces.

'Oho,' said the man slowly, 'me young cock-sparra. That's what ye'd be at, is it?'

Then Dan, weeping, appeared over the edge of the wall. By good fortune he was not badly hurt. Kick and fall had bruised and winded him: his forehead was scraped, and the blood was trickling from a cut on his shin: but his spirit was unbroken, and as his breath came back he cursed the man through his sobs with an expert profanity.

So they stood, a strange group: three laughing men, two weeping, furious boys; but the men were somehow ill at ease, and Dan's assailant felt a need to justify his action. He leaned upon morality.

'That'll larn ye to ill-trate them that's smaller than yeerself!' he pronounced solemnly. 'Be off with ye now, or I'll sarve ye worse.' And he made a threatening gesture with his hand.

Dan confronted him.

'Ye will, will ye?' he cried. 'Wait till I tell me da what ye done. Wait, ye big bloody brute, ye! Wait till ye get a puck of Jem Foster's fist in yer gob, and then we'll see what ye'll do.'

Jem Foster, bedad! The men looked at one another uneasily; and the leader's face lengthened. He hadn't bargained for this. Jem Foster! This might turn out a nasty business. A bad man to quarrel with, Jem Foster. True, he wasn't famous for any great love of his children; but a bad man to cross. It would be well to run no risks with his like.

The assailant changed his tone, and the boys at once perceiving it, began to dance up and down before him and to chant their father's name as though it were a kind of incantation.

'Are ye hurted?' asked the man with affected unconcern, coming forward to investigate; but Dan backed away and spat at him. 'Ah, well,' the man went on, 'maybe I hurted ye more than I meaned. I didn't mean for ye to fall on the rocks—though, mind ye, ye richly desarved it. Didn't he, boys?'

'Richly desarved it!' echoed the other two. 'Oh, begad, he did.'

'Still, seein' I've hurted ye more nor I meaned, I'll try what can I do to make it up to ye.'

Magnanimously the man put his hand in his pocket.

'We'll make it up to him, won't we, boys?'

'Aye, sure, we will.'

Between them they collected a sixpence and a handful of coppers. Dan and Johnny ceased their noise at once, and watched attentively.

'Now,' said the man, holding out the coins, 'do you take these, and say nothin' to yeer da. What do ye say?'

'Johnny's eyes were round. He looked at the money, and then at his brother. Dan wavered; all his resentment seemed suddenly to have left him, and he answered almost sadly.

'I can't take yeer money,' he said. 'Me da would never suffer me to take a gift of money.'

The man cajoled him. 'Ah, come on, now, alanna. Take it, and yeer da'll be none the wiser.' Dan shook his head.

'I can't take a gift,' he repeated. 'I've nothin' to give ye in exchange.'

Suddenly, as if he had been stung, Johnny went down on all fours, and in a moment was on the rocks under the wall, ferreting about feverishly. The man stopped to stare at him.

'What the—' he began.

'The prongs,' cried Johnny. 'The prongs, Dan darlin' —me lovely prongs. Look at here: I have the best of them still. Here, take them, and give them to the gentleman—and ye can take the money, then. Isn't that so, mister?' His small face wrinkled up at the man in eager inquiry. 'Isn't that so?'

'It is indeed,' replied the man. 'What is it ye have?

Praans, is it? Indeed, and I'll buy them off o' ye, and glad to do it. I have a great likin' for praans.'

'Here they are.' Johnny poured the limp green creatures into the big brown hand, opened dubiously to receive them.

'There's one trodden on, but ye can still ate him.'

'Faith, and I can so.' The man looked into his palm with pretended enthusiasm. 'And here's yeer money.'

He tipped the coins into Dan's still shaking hand.

'And ye'll say nothin' to yeer da?'

'Nothin'.'

The man saw that he could be trusted; and so it came about that, a minute later, the three were congratulating themselves on having got out from a nasty position, and the two boys were hurrying homeward, Johnny trotting at his brother's side, from time to time looking anxiously up at his face.

They were terribly late for the meal. Jem was in. He scowled at them as they entered, and began fumbling at his belt; their mother's face showed pale in the gloom behind him.

But Johnny gave him no time.

'I'm terrible sorry we're late, da,' he babbled hurriedly. 'We was catchin' prongs—and—and a gintleman said he'd buy them off of us—and we stayed on and catched a lot—and Dan has the money here. Looka, da!'

Jem eyed them and the money, in two minds. Ordinarily there would have been an outburst; but he was very dry, and the money was there, right enough; so he grabbed it, and with a growl motioned the boys away. The woman's face showed piteous relief, and the two, glad enough to escape, hastily followed her out to the yard, where she had a meal of potatoes and buttermilk waiting for them.

After they had eaten, they climbed a little way up the hill, past the tethered goat, to a grassy place between grey rocks, from which they had a wide view of the harbour and the sea—climbing slowly, for Dan's hurts were stiffening, and he hobbled painfully on the slope. They sat down together, facing the sea, in silence. It was a dead calm, and very clear. The horizon was a dark line drawn between sea and sky, and a ship which had sunk below it left a dark-blue smudge of smoke, faint, motionless, incredibly distant.

Presently Johnny moved closer to his brother.

'I'm sorry, Danny,' he whispered. 'Is your hurts painin' ye? I'm sorry.'

Dan did not seem to have heard; he still looked out to sea; but after a few moments his arm moved around Johnny's neck, and he began absent-mindedly to stroke his hair. With a sigh of happiness, the little boy snuggled closer, and shut his eyes.

Unholy Living and Half Dying

SEÁN O'FAOLÁIN

(b. 1900)

JACKY CARDEW is one of those club bachelors who are so well groomed, well preserved, pomaded, medicated, and self-cosseted that they seem ageless—the sort of fixture about whom his pals will say when he comes unstuck around the age of eighty, 'Well, well! Didn't poor old Jacky Cardew go off *very* fast in the end?'

For thirty years or so he has lived in what are called Private Hotels; last winter he said to his friends,

'These bloody kips are neither private nor hotels, I'm going to take a flat.' What he got in the end was the sort of makeshift thing that goes by the name of a flat in Irish cities—two rooms (that is, one room cut in two), with the W.C. on the ground floor and the bathroom on the top floor; and in the bathroom an unpleasant, greasy-looking gas-stove such as Prince Albert might have unveiled at the Great Crystal Palace Exhibition of 1851.

But Jacky was delighted. At least he now had privacy. Nobody lived in the house but himself and his own landlady; for a tinsmith had the ground floor (rather noisy and smelling of solder), there were solicitors' offices on the second floor, the old lady lived under the slates, above Jacky's flat, and he hardly ever saw her except when he paid his rent.

About two o'clock one bad February morning just as Jacky and a few friends were settling down for the fourth time to their last game of solo they gradually became aware that a dog was beating his tail on the floor above. There was no other sound then—for a while—but the flick of the cards and the rain spitting on the window and the slight exclamations of the players. Then they heard the rapping again.

'Better go easy, boys,' somebody said, playing a card, 'we're keeping the old lady upstairs awake.'

They played on intently. Again they heard the rapping, this time insistent and loud. Jacky glanced around at the lifted eyebrows, at his wrist-watch, at the dying fire, at the drops sparkling on the pane in the arclight of the Square below, and went out with the sort of frown he would have turned on a junior in the bank who had not been soapy enough. Striking matches he climbed the stairs. The nail-heads shone. Hearing him stumble and curse she called his name, and he

made his way towards the voice, stooping under the
great rafters of the attics, elbowing aside the damp
washing that she had hung there to dry, feeling the
cold within a few inches of his poll. He found her
room, a bare attic. He was affronted by its poverty, its
cold stuffiness, its sloping attic-window that wept in
ripples with the lights of the city.

In the match-light he saw her pale eyes staring up
at him in terror from the pillow; he saw her hollowed
cheeks; the white beard on her chin; her two pigtails
tied with bits of red wool. The match burned his
fingers. Through the dark he heard her whisper,

'Mr. Cardew, I'm dying.'

He was so frightened that he immediately lit another
match. He was even more frightened by what she
replied when he asked her if he could call in one of
her friends:

'God help us,' she panted. 'Friends how are ye? I
haven't a friend to wet me lips. Not a friend. In the
world.'

He raced down the stairs. One of his pals was a
doctor; he went up and examined her, soothed her,
came down, said there was nothing much wrong with
her except old age and perhaps a touch of indigestion,
and ordered two aspirins and a hot-water bottle on
her stomach. They made her comfortable for the night
and the party went home, heads down to the rain,
shouting commiserations all round.

Jacky came back to his dishevelled room and sat by
the cold fireplace. He heard every quarter-hour strike
from the City Hall, sometimes bold and clear, sometimes faint and sad, according to the mood of the
wintry wind. He suddenly remembered that his own
mother had gone on a night like this. He wondered
who would attend to the old woman if she died, and

for the first time he took notice of the family photographs hung around the walls, mainly young men and women and vacant-looking babies with their mouths open. There was a big black enlargement of a man with a grey moustache and a bald head. He reminded him of old Cassidy, his last Manager, who now dined regularly every Tuesday of the year with another retired banker called Enright. As Jacky poked the dead cinders it came to him that Cassidy probably had no other friend in the world, and, begod, anyway, once you turn fifty what is it but a gallop down the bloody straight?

At half-past three he went up to have another look at her. She was asleep, breathing heavily. He tried to feel her pulse but could not remember what a normal beat is and felt hers was as slow as a hearse. He returned to his cold room. The rain still spat. The Square outside shone. He felt a dull pain in his groin and wondered, could it be appendicitis? He thought that he should have called in the priest to her and he counted the years since he last went to Confession. At half-past four he had another look at her and found her breathing easily and decided she was all right. As he pulled up his pyjamas he gave his paunch a dirty look.

He was awakened at his usual hour by the old lady herself, bringing him his usual hot cup of tea and buttered toast. She had a prayer-book under one arm and was dressed for the street.

'Good Heavens,' he gulped, 'I thought you were....'

Her tall lean body swayed over like a reed with the gusts of laughter.

'Mr. Cardew, 'tis well known you can't kill a bad thing. My little hot seat in Purgatory isn't ready for me yet. Ah, I knew I'd pay for that load of bacon and cabbage I ate yesterday.' An inelegant gesture from her stomach to her throat made him hastily lay down the buttered toast. 'I was all swelled up with it the day long.'

Jacky dressed, blaspheming. On his way out he decided to have a serious word with the woman. She had returned from chapel and was sitting in her kitchen sucking up a big basin of soup.

'Look here, Mrs. Canty,' he said severely, 'is it an actual fact that you have no friends whatsoever?'

'I have plenty friends, Mr. Cardew,' she smiled happily. 'The best friends any woman ever had.' She laid her bony hands on a pile of prayer-books—there must have been about twelve of them, a pile a foot high, all in shiny black cloth coverings. 'Haven't I the souls suffering in Purgatory? I have Saint Anthony.' Her glance directed his to a big brown-and-cream statue on the dresser. 'And haven't I the Sacred Heart?' He eyed the red-and-gold statue over the sink with the withered palms of last Easter crossed before it. 'Look at the Little Flower smiling at me. And what about Saint Joseph and Saint Monica?'

Jacky's head was going around like a weather-cock.

'And amn't I only after coming in from praying to the Left Shoulder? Friends, Mr. Cardew?'

She smiled pityingly at him. He strode out, to prevent himself from saying, 'Then why the hell didn't you call on them last night instead of rapping me up to you?' Instead he took it out of his secretary at the bank.

'Pure damn superstition, that's what I call it. Craw-thumpin' by day and bellyachin' by night. The usual Irish miserere. All based on fear of hell-fire and damnation. It would turn anybody into an atheist!'

The girl talked up to him; they almost quarrelled; she told him he should be ashamed of himself; she even told him his 'day would come'; she drove him beside himself by telling him she 'would pray for him'. At lunch he got into a violent argument about religion during which he kept on using the word, 'Benighted! Benighted!' He was still at it that night in the club, but he had to go easy there as most of the members were Knights of Columbanus and business is business. He took the middle line of:

'Mind you, I have a great regard for what I call *real* religion. And, mind you, I'm no saint. I'm honest about that. Though I suppose I'm no worse than the general run, and maybe a bit better if the truth were told. And I'll say this for it, religion is a great consolation for old age. But if religion doesn't go with *character*— character first and before all—then it crumbles away into formalism and superstition!'

They all considered it safe to agree with that. He surveyed his cards contentedly.

'I think it's your lead, Maguire.'

He found himself strolling homewards with Maguire: a gentle night after all the rain, and a delicate spring touch in the air.

'We won't know where we are now,' said Maguire, 'until Easter is on us.' And he gave an uncomfortable little laugh.

'What's the joke?'

'Wisha, I was just thinking there tonight when you were gassing about religion that . . . begod, do you know, 'tis a year since I was at confession. With Easter coming on now I suppose we'll have to get the culd skillet cleaned again. Easter Duty, you know. Where do you go? I always pop up to Rathfarnham to the S.J.'s. Men of the world. Nobody like 'em.'

'I usually go there, too,' lied Jacky. 'You can talk to those fellows.'

And he began to wonder, would he or would he not make a dash for it this year?

On the Thursday of Holy Week, just after midnight, Jacky and the boys were in the middle of a hot game of nap when a faint knocking percolated through the ceiling.

'No bloody fear,' he grunted. 'Once bitten twice shy. More cod-acting.'

They gathered up their hands and began to play. Through the slap of the cards the rapping came again, this time more faintly.

'That one now,' said Jacky. 'You play, Jim. That one.... God, have you nothing but the Ace? That one is a typical example of the modern Irish crawthumper. Behind all this piety, believe you me.... Who said I reneged? What are you talking about, didn't I put the seven on Redmond's deuce? Behind all this so-called piety there's nothing but a child's fear of the dark.'

Maguire laughed at him.

'Now, Jacky, there's no earthly use your beefing about religion. The stamp of the Church is on you. 'Tis on all of us. 'Tis on you since the day you were born and sooner or later they'll get you and you may as well give in and be done with it. Mark my words, I'll live to see the day you'll have holy pictures all around your bloody bedroom! The stamp is on you! The stamp is on you.'

Jacky flared. Here was a fellow who barely confessed once a year and he was talking as if he were a blooming saint.

'Stop wagging your finger at me, please. And, anyway, with all your guff, when were you at confession last, I'd like to know?'

Maguire laughed smugly.

'I don't in the least mind telling you. I was there three days ago. A grand old priest.' He clicked his fingers and looked around him at the group. 'He let me off like that. I think if I'd told him I'd committed murder all he'd say would be, "Any other little thing troubling you, my child?"'

They laughed approvingly.

'Ah, there's nothing like an S.J.,' Maguire went on. 'Listen, did ye ever hear the one about the fellow that went to confession the time of the Troubles here and said, "Father, I shot a Black and Tan." Do you know what the priest said? "My child," says he, "You may omit your venial sins." Honest to God, I believe 'tis a fact.'

They all laughed again although they had heard the yarn many times before: it is the sort of story every hardy sinner likes to hear. Through their laughter the knocking came again.

'I'm afraid, Jacky,' said another of them, a commercial named Sullivan, 'You'll have to have a look at the ould geezer.'

With a curse Jacky flung down his cards. He climbed to the attic. He struck a match and gave one look at her and at once he knew that she was bad. Her forehead was beaded. Her chest rose and fell rapidly.

'Mr. Cardew. I'm finished. Get me the priest. For God's sake.'

'Certainly. Certainly. Right away. And I'll get the doctor.'

He belted down the stairs and burst in on them.

'God, lads, 'tis no joke this time. She's for it. I can tell it. I can see it. Maguire, run out for the priest like a good man. Sullivan, there's a telephone down by the kiosk, call the doctor, get Cantillon, Hanley, Casey, any of 'em. Hurry, hurry!'

He brought her up a stiff whisky but she was too weak to sip it. When the priest came, a young man with the sad eyes and bent head of a Saint Francis, the gamblers huddled outside under the rafters, looking through the skylight at the wide Easter moon. They were all middle-aged men, younger than Jacky, but replicas in every other way.

'Oh,' whispered Maguire. ''Tis true. Just as the old priest told me. Like a thief in the night. We never know the day or the hour.'

''Twas a terrible winter,' whispered Sullivan. 'I never saw so many people popping off. I see where old Sir John Philpott went off yesterday.'

'Ah, God, no?' begged Jacky, shocked at the news. 'You don't mean Philpott of Potter and Philpotts? I was talking to him in the club only three days ago.' (He said it as if he were affronted at Sir John's giving him no previous warning of the event.) 'But he was a comparatively young man! Was he sixty-two itself?'

'Heart,' whispered Wilson. 'He went off very fast in the end.'

'Here today,' sighed Maguire. 'Gone tomorrow.'

'The best way to go,' murmured Sullivan. 'No trouble to anybody.'

'That is,' whispered Maguire, 'provided our ticket's been punched for—' And he pointed respectfully upwards. 'I heard a preacher say one time that he knew a man who came into his confession-box after being twenty years away. He said he had just lifted his finger and said the *Absolvo te*'—here Maguire lifted his two first fingers—'when the man dropped dead at his feet in the box! There was a close shave for you!'

Jacky moved uneasily; he knew the story was just a preacher's yarn, but he had not the spirit to say it.

'The best death of all,' murmured Sullivan, 'is the soldier's. I believe, just before a battle, a priest can give a whole regiment a General Absolution, and if a man is killed he goes straight up to heaven. That's what makes Irishmen such good soldiers. Straight up to heaven!'

'Grand in attack,' said Jacky judiciously, 'not so good in defence.'

'And that's why!' said Sullivan. 'And, what's more, I wouldn't be surprised if that isn't why the English are better on the defensive than in the charge. Sure any man would fight like a divil if he knew what was coming after? Death has no terrors for a man in a situation like that.'

They fell silent. A cloudlet dimmed the moon. Then all their faces were illumined again. The city's roofs shone. The priest's voice murmured softly.

'He's taking a long time,' said Jacky. 'And it isn't,' he whispered, trying to make a little joke, 'as if she had so much to tell. *She's* all right anyway.'

'And,' said Maguire piously, 'on Good Friday. A lovely death!'

'So it is,' said Wilson. 'Good Friday!'

They all sighed deeply. The priest came out, stooping under the beams, removing his stole and kissing it. Maguire asked him, 'Will she last, father?' The priest sighed, 'A saint, a saint,' as if he were sighing for all the sinners of the world. Jacky showed him out, and as he walked away the doctor came down. Jacky shut him into his car and shoved in his head anxiously.

'Is she bad, doctor?'

'Anno Domini. We can't live for ever. The works give out—just like an old motor-car. All we can do at that age is wait for the call,' and he beckoned with one finger. Jacky drew back hastily. The headlamps whirled and the car purred away across the empty Square as if its red tail-light were running away with somebody.

Jacky was left alone in his room. He sank into an arm-chair by the open window. The spring night was gentle. The blood of life was pulsing through everything. Even the three old London planes in the middle of the Square had their little throb and the high Easter moon was delicately transparent as if with youth. He leaped up and began to circle the room. He had never seen anything so lovely, it seemed to him, as those little babies gazing at him out of their big eyes, with their soft little lips parted. He was looking again over the shining roofs and the blank chimney-pots, and as if a shutter flicked he felt for one moment the intense vacancy and loneliness of his life and saw it, as the years went by, becoming more lonely and more empty. And when he was gone, that moon out there, the old trees below, would still be there, still throbbing. A little wind scurried furtively in the dust of the Square. He looked at the decanter. Low tide. Like his own life. He'd be able to rest tomorrow anyway. He paused before the black enlargement. Good Friday morning. One more day to Easter. A veined, red face with a blue nose, thin ruffled hair, bags under the eyes was looking at him out of the mirror. He licked his lips and got a horrible taste in his mouth and felt an uneven thumping in his heart.

He sat down heavily by the open window, before the moon's indifferent beauty, and began to go back over the years. There were a couple of things it wasn't going to be too easy to. . . .

'Not, mind you,' he assured the empty Square, with

bravado, 'that I'm going to hand myself over to some bogtrot from the County Meath. Pick the right man and. . . . "Well, Father,"' he rehearsed, flicking a grain of ash from his pants and pulling his ear, 'I'm afraid, er, I've got more than a few little peccadilloes to tell you. We're only human, Father. Children of Adam, and all to that and so on.' That was the ticket. Frank and open. Two men of the world. 'Of course, there's been a spot of liquor, Father. And, er . . . Well, er . . . I mean, er. . . .' Jacky coughed and ran his finger around inside his collar. This thing was going to take a bit of doing. He closed his eyes and began to think of all those nights that had seemed such grand nights—at the time.

When he opened his eyes again the sun was warm on his face, the Square was gay with sunlight, somebody was shaking his shoulder. It was his landlady smilingly handing him his tea and buttered toast.

'Well, Mr. Cardew,' she cackled, 'since I didn't go last night I'll live to be a hundred!'

As Jacky looked blearily down at the three plane trees the misery of the night flooded on him. He gave her one maddened look, banged down the cup, and started to tell her just what he thought of her. An unholy gripe pierced a red-hot needle through the small of his back.

'Oh, Mr. Cardew, what on earth made you sit by the open window!'

But now the pain ran across the back of his neck, and with a hand to his back and a hand to his neck all he could do was to crawl away moaning and cursing to his bed.

As he lay there through the holidays he found himself being petted and cosseted as he had never been in his life before. She rubbed his back and she rubbed

his chest and she brought him hot punch and fed him
with Easter delicacies until, gradually, if sourly, he
decided that he would be a fool to change his landlady. At the same time, and especially on Easter Sunday morning as he lay with the sun slanting warmly
across his chest, his hands behind his head, smoking
his after-breakfast cigarette, his Sunday paper on his
lap, listening to the silvery bells of all the churches of
the city, he was aware of a certain slight feeling of
discomfort—nothing much, just a coiled shadow at
the back of his mind, the merest hint of apprehension.
Cautiously he turned his stiff shoulders to look at the
mantelpiece where she had placed a little spray of
Palm in a glass vase, and beside it a little glass bowl
of Holy Water. He grunted as he considered them.
He'd get rid of those things all right when he got on
his feet again! Just then he remembered Maguire, and
all that about the stamp being on you. He smiled un-
comfortably. Oh, well! He flicked his ash on the
carpet. Some day, no doubt. Some day.

How lovely the sun was. It was nice to hear all the
footsteps across the Square below, going to Mass.
Their shadowy reflections passed softly on the ceiling,
and the silvery bells went on calling everybody to be
happy because Christ was risen.

He took up the paper and began to study Form.

The Trout

SEÁN O'FAOLÁIN
(b. 1900)

ONE of the first places Julia always ran to when they
arrived in G—— was The Dark Walk. It is a laurel
walk, very old; almost gone wild, a lofty midnight

167

tunnel of smooth, sinewy branches. Underfoot the tough brown leaves are never dry enough to crackle: there is always a suggestion of damp and cool trickle.

She raced right into it. For the first few yards she always had the memory of the sun behind her, then she felt the dusk closing swiftly down on her so that she screamed with pleasure and raced on to reach the light at the far end; and it was always just a little too long in coming so that she emerged gasping, clasping her hands, laughing, drinking in the sun. When she was filled with the heat and glare she would turn and consider the ordeal again.

This year she had the extra joy of showing it to her small brother, and of terrifying him as well as herself. And for him the fear lasted longer because his legs were so short and she had gone out at the far end while he was still screaming and racing.

When they had done this many times they came back to the house to tell everybody that they had done it. He boasted. She mocked. They squabbled.

'Cry babby!'

'You were afraid yourself, so there!'

'I won't take you any more.'

'You're a big pig.'

'I hate you.'

Tears were threatening so somebody said, 'Did you see the well?' She opened her eyes at that and held up her long lovely neck suspiciously and decided to be incredulous. She was twelve and at that age little girls are beginning to suspect most stories: they have already found out too many, from Santa Claus to the Stork. How could there be a well! In The Dark Walk? That she had visited year after year? Haughtily she said, 'Nonsense.'

But she went back, pretending to be going some-

where else, and she found a hole scooped in the rock
at the side of the walk, choked with damp leaves, so
shrouded by ferns that she only uncovered it after
much searching. At the back of this little cavern there
was about a quart of water. In the water she suddenly
perceived a panting trout. She rushed for Stephen and
dragged him to see, and they were both so excited that
they were no longer afraid of the darkness as they
hunched down and peered in at the fish panting in his
tiny prison, his silver stomach going up and down like
an engine.

Nobody knew how the trout got there. Even old
Martin in the kitchen-garden laughed and refused to
believe that it was there, or pretended not to believe,
until she forced him to come down and see. Kneeling
and pushing back his tattered old cap he peered in.

'Be cripes, you're right. How the divil in hell did
that fella get there?'

She stared at him suspiciously.

'You knew?' she accused; but he said, 'The divil a
know'; and reached down to lift it out. Convinced she
hauled him back. If she had found it then it was her
trout.

Her mother suggested that a bird had carried the
spawn. Her father thought that in the winter a small
streamlet might have carried it down there as a baby,
and it had been safe until the summer came and the
water began to dry up. She said, 'I see,' and went back
to look again and consider the matter in private. Her
brother remained behind, wanting to hear the whole
story of the trout, not really interested in the actual
trout but much interested in the story which his
mummy began to make up for him on the lines of, 'So
one day Daddy Trout and Mammy Trout . . .' When
he retailed it to her she said, 'Pooh.'

It troubled her that the trout was always in the same position; he had no room to turn; all the time the silver belly went up and down; otherwise he was motionless. She wondered what he ate and in between visits to Joey Pony, and the boat and a bathe to get cool, she thought of his hunger. She brought him down bits of dough; once she brought him a worm. He ignored the food. He just went on panting. Hunched over him she thought how, all the winter, while she was at school he had been in there. All the winter, in The Dark Walk, all day, all night, floating around alone. She drew the leaf of her hat down around her ears and chin and stared. She was still thinking of it as she lay in bed.

It was late June, the longest days of the year. The sun had sat still for a week, burning up the world. Although it was after ten o'clock it was still bright and still hot. She lay on her back under a single sheet, with her long legs spread, trying to keep cool. She could see the D of the moon through the fir-tree—they slept on the ground floor. Before they went to bed her mummy had told Stephen the story of the trout again, and she, in her bed, had resolutely presented her back to them and read her book. But she had kept one ear cocked.

'And so, in the end, this naughty fish who would not stay at home got bigger and bigger and bigger, and the water got smaller and smaller. . . .'

Passionately she had whirled and cried, 'Mummy, don't make it a horrible old moral story!' Her mummy had brought in a Fairy Godmother, then, who sent lots of rain, and filled the well, and a stream poured out and the trout floated away down to the river below. Staring at the moon she knew that there are no such things as Fairy Godmothers and that the trout, down in The Dark Walk, was panting like an engine. She heard somebody unwind a fishing-reel. Would the *beasts* fish him out!

She sat up. Stephen was a hot lump of sleep, lazy thing. The Dark Walk would be full of little scraps of moon. She leaped up and looked out of the window, and somehow it was not so lightsome now that she saw the dim mountains far away and the black firs against the breathing land and heard a dog say, bark-bark. Quietly she lifted the ewer of water, and climbed out the window and scuttled along the cool but cruel gravel down to the maw of the tunnel. Her pyjamas were very short so that when she splashed water it wet her ankles. She peered into the tunnel. Something alive rustled inside there. She raced in, and up and down she raced, and flurried, and cried aloud, 'Oh, Gosh, I can't find it,' and then at last she did. Kneeling down in the damp she put her hand into the slimy hole. When the body lashed they were both mad with fright. But she gripped him and shoved him into the ewer and raced, with her teeth ground, out to the other end of the tunnel and down the steep paths to the river's edge.

All the time she could feel him lashing his tail against the side of the ewer. She was afraid he would jump right out. The gravel cut into her soles until she came to the cool ooze of the river's bank where the moon-mice on the water crept into her feet. She poured out watching until he plopped. For a second he was visible in the water. She hoped he was not dizzy. Then all she saw was the glimmer of the moon in the silent-flowing river, the dark firs, the dim mountains, and the radiant pointed face laughing down at her out of the empty sky.

She scuttled up the hill, in the window, plonked

down the ewer, and flew through the air like a bird into bed. The dog said bark-bark. She heard the fishing-reel whirring. She hugged herself and giggled. Like a river of joy her holiday spread before her.

In the morning Stephen rushed to her, shouting that 'he' was gone, and asking 'where' and 'how'. Lifting her nose in the air she said superciliously, 'Fairy Godmother, I suppose?' and strolled away patting the palms of her hands.

Guests of the Nation

FRANK O'CONNOR

(1903–1966)

I

AT dusk the big Englishman, Belcher, would shift his long legs out of the ashes and say, 'Well, chums, what about it?' and Noble or me would say, 'All right, chum' (for we had picked up some of their curious expressions), and the little Englishman, Hawkins, would light the lamp and bring out the cards. Sometimes Jeremiah Donovan would come up and supervise the game and get excited over Hawkins's cards, which he always played badly, and shout at him as if he was one of our own, 'Ah, you divil, you, why didn't you play the tray?'

But ordinarily Jeremiah was a sober and contented poor devil like the big Englishman, Belcher, and was looked up to only because he was a fair hand at documents, though he was slow enough even with them. He wore a small cloth hat and big gaiters over his long pants, and you seldom saw him with his hands out of his pockets. He reddened when you talked to him, tilting from toe to heel and back, and looking down all the time at his big farmer's feet. Noble and me used to make fun of his broad accent, because we were from the town.

I couldn't at the time seen the point of me and Noble guarding Belcher and Hawkins at all, for it was my belief that you could have planted that pair down anywhere from this to Claregalway and they'd have taken root there like a native weed. I never in my short experience seen two men to take to the country as they did.

They were handed on to us by the Second Battalion when the search for them became too hot, and Noble and myself, being young, took over with a natural feeling of responsibility, but Hawkins made us look like fools when he showed that he knew the country better than we did.

'You're the bloke they calls Bonaparte,' he says to me. 'Mary Brigid O'Connell told me to ask you what you done with the pair of her brother's socks you borrowed.'

For it seemed, as they explained it, that the Second used to have little evenings, and some of the girls of the neighbourhood turned in, and, seeing they were such decent chaps, our fellows couldn't leave the two Englishmen out of them. Hawkins learned to dance 'The Walls of Limerick', 'The Siege of Ennis', and 'The Waves of Tory' as well as any of them, though, naturally, he couldn't return the compliment, because our lads at that time did not dance foreign dances on principle.

So whatever privileges Belcher and Hawkins had with the Second they just naturally took with us, and after the first day or two we gave up all pretence of keeping a close eye on them. Not that they could have got far, for they had accents you could cut with a knife and wore khaki tunics and overcoats with civilian pants and boots. But it's my belief that they never had any idea of escaping and were quite content to be where they were.

It was a treat to see how Belcher got off with the old woman of the house where we were staying. She was a great warrant to scold, and cranky even with us, but before ever she had a chance of giving our guests, as I may call them, a lick of her tongue, Belcher had made her his friend for life. She was breaking sticks, and Belcher, who hadn't been more than ten minutes in the house, jumped up from his seat and went over to her.

'Allow me, madam,' he says, smiling his queer little smile, 'please allow me'; and he takes the bloody hatchet. She was struck too paralytic to speak, and after that, Belcher would be at her heels, carrying a bucket, a basket, or a load of turf, as the case might be. As Noble said, he got into looking before she leapt, and hot water, or any little thing she wanted, Belcher would have it ready for her. For such a huge man (and though I am five foot ten myself I had to look up at him) he had an uncommon shortness—or should I say lack?—of speech. It took us some time to get used to him, walking in and out, like a ghost, without a word. Especially because Hawkins talked enough for a platoon, it was strange to hear big Belcher with his toes in the ashes come out with a solitary 'Excuse me, chum,' or 'That's right, chum.' His one and only passion was cards, and I will say for him that he was a good card-player. He could have fleeced myself and Noble, but whatever we lost to him Hawkins lost to us, and Hawkins played with the money Belcher gave him.

174

Hawkins lost to us because he had too much old gab, and we probably lost to Belcher for the same reason. Hawkins and Noble would spit at one another about religion into the early hours of the morning, and Hawkins worried the soul out of Noble, whose brother was a priest, with a string of questions that would puzzle a cardinal. To make it worse, even in treating of holy subjects, Hawkins had a deplorable tongue. I never in all my career met a man who could mix such a variety of cursing and bad language into an argument. He was a terrible man, and a fright to argue. He never did a stroke of work, and when he had no one else to talk to, he got stuck in the old woman.

He met his match in her, for one day when he tried to get her to complain profanely of the drought, she gave him a great come-down by blaming it entirely on Jupiter Pluvius (a deity neither Hawkins nor I had ever heard of, though Noble said that among the pagans it was believed that he had something to do with the rain). Another day he was swearing at the capitalists for starting the German war when the old lady laid down her iron, puckered up her little crab's mouth, and said: 'Mr. Hawkins, you can say what you like about the war, and think you'll deceive me because I'm only a simple poor countrywoman, but I know what started the war. It was the Italian Count that stole the heathen divinity out of the temple in Japan. Believe me, Mr. Hawkins, nothing but sorrow and want can follow the people that disturb the hidden powers.'

A queer old girl, all right.

II

We had our tea one evening, and Hawkins lit the lamp and we all sat into cards. Jeremiah Donovan came in too, and sat down and watched us for a while, and it suddenly struck me that he had no great love for the two Englishmen. It came as a great surprise to me, because I hadn't noticed anything about him before.

Late in the evening a really terrible argument blew up between Hawkins and Noble, about capitalists and priests and love of your country.

'The capitalists,' says Hawkins with an angry gulp, 'pays the priests to tell you about the next world so as you won't notice what the bastards are up to in this.'

'Nonsense, man!' says Noble, losing his temper. 'Before ever a capitalist was thought of, people believed in the next world.'

Hawkins stood up as though he was preaching a sermon.

'Oh, they did, did they?' he says with a sneer. 'They believed all the things you believe, isn't that what you mean? And you believe that God created Adam, and Adam created Shem, and Shem created Jehoshophat. You believe all that silly old fairytale about Eve and Eden and the apple. Well, listen to me, chum. If you're entitled to hold a silly belief like that, I'm entitled to hold my silly belief—which is that the first thing your God created was a bleeding capitalist, with morality and Rolls-Royce complete. Am I right, chum?' he says to Belcher.

'You're right, chum,' says Belcher with his amused smile, and got up from the table to stretch his long legs into the fire and stroke his moustache. So, seeing that Jeremiah Donovan was going, and that there was no knowing when the argument about religion would be over, I went out with him. We strolled down to the village together, and then he stopped and started blushing and mumbling and saying I ought to be

176

behind, keeping guard on the prisoners. I didn't like
the tone he took with me, and anyway I was bored
with life in the cottage, so I replied by asking him
what the hell we wanted guarding them at all for. I
told him I'd talked it over with Noble, and that we'd
both rather be out with a fighting column.

'What use are those fellows to us?' says I.

He looked at me in surprise and said: 'I thought
you knew we were keeping them as hostages.'

'Hostages?' I said.

'The enemy have prisoners belonging to us,' he says,
'and now they're talking of shooting them. If they
shoot our prisoners, we'll shoot theirs.'

'Shoot them?' I said.

'What else did you think we were keeping them
for?' he says.

'Wasn't it very unforeseen of you not to warn Noble
and myself of that in the beginning?' I said.

'How was it?' says he. 'You might have known it.'

'We couldn't know it, Jeremiah Donovan,' says I.
'How could we when they were on our hands so long?'

'The enemy have our prisoners as long and longer,'
says he.

'That's not the same thing at all,' says I.

'What difference is there?' says he.

I couldn't tell him, because I knew he wouldn't
understand. If it was only an old dog that was going
to the vet's, you'd try and not get too fond of him, but
Jeremiah Donovan wasn't a man that would ever be
in danger of that.

'And when is this thing going to be decided?' says I.

'We might hear tonight,' he says. 'Or tomorrow or
the next day at latest. So if it's only hanging round
here that's a trouble to you, you'll be free soon
enough.'

It wasn't the hanging round that was a trouble to me at all by this time. I had worse things to worry about. When I got back to the cottage the argument was still on. Hawkins was holding forth in his best style, maintaining that there was no next world, and Noble was maintaining that there was; but I could see that Hawkins had had the best of it.

'Do you know what, chum?' he was saying with a saucy smile. 'I think you're just as big a bleeding unbeliever as I am. You say you believe in the next world, and you know just as much about the next world as I do, which is sweet damn-all. What's heaven? You don't know. Where's heaven? You don't know. You know sweet damn-all! I ask you again, do they wear wings?'

'Very well, then,' says Noble, 'they do. Is that enough for you? They do wear wings.'

'Where do they get them, then? Who makes them? Have they a factory for wings? Have they a sort of store where you hands in your chit and takes your bleeding wings?'

'You're an impossible man to argue with,' says Noble. 'Now, listen to me—' And they were off again.

It was long after midnight when we locked up and went to bed. As I blew out the candle I told Noble what Jeremiah Donovan was after telling me. Noble took it very quietly. When we'd been in bed about an hour he asked me did I think we ought to tell the Englishmen. I didn't think we should, because it was more than likely that the English wouldn't shoot our men, and even if they did, the brigade officers, who were always up and down with the Second Battalion and knew the Englishmen well, wouldn't be likely to want them plugged. 'I think so too,' says Noble. 'It would be great cruelty to put the wind up them now.

178

'It was very unforeseen of Jeremiah Donovan any-how,' says I.

It was next morning that we found it so hard to face Belcher and Hawkins. We went about the house all day scarcely saying a word. Belcher didn't seem to notice; he was stretched into the ashes as usual, with his usual look of waiting in quietness for something unforeseen to happen, but Hawkins noticed and put it down to Noble's being beaten in the argument of the night before.

'Why can't you take a discussion in the proper spirit?' he says severely. 'You and your Adam and Eve! I'm a Communist, that's what I am. Communist or anarchist, it all comes to much the same thing.' And for hours he went round the house, muttering when the fit took him. 'Adam and Eve! Adam and Eve! Nothing better to do with their time than picking bleeding apples!'

III

I don't know how we got through that day, but I was very glad when it was over, the tea things were cleared away, and Belcher said in his peaceable way: 'Well, chums, what about it?' We sat round the table and Hawkins took out the cards, and just then I heard Jeremiah Donovan's footstep on the path and a dark presentiment crossed my mind. I rose from the table and caught him before he reached the door.

'What do you want?' I asked.

'I want those two soldier friends of yours,' he says, getting red.

'Is that the way, Jeremiah Donovan?' I asked.

'That's the way. There were four of our lads shot this morning, one of them a boy of sixteen.'

'That's bad,' I said.

At that moment Noble followed me out, and the three of us walked down the path together, talking in whispers. Feeney, the local intelligence officer, was standing by the gate.

'What are you going to do about it?' I asked Jeremiah Donovan.

'I want you and Noble to get them out; tell them they're being shifted again; that'll be the quietest way.'

'Leave me out of that,' says Noble under his breath.

Jeremiah Donovan looks at him hard.

'All right,' he says. 'You and Feeney get a few tools from the shed and dig a hole by the far end of the bog. Bonaparte and myself will be after you. Don't let anyone see you with the tools. I wouldn't like it to go beyond ourselves.'

We saw Feeney and Noble go round to the shed and went in ourselves. I left Jeremiah Donovan to do the explanations. He told them that he had orders to send them back to the Second Battalion. Hawkins let out a mouthful of curses, and you could see that though Belcher didn't say anything, he was a bit upset too. The old woman was for having them stay in spite of us, and she didn't stop advising them until Jeremiah Donovan lost his temper and turned on her. He had a nasty temper, I noticed. It was pitch-dark in the cottage by this time, but no one thought of lighting the lamp, and in the darkness the two Englishmen fetched their top-coats and said good-bye to the old woman.

'Just as a man makes a home of a bleeding place, some bastard at headquarters thinks you're too cushy and shunts you off,' says Hawkins, shaking her hand.

'A thousand thanks, madam,' says Belcher. 'A thousand thanks for everything'—as though he'd made it up.

We went round to the back of the house and down towards the bog. It was only then that Jeremiah Donovan told them. He was shaking with excitement.

'There were four of our fellows shot in Cork this morning and now you're to be shot as a reprisal.'

'What are you talking about?' snaps Hawkins. 'It's bad enough being mucked about as we are without having to put up with your funny jokes.'

'It isn't a joke,' says Donovan, 'I'm sorry, Hawkins, but it's true,' and begins on the usual rigmarole about duty and how unpleasant it is.

I never noticed that people who talk a lot about duty find it much of a trouble to them.

'Oh, cut it out!' says Hawkins.

'Ask Bonaparte,' says Donovan, seeing that Hawkins isn't taking him seriously. 'Isn't it true, Bonaparte?'

'It is,' I say, and Hawkins stops.

'Ah, for Christ's sake, chum!'

'I mean it, chum,' I say.

'You don't sound as if you meant it.'

'If he doesn't mean it, I do,' says Donovan, working himself up.

'What have you against me, Jeremiah Donovan?'

'I never said I had anything against you. But why did your people take out four of our prisoners and shoot them in cold blood?'

He took Hawkins by the arm and dragged him on, but it was impossible to make him understand that we were in earnest. I had the Smith and Wesson in my pocket and I kept fingering it and wondering what I'd do if they put up a fight for it or ran, and wishing to God they'd do one or the other. I knew if they did run for it, that I'd never fire on them. Hawkins wanted to know was Noble in it, and when we said yes, he asked us why Noble wanted to plug him. Why did any of us want to plug him? What had he done to us? Weren't we all chums? Didn't we understand him and didn't he understand us? Did we imagine for an instant that he'd shoot us for all the so-and-so officers in the so-and-so British Army?

By this time we'd reached the bog, and I was so sick I couldn't even answer him. We walked along the edge of it in the darkness, and every now and then Hawkins would call a halt and begin all over again, as if he was wound up, about our being chums, and I knew that nothing but the sight of the grave would convince him that we had to do it. And all the time I was hoping that something would happen; that they'd run for it or that Noble would take over the responsibility from me. I had the feeling that it was worse on Noble than on me.

IV

At last we saw the lantern in the distance and made towards it. Noble was carrying it, and Feeney was standing somewhere in the darkness behind him, and the picture of them so still and silent in the bogland brought it home to me that we were in earnest, and banished the last bit of hope I had.

Belcher, on recognizing Noble, said: 'Hallo, chum,' in his quiet way, but Hawkins flew at him at once, and the argument began all over again, only this time Noble had nothing to say for himself and stood with his head down, holding the lantern between his legs.

It was Jeremiah Donovan who did the answering.

For the twentieth time, as though it was haunting his mind, Hawkins asked if anybody thought he'd shoot Noble.

'Yes, you would,' says Jeremiah Donovan.

'No, I wouldn't, damn you!'

'You would, because you'd know you'd be shot for not doing it.'

'I wouldn't, not if I was to be shot twenty times over. I wouldn't shoot a pal. And Belcher wouldn't— isn't that right, Belcher?'

'That's right, chum,' Belcher said, but more by way of answering the question than of joining in the argument. Belcher sounded as though whatever unforeseen thing he'd always been waiting for had come at last.

'Anyway, who says Noble would be shot if I wasn't? What do you think I'd do if I was in his place, out in the middle of a blasted bog?'

'What would you do?' asks Donovan.

'I'd go with him wherever he was going, of course. Share my last bob with him and stick by him through thick and thin. No one can ever say of me that I let down a pal.'

'We had enough of this,' says Jeremiah Donovan, cocking his revolver. 'Is there any message you want to send?'

'No, there isn't.'

'Do you want to say your prayers?'

Hawkins came out with a cold-blooded remark that even shocked me and turned on Noble again.

'Listen to me, Noble,' he says. 'You and me are chums. You can't come over to my side, so I'll come over to your side. That show you I mean what I say? Give me a rifle and I'll go along with you and the other lads.'

Nobody answered him. We knew that was no way out.

'Hear what I'm saying?' he says. 'I'm through with it. I'm a deserter or anything else you like. I don't believe in your stuff, but it's no worse than mine. That satisfy you?'

Noble raised his head, but Donovan began to speak and he lowered it again without replying.

'For the last time, have you any messages to send?' says Donovan in a cold, excited sort of voice.

'Shut up, Donovan! You don't understand me, but these lads do. They're not the sort to make a pal and kill a pal. They're not the tools of any capitalist.'

I alone of the crowd saw Donovan raise his Webley to the back of Hawkins's neck, and as he did so I shut my eyes and tried to pray. Hawkins had begun to say something else when Donovan fired, and as I opened my eyes at the bang, I saw Hawkins stagger at the knees and lie out flat at Noble's feet, slowly and as quiet as a kid falling asleep, with the lantern-light on his lean legs and bright farmer's boots. We all stood very still, watching him settle out in the last agony.

Then Belcher took out a handkerchief and began to tie it about his own eyes (in our excitement we'd forgotten to do the same for Hawkins), and, seeing it wasn't big enough, turned and asked for the loan of mine. I gave it to him and he knotted the two together and pointed with his foot at Hawkins.

'He's not quite dead,' he says. 'Better give him another.'

Sure enough, Hawkins's left knee is beginning to rise. I bend down and put my gun to his head; then, recollecting myself, I get up again. Belcher understands what's in my mind.

'Give him his first,' he says. 'I don't mind. Poor

bastard, we don't know what's happening to him now.'

I knelt and fired. By this time I didn't seem to know what I was doing. Belcher, who was fumbling a bit awkwardly with the handkerchiefs, came out with a laugh as he heard the shot. It was the first time I heard him laugh and it sent a shudder down my back; it sounded so unnatural.

'Poor bugger!' he said quietly. 'And last night he was so curious about it all. It's very queer, chums, I always think. Now he knows as much about it as they'll ever let him know, and last night he was all in the dark.'

Donovan helped him to tie the handkerchiefs about his eyes. 'Thanks, chum,' he said. Donovan asked if there were any messages he wanted sent.

'No, chum,' he says. 'Not for me. If any of you would like to write to Hawkins's mother, you'll find a letter from her in his pocket. He and his mother were great chums. But my missus left me eight years ago. Went away with another fellow and took the kid with her. I like the feeling of a home, as you may have noticed, but I couldn't start again after that.'

It was an extraordinary thing, but in those few minutes Belcher said more than in all the weeks before. It was just as if the sound of the shot had started a flood of talk in him and he could go on the whole night like that, quite happily, talking about himself. We stood round like fools now that he couldn't see us any longer. Donovan looked at Noble, and Noble shook his head. Then Donovan raised his Webley, and at that moment Belcher gives his queer laugh again. He may have thought we were talking about him, or perhaps he noticed the same thing I'd noticed and couldn't understand it.

'Excuse me, chums,' he says. 'I feel I'm talking the hell of a lot, and so silly, about my being so handy about a house and things like that. But this thing came on me suddenly. You'll forgive me, I'm sure.'

'You don't want to say a prayer?' asks Donovan.

'No, chum,' he says. 'I don't think it would help. I'm ready, and you boys want to get it over.'

'You understand that we're only doing our duty?' says Donovan.

Belcher's head was raised like a blind man's, so that you could only see his chin and the tip of his nose in the lantern-light.

'I never could make out what duty was myself,' he said. 'I think you're all good lads, if that's what you mean. I'm not complaining.'

Noble, just as if he couldn't bear any more of it, raised his fist at Donovan, and in a flash Donovan raised his gun and fired. The big man went over like a sack of meal, and this time there was no need of a second shot.

I don't remember much about the burying, but that it was worse than all the rest because we had to carry them to the grave. It was all mad lonely with nothing but a patch of lantern-light between ourselves and the dark, and birds hooting and screeching all round, disturbed by the guns. Noble went through Hawkins's belongings to find the letter from his mother, and then joined his hands together. He did the same with Belcher. Then, when we'd filled in the grave, we separated from Jeremiah Donovan and Feeney and took our tools back to the shed. All the way we didn't speak a word. The kitchen was dark and cold as we'd left it, and the old woman was sitting over the hearth, saying her beads. We walked past her into the room, and Noble struck a match to light the lamp. She rose

186

quietly and came to the doorway with all her cantankerousness gone.

'What did ye do with them?' she asked in a whisper, and Noble started so that the match went out in his hand.

'What's that?' he asked without turning round.

'I heard ye,' she said.

'What did you hear?' asked Noble.

'I heard ye. Do ye think I didn't hear ye, putting the spade back in the houseen?'

Noble struck another match and this time the lamp lit for him.

'Was that what ye did to them?' she asked.

Then, by God, in the very doorway, she fell on her knees and began praying, and after looking at her for a minute or two Noble did the same by the fireplace. I pushed my way out past her and left them at it. I stood at the door, watching the stars and listening to the shrieking of the birds dying out over the bogs. It is so strange what you feel at times like that that you can't describe it. Noble says he saw everything ten times the size, as though there were nothing in the whole world but that little patch of bog with the two Englishmen stiffening into it, but with me it was as if the patch of bog where the Englishmen were was a million miles away, and even Noble and the old woman, mumbling behind me, and the birds and the bloody stars were all far away, and I was somehow very small and very lost and lonely like a child astray in the snow. And anything that happened me afterwards, I never felt the same about again.

My Œdipus Complex

FRANK O'CONNOR

(1903–1966)

FATHER was in the army all through the war—the first war, I mean—so, up to the age of five, I never saw much of him, and what I saw did not worry me. Sometimes I woke and there was a big figure in khaki peering down at me in the candlelight. Sometimes in the early morning I heard the slamming of the front door and the clatter of nailed boots down the cobbles of the lane. These were Father's entrances and exits. Like Santa Claus he came and went mysteriously.

In fact, I rather liked his visits, though it was an uncomfortable squeeze between Mother and him when I got into the big bed in the early morning. He smoked, which gave him a pleasant musty smell, and shaved, an operation of astounding interest. Each time he left a trail of souvenirs—model tanks and Gurkha knives with handles made of bullet cases, and German helmets and cap badges and button-sticks, and all sorts of military equipment—carefully stowed away in a long box on top of the wardrobe, in case they ever came in handy. There was a bit of the magpie about Father; he expected everything to come in handy. When his back was turned, Mother let me get a chair and rummage through his treasures. She didn't seem to think so highly of them as he did.

The war was the most peaceful period of my life. The window of my attic faced south-east. My mother had curtained it, but that had small effect. I always woke with the first light and, with all the responsibilities of the previous day melted, feeling myself rather like the sun, ready to illumine and rejoice. Life never

seemed so simple and clear and full of possibilities as
then. I put my feet out from under the clothes—I
called them Mrs. Left and Mrs. Right—and invented
dramatic situations for them in which they discussed
the problems of the day. At least Mrs. Right did; she
was very demonstrative, but I hadn't the same control
of Mrs. Left, so she mostly contented herself with
nodding agreement.

They discussed what Mother and I should do during
the day, what Santa Claus should give a fellow for
Christmas, and what steps should be taken to brighten
the home. There was that little matter of the baby, for
instance. Mother and I could never agree about that.
Ours was the only house in the terrace without a new
baby, and Mother said we couldn't afford one till
Father came back from the war because they cost
seventeen and six. That showed how simple she was.
The Geneys up the road had a baby, and everyone
knew they couldn't afford seventeen and six. It was
probably a cheap baby, and Mother wanted something really good, but I felt she was too exclusive. The
Geneys baby would have done us fine.

Having settled my plans for the day, I got up, put a
chair under the attic window, and lifted the frame
high enough to stick out my head. The window over-
looked the front gardens of the terrace behind ours,
and beyond these it looked over a deep valley to the
tall, red-brick houses terraced up the opposite hill-
side, which were all still in shadow, while those at our
side of the valley were all lit up, though with long
strange shadows that made them seem unfamiliar;
rigid and painted.

After that I went into Mother's room and climbed
into the big bed. She woke and I began to tell her of
my schemes. By this time, though I never seem to have

noticed it, I was petrified in my nightshirt, and I thawed as I talked until, the last frost melted, I fell asleep beside her and woke again only when I heard her below in the kitchen, making the breakfast.

After breakfast we went into town; heard Mass at St. Augustine's and said a prayer for Father, and did the shopping. If the afternoon was fine we either went for a walk in the country or a visit to Mother's great friend in the convent, Mother St. Dominic. Mother had them all praying for Father, and every night, going to bed, I asked God to send him back safe from the war to us. Little, indeed, did I know what I was praying for!

One morning, I got into the big bed, and there, sure enough, was Father in his usual Santa Claus manner, but later, instead of uniform, he put on his best blue suit, and Mother was as pleased as anything. I saw nothing to be pleased about, because, out of uniform, Father was altogether less interesting, but she only beamed, and explained that our prayers had been answered, and off we went to Mass to thank God for having brought Father safely home.

The irony of it! That very day when he came in to dinner he took off his boots and put on his slippers, donned the dirty old cap he wore about the house to save him from colds, crossed his legs, and began to talk gravely to Mother, who looked anxious. Naturally, I disliked her looking anxious, because it destroyed her good looks, so I interrupted him.

'Just a moment, Larry!' she said gently.

This was only what she said when we had boring visitors, so I attached no importance to it and went on talking.

'Do be quiet, Larry!' she said impatiently. 'Don't you hear me talking to Daddy?'

This was the first time I had heard those ominous words, 'talking to Daddy', and I couldn't help feeling that if this was how God answered prayers, He couldn't listen to them very attentively.

'Why are you talking to Daddy?' I asked with as great a show of indifference as I could muster.

'Because Daddy and I have business to discuss. Now, don't interrupt again!'

In the afternoon, at Mother's request, Father took me for a walk. This time we went into town instead of out the country, and I thought at first, in my usual optimistic way, that it might be an improvement. It was nothing of the sort. Father and I had quite different notions of a walk in town. He had no proper interest in trams, ships, and horses, and the only thing that seemed to divert him was talking to fellows as old as himself. When I wanted to stop he simply went on, dragging me behind him by the hand; when he wanted to stop I had no alternative but to do the same. I noticed that it seemed to be a sign that he wanted to stop for a long time whenever he leaned against a wall. The second time I saw him do it I got wild. He seemed to be settling himself forever. I pulled him by the coat and trousers, but, unlike Mother who, if you were too persistent, got into a wax and said: 'Larry, if you don't behave yourself, I'll give you a good slap,' Father had an extraordinary capacity for amiable in-attention. I sized him up and wondered would I cry, but he seemed to be too remote to be annoyed even by that. Really, it was like going for a walk with a mountain! He either ignored the wrenching and pummelling entirely, or else glanced down with a grin of amusement from his peak. I had never met anyone so absorbed in himself as he seemed.

At teatime, 'talking to Daddy' began again, com-

plicated this time by the fact that he had an evening
paper, and every few minutes he put it down and told
Mother something new out of it. I felt this was foul
play. Man for man, I was prepared to compete with
him any time for Mother's attention, but when he had
it all made up for him by other people it left me no
chance. Several times I tried to change the subject
without success.

'You must be quiet while Daddy is reading, Larry,'
Mother said impatiently.

It was clear that she either genuinely liked talking
to Father better than talking to me, or else that he had
some terrible hold on her which made her afraid to
admit the truth.

'Mummy,' I said that night when she was tucking
me up, 'do you think if I prayed hard God would send
Daddy back to the war?'

She seemed to think about that for a moment.

'No, dear,' she said with a smile. 'I don't think He
would.'

'Why wouldn't he, Mummy?'

'Because there isn't a war any longer, dear.'

'But, Mummy, couldn't God make another war, if
He liked?'

'He wouldn't like to, dear. It's not God who makes
wars, but bad people.'

'Oh!' I said.

I was disappointed about that. I began to think that
God wasn't quite what He was cracked up to be.

Next morning I woke at my usual hour, feeling like
a bottle of champagne. I put out my feet and invented
a long conversation in which Mrs. Right talked of the
trouble she had with her own father till she put him
in the Home. I didn't quite know what the Home was
but it sounded the right place for Father. Then I got

my chair and stuck my head out of the attic window. Dawn was just breaking, with a guilty air that made me feel I had caught it in the act. My head bursting with stories and schemes, I stumbled in next door, and in the half-darkness scrambled into the big bed. There was no room at Mother's side so I had to get between her and Father. For the time being I had forgotten about him, and for several minutes I sat bolt upright, racking my brains to know what I could do with him. He was taking up more than his fair share of the bed, and I couldn't get comfortable, so I gave him several kicks that made him grunt and stretch. He made room all right, though. Mother waked and felt for me. I settled back comfortably in the warmth of the bed with my thumb in my mouth.

'Mummy!' I hummed, loudly and contentedly.

'Sssh! dear,' she whispered. 'Don't wake Daddy!'

This was a new development, which threatened to be even more serious than 'talking to Daddy'. Life without my early-morning conferences was unthinkable.

'Why?' I asked severely.

'Because poor Daddy is tired.'

This seemed to me a quite inadequate reason, and I was sickened by the sentimentality of her 'poor Daddy'. I never liked that sort of gush; it always struck me as insincere.

'Oh!' I said lightly. Then in my most winning tone: 'Do you know where I want to go with you today, Mummy?'

'No, dear,' she sighed.

'I want to go down the Glen and fish for thornybacks with my new net, and then I want to go out to the Fox and Hounds, and—'

'Don't-wake-Daddy!' she hissed angrily, clapping her hand across my mouth.

But it was too late. He was awake, or nearly so. He grunted and reached for the matches. Then he stared incredulously at his watch.

'Like a cup of tea, dear?' asked Mother in a meek, hushed voice I had never heard her use before. It sounded almost as though she were afraid.

'Tea?' he exclaimed indignantly. 'Do you know what the time is?'

'And after that I want to go up the Rathcooney Road,' I said loudly, afraid I'd forget something in all those interruptions.

'Go to sleep at once, Larry!' she said sharply.

I began to snivel. I couldn't concentrate, the way that pair went on, and smothering my early-morning schemes was like burying a family from the cradle.

Father said nothing, but lit his pipe and sucked it, looking out into the shadows without minding Mother or me. I knew he was mad. Every time I made a remark Mother hushed me irritably. I was mortified. I felt it wasn't fair; there was even something sinister in it. Every time I had pointed out to her the waste of making two beds when we could both sleep in one, she had told me it was healthier like that, and now here was this man, this stranger, sleeping with her without the least regard for her health!

He got up early and made tea, but though he brought Mother a cup he brought none for me.

'Mummy,' I shouted, 'I want a cup of tea, too.'

'Yes, dear,' she said patiently. 'You can drink from Mummy's saucer.'

That settled it. Either Father or I would have to leave the house. I didn't want to drink from Mother's saucer; I wanted to be treated as an equal in my own home, so, just to spite her, I drank it all and left none for her. She took that quietly, too.

But that night when she was putting me to bed she said gently:

'Larry, I want you to promise me something.'

'What is it?' I asked.

'Not to come in and disturb poor Daddy in the morning. Promise?'

'Poor Daddy' again! I was becoming suspicious of everything involving that quite impossible man.

'Why?' I asked.

'Because poor Daddy is worried and tired and he doesn't sleep well.'

'Why doesn't he, Mummy?'

'Well, you know, don't you, that while he was at the war Mummy got the pennies from the Post Office?'

'From Miss MacCarthy?'

'That's right. But now, you see, Miss MacCarthy hasn't any more pennies, so Daddy must go out and find us some. You know what would happen if he couldn't?'

'No,' I said, 'tell us.'

'Well, I think we might have to go out and beg for them like the poor old woman on Fridays. We wouldn't like that, would we?'

'No,' I agreed. 'We wouldn't.'

'So you'll promise not to come in and wake him?'

'Promise.'

Mind you, I meant that. I knew pennies were a serious matter, and I was all against having to go out and beg like the old woman on Fridays. Mother laid out all my toys in a complete ring round the bed so that, whatever way I got out, I was bound to fall over one of them.

When I woke I remembered my promise all right. I got up and sat on the floor and played—for hours, it seemed to me. Then I got my chair and looked out the attic window for more hours. I wished it was time for Father to wake; I wished someone would make me a cup of tea. I didn't feel in the least like the sun; instead, I was bored and so very, very cold! I simply longed for the warmth and depth of the big feather-bed.

At last I could stand it no longer. I went into the next room. As there was still no room at Mother's side I climbed over her and she woke with a start.

'Larry,' she whispered, gripping my arm very tightly, 'what did you promise?'

'But I did, Mummy,' I wailed, caught in the very act. 'I was quiet for ever so long.'

'Oh, dear, and you're perished!' she said sadly, feeling me all over. 'Now, if I let you stay will you promise not to talk?'

'But I want to talk, Mummy,' I wailed.

'That has nothing to do with it,' she said with a firmness that was new to me. 'Daddy wants to sleep. Now, do you understand that?'

I understood it only too well. I wanted to talk, he wanted to sleep—whose house was it, anyway?

'Mummy,' I said with equal firmness, 'I think it would be healthier for Daddy to sleep in his own bed.'

That seemed to stagger her, because she said nothing for a while.

'Now, once for all,' she went on, 'you're to be perfectly quiet or go back to your own bed. Which is it to be?'

The injustice of it got me down. I had convicted her out of her own mouth of inconsistency and unreasonableness, and she hadn't even attempted to reply. Full of spite, I gave Father a kick, which she didn't notice but which made him grunt and open his eyes in alarm.

'What time is it?' he asked in a panic-stricken voice, not looking at Mother but at the door, as if he saw someone there.

'It's early yet,' she replied soothingly. 'It's only the child. Go to sleep again. . . . Now, Larry,' she added, getting out of bed, 'you've wakened Daddy and you must go back.'

This time, for all her quiet air, I knew she meant it, and knew that my principal rights and privileges were as good as lost unless I asserted them at once. As she lifted me, I gave a screech, enough to wake the dead, not to mind Father. He groaned.

'That damn child! Doesn't he ever sleep?'

'It's only a habit, dear,' she said quietly, though I could see she was vexed.

'Well, it's time he got out of it,' shouted Father, beginning to heave in the bed. He suddenly gathered all the bedclothes about him, turned to the wall, and then looked back over his shoulder with nothing showing only two small, spiteful, dark eyes. The man looked very wicked.

To open the bedroom door, Mother had to let me down, and I broke free and dashed for the farthest corner, screeching. Father sat bolt upright in bed.

'Shut up, you little puppy!' he said in a choking voice.

I was so astonished that I stopped screeching. Never, never had anyone spoken to me in that tone before. I looked at him incredulously and saw his face convulsed with rage. It was only then that I fully realized how God had codded me, listening to my prayers for the safe return of this monster.

'Shut up, you!' I bawled, beside myself.

'What's that you said?' shouted Father, making a wild leap out of the bed.

197

'Mick, Mick!' cried Mother. 'Don't you see the child isn't used to you?'

'I see he's better fed than taught,' snarled Father, waving his arms wildly. 'He wants his bottom smacked.'

All his previous shouting was as nothing to these obscene words referring to my person. They really made my blood boil.

'Smack your own!' I screamed hysterically. 'Smack your own! Shut up! Shut up!'

At this he lost his patience and let fly at me. He did it with the lack of conviction you'd expect of a man under Mother's horrified eyes, and it ended up as a mere tap, but the sheer indignity of being struck at all by a stranger, a total stranger who had cajoled his way back from the war into our big bed as a result of my innocent intercession, made me completely dotty. I shrieked and shrieked, and danced in my bare feet, and Father, looking awkward and hairy in nothing but a short grey army shirt, glared down at me like a mountain out for murder. I think it must have been then that I realized he was jealous too. And there stood Mother in her nightdress, looking as if her heart was broken between us. I hoped she felt as she looked. It seemed to me that she deserved it all.

From that morning out my life was a hell. Father and I were enemies, open and avowed. We conducted a series of skirmishes against one another, he trying to steal my time with Mother and I his. When she was sitting on my bed, telling me a story, he took to looking for some pair of old boots which he alleged he had left behind him at the beginning of the war. While he talked to Mother I played loudly with my toys to show my total lack of concern. He created a terrible scene one evening when he came in from work and found me at his box, playing with his regimental badges, Gurkha knives, and button-sticks. Mother got up and took the box from me.

'You mustn't play with Daddy's toys unless he lets you, Larry,' she said severely. 'Daddy doesn't play with yours.'

For some reason Father looked at her as if she had struck him and then turned away with a scowl.

'Those are not toys,' he growled, taking down the box again to see had I lifted anything. 'Some of those curios are very rare and valuable.'

But as time went on I saw more and more how he managed to alienate Mother and me. What made it worse was that I couldn't grasp his method or see what attraction he had for Mother. In every possible way he was less winning than I. He had a common accent and made noises at his tea. I thought for a while that it might be the newspapers she was interested in, so I made up bits of news of my own to read to her. Then I thought it might be the smoking, which I personally thought attractive, and took his pipes and went round the house dribbling into them till he caught me. I even made noises at my tea, but Mother only told me I was disgusting. It all seemed to hinge round that unhealthy habit of sleeping together, so I made a point of dropping into their bedroom and nosing round, talking to myself, so that they wouldn't know I was watching them, but they were never up to anything that I could see. In the end it beat me. It seemed to depend on being grown-up and giving people rings, and I realized I'd have to wait.

But at the same time I wanted him to see that I was only waiting, not giving up the fight. One evening when he was being particularly obnoxious, chattering away well above my head, I let him have it.

'Mummy,' I said, 'do you know what I'm going to do when I grow up?'

'No, dear,' she replied. 'What?'

'I'm going to marry you,' I said quietly.

Father gave a great guffaw out of him, but he didn't take me in. I knew it must only be pretence. And Mother, in spite of everything, was pleased. I felt she was probably relieved to know that one day Father's hold on her would be broken.

'Won't that be nice?' she said with a smile.

'It'll be very nice,' I said confidently. 'Because we're going to have lots and lots of babies.'

'That's right, dear,' she said placidly. 'I think we'll have one soon, and then you'll have plenty of company.'

I was no end pleased about that because it showed that in spite of the way she gave in to Father she still considered my wishes. Besides, it would put the Geneys in their place.

It didn't turn out like that, though. To begin with, she was very preoccupied—I supposed about where she would get the seventeen and six—and though Father took to staying out late in the evenings it did me no particular good. She stopped taking me for walks, became as touchy as blazes, and smacked me for nothing at all. Sometimes I wished I'd never mentioned the confounded baby—I seemed to have a genius for bringing calamity on myself.

And calamity it was! Sonny arrived in the most appalling hullabaloo—even that much he couldn't do without a fuss—and from the first moment I disliked him. He was a difficult child—so far as I was concerned he was always difficult—and demanded far too much attention. Mother was simply silly about him, and couldn't see when he was only showing off.

As company he was worse than useless. He slept all day, and I had to go round the house on tiptoe to avoid waking him. It wasn't any longer a question of not waking Father. The slogan now was 'Don't-wake-Sonny!' I couldn't understand why the child wouldn't sleep at the proper time, so whenever Mother's back was turned I woke him. Sometimes to keep him awake I pinched him as well. Mother caught me at it one day and gave me a most unmerciful flaking.

One evening, when Father was coming in from work, I was playing trains in the front garden. I let on not to notice him; instead, I pretended to be talking to myself, and said in a loud voice: 'If another bloody baby comes into this house, I'm going out.'

Father stopped dead and looked at me over his shoulder.

'What's that you said?' he asked sternly.

'I was only talking to myself,' I replied, trying to conceal my panic. 'It's private.'

He turned and went in without a word. Mind you, I intended it as a solemn warning, but its effect was quite different. Father started being quite nice to me. I could understand that, of course. Mother was quite sickening about Sonny. Even at meal-times she'd get up and gawk at him in the cradle with an idiotic smile, and tell Father to do the same. He was always polite about it, but he looked so puzzled you could see he didn't know what she was talking about. He complained of the way Sonny cried at night, but she only got cross and said that Sonny never cried except when there was something up with him—which was a flaming lie, because Sonny never had anything up with him, and only cried for attention. It was really painful to see how simple-minded she was. Father wasn't attractive, but he had a fine intelligence. He

201

saw through Sonny, and now he knew that I saw through him as well.

One night I woke with a start. There was someone beside me in the bed. For one wild moment I felt sure it must be Mother, having come to her senses and left Father for good, but then I heard Sonny in convulsions in the next room, and Mother saying: 'There! There! There!' and I knew it wasn't she. It was Father. He was lying beside me, wide awake, breathing hard and apparently as mad as hell.

After a while it came to me what he was mad about. It was his turn now. After turning me out of the big bed, he had been turned out himself. Mother had no consideration now for anyone but that poisonous pup, Sonny. I couldn't help feeling sorry for Father. I had been through it all myself, and even at that age I was magnanimous. I began to stroke him down and say: 'There! There!' He wasn't exactly responsive.

'Aren't you asleep either?' he snarled.

'Ah, come on and put your arm around us, can't you?' I said, and he did, in a sort of way. Gingerly, I suppose, is how you'd describe it. He was very bony but better than nothing.

At Christmas he went out of his way to buy me a really nice model railway.

The Jury Case

ERIC CROSS

(b. 1905)

'WAS I ever telling you about the jury case we had up at the hotel? It wasn't really a trial, but a coroner's inquest, but they had a system very much like a trial in a court-house. There was a jury, and they had to listen to the evidence, and find out what had happened to the man and give their opinion.

'It all happened over a man who was found dead on the island. He had fallen over a bank, and a slab had fallen on top of him and broke his neck.

'Well, the following morning the coroner and the sergeant came along collecting a jury. There were twelve of us. There was the Sheep and Cork Echo and Dan Bedam and the Rocky Mountaineer and several others. Some of them are dead now—may the Lord have mercy on them.

'There was a priest once preached a sermon on the twelve apostles, and it was failing him to describe what type of men they were at all. He wanted to tell the people that they were just ordinary folk: that there was nothing grand or smart about them. So after he had thought for a while he said, "They were twelve working men. Farmers and fishermen and such class of people. They were twelve ignorant men—as ignorant as any twelve men you would find in this parish, and, God knows, that wouldn't be difficult."

'Well, the twelve apostles were like the jury we had that day—as ignorant as any twelve men you would find in this parish. The divil a bit but we all assembled, and we struck away to the hotel. They hadn't an idee what was going to happen to them. Some of them thought that they were going to be tried for killing the man. Others thought that they were going to his wake. And more of them thought that they were going to "shoulder" him to his grave. You see it was the first time that there had been a jury case in the district for many a long year, and it was all a mystery to them, for none of them, except myself, had ever travelled.

'Good enough! We got to the hotel, and the body

was lying in a room, and we all had a look at it. The poor fellow was dead enough. There was no doubt about that—God rest his soul. The coroner asked if we recognized the man, and we did, for he was well known to most of us.

'After we had all had our fill of the sight, we had a couple more drinks, and then we went into the room where the case was to be tried. There were chairs for each of us, and the sergeant and the coroner were there.

'The sergeant told the others that they would have to take the oath and swear on the book. Then Cork Echo spoke up. He hadn't said a word till this. He said that he would not swear, because swearing was a sin, and he started quoting bits out of the catechism. He wasn't going to swear with his eyes open. It would be altogether different if he did it unknownst to himself, but he had not enough drink taken yet.

'The sergeant started quoting bits from a book he had in his pocket, and then the coroner joined in, but they were only making a poor hand of the business. I explained it to him and all about the business, and that battle was done with.

'To save time we held the book in threes, and took the oath together. When it came to Dan Bedam he said that he wanted to swear alone, and he would not put his hand on the book with anyone else. So he swore alone. He held the book as though it was going to bite him, and when he had his swearing done he looked behind him as though he expected the devil was waiting there waiting to take him.

'The sergeant and the coroner got their notebooks ready, and we were all set for the business. Just as we were going to start, the Sheep got up and started to go out. The Coroner wanted to know where the hell he thought he was going, and the Sheep explained that he was "going behind", for he had drink taken and his bladder was weak.

'So we waited for the Sheep to return, and when he'd returned and sat down and lighted his pipe we started again.

'The sergeant read his statement, and we listened. Then the man who had found the body told how he had come to find it, and the coroner asked if we accepted that.

'The year before the man who had found the body had sold the Rocky Mountaineer a mare, and the mare was faulty. The Rocky Mountaineer did not find this out until after the deal was made, and he could do nothing but wait till he got the chance of his man again, and this was his chance.

'I declare to God, didn't he say that the man was a liar, and that there was no one there at the time but him, and he might have pushed the man over the wall. Well, they had a few words, and the sergeant called the meeting to order, and the coroner was not able to make out what had happened till the sergeant explained the affair to him, and then the coroner understood and the business proceeded.

'The coroner explained what had happened, and what sort of a verdict we could bring in—either death by misadventure or *felo de se*, or murder by person unknown, and he explained his own opinion.

'The Rocky Mountaineer jumped up, and said it was plain murder, and he did not care a damn what anyone else said, for he had had dealings with the man who found the body, and he had swindled him over the sale of a horse, and if he would do that, murder was nothing to him. So we had that all over again.

'It was a very warm day and the room was small, and what with the smoke and the arguments we decided that a drink or two would not do anyone any harm. So we retired for a drink or two, and when we came back we took up the business where we had left off. The coroner counted and found one missing. "Sky high", who was one of the jury, had not come back. The sergeant went off to find him, and found him on his way home and brought him back. He said that it wasn't in his line at all. That he did not understand it, and he had a cow at home that was due to calve, and he would be better there. But the coroner made him stay.

'The coroner talked to them about *felo de se*, and he explained all about it to us. When he had finished, Dan Bedam got up and said that he could not understand it at all. How could the fellow fall into the sea, he asked, when the sea was fifteen miles away as the crow flies?

'"Bedam, I couldn't agree to that at all. Bedam, it could be 'fell into the lake', but, bedam, it could never be 'fell into the sea'."

'The coroner explained again, but Dan Bedam could not understand him still.

'"Bedam, if the fellow fell into the sea he would be wet, wouldn't he? Bedam, but his clothes were quite dry. Bedam, it couldn't be that at all, but some other thing."

'The coroner explained suicide, too, but Dan Bedam had not heard of that either. He wanted to know if it was Irish. In the middle of this argument there was a knock at the door, and in walked "Ball o' Wax's" wife with his dinner.

'She's the divil of a great pounder of a woman, who would make a grand door for a car-house. "Ball o'

Wax" is only a small class of a man, but he had a fierce appetite, and his wife was afraid that he would die if he did not have his dinner. He was a great friend of Dan's, and the two of them started on the dinner and forgot all about the inquest. Not that it mattered much, for the two of them were ever better at eating than they were at thinking, and the wife had brought up a grand "potash" of pig's head and cabbage and potatoes.

'At last the business was coming to a head, and the coroner asked us to consider our verdict. Then the fun started. One said one thing and one another. The effects of the drink had worn off the Rocky Mountaineer, and he was all for murder again. The Sheep said that he did not understand it at all, and he would not care to give his opinion. That was with the height of meanness. He would not even give his opinion unless he was paid for it.

'Cork Echo thought that the business was all wrong, and that no good would ever come of it, and the less we had to do with it the better. He had not got over the swearing part of it yet. I tried to knock sense into their heads, but it was failing me.

'Now that Dan Bedam had a bellyful of food he had an idee.

'"Bedam!" said he, "doesn't the man say that it was death by misadventure? Bedam! isn't he from the Government? Bedam! it would not be right to agree with him so. We must say something else, bedam!"

'There were others of them with queer notions, and there were some of them so scared stiff that they were just sitting like dummies and saying nothing at all. Twelve good men and true! Am Bostha! you'd search the earth before you would find an equal pack of mugwumps of bladdergashes!

'I went to the coroner, who was a decent, sensible type of a man, and explained the position to him. We sent the rest of them into the bar for a drink, and I and the coroner settled the business, and we brought in a verdict of death by misadventure, and I added a vote of sympathy with the poor fellow's relations in their trouble, and we left the jury to drink itself stupid. But they could never do that if they were drinking to this day, for they were stupid before they started.

'Twelve men, as ignorant as any twelve men you would find in this parish, and God knows that would be easy enough—with their weak bladders, and their sins, and their cows calving, and their pig's head and cabbage, and their "fell in the sea"!'

The Poteen Maker

MICHAEL MCLAVERTY
(b. 1907)

WHEN he taught me some years ago he was an old man near his retirement, and when he would pass through the streets of the little town on his way from school you would hear the women talking about him as they stood at their doors knitting or nursing their babies: 'Poor man, he's done. . . . Killing himself. . . . Digging his own grave!' With my bag of books under my arm I could hear them, but I could never understand why they said he was digging his own grave, and when I would ask my mother she would scold me: 'Take your dinner, like a good boy, and don't be listening to the hard back-biters of this town. Your father has always a good word for Master Craig—so that should be enough for you!'

'But why do they say he's killing himself?'

'Why do who say? Didn't I tell you to take your dinner and not be repeating what the idle gossips of this town are saying? Listen to me, son! Master Craig is a decent, good-living man—a kindly man that would go out of his way to do you a good turn. If Master Craig was in any other town he'd have got a place in the new school at the Square instead of being stuck for ever in that wee poky bit of a school at the edge of the town!'

It was true that the school was small—a two-roomed ramshackle of a place that lay at the edge of the town beyond the last street lamp. We all loved it. Around it grew a few trees, their trunks hacked with boys' names and pierced with nibs and rusty drawing-pins. In summer when the windows were open we could hear the leaves rubbing together and in winter see the raindrops hanging on the bare twigs.

It was a draughty place and the master was always complaining of the cold, and even in the early autumn he would wear his overcoat in the classroom and rub his hands together: 'Boys, it's very cold today. Do you feel it cold?' And to please him we would answer: 'Yes, sir, 'tis very cold.' He would continue to rub his hands and he would look out at the old trees casting their leaves or at the broken spout that flung its tail of rain against the window. He always kept his hands clean and three times a day he would wash them in a basin and wipe them on a roller towel affixed to the inside of his press. He had a hanger for his coat and a brush to brush away the chalk that accumulated on the collar in the course of the day.

In the wet, windy month of November three buckets were placed on the top of the desks to catch the drips that plopped here and there from the ceiling, and those drops made different music according to the direction of the wind. When the buckets were filled the master always called me to empty them, and I would take them one at a time and swirl them into the drain at the street and stand for a minute gazing down at the wet roofs of the town or listen to the rain pecking at the lunch-papers scattered about on the cinders.

'What's it like outside?' he always asked when I came in with the empty buckets.

'Sir, 'tis very bad.'

He would write sums on the board and tell me to keep an eye on the class, and out to the porch he would go and stand in grim silence watching the rain nibbling at the puddles. Sometimes he would come in and I would see him sneak his hat from the press and disappear for five or ten minutes. We would fight then with rulers or paper-darts till our noise would disturb the mistress next door and in she would come and stand with her lips compressed, her finger in her book. There was silence as she upbraided us: 'Mean, low, good-for-nothing corner boys. Wait'll Mister Craig comes back and I'll let him know the angels he has. And I'll give him special news about *you*!'—and she shakes her book at me: 'An altar boy on Sunday and a corner boy for the rest of the week!' We would let her barge away, the buckets plink-plonking as they filled up with rain and her own class beginning to hum, now that she was away from them.

When Mr. Craig came back he would look at us and ask if we disturbed Miss Lagan. Our silence or our tossed hair always gave him the answer. He would correct the sums on the board, flivell the pages of a book with his thumb, and listen to us reading; and occasionally he would glance out of the side-window

210

at the river that flowed through the town and, above it, the bedraggled row of houses whose tumbling yard-walls sheered to the water's edge. 'The loveliest county in Ireland is County Down!' he used to say, with a sweep of his arm to the river and the tin cans and the chalked walls of the houses.

During that December he was ill for two weeks and when he came back amongst us he was greatly failed. To keep out the draughts he nailed perforated ply-wood over the ventilators and stuffed blotting paper between the wide crevices at the jambs of the door. There were muddy marks of a ball on one of the windows and on one pane a long crack with fangs at the end of it: 'So someone has drawn the River Ganges while I was away,' he said; and whenever he came to the geography of India he would refer to the Ganges delta by pointing to the cracks on the pane.

When our ration of coal for the fire was used up he would send me into the town with a bucket, a coat over my head to keep off the rain, and the money in my fist to buy a stone of coal. He always gave me a penny to buy sweets for myself, and I can always remember that he kept his money in a waistcoat pocket. Back again I would come with the coal and he would give me disused exercise books to light the fire. 'Chief stoker!' he called me, and the name has stuck to me to this day.

It was at this time that the first snow had fallen, and someone by using empty potato bags had climbed over the glass-topped wall and stolen the school coal, and for some reason Mr. Craig did not send me with the bucket to buy more. The floor was continually wet from our boots, and our breaths frosted the windows. Whenever the door opened a cold draught would rush in and gulp down the breath-warmed air in the room.

We would jig our feet and sit on our hands to warm them. Every half-hour Mr. Craig would make us stand and while he lilted *O'Donnell Abu* we did a series of physical exercises which he had taught us, and in the excitement and the exaltation we forgot about our sponging boots and the snow that pelted against the windows. It was then that he did his lessons on Science; and we were delighted to see the bunsen burner attached to the gas bracket which hung like an inverted T from the middle of the ceiling. The snoring bunsen seemed to heat up the room and we all gathered round it, pressing in on top of it till he scattered us back to our places with the cane: 'Sit down!' he would shout. 'There's no call to stand. Everybody will be able to see!'

The cold spell remained, and over and over again he repeated one lesson in Science, which he called: *Evaporation and Condensation.*

'I'll show you how to purify the dirtiest of water,' he had told us. 'Even the filthiest water from the old river could be made fit for drinking purposes.' In a glass trough he had a dark brown liquid and when I got his back turned I dipped my finger in it and it tasted like treacle or burnt candy, and then I remembered about packets of brown sugar and tins of treacle I had seen in his press.

He placed some of the brown liquid in a glass retort and held it aloft to the class: 'In the retort I have water which I have discoloured and made impure. In a few minutes I'll produce from it the clearest of spring water.' And his weary eyes twinkled, and although we could see nothing funny in that, we smiled because he smiled.

The glass retort was set up with the flaming bunsen underneath, and as the liquid was boiling, the steam was trapped in a long-necked flask on which I sponged cold water. With our eyes we followed the bubbling mixture and the steam turning into drops and dripping rapidly into the flask. The air was filled with a biscuity smell, and the only sound was the snore of the bunsen. Outside was the cold air and the falling snow. Presently the master turned out the gas and held up the flask containing the clear water.

'As pure as crystal!' he said, and we watched him pour some of it into a tumbler, hold it in his delicate fingers, and put it to his lips. With wonder we watched him drink it and then our eyes travelled to the dirty, cakey scum that had congealed on the glass sides of the retort. He pointed at this with his ruler: 'The impurities are sifted out and the purest of pure water remains.' And for some reason he gave his roguish smile. He filled up the retort again with the dirty brown liquid and repeated the experiment until he had a large bottle filled with the purest of pure water.

The following day it was still snowing and very cold. The master filled up the retort with the clear liquid which he had stored in the bottle: 'I'll boil this again to show you that there are no impurities left.' So once again we watched the water bubbling, turning to steam, and then to shining drops. Mr. Craig filled up his tumbler: 'As pure as crystal,' he said, and then the door opened and in walked the Inspector. He was muffled to the ears and snow covered his hat and his attaché case. We all stared at him—he was the old, kind man whom we had seen before. He glanced at the bare firegrate and at the closed windows with their sashes edged with snow. The water continued to bubble in the retort, giving out its pleasant smell.

The Inspector shook hands with Mr. Craig and they talked and smiled together, the Inspector now and again looking towards the empty grate and shaking his head. He unrolled his scarf and flicked the snow from off his shoulders and from his attaché case. He sniffed the air, rubbed his frozen hands together, and took a black notebook from his case. The snow ploofed against the windows and the wind hummed under the door.

'Now, boys,' Mr. Craig continued, holding up the tumbler of water from which a thread of steam wriggled in the air. He talked to us in a strange voice and told us about the experiment as if we were seeing it for the first time. Then the Inspector took the warm tumbler and questioned us on our lesson. 'It should be perfectly pure water,' he said, and he sipped at it. He tasted its flavour. He sipped at it again. He turned to Mr. Craig. They whispered together, the Inspector looking towards the retort which was still bubbling and sending out its twirls of steam to be condensed to water of purest crystal. He laughed loudly, and we smiled when he again put the tumbler to his lips and this time drank it all. Then he asked us more questions and told us how, if we were shipwrecked, we could make pure water from the salt sea water.

Mr. Craig turned off the bunsen and the Inspector spoke to him. The master filled up the Inspector's tumbler and poured out some for himself in a cup. Then the Inspector made jokes with us, listened to us singing, and told us we were the best class in Ireland. Then he gave us a few sums to do in our books. He put his hands in his pockets and jingled his money, rubbed a little peep-hole in the breath-covered window and peered out at the loveliest sight in Ireland. He spoke to Mr. Craig again and Mr. Craig shook hands with him and they both laughed. The Inspector looked at his watch. Our class was let out early, and while I remained behind to tidy up the Science apparatus the master gave me an empty treacle tin to throw in the bin and told me to carry the Inspector's case up to the station. I remember that day well as I walked behind them through the snow, carrying the attaché case, and how loudly they talked and laughed as the snow whirled cold from the river. I remember how they crouched together to light their cigarettes, how match after match was thrown on the road, and how they walked off with the unlighted cigarettes still in their mouths. At the station Mr. Craig took a penny from his waistcoat pocket and as he handed it to me it dropped on the snow. I lifted it and he told me I was the best boy in Ireland. . . .

When I was coming from his funeral last week— God have mercy on him—I recalled that wintry day and the feel of the cold penny and how much more I know now about Mr. Craig than I did then. On my way out of the town—I don't live there now—I passed the school and saw a patch of new slates on the roof and an ugly iron barrier near the door to keep the home-going children from rushing headlong on to the road. I knew if I had looked at the trees I'd have seen rusty drawing-pins stuck into their rough flesh. But I passed by. I heard there was a young teacher in the school now, with an array of coloured pencils in his breast pocket.

Exile's Return

BRYAN MACMAHON

(b. 1909)

FAR away the train whistled. The sound moved in rings through the rain falling on the dark fields.

On hearing the whistle the little man standing on the railway bridge gave a quick glance into the up-line darkness and then began to hurry downwards towards the station. Above the metal footbridge the lights came on weak and dim as he hurried onwards. The train beat him to the station; all rattle and squeak and bright playing cards placed in line, it drew in beneath the bridge. At the station's end the engine lurched uneasily: then it puffed and huffed, blackened and whitened, and eventually, after a loud release of steam, stood chained.

One passenger descended—a large man resembling Victor McLaglen. He was dressed in a new cheap suit and overcoat. A black stubble of beard littered his scowling jowls. The eyes under the cap were black and daft. In his hand he carried a battered attaché case tied with a scrap of rope. Dourly slamming the carriage door behind him, he stood glaring up and down the platform.

A passing porter looked at him, abandoned him as being of little interest, then as on remembrance glanced at him a second time. As he walked away the porter's eyes still lingered on the passenger. A hackney-driver, viewing with disgust the serried unprofitable door-handles, smiled grimly to himself at the sight of the big fellow. Barefooted boys grabbing cylinders of magazines that came hurtling out of the luggage van took no notice whatsoever of the man standing alone. The rain's falling was visible in the pocking of the cut limestone on the platform's edge.

Just then the little man hurried in by the gateway of the station. His trouser-ends were tied over clay-daubed boots above which he wore a cast-off green Army great-coat. A sweat-soiled hat sat askew on his poll. After a moment of hesitation he hurried forward to meet the swaying newcomer.

'There you are, Paddy!' the small man wheezed brightly, yet not coming too close to the big fellow.

The big fellow did not answer. He began to walk heavily out of the station. The little man moved hoppingly at his side, pelting questions to which he received no reply.

'Had you a good crossing, Paddy?' 'Is it true that the Irish Sea is as wicked as May Eve?' 'There's a fair share of Irish in Birmingham, I suppose?' Finally, in a tone that indicated that this question was closer to the bone than its fellows: 'How long are you away now, Paddy? Over six year, eh?'

Paddy ploughed ahead without replying. When they had reached the first of the houses of the country town, he glowered over his shoulder at the humpy bridge that led over the railway line to the open country: after a moment or two he dragged his gaze away and looked at the street that led downhill from the station.

'We'll have a drink, Timothy!' the big man said dourly.

'A drink, Paddy!' the other agreed.

The pub glittered in the old-fashioned way. The embossed wallpaper between the shelving had been painted lime-green. As they entered the bar, the publi-

can was in the act of turning with a full pint-glass in
his hand. His eyes hardened on seeing Paddy: he
delayed the fraction of a second before placing the
glass on the high counter in front of a customer.

Wiping his hands in a blue apron, his face working
overtime, 'Back again, eh, Paddy?' the publican asked,
with false cheer. A limp handshake followed.

Paddy grunted, then lurched towards the far corner
of the bar. There, sitting on a high stool, he crouched
against the counter. Timothy took his seat beside him,
seating himself sideways to the counter as if protecting
the big fellow from the gaze of the other customers.
Paddy called for two pints of porter: he paid for his
call from an old-fashioned purse bulky with English
treasury notes. Timothy raised his full glass—its size
tended to dwarf him—and ventured: 'Good health!'
Paddy growled a reply. Both men tilted the glasses
on their heads and gulped three-quarters of the
contents. Paddy set down his glass and looked moodily
in front of him. Timothy carefully replaced his glass
on the counter, then placed his face closer to the
other's ear.

'Yeh got my letter, Paddy?'

'Ay!'

'You're not mad with me?'

'Mad with *you*?' The big man's guffaw startled the
bar.

There was a long silence.

'I got yer letter!' Paddy said abruptly. He turned
and for the first time looked his small companion
squarely in the face. Deliberately he set the big
battered index finger of his right hand inside the
other's collar-stud. As, slowly, he began to twist his
finger, the collar-band tightened. When it was taut
Paddy drew the other's face close to his own. So inti-

mately were the two men seated that the others in the
bar did not know what was going on. Timothy's face
changed colour, yet he did not raise his hands to try
to release himself.

'Yer swearin' 'tis true?' Paddy growled.

Gaspingly: 'God's gospel, it's true!'

'Swear it!'

'That I may be struck down dead if I'm tellin' you
a word of a lie! Every mortal word I wrote you is
true!'

'Why didn't you send me word afore now?'

'I couldn't rightly make out where you were, Paddy.
Only for Danny Greaney comin' home I'd never have
got your address. An' you know I'm not handy with
the pen.'

'Why didn't you let me as I was—not knowin' at
all?'

'We to be butties always, Paddy. I thought it a
shame you to keep sendin' her lashin's o' money an'
she to be like that! You're chokin' me, Paddy!'

As Paddy tightened still more, the button-hole
broke and the stud came away in the crook of his
index finger. He looked at it stupidly. Timothy quietly
put the Y of his hand to his chafed neck. Paddy threw
the stud behind him. It struck the timbered encase-
ment of the stairway.

'Ach!' he said harshly. He drained his glass and
with its heel tapped on the counter. The publican
came up to refill the glasses.

Timothy, whispering: 'What'll you do, Paddy?'

'What'll I do?' Paddy laughed. 'I'll drink my pint,'
he said. He took a gulp. 'Then, as likely as not, I'll
swing for her!'

'Sssh!' Timothy counselled.

Timothy glanced into an advertising mirror: behind

the picture of little men loading little barrels on to a little lorry he saw the publican with his eyes fast on the pair of them. Timothy warned him off with a sharp look. He looked swiftly around: the backs of the other customers were a shade too tense for his liking. Then suddenly the publican was in under Timothy's guard.

Swabbing the counter: 'What way are things over, Paddy?'

'Fair enough!'

'I'm hearin' great accounts of you from Danny Greaney. We were all certain you'd never again come home, you were doin' so well. How'll you content yourself with a small place like this, after what you've seen? But then, after all, home is home!'

The publican ignored Timothy's threatening stare. Paddy raised his daft eyes and looked directly at the man behind the bar. The swabbing moved swiftly away.

'Swing for her, I will!' Paddy said again. He raised his voice. 'The very minute I turn my back. . . .'

'Sssh!' Timothy intervened. He smelled his almost empty glass, then said in a loud whisper: 'The bloody stout is casky. Let's get away out o' this!'

The word 'casky' succeeded in moving Paddy. It also nicked the publican's pride. After they had gone the publican, on the pretence of closing the door, looked after them. He turned and threw a joke to his customers. A roar of laughter was his reward.

Paddy and Timothy were now wandering towards the humpy bridge that led to the country. Timothy was carrying the battered case: Paddy had his arm around his companion's shoulder. The raw air was testing the sobriety of the big fellow's legs.

'Nothing hasty!' Timothy was advising. 'First of all we'll pass out the cottage an' go on to my house. You'll sleep with me tonight. Remember, Paddy, that I wrote that letter out o' pure friendship!'

Paddy lifted his cap and let the rain strike his forehead. 'I'll walk the gallows high for her!' he said.

'Calm and collected, that's my advice!'

'When these two hands are on her throat, you'll hear her squealin' in the eastern world!'

'Nothin' hasty, Paddy: nothin' hasty at all!'

Paddy pinned his friend against the parapet of the railway bridge. 'Is six years hasty?' he roared.

'For God's sake, let go o' me, Paddy! I'm the only friend you have left! Let go o' me!'

The pair lurched with the incline. The whitethorns were now on each side of them, releasing their raindrops from thorn to thorn in the darkness. Far away across the ridge of the barony a fan of light from a lighthouse swung its arc on shore and sea and sky. Wherever there was a break in the hedges a bout of wind mustered its forces and vainly set about capsizing them.

Paddy began to growl a song with no air at all to it.

'Hush, man, or the whole world'll know you're home,' Timothy said.

'As if to sweet hell I cared!' Paddy stopped and swayed. After a pause he muttered: 'Th' other fellah —is he long gone?'

Timothy whinnied. 'One night only it was, like Duffy's Circus.' He set his hat farther back on his poll and then, his solemn face tilted to the scud of the moon, said: 'You want my firm opinion, Paddy? 'Twas nothin' but a chance fall. The mood an' the man meetin' her. 'Twould mebbe never again happen in a million years. A chance fall, that's all it was, in my considered opinion.'

Loudly: 'Did you ever know me to break my word?'

'Never, Paddy!'

'Then I'll swing for her! You have my permission to walk into the witness-box and swear that Paddy Kinsella said he'd swing for her!'

He resumed his singing.

'We're right beside the house, Paddy. You don't want to wake your own children, do you? Your own fine lawful-got sons! Eh, Paddy? Do you want to waken them up?'

Paddy paused: 'Lawful-got is right!—you've said it there!'

'Tomorrow is another day. We'll face her tomorrow and see how she brazens it out. I knew well you wouldn't want to disturb your own sons.'

They lurched on through the darkness. As they drew near the low thatched cottage that was slightly below the level of the road, Timothy kept urging Paddy forward. Paddy's boots were more rebellious than heretofore. Timothy grew anxious at the poor progress they were making. He kept saying: 'Tomorrow is the day, Paddy! I'll put the rope around her neck for you. Don't wake the lads tonight.'

Directly outside the cottage, Paddy came to a halt. He swayed and glowered at the small house with its tiny windows. He drew himself up to his full height.

'She's in bed?' he growled.

'She's up at McSweeney's. She goes there for the sake of company. Half an hour at night when the kids are in bed—you'll not begrudge her that, Paddy?'

'I'll not begrudge her that!' Paddy yielded a single step, then planted his shoes still more firmly on the roadway. He swayed.

'The . . . ?' he queried.

'A girl, Paddy, a girl!'

A growl, followed by the surrender of another step.

'Goin' on six year, is it?'

'That's it, Paddy. Six year.'

Another step. 'Like the ma, or . . . the da?'

'The ma, Paddy. Mostly all the ma. Come on now, an' you'll have a fine sleep tonight under my roof.'

Paddy eyed the cottage. Growled his contempt of it, then spat on the roadway. He gave minor indications of his intention of moving forward. Then unpredictably he pounded off the restraining hand of Timothy, pulled violently away, and went swaying towards the passage that led down to the cottage.

After a fearful glance uproad, Timothy wailed: 'She'll be back in a minute!'

'I'll see my lawful-got sons!' Paddy growled.

When Timothy caught up with him the big fellow was fumbling with the padlock on the door. As on a thought he lurched aside and groped in vain in the corner of the window sill.

'She takes the key with her,' Timothy said. 'For God's sake leave it till mornin'.'

But Paddy was already blundering on the cobbled pathway that led around by the gable of the cottage. Finding the back door bolted, he stood back from it angrily. He was about to smash it in when Timothy discovered that the hinged window of the kitchen was slightly open. As Timothy swung the window open the smell of turf-smoke emerged. Paddy put his boot on an imaginary niche in the wall and dug in the plaster until he gained purchase of a sort. 'Gimme a leg!' he ordered harshly.

Timothy began clawing Paddy's leg upwards. Belabouring the small man's shoulders with boot and hand, the big fellow floundered through the open window. Spreadeagled on the kitchen table he remained breathing harshly for a full minute, then laboriously he grunted his way via a *súgán* chair to the floor.

'You all right, Paddy?'

A grunt.

'Draw the bolt of the back door, Paddy.'

A long pause followed. At last the bolt was drawn. 'Where the hell's the lamp?' Paddy asked as he floundered in the darkness.

'She has it changed. It's at the right of the window now.'

Paddy's match came erratically alight. He held it aloft. Then he slewed forward and removed the lamp-chimney and placed it on the table. ''Sall right!' he said, placing a match to the wick and replacing the chimney. Awkwardly he raised the wick. He began to look here and there about the kitchen.

The fire was raked in its own red ashes. Two *súgán* chairs stood one on each side of the hearth-stone. Delph glowed red, white, and green on the wide dresser. The timber of the chairs and the deal table were white from repeated scrubbings. Paddy scowled his recognition of each object. Timothy stood watching him narrowly.

'See my own lads!' Paddy said, focusing his gaze on the bedroom door at the rear of the cottage.

'Aisy!' Timothy counselled.

Lighting match held aloft, they viewed the boys. Four lads sleeping in pairs in iron-headed double-beds. Each of the boys had a mop of black hair and a pair of heavy eyebrows. The eldest slept with the youngest and the two middle-aged lads slept together. They sprawled anyhow in various postures.

Paddy had turned surprisingly sober. ''Clare to God!' he said. 'I'd pass 'em on the road without knowin' 'em!'

'There's a flamin' lad!' Timothy caught one of the middle-aged boys by the hair and pivoted the sleep-loaded head. Transferring his attention to the other of this pair: 'There's your livin' spit, Paddy!' Indicating the eldest: 'There's your own ould fellah born into the world a second time, devil's black temper an' all!' At the youngest: 'Here's Bren—he was crawlin' on the floor the last time you saw him. Ay! Bully pups all!'

'Bully pups all!' Paddy echoed loudly. The match embered in his fingers. When there was darkness: 'My lawful-got sons!' he said bitterly.

Timothy was in the room doorway. 'We'll be off now, Paddy!' he said. After a growl, Paddy joined him.

Timothy said: 'One of us'll have to go out by the window. Else she'll spot the bolt drawn.'

Paddy said nothing.

'You'll never manage the window twice.'

'I'll be after you,' Paddy said.

Timothy turned reluctantly away.

'Where's the . . . ?' Paddy asked. He was standing at the kitchen's end.

'The . . . ?'

'Yeh!'

'She's in the front room. You're not goin' to . . . ?' Paddy was already at the door of the other room.

'She sleeps like a cat!' Timothy warned urgently. 'If she tells the mother about me, the fat'll be in the fire!'

Paddy opened the door of the front room. Breathing heavily he again began fumbling with the match-box. Across the window moved the scudding night life of the sky. The matchlight came up and showed a quilt patterned with candle-wick. Then abruptly where the bed-clothes had been a taut ball there was no longer a

225

ball. As if playing a merry game, the little girl, like Jill-in-the-box, flax-curled and blue-eyed, sprang up.

'Who is it?' she asked fearlessly.

The matchlight was high above her. Paddy did not reply.

The girl laughed ringingly. 'You're in the kitchen, Timothy Hannigan,' she called out. 'I know your snuffle.'

'Holy God!' Timothy breathed.

'I heard you talking too, boyo,' she said gleefully as the matchlight died in Paddy's fingers.

''Tis me all right, Maag,' said Timmy, coming apologetically to the doorway of the room. 'Come on away!' he said in a whisper to Paddy.

'Didn't I know right well 'twas you, boyo!' Maag laughed. She drew up her knees and locked her hands around them in a mature fashion.

Another match sprang alive in Paddy's fingers.

'Who's this fellah?' Maag inquired of Timothy.

Timothy put his head inside the room. 'He's your . . . your uncle!'

'My uncle what?'

'Your uncle . . . Paddy!'

Paddy and Maag looked fully at one another.

Timothy quavered: 'You won't tell your mother I was here?'

'I won't so!' the girl laughed. 'Wait until she comes home!'

Timothy groaned. 'C'm'on away to hell outa this!' he said, showing a spark of spirit. Surprisingly enough, Paddy came. They closed the room door behind them.

'Out the back door with you,' Timothy said. 'I'll manage the lamp and the bolt.'

'Out, you!' Paddy growled. He stood stolidly like an ox.

226

Dubiously: 'Very well!'

Timothy went out. From outside the back door he called: 'Shoot the bolt quick, Paddy. She'll be back any minute.'

Paddy shot the bolt.

'Blow out the lamp, Paddy!' Timothy's head and shoulders were framed in the window.

After a pause Paddy blew out the lamp.

'Hurry, Paddy! Lift your leg!'

No reply.

'Hurry, Paddy, I tell you. What's wrong with you, man?'

Paddy gave a deep growl. 'I'm sorry now I didn't throttle you.'

'Throttle me! Is that my bloody thanks?'

'It was never in my breed to respect an informer.'

'Your breed!' Timothy shouted. 'You, with a cuckoo in your nest.'

'If my hands were on your throat. . . .'

'Yehoo! You, with the nest robbed.'

'Go, while you're all of a piece. The drink has me lazy. I'll give you while I'm countin' five. One, two....'

Timothy was gone.

Paddy sat on the rough chair at the left of the hearth. He began to grope for the tongs. Eventually he found it. He drew the red coals of turf out of the ashes and set them together in a kind of pyramid. The flames came up.

The door of the front bedroom creaked open. Maag was there, dressed in a long white nightdress.

'Were you scoldin' him?'

'Ay!' Paddy answered.

'He wants scoldin' badly. He's always spyin' on my Mom.'

After a pause, the girl came to mid-kitchen.

'Honest,' she asked, 'are you my uncle?'

'In a class of a way!'

'What class of a way?' she echoed. She took a step closer.

'Are you cold, girlie?' Paddy asked.

'I am an' I am not. What class of a way are you my uncle?'

There was no reply.

'Mebbe you're my ould fellah back from England?' she stabbed suddenly.

'Mebbe!'

The girl's voice was shaken with delight. 'I knew you'd be back! They all said no, but I said yes—that you'd be back for sure.' A pause. A step nearer. 'What did you bring me?'

Dourly he put his hand into his pocket. His fingers encountered a pipe, a half-quarter of tobacco, a six-inch nail, a clotted handkerchief, and the crumpled letter from Timothy.

'I left it after me in the carriage,' he said limply.

Her recovery from disappointment was swift. 'Can't you get it in town a Saturday?' she said, drawing still closer.

'That's right!' he agreed. There was a short pause. Then: 'Come hether to the fire,' he said.

She came and stood between his knees. The several hoops of her curls were between him and the fire-light. She smelled of soap. His fingers touched her arms. The mother was in her surely. He knew it by the manner in which her flesh was sure and unafraid.

They remained there without speaking until the light step on the road sent her prickling alive. 'Mom'll kill me for bein' out of bed,' she said. Paddy's body stiffened. As the girl struggled to be free, he held her fast. Of a sudden she went limp, and laughed: 'I for-

got!' she whispered. 'She'll not touch me on account
of you comin' home.' She rippled with secret laughter.
'Wasn't I the fooleen to forget?'

The key was in the padlock. The door moved open.
The woman came in, her shawl down from her
shoulders. 'Maag!' she breathed. The girl and the
man were between her and the firelight.

Without speaking the woman stood directly inside
the door. The child said nothing but looked from one
to the other. The woman waited for a while. Slowly
she took off her shawl, then closed the door behind
her. She walked carefully across the kitchen. A match-
box noised. She lighted the warm lamp. As the lamp-
light came up Paddy was seen to be looking steadfastly
into the fire.

'You're back, Paddy?'

'Ay!'

'Had you a good crossin'?'

'Middlin!'

'You hungry?'

'I'll see . . . soon!'

There was a long silence. Her fingers restless, the
woman stood in mid-kitchen.

She raised her voice: 'If you've anything to do or
say to me, Paddy Kinsella, you'd best get it over. I'm
not a one for waitin'!'

He said nothing. He held his gaze on the fire.

'You hear me, Paddy? I'll not live cat and dog with
you. I know what I am. Small good your brandin' me
when the countryside has me well branded before
you.'

He held his silence.

'Sayin' nothin' won't get you far. I left you down,
Paddy. Be a man an' say it to my face!'

Paddy turned: 'You left me well down,' he said

clearly. He turned to the fire and added, in a mutter: 'I was no angel myself!'

Her trembling lips were unbelieving. 'We're quits, so?' she ventured at last.

'Quits!'

'You'll not keep firin' it in my face?'

'I'll not!'

'Before God?'

'Before God!'

The woman crossed herself and knelt on the floor. 'In the presence of my God,' she said, 'because you were fair to me, Paddy Kinsella, I'll be better than three wives to you. I broke my marriage-mornin' promise, but I'll make up for it. There's my word, given before my Maker!'

Maag kept watching with gravity. The mother crossed herself and rose.

Paddy was dourly rummaging in his coat-pocket. At last his fingers found what he was seeking. 'I knew I had it somewhere!' he said. He held up a crumpled toffee-sweet. 'I got it from a kid on the boat.'

Maag's face broke in pleasure: ''Twill do—till Saturday!' she said.

The girl's mouth came down upon the stripped toffee. Then, the sweet in her cheek, she broke away and ran across the kitchen. She flung open the door of the boys' bedroom.

'Get up outa that!' she cried out. 'The ould fellah is home!'

The Will

MARY LAVIN
(b. 1912)

'I COULDN'T say what I thought while he was here!'
said Kate, the eldest of the family, closing the door
after the solicitor, who had just read their mother's
will to the Conroy family. She ran over to her youngest
sister and threw out her hands. 'I cannot tell you how
shocked I am, Lally. We had no idea that she felt as
bitter against you as all that. Had we?' She turned
and appealed to the other members of the family who
stood around the large red mahogany table, in their
stiff black mourning clothes.

'I knew she felt bitter,' said Matthew, the eldest of
the sons. 'We couldn't mention your name without
raising a row!'

'She knocked over the lamp, once,' said Nonny, the
youngest of the unmarried members. 'Of late years she
always kept a stick beside her on the counterpane of
the bed and she tapped with it on the floor when she
wanted anything, and then one day someone said
something about you, I forget what it is they said, but
she caught up the stick and drove it through the air
with all her force. The next thing we knew the lamp
was reeling off the table! The house would have been
burned down about us if the lamp hadn't quenched
with the draught of falling through the air!'

'Still, even after that we never thought that she'd
leave your name out of the parchment altogether. Did
we?' Kate corroborated every remark by an appeal to

231

the rest of the group. 'We thought she'd leave you something anyway, no matter how small it might be!'

'But I don't mind,' said Lally. 'Honestly I don't. I wish you didn't feel so bad about it, all of you.' She looked around from one to the other beseechingly.

'Why wouldn't we feel bad!' said Matthew. 'You're our own sister after all. She was your mother as well as ours, no matter what happened.'

'The only thing I regret,' said Lally, 'was that I didn't get here before she died.' The tears started into her eyes.

'I don't think it would have made any difference whether you got here in time or not before she went. The will was made years ago.'

'Oh, I didn't mean anything like that!' said Lally in dismay, and a red blush struggled through the thickened cells of her skin. 'I only meant to say that I'd like to have seen her, no matter what, before she went.'

The tears streamed down her face then, and they ran freely, for her mind was far away thinking of the days before she left home at all. She made no attempt to dry her eyes. But the tears upset the others, who felt no inclination to cry. Having watched the old lady fade away in a long lingering illness, they had used up their emotional energy in anticipating grief. Their minds were filled now with practical arrangements.

'Don't upset yourself, Lally,' said Kate. 'Perhaps it all turned out for the best. If she had seen you she might only have flown into one of her rages and died sitting up in the bed from a rush of blood to the forehead, instead of the nice natural death that she did get, lying straight out with her hands folded better than any undertaker could have folded them. Everything happened for the best.'

'I don't suppose she mentioned my name, did she? Near the end I mean.'

'No, the last time she spoke about you was so long ago I couldn't rightly say now when it was. It was one night that she was feeling bad. She hadn't slept well the night before. I was tidying her room for her, plumping up her pillows and one thing and another, and she was looking out of the window. Suddenly she looked at me and asked me how old you were now. It gave me such a start to hear her mention your name after all those years that I couldn't remember what age you were, so I just said the first thing that came into my head.'

'What did she say?'

'She said nothing for a while, and then she began to ramble about something under her breath. I couldn't catch the meaning. She used to wander a bit in her mind, now and again, especially if she had lost her sleep the night before.'

'Do you think it was me she was talking about under her breath?' said Lally, and her eyes and her open lips and even the half-gesture of her outstretched hands seemed to beg for an answer in the affirmative.

'Oh, I don't know what she was rambling about,' said Kate. 'I had my mind fixed on getting the bed straightened out so she could lie back at her ease. I wasn't listening to what she was saying. All I remember is that she was saying something about blue feathers. Blue feathers! Her mind was astray for the time being, I suppose.'

The tears glistened in Lally's eyes again.

'I had two little blue feathers in my hat the morning I went into her room to tell her I was getting married. I had nothing new to put on me. I was wearing my old green silk costume, and my old green hat, but I bought two little pale blue feathers and pinned them on the front of the hat. I think the feathers upset her more than going against her wishes with the marriage. She kept staring at them all the time I was in the room, and even when she ordered me to get out of her sight it was at the feathers in my hat she was staring and not at me.'

'Don't cry, Lally.' Kate felt uncomfortable. 'Don't cry. It's all over long ago. Don't be going back to the past. What is to be, is to be. I always believe that.'

Matthew and Nonny believed that too. They told her not to cry. They said no good could be done by upsetting yourself.

'I never regretted it!' said Lally. 'We had a hard time at the beginning, but I never regretted it.'

Kate moved over and began to straighten the red plush curtains as if they had been the sole object of her change in position, but the movement brought her close to her thin brother Matthew where he stood fingering his chin uncertainly. Kate gave him a sharp nudge.

'Say what I told you,' she said, speaking rapidly in a low voice.

Matthew cleared his throat. 'You have no need for regret as far as we are concerned, Lally,' he said, and he looked back at Kate who nodded her head vigorously for him to continue. 'We didn't share our poor mother's feelings. Of course we couldn't help thinking that you could have done better for yourself but it's all past mending now, and we want you to know that we will do all in our power for you.' He looked again at his sister Kate who nodded her head still more vigorously indicating that the most important thing had still been left unsaid. 'We won't see you in want,' said Matthew.

When this much had been said, Kate felt that her brother's authority had been deferred to sufficiently, and she broke into the conversation again.

'We won't let it be said by anyone that we'd see you in want, Lally. We talked it all over. We can make an arrangement.' She looked across at Matthew again with a glance that seemed to toss the conversation to him as one might toss a ball.

'We were thinking,' said Matthew, 'that if each one of us was to part with a small sum the total would come to a considerable amount when it was all put together.'

But Lally put up her hands again.

'Oh no, no, no,' she said. 'I wouldn't want anything that didn't come to me by rights.'

'It would only be a small sum from each one,' said Nonny placatingly. 'No one would feel any pinch.'

'No, no, no,' said Lally. 'I couldn't let you do that. It would be going against her wishes.'

'It's late in the day you let the thought of going against her wishes trouble you!' said Kate with an involuntary flash of impatience for which she hurried to atone by the next remark. 'Why wouldn't you take it! It's yours as much as ours!'

'You might put it like that, anyhow,' said Matthew, 'as long as we're not speaking legally.'

'No, no, no,' said Lally for the third time. 'Don't you see? I'd hate taking it and knowing all the time that she didn't intend me to have it. And anyway, you have to think of yourselves.' She looked at Kate. 'You have your children to educate,' she said. 'You have this place to keep up, Matthew! And you have no one to look after you at all, Nonny. I won't take a penny from any of you.'

'What about your own children?' said Kate. 'Are you forgetting them?'

'Oh, they're all right,' said Lally. 'Things are different in the city. In the city there are plenty of free schools. And I'm doing very well. Every room in the house is full.'

There was silence after that for a few minutes, but glances passed between Kate and Nonny. Kate went over to the fire and picked up the poker. She drove it in among the blazing coals and rattled them up with such unusual violence that Matthew looked around at her where she knelt on the red carpet.

'Do you have to be prompted at every word?' said Kate when she got his attention.

Matthew cleared his throat again, and this time, at the sound, Lally turned towards him expectantly.

'There is another thing that we were talking about before you arrived,' he said, speaking quickly and nervously. 'It would be in the interests of the family, Lally, if you were to give up keeping lodgers.' He looked at her quickly to see how she took what he said, and then he stepped back a pace or two like an actor who had said his lines and made way for another person to say his.

While he was speaking Kate had remained kneeling at the grate with the poker in her hand, but when he stopped she made a move to rise quickly. Her stiff new mourning skirt got in her way, however, and the cold and damp at the graveside had brought about an unexpected return of rheumatism, and so as she went to rise up quickly she listed forward with the jerky movement of a camel. It couldn't be certain whether Lally was laughing at Matthew's words, or at the camelish appearance of Kate. Kate, however, was the first to take offence. But she attributed the laughing to Matthew's words.

'I don't see what there is to laugh at, Lally,' she said. 'It's not a very nice thing for us to feel that our sister is a common landlady in the city. Mother never forgave that! She might have forgiven your marriage in time, but she couldn't forgive you for lowering yourself to keeping lodgers.'

'We had to live somehow,' said Lally, but she spoke lightly, and as she spoke she was picking off the green-flies from the plant on the table.

'I can't say I blame Mother!' said Nonny, breaking into the discussion with a sudden venom. 'I don't see why you were so anxious to marry him when it meant keeping lodgers.'

'It was the other way round, Nonny,' said Lally. 'I was willing to keep lodgers because it meant I could marry him.'

'Easy now!' said Matthew. 'There's no need to quarrel. We must talk this thing over calmly. We'll come to some arrangement. But there's no need in doing everything the one day. Tomorrow is as good as today, and better. Lally must be tired after travelling all the way down and then going on to the funeral without five minutes rest. We'll talk it all over in the daylight tomorrow.'

Lally looked back and forth from one face to another as if she was picking the face that looked most lenient before she spoke again. At last she turned back to Matthew.

'I won't be here in the morning,' she said hurriedly, as if it was a matter of no consequence. 'I am going back tonight. I only came down for the burial. I can't stay any longer.'

'Why not?' demanded Kate, and then as if she knew

the answer to the question and did not want to hear it upon her sister's lips, she continued to speak hurriedly. 'You've got to stay,' she said, stamping her foot. 'You've got to stay. That's all there is to say about the matter.'

'There is nothing to be gained by my staying, anyway,' said Lally. 'I wouldn't take the money, no matter what was said, tonight or tomorrow!'

Matthew looked at his other sisters. They nodded at him.

'There's nothing to be gained by being obstinate, Lally,' he said lamely.

'You may think you are behaving unselfishly,' said Kate, 'but let me tell you it's not a nice thing for my children to feel that their first cousins are going to free schools in the city and mixing with the lowest of the low, and running messages for your dirty lodgers. And as if that isn't bad enough, I suppose you'll be putting them behind the counter in some greengrocers, one of these days!'

Lally said nothing.

'If you kept an hotel, it wouldn't seem so bad,' said Matthew looking up suddenly with an animation that betrayed the fact that he was speaking for the first time upon his own initiative. 'If you kept an hotel we could make it a limited company. We could all take shares. We could recommend it to the right kind of people. We could stay there ourselves whenever we were in the city.' His excitement grew with every word he uttered. He turned from Lally to Kate. 'That's not a bad idea. Is it?' He turned back to Lally again. 'You'll have to stay the night, now,' he said, enthusiastically, showing that he had not believed before that it was worth her while to comply with their wishes.

'I can't stay,' said Lally faintly.

'Of course you can.' Matthew dismissed her difficulties unheard. 'You'll have to stay,' he said. 'Your room is ready. Isn't it?'

'It's all ready,' said Nonny. 'I told them to light a fire in it and to put a hot jar in the bed.' As an afterthought she explained further. 'We were going to fix up a room for you here, but with all the fuss we didn't have time to attend to it, and I thought that the simplest thing to do was to send out word to the Station Hotel that they were to fix up a nice room for you. They have the room all ready. I went out to see it. It's a big airy room with a nice big bed. It has two windows, and it looks out on the ball-alley. You'll be more comfortable there than here. Of course, I could put a stretcher into my room if you liked, but I think for your own sake you ought to leave things as I arranged them. You'll get a better night's rest. If you sleep here it may only remind you of things you'd rather forget.'

'I'm very grateful to you Nonny for all the trouble you took. I'm grateful to all of you. But I can't stay.'

'Why?' said someone then, voicing the look in every face.

'I have things to attend to!'

'What things?'

'Different things. You wouldn't understand.'

'They can wait.'

'No,' said Lally. 'I must go. There is a woman coming tonight to the room on the landing, and I'll have to be there to help her settle in her furniture.'

'Have you got her address?' said Matthew.

'Why?' said Lally.

'You could send her a telegram cancelling the arrangement.'

'Oh, but that would leave her in a hobble,' said Lally.

'What do you care. You'll never see her again. When we start the hotel you'll be getting a different class of person altogether.'

'I'll never start an hotel,' said Lally. 'I won't make any change now. I'd hate to be making a lot of money and Robert gone where he couldn't profit by it. It's too late now. I'm too old now.'

She looked down at her thin hands, with the broken finger-nails, and the fine web of lines deepened by dirt. And as she did so the others looked at her too. They all looked at her; at this sister that was younger than all of them, and a chill descended on them as they read their own decay in hers. They had been better preserved, that was all; hardship had hastened the disintegration of her looks, but the undeniable bending of the bone, the tightening of the skin, and the fading of the eye could not be guarded against. A chill fell on them. A grudge against her gnawed at them.

'I begin to see,' said Matthew, 'that Mother was right. I begin to see what she meant when she said that you were as obstinate as a tree.'

'Did she say that?' said Lally, and her face lit up for a moment with the sunlight of youth, as her mind opened wide in a wilful vision of tall trees, leafy, and glossy with light, against a sky as blue as the feathers in a young girl's hat.

Nonny stood up impatiently. 'What is the use of talking?' she said. 'No one can do anything for an obstinate person. They must be left to go their own way. But no one can say we didn't do our best.'

'I'm very grateful,' said Lally again.

'Oh, keep your thanks to yourself!' said Nonny. 'As Matthew said we didn't do it for your sake. It's not very nice to have people coming back from the city saying that they met you, and we knowing all the time the old clothes you were likely to be wearing, and your hair all tats and taws, and your face dirty maybe, if all was told!'

'Do you ever look at yourself in a mirror?' said Matthew.

'What came over you that you let your teeth go so far?' said Kate. 'They're disgusting to look at.' She shivered.

'I'd be ashamed to be seen talking to you,' said Nonny.

Through the silent evening air there was a far sound of a train shunting. Through the curtains the signal lights on the railway line could be seen changing from red to green. Even when the elderly maidservant came in with the heavy brass lamp the green light shone through the pane, insistent as a thought.

'What time is it?' said Lally.

'You have plenty of time,' said Matthew; his words marked the general acceptance of the fact that she was going.

Tea was hurried in on a tray. A messenger was sent running upstairs to see if Lally's gloves were on the bed in Kate's room.

'Where did you leave them?' someone kept asking every few minutes and going away in the confusion without a satisfactory answer.

'Do you want to have a wash?' Nonny asked. 'It will freshen you for the journey. I left a jug of water on the landing.'

And once or twice, lowering his voice to a whisper, Matthew leaned across the table and asked her if she was absolutely certain that she was all right for the journey back. Had she a return ticket? Had she loose change for the porters?

But Lally didn't need anything, and when it came nearer to the time of the train, it appeared that she did not even want the car to take her to the station.

'But it's wet!' said Matthew.

'It's as dark as a pit outside,' said Kate.

And all of them, even the maidservant who was clearing away the tray, were agreed that it was bad enough for people to know she was going back the very night that her mother was lowered into the clay, without adding to the scandal by giving people a chance to say that her brother Matthew wouldn't drive her to the train in his car, and it pouring rain.

'They'll say we had a difference of opinion over the will,' said Nonny, who retained one characteristic at least of youth, its morbid sensitivity.

'What does it matter what they say?' said Lally, 'as long as we know it isn't true?'

'If everyone took that attitude it would be a queer world,' said Matthew.

'There's such a thing as keeping up appearances,' said Kate, and she threw a hard glance at Lally's coat. 'Is that coat black or is it blue?' she asked suddenly, catching the sleeve of it and pulling it nearer to the lamp.

'It's almost black,' said Lally. 'It's a very dark blue. I didn't have time to get proper mourning, and the woman next door lent me this. She said you couldn't tell it from black.'

Nonny shrugged her shoulders and addressed herself to Matthew. 'She's too proud to accept things from her own, but she's not too proud to accept things from strangers.'

A train whistle shrilled through the air.

'I must go,' said Lally.

She shook hands with them all. She looked up the

stairway that the coffin had been carried down that morning. She put her hand on the door. While they were persuading her again to let them take her in the car, she opened the door and ran down the street.

They heard her footsteps on the pavement in the dark, as they had heard them often when she was a young girl running up the town on a message for their mother. And just as in those days, when she threw a coat over her head with the sleeves dangling, and ran out, the door was wide open upon the darkness. Matthew hesitated for a minute, and then he closed the door.

'Why didn't you insist?' said Kate.

'With people like Lally there is no use wasting your breath. They have their own ways of looking at things and nothing will change them. You might as well try to catch a falling leaf as try to find out what's at the back of Lally's mind.'

They stood in the cold hallway. Suddenly Kate began to cry awkwardly.

'Why are you crying now?' said Nonny. 'You were great at the cemetery. You kept us all from breaking down. Why are you crying now?' Her own voice had thinned and she dug her fingers into Matthew's sleeve.

'It's Lally!' said Kate. 'None of you remember her as well as I do. I made her a dress for her first dance. It was white muslin with blue bows all down the front. Her hair was like light.' Kate sobbed with thick hurtful sobs that shook her whole frame and shook Matthew's thin dried-up body when he put his arm around her.

Lally ran along the dark streets of the country town as she had run along them long ago as a young girl, and hardly remembered to slacken into a walking pace when she came to the patches of yellow lamplight that flooded out from shop windows and the open doors of houses near the Square. But the excitement of running now was caused by the beat of blood in her temple and the terrible throbbing of her heart. As a child it had been an excitement of the mind, for then it had seemed that the bright world ringed the town around, and that somewhere outside the darkness lay the mystery of life; one had only to run on, on past the old town gate, on under the dark railway bridge, on a little way out the twisty road, and you would reach the heart of that mystery. Some day she would go.

And one day she went. But there was no mystery now; anywhere. Life was just the same in the town, in the city, and in the twisty countryside. Life was the same in the darkness and the light. It was the same for the spinster and for the draggled mother of a family. You were yourself always, no matter where you went or what you did. You didn't change. Her brothers and sisters were the same as they always were. She herself was the same as she always was, although her teeth were rotted, and a blue feather in her hat now would make her look like an old hag in a pantomime. Nothing you did made any real change in you. You might think beforehand that it would make a great change, but it wouldn't make any change. There was only one thing that could change you, and that was death. And no one knew what that change would be like.

No one knew what death was like, but people made terrible torturing guesses. Fragments of the old penny catechism she had learned by rote in school came back to her, distorted by a bad memory and a confused emotion. Pictures of flames and screaming souls writhing on gridirons, rose before her mind as she ran down the street to the station. The whistle of the train when it screamed in the darkness gave a reality to her racing thoughts, and she paused and listened to it for a moment. Then turning rapidly around she ran a few paces in the way that she had come, and groped along the dark wall that lined the street at this point.

The wet black railings of a gate came in contact with her fingers. This was the gate leading into the residence of the Canon. She banged the gate back against the piers with the fierce determination with which she opened it. She ran up the wet gravelly drive to the priest's house.

In the dark she could not find the brass knocker and she beat against the panels of the door with her hard hands. The door was thrown open after a minute with a roughness that matched the rough knocking.

'What in the Name of God do you want?' said an elderly woman with an apron that blazed white in the darkness.

'I want to see the Canon!' said Lally.

'He's at his dinner,' said the woman, aggressively, and went to close the door.

'I must see him,' said Lally, and she stepped into the hall-way.

'I can't disturb him at his meals,' said the woman, but her anger had softened somewhat at seeing that Lally was a stranger to her. Two emotions cannot exist together and a strong curiosity possessed her at the moment. 'What name?' she said.

'Lally Conroy,' said Lally, the old associations being so strong that her maiden name came more naturally to her lips than the name she had carried for twenty-four years.

The housekeeper went across the hall and opened a door on the left. She closed it after her, but the lock did not catch and the door slid open again. Lally heard the conversation distinctly, but with indifference, as she sat down on the polished mahogany chair in the hall.

'There's a woman outside who insists on seeing you, Father.'

'Who is she?' said the priest, his voice muffled, as if by a serviette wiped across his mouth.

'She gave her name as Conroy,' said the woman, 'and she has a look of Matthew Conroy, but I never saw her before and she's dressed like a pauper.'

The priest's voice was slow and meditative. 'I heard that there was another sister,' he said, 'but there was a sad story about her, I forget what it was.' A chair scraped back. 'I'll see her,' he said. And his feet sounded on the polished floor as he crossed the room towards the hall.

Lally was sitting on the stiff chair with the wooden seat, shielding her face from the heat of the flames that dragged themselves like serpents along the logs in the fireplace.

'Father, I'm in a hurry. I'm going away on this train.'

The train had shrilled its whistle once again in the darkness outside.

'I'm sorry to disturb you. I only wanted to ask a question.' Her short phrases leaped uncontrollably as the leaping flames in the grate. 'I want to know if you will say a mass for my mother first thing in the morning? My name is Lally Conroy. I'll send you the offering money the minute I get back to the city. I'll post it tonight. Will you do that, Father? Will you?' As if the interview was over she stood up and began to go towards the door, backwards, without waiting for an answer, repeating her urgent question, 'Will you?

Will you do that, Father? First thing in the morning!'

The Canon took out a watch from under the cape of his shiny canonical robes.

'You have six minutes, yet,' he said. 'Sit down. Sit down.'

'No, no, no,' said Lally. 'I mustn't miss the train.'

The whistle blew again and the sound seemed to race her thoughts to a gallop.

'I want three masses to be said,' she explained, 'but I want the first one to be said at once, tomorrow, first thing in the morning. You'll have the offering money as soon as I get back. I'll post it, tonight.'

The Canon looked at the shabby boots and the thick stockings, the rubbed coat with the faded stitching on it.

'There is no need to worry about masses. She was a good woman,' he said. 'And I understand that she left a large sum in her will for masses to be said for her after her death. Three hundred pounds I believe, or thereabouts; a very considerable sum, at any rate. There is no need for worry on that score.'

'It's not the same thing to leave money yourself for masses. It's the masses that other people have said for you that count.' Her excitement leaped like the leaping flames. 'I want a mass said for her with my money! With my money!'

The priest leaned forward with an unusual and ungovernable curiosity.

'Why?' he said.

'I'm afraid,' said Lally. 'I'm afraid she might suffer. I'm afraid for her soul.' The eyes that stared into the flaming heart of the fire were indeed filled with fear, and as a coal fell, revealing a gaping abyss of fire, those eyes filled with absolute horror. The reflection of the flames leaped in them. 'She was very bitter,' Lally Conroy sobbed for the first time since she had news of her mother's death. 'She was very bitter against me all the time, and she died without forgiving me. I'm afraid for her soul.' She looked up at the priest. 'You'll say them as soon as ever you can, Father?'

'I'll say them,' said the priest. 'But don't worry about the money. I'll offer them from myself.'

'That's not what I want?' said Lally, angrily. 'I want them to be paid for with my money. That is what will count most; that they are paid for out of my money.'

Humbly the priest in his stiff canonical robes, piped with red, accepted the dictates of the draggled woman in front of him.

'I will do as you wish,' he said. 'Is there anything else troubling you?'

'The train! The train!' said Lally, and she fumbled the catch of the door.

The priest took out his watch again.

'You have just time to catch it,' he said, 'if you hurry.' And he opened the door. Lally ran out into the dark again.

For a moment she felt peace at the thought of what she had done, and running down the wet gravelly drive with the cold rain beating on her flushed face, her mind was filled with practical thoughts about the journey home. But when she got into the hot and stuffy carriage of the train, where there was an odour of dust and of wet soot, the tears began to stream down her face again, and she began to wonder if she had made herself clear to the Canon. She put her head out of the carriage window as the train began to leave the platform and she called out to a porter who stood with a green flag in his hand.

'What time does this train arrive in the city?' she asked, but the porter could not hear her. He put his hand to his ear but just then the train rushed into the darkness under the railway bridge. Lally let the window up and sat back in the seat.

If the train got in before midnight, she thought, she would ring the night bell at the Franciscan Friary and ask for a mass to be said there and then for her mother's soul. She had heard that masses were said night and day in the Friary. She tried to remember where she had heard that, and who had told her, but her thoughts were in confusion. She leaned her head back against the cushions as the train roared into the night, and feverishly she added the prices she would get from the tenants in the top rooms and subtracted the amount that would be needed to buy food for herself and the children for the week. She would have a clear two pound ten. She could have ten masses said at least for that. There might even be money over to light some holy lamps at the Convent of Perpetual Reparation. She tried to comfort herself by these calculations, but as the dark train rushed through the darkness she sat more upright on the red-carpeted seats that smelled of dust, and clenched her hands tightly as she thought of the torments of Purgatory. Bright red sparks from the engine flew past the carriage window, and she began to pray with rapid unformed words that jostled themselves in her mind like sheaves of burning sparks.

A Wet Day

MARY LAVIN

(b. 1912)

'How is your lettuce, Ma'am?' asked the old Parish Priest. 'I hear it's been bad everywhere this year.' He paused and blew his nose loudly, and then he looked around him. 'Slugs!' he said then, very sternly, and went on a few paces after my aunt. We hadn't room to walk abreast on the narrow garden path. We went in single file; the three of us. After a minute the old man turned around and looked back at me.

'Slugs,' he said again, and only the fact that he put the word in the plural kept me from feeling that this sturdy and blunt old man was calling me names.

'Our lettuce is very good this year,' said my aunt, as all three of us somewhat unconsciously turned down towards the sodden path that led to the kitchen garden, and she took a firm grip of my arm although it meant that both of us got our legs wet by the border grasses. Father Gogarty distrusted students and my aunt probably linked me in case I might take offence at some remark of his, although it is scarcely likely that this would have happened. My aunt was always nervous when the local clergy called because we had had a couple of brisk arguments, she and I, about one thing and another, and she was beginning to realize that in my estimate of a man's worth I did not allow credit for round collars and tussore. I met some fine men who were in clerical clothes, but my respect for them had nothing to do with their dress. My aunt, however, had no use for anything I said on certain subjects. She

250

banged the door against all my arguments. Sometimes she went as far as saying that she doubted the wisdom of my parents in sending me to the University at all. It was there that I got my ideas, she said; ideas she distrusted. When she wasn't too angry to listen, she kept interrupting so much that she couldn't hear half what I said. Cheap anti-clericalism was the phrase she used most often to batter a way through my remarks. But as a matter of fact I believe that secretly she enjoyed these encounters that we had, and that they gave her a feeling of satisfaction as if she were Fighting for the Faith. I could understand, of course, that she wouldn't care to have outsiders overhear my views. And she lived in terror of my offending the local clergy.

That was why she linked me so close as we went into the kitchen garden. She wanted to keep me near her so that she could squeeze my arm, and nudge me, and, in general, keep a guide over my conversation and demeanour.

We walked along the garden path.

Just inside the kitchen garden was a large ramshackle fuchsia bush that hung out, heavy with raindrops, over the gravel path. Our legs were sprinkled with wet.

'You ought to clip back those bushes, Ma'am,' said the parish priest. 'Nothing would give you a cold quicker than wet feet.'

'I know that, Father,' said my aunt, deferentially, 'but they look very pretty on a sunny day; so shaggy and unpretentious.'

'On a sunny day!' said the old man. 'And when do we get a sunny day in this country I'd like to know? As far as I can see it's rain, rain, rain.'

He shook the bush with petulant strokes of his walking-stick, while he was talking, and we knew that his thoughts were back in the days before his ordination, when he wandered along the blistered roads in Rome, and wiped the sweat from his red young face.

He often told us stories about those days, and all his stories had flashes of sunlight in them, that made up for the absence of humour. We thought, involuntarily, of sun-pools lying on hot, city pavements, between the chill shadows of lime leaves. We thought of barrows of melons and pawpaws and giant vegetable marrows; huge, waxy growths of red and yellow. We thought of the young priest from Ireland in his shining black alpaca, laying his hands on them, and smiling to find them warm; for at home they were always chill to the touch, with a mist of moisture on them.

It was extraordinary the way we thought of his youth like that every time we saw him, because it was forty-five years, at the very least, since those days when he knelt to the Pope in Rome, and out of those forty-five years we, ourselves, had only known him for ten; the last ten. And those ten years were the years least likely to make us think of his hot, healthy youth, because during all that time he was delicate and suffering, and the duties of the parish put a great strain on him.

He always looked cold, and although his face was rosy-appled over with broken veins, it nevertheless looked blue and chilly to us as we sat watching him in the bleak, concrete church where he went through Mass perfunctorily, and gave out a hard dry sermon, with a blackened silver watch in his hand, and his eye darting from one side of the church to the other, from the back to the front, from the organ-stall to the gallery steps, according to wherever a cough or a sneeze escaped from some incautious person. There was always someone coughing, or stifling a cough. He used to say that he would like to preach a sermon some day on avoiding colds; he'd like to tell the ignorant people at the back of the church to close the door quickly when they came in, and not to hold it open for someone half-way down the outside path. There were more colds contracted by false politeness, he explained, than by any other way. He'd like to tell his congregation to cover their mouths when they sneezed. But he knew that a sermon of this kind would not be taken in the spirit in which it was meant, and so he had to content himself with stopping in the middle of a sentence, whenever anyone coughed, and staring at the offender till his stare became a glare. They probably thought that he was annoyed at the interruption, but they might have known, had they any wits awake at all at that hour of the morning, that nothing could interrupt the perfect machinery of his sentences. They ran smoothly in the tracks they had cut for themselves through dogma and doctrine, over forty years before, when he was a careful curate, working under a careful pastor.

It was very remarkable the way Father Gogarty could pause to glare around the church, or even pause for a longer while, to take out his handkerchief, shake it, blow his nose in it for a considerable time, and finally fold it carefully and tuck it back in the pleats of his surplice, before he finished a sentence. And yet he always went on at the exact place where he had stopped, and never repeated as much as a preposition of what he had already said.

Once in a while he dropped hints in his sermons about the damp of the church, hoping perhaps that some confraternity would get up a subscription for a heating apparatus. The confraternity members, however, thought that the cold of the chapel and the draught that came in under the badly hung door and, yes, even the fact that you might get a splinter in your knee any minute from the rotten wood of the kneelers, were all additional earthly endurances that enhanced the beauty of their souls in the eyes of the Lord. The last thing that would have occurred to them would have been the installation of any form of comfort into the concrete church, although there were large subscriptions raised every other year or so, for silk banners with gilt tassels, for brass candelabra, or for yards of confraternity ribbon with fringes and picot edging.

'It's a pity, you know,' the old priest used to say, 'that the Irish people make no effort to counteract the climate, because it's a most unhealthy climate. It's damp. It's heavy. It is, as I say, very unhealthy to live in.'

It may have been his constant talk of health that made us associate him with the pagans of southern Europe, and made us feel a certain sympathy for him, trapped in a land of mist, where most of the days were sunless and where the nights were never without their frost or rain. My aunt often looked out at the sky and sighed.

'It looks like rain,' she would say. 'Poor Father Gogarty. This kind of weather is very injurious to him.'

And when he came to call, the conversation was mainly about goloshes and leaking roofs and the value of wool next the skin. He was a diabetic. My aunt, of course, had a great sympathy for him, but it would not have exceeded mine, had it not been for the fact that she deliberately exploited his delicacy to gain merit for his calling.

'He's a martyr!' she often said, when we were sitting down to a well-cooked dinner. 'Can you imagine having nothing for your meal but a soup-plate of cabbage?'

'Or rhubarb,' I'd say, because I did feel sorry for the old man.

'Rhubarb is not so bad,' my aunt would say, pouring the melted butter over her fish.

'Without sugar?' I would inquire.

'Without sugar?' my aunt would say, looking up. 'Are you sure?'

'Of course I'm sure. Diabetics can't have sugar in any form. They can't even have green peas, or beans.'

'You don't tell me! I thought they could eat any vegetable they liked as long as it was a vegetable.'

And while I was explaining the differences between certain vegetables she would listen carefully, and on these occasions she looked as if she was pleased that I was going to the University and getting such general knowledge.

'Let's not talk about the poor man,' she would say at last. 'He is a martyr, that is the truth. How the rest of us can expect to reach heaven, is more than I can tell!' And here, she would call back Ellen, the parlour-maid, before she retired behind the service-screen, to ask her if the cheese soufflé had been sent back to the kitchen. 'It hasn't?' she'd say. 'Good! I think I could manage a little more. It's so good today,' and then, as she scraped the sides of the silver dish, and looked sideways at me to ask if I was quite sure, absolutely sure, that I wouldn't have another spoonful, she would send a message to the kitchen. 'My compliment to the cook!' she would cry.

If the old parish priest happened to call, as he sometimes did, after a conversation like that, we would both go out to the garden with him and walk around the sodden paths, urging him to take another head of

sea-kale, or prising open the green curls of the cauli-
flower plants to see if even the smallest head had
formed there, that he could have, as a change from
what he called the Eternal Cabbage. Father Gogarty
was supplied with vegetables from every little plot in
the parish, but my aunt tried to keep him supplied
with the kinds that were more difficult of culture, and
which he would be unlikely to get elsewhere.

On this particular day in September, when he
showed such solicitude for our lettuce, the weather
was at its dirtiest, and of all places on earth to feel
the dismay of rain I think a garden is the worst. The
asters alone would depress the most steadfast heart.
They were logged to the ground with rain and their
shaggy petals of blue and pink and purple trailed
dismally in the mud that streaked them all over. As
we went slowly round the garden, and printed the
path with our footprints, we left in our wake great
heaps of vegetable, lettuce here, spinach there, to be
collected by the gardener and put into the priest's car.

The gardener shared our sympathy for the old man
and when my aunt would be ordering seeds from the
catalogue that was sent to her every year from the
city, he would often throw in a suggestion for some
vegetable that we ourselves did not particularly like.

'What do we want with that?' my aunt would cry,
impulsively, but she nearly always checked herself,
quickly, before the gardener had time to explain that
the old man had a partiality for it. 'You are quite right,
Mike. I'm glad you reminded me. Put down a large
patch of that too. And I think we could put in more
spinach this year. It ran out towards the end of last
year.'

The gardener was very fond of Father Gogarty, and
when the old man came they always had a chat.

'We must keep the old machine going, Mike. Isn't that right?' Father Gogarty would say.

'That's right, Father,' Mike used to say. 'Mind your health. It's the only thing that will stand to you at the finish.'

'Perhaps you'd better throw in a few more of those cabbages,' Father Gogarty would say. 'And, by the way! while I think of it, I have been trying to keep it in my mind for a long time, to ask you a question, Mike!'

'Certainly Father. Anything at all I can tell you.'

'It's about lettuce. I wonder, Mike, is there any way of keeping lettuce fresh? My housekeeper says it should be kept airtight, but it gets all dried up, I notice, if you do that. I heard other people say they put it in water, but when that is done, I find, it gets yellow and flabby. I thought maybe that you might know of some knack for keeping it fresh. Do you now?'

'I can't say I do, Father, but why do you bother trying to keep it, can't you always get a bit fresh from here any time you want? What is the need in trying to preserve it? There's always plenty here.'

Mike would speak from his own bounty, but he would look over the priest's shoulder as he spoke, and talk loudly for my aunt to hear. On these occasions she would nod her approval.

'You're working for a kind woman, Mike. There aren't many like her going the way nowadays. She spoils us all. She spoils us all.' The old man sighed. 'I suppose it isn't right for me to let her spoil me like this. Eh, Mike?'

'Ah! Why wouldn't you let her spoil you, Father? She loves giving you the few poor vegetables!'

'She does, indeed. She does. I know that, Mike. I

can see that. Isn't it a grand thing the way the Irish women are so good to the clergy?'

'Why wouldn't they be, Father? Where would we be only for the priests?'

'I suppose you're right, Mike, but sometimes I say to myself that I shouldn't be taking such care of myself, an old man like me. "I'll sit down and eat a bit of steak tonight," I say to myself, sometimes—"What harm if it kills me, amn't I near the end, anyway!" But then I say to myself that it's everyone's duty to guard the bit of life that's left in him, no matter what happens, and to keep it from giving out till the very last minute.'

'You've no need to talk of dying, Father. I never saw you looking better.'

'None of your flattery now, Mike,' he'd say, to round off the conversation, turning out of the greenhouse to where my aunt and I would be waiting for him. My aunt felt that the few words the priest had with any of the men or women on the place was, in some way, a part of his priestly duty, and she never liked to interrupt.

'Let him have a few words with Mike,' she would say to me, and she would busy herself until he came out of the greenhouse, by shaking the clay off the lettuce heads, or flicking slugs off with her long forefinger.

The end of the conversations with Mike, all of which were of a remarkable similarity, took place half-way in and half-way out of the glasshouse.

'It's up to all of us to keep going up to the very last minute, isn't that right, Mike?'

'That's right, Father. We should try to guard the bit of health we have. I've always heard that said.'

'Is that so? I'm glad to hear that now, Mike. I must remember that, now.'

Yes, the conversations were all alike, almost word for word alike upon every visit he made. But on this particular day that I mention, the day of rain and draggled fuchsias, Father Gogarty stopped and turned back suddenly to Mike, who was picking up a watering-can and going back into the greenhouse.

'Aren't you from somewhere around Mullingar, Mike?' he said.

'I'm from three miles the other side, Father.'

'I thought that, mind you! Did you know a young farmer there by the name of Molloy?'

'I did, Father. I knew him well, Father.'

'I hear he's dead, the poor fellow,' said Father Gogarty.

'I'm sorry to hear that now,' said Mike. 'He was a fine strong fellow, if I remember rightly.'

'A big broad-shouldered fellow?' said the priest.

'Yes,' said Mike. 'A big broad-shouldered fellow is right.'

'Reddish hair?'

'Red hair would be right.'

'About twenty-five years of age?'

'That's him,' said Mike.

'Yes, that would be him, all right,' said Father Gogarty. 'Well, he's dead.'

'Is that so?' said Mike and he left the watering-can on the ground. 'It just shows you can never tell the day nor the hour. Isn't that so, Father?'

Mike shook his head. Father Gogarty came out of the greenhouse and joined us on the wet gravel.

'I heard you talking to Mike, Father,' said my aunt sympathetically. 'I heard you talking about some young man who died. I hope he wasn't a relative of yours?'

'No,' said Father Gogarty. 'No, but it was a very sad case.' He shook his head dolefully, and then he became more cheerful. 'Do you know!' he said, impulsively, 'I'm a lucky man that it's not me that is under the sod this minute, instead of him.'

'God between us and all harm!' said my aunt. 'Tell us about it, quick.'

'I suppose you often heard me speak of my niece Lottie?' said Father Gogarty. 'She's my sister's daughter, you know, and she comes to see me once in a while. Every six months or so. She's a nurse up in Dublin. Well, anyway, to tell you about the young fellow that's dead. Lottie got engaged a few weeks back to this young fellow from Mullingar. They were planning on getting married next month.'

'Oh, how tragic!' said my aunt.

'Wait till you hear!' said the priest, looking back to make sure that Mike was coming after us with the basket of vegetables to put in the car. 'As I was saying, anyway,' he continued, 'they were planning on getting married next month, and nothing would do Lottie but that I'd see him before they were married. She wrote to say she was bringing him down. I suppose she had an eye to the wedding present, too, you know, but, however it was anyway, I was expecting them last Thursday, and I told my housekeeper to fix up a bit of dinner for them, to get a bit of meat and the like, as well as the dirty old cabbage and rhubarb that I have to eat. I told her to think up a bit of a sweet for them too. She's a good woman, this housekeeper of mine, and she is a great cook; not that her cooking gets any great strain put on it with me in the state of health I'm in! But anyway, she put a nice dinner together.

The smell of it nearly drove me out of the house. And when I saw her throwing it out in the pigs' bucket next morning, I could have cried. I could. That's a fact.'

'Didn't they come?'

'They came all right, but wait till you hear. It appears he had a cold on him for a day or two past, and coming down in the car he must have got a chill, because the fellow wasn't able to speak when they drew up to the door. The car was a ramshackle affair. You wouldn't wonder at what would happen to anyone in it. I wouldn't ride down the drive in it much less the journey they had made. The niece was very upset and she was fussing over him like as if they were married for fifteen years. Tea, she wanted for him, if you please; right away.

'"Don't mind about dinner," she said, "he couldn't look at a bit of food." Pillows, she wanted for him, if you please. "Get him a pillow so, if you haven't any cushions!" she said to the housekeeper, pushing her out of the way and going over to the sideboard and opening it wide. "Is there a drop of brandy here?" she said, "or where will I look for it? I want to rub it on his chest." I was pretty well sick of the fussing by this time, Ma'am, as you can imagine, and I gave it as my opinion that the best thing she could do would be to take him back to Dublin as quick as ever she could, where he could be given the proper attention.

'"But the drive back?" said Lottie, and I saw in a flash what was in the back of her mind.

'"The harm is done now,' I said, "another hour or so won't make any difference. A strange bed might be the death of him. Wrap him up warm," I said, "I'll lend you my overcoat." It was my big frieze coat, Ma'am, you know the one? It was a good warm coat.

But Lottie was fidgeting about. She didn't know what was best to do, she said. I was getting pretty uneasy by this time, I need not tell you. What on earth would I have done if they insisted on staying. The whole house would have been upset. There's only one hot jar. Where would I get blankets enough to cover a big fellow like that? There's only the one woman to do everything and she has her hands full looking after me. I couldn't stand the excitement. There would be running up and down the stairs all the night. There'd be noise. There'd be talking till all hours. The doctor would be there. The doctor would have to have a meal. Oh, I could see it all! I could see it all! I have to be careful at my age, you know. I have to have everything regular. I have to have quiet. "If you know what is right," I said to Lottie, "you'll take that man right back where he came from, and get good medical care for him," and as I was saying it, I was thinking to myself that if anyone knew what was right and what was wrong it ought to be her, with her hospital training. And sure enough, there were no flies on her. "I'll tell you what I'll do," she said, "I'll take his temperature, and if he has no temperature I'll take him back to the city and telephone to the hospital. If he has a temperature, of course, it would be madness to undertake the journey back. I suppose the doctor here is passable?" She was pulling out the drawers of the desk while she was talking, looking for the thermometer, I suppose. "Where do you keep the thermometer?" she said, looking round at me.

'"I haven't one," I said, but she wasn't listening to me. "His forehead is very hot, isn't it?" she said. "Why wouldn't it be," said I, "with your hand on it." And the poor fellow himself didn't see the joke, any more than her, he was so sick. "Where did you say the

thermometer was?" she said again. "I said I haven't
got such a thing," said I, and she was so vexed she
could hardly speak. "Every house should have a thermometer," she said, "it's a downright shame not to
have one." But she began to gather up rugs and pillows
while she was giving out to me. "As long as you haven't
one, I suppose I'd better not waste any more time but
start getting him back to the city." She went over to
the poor fellow. "Do you feel able for the journey
back?" she asked, feeling his pulse and frowning.

'"I'm all right," said he. He was a nice lad, not
wanting to cause any commotion; and different from
her altogether.

'"We'll come down another day, Father," said
Lottie, "I hope you hadn't made a lot of preparations
for us?"

'"I'll make greater preparations next time," I said,
just in order to cheer the poor fellow she was wrap-
ping up with rugs and blankets in the back of the car.
I wanted to cheer him up because I had a kind of
feeling that he was worse than she thought he was.
"I'll send you down a thermometer," she shouted back
at me, as they went down the drive. "Everyone should
keep a thermometer."'

'That was true for her,' my aunt interposed impulsively at this point, and I could see she was wondering
if we had a second one in the house that she could
give him.

'I know it was true for her, Ma'am. All I can say is
I hope she won't send me one though. You don't think
that a man like me would be without such a necessary
thing as a thermometer, do you?' He looked at us
sternly.

'You had one all the time?' my aunt asked, falter-
ingly.

'Three!' he said. 'I had three of them, no less than three, but I wasn't going to let on to her that I had.' His face was criss-crossed with lines of aged cunning. 'Didn't I know by the feel of the fellow's hand that he had a temperature, but I wasn't going to let myself in for having him laid up in the presbytery for a couple of weeks, as he would have been, you know, with pneumonia.'

'Pneumonia?'

'That's right, Ma'am. He had pneumonia. Double pneumonia, I should say. He was dead the following evening. I was very sorry for the poor fellow. He was a nice lad. I was extremely sorry for him. I can't say that I was so sorry for my niece. It was a very inconsiderate thing, I think you will agree, Ma'am, to come along and visit anyone and bring a man that wasn't able to stand on his feet with a cold? People nowadays have no consideration at all; that's the long and the short of it; no consideration. I sent down to the chemists and got him to send up a bottle of strong disinfectant to sprinkle on the carpets after they went out. You can't afford to take risks. I consider I am a very lucky man to be alive today, a man in my state of health would have been gone in the twinkling of an eye if I was burthened with a young fellow like that in the house, for maybe a month. He might even have died there in any case, even if he didn't have the journey back, and then think of the fuss! I'd be in the grave along with him. There is no doubt in my mind whatsoever on that score.' He stood up. 'Here is Mike with the vegetables,' he said. 'Put the lettuce on the front seat, Mike, I don't want it to get crushed. "Eat plenty of lettuce" the doctor says to me at every visit.' He shook hands with us. 'I'm getting too old to be gadding about in a car,' he said, smiling out the car window at us, before he swung the car around and went off down the drive.

'I'll go for a walk,' I said to my aunt. 'I'll be back in time for dinner.' I thought the least said the better.

And when I came back from my walk, I had indeed forgotten all about the incident. The evening had been very sweet and scented after the recent rain. You'd forget anything walking along the roads and hearing the heavy drops fall from the trees on to the dead leaves in the wood, while the sky over your head was bright and blue and cloudless. And when I came back I was hungry. I was looking forward to my dinner. When Ellen came in with a bowl of salad I hoped my aunt would not take too big a helping because I felt I could eat the whole bowlful. But what do you think? Before the girl had time to set the bowl before us, my aunt snapped at her and rapped the table with her wrist.

'Take away that lettuce,' she said. 'We don't want any tonight.'

I was going to protest when I caught her eye, and held my tongue. We didn't mention that story of the big red-haired farmer, either then, or since, but isn't it a funny thing, I have been on better terms with my aunt since that day. We get on better. And we have less fights about books and politics and one thing and another.

The Eagles and the Trumpets

JAMES PLUNKETT

(b. 1920)

I

WHEN the girl crossed from the library, the square was bathed in August sunshine. The folk from the outlying areas who had left their horses and carts tethered about the patriotic monument in the centre were still in the shops, and the old trees which lined either side emphasized the stillness of the morning. She went down a corridor in the Commercial Hotel and turned left into the bar. She hardly noticed its quaintness, the odd layout of the tables, its leather chairs in angles and corners, the long low window which looked out on the dairy yard at the back. After six years in the town she was only aware of its limitations. But the commercial traveller startled her. She had not expected to find anyone there so early. He raised his eyes and when he had stared at her gloomily for a moment, he asked, 'Looking for Cissy?'

One of the things she had never got used to was this easy familiarity of the country town. But she accepted it. One either accepted or became a crank.

'No,' she answered, 'Miss O'Halloran.'

'You won't see her,' he said. 'It's the first Friday. She goes to the altar and has her breakfast late.' He had a glass of whiskey in front of him and a bottle of Bass. He gulped half the whiskey and then added, 'I'll ring the bell for you.'

'Thank you.'

266

His greyish face with its protruding upper lip was vaguely familiar. Probably she had passed him many times in her six years without paying much attention. Now she merely wondered about his black tie. She heard the bell ringing remotely and after a moment Cissy appeared. The girl said:

'I really wanted Miss O'Halloran. It's a room for a gentleman tonight.' She hesitated. Then reluctantly she added, 'Mr. Sweeney.' As she had expected, Cissy betrayed immediate curiosity.

'Not Mr. Sweeney that stayed here last autumn?'

'Yes. He hopes to get in on the afternoon bus.'

Cissy said she would ask Miss O'Halloran. When she had gone to inquire, the girl turned her back on the traveller and pretended interest in an advertisement for whiskey which featured two dogs, one with a pheasant in its mouth. The voice from behind her asked.

'Boy friend?'

She had expected something like that. Without turning she said, 'You're very curious.'

'Sorry. I didn't mean that. I don't give a damn. Do you drink?'

'No, thank you.'

'I was going to offer you something better than a drink. Good advice.' The girl stiffened. She was the town librarian, not a chambermaid. Then she relaxed and almost smiled.

'If you ever do,' the voice added sadly, 'don't mix the grain with the grape. That's what happened to me last night.'

Cissy returned and said Mr. Sweeney could have room seven. Miss O'Halloran was delighted. Mr. Sweeney had been such a nice young man. Her eye caught the traveller and she frowned.

'Mr. Cassidy,' she said pertly, 'Miss O'Halloran says your breakfast's ready.'

The traveller looked at her with distaste. He finished his whiskey and indicated with a nod of his head the glass of Bass which he had taken in his hand.

'Tell Miss O'Halloran I'm having my breakfast,' he said. But Cissy was admiring the new dress.

'You certainly look pretty,' she said enviously.

'Prettiest girl in town,' the traveller added for emphasis.

The girl flushed. Cissy winked and said, 'Last night he told me I was.'

'Did I?' the traveller said, finishing his Bass with a grimace of disgust. 'I must have been drunk.'

On the first Friday of every month, precisely at 11.45, the chief clerk put on his bowler hat, hung his umbrella on his arm, and left to spend the rest of the day inspecting the firm's branch office. It was one of the few habits of the chief clerk which the office staff approved. It meant that for the rest of the evening they could do more or less as they pleased. Sweeney, who had been watching the monthly ceremony from the public counter with unusual interest, turned around to find Higgins at his elbow.

'You're wanted,' he was told.

'Who?'

'Our mutual musketeer—Ellis. He's in his office.'

That was a joke. It meant Ellis was in the store-room at the top of the building. Part of the duties assigned to Ellis was the filing away of forms and documents. The firm kept them for twenty-five years, after which they were burned. Ellis spent interminable periods in the store-room, away from supervision and interference. It was a much-coveted position.

Sweeney, disturbed in his day-dreaming, frowned at Higgins and said:

'Why the hell can't he come down and see me?' It was his habit to grumble. He hated the stairs up to the store-room and he hated the store-room. He disliked most of the staff, especially the few who were attending night-school classes for accountancy and secretarial management in order to get on in the job. Put into the firm at nineteen years of age because it was a good, safe, comfortable job, with a pension scheme and adequate indemnity against absences due to ill health, he realized now at twenty-six that there was no indemnity against the boredom, no contributory scheme which would save his manhood from rotting silently inside him among the ledgers and the comptometer machines. From nine to five he decayed among the serried desks with their paper baskets and their telephones, and from five onwards there was the picture house, occasional women, and drink when there was money for it.

The store-room was a sort of paper tomb, with tiers of forms and documents in dusty bundles, which exhaled a musty odour. He found Ellis making tea. A paper-covered book had been flung to one side. On the cover he could make out the words *Selected Poems*, but not whose they were. He was handed a cup with a chocolate biscuit in the saucer.

'Sit down,' Ellis commanded.

Sweeney, surprised at the luxury of the chocolate biscuit, held it up and inspected it with raised eyebrows.

Ellis offered milk and sugar.

'I pinched them out of Miss Bouncing's drawers,' he said deliberately.

Sweeney, secure in the knowledge that the chief

clerk was already on his way across town, munched the biscuit contentedly and looked down into the street. It was filled with sunshine. Almost level with his eyes, the coloured flags on the roof of a cinema lay limp and unmoving, while down below three charwomen were scrubbing the entrance steps. He took another biscuit and heard Ellis saying conversationally, 'I suppose you're looking forward to your weekend in the country.'

The question dovetailed unnoticed in Sweeney's thought.

'I've been wanting to get back there since last autumn. I told you there was a girl. . . .'

'With curly eyes and bright blue hair.'

'Never mind her eyes and her hair. I've tried to get down to see her twice but it didn't come off. The first time you and I drank the money—the time Dacey got married. The second, I didn't get it saved in time. But I'm going today. I've just drawn the six quid out of Miss Bouncing's holiday club.'

'What bus are you getting?'

'The half past two. His nibs has gone off so I can slip out.'

'I see,' Ellis said pensively.

'I want you to sign me out at five.'

They had done things like that for one another before. Turning to face him, Ellis said, 'Is there a later bus?'

'Yes. At half-past eight. But why?'

'It's . . . well, it's a favour,' Ellis said uncertainly. With sinking heart Sweeney guessed at what was coming.

'Go on,' he invited reluctantly.

'I'm in trouble,' Ellis said. 'The old man was away this past two weeks and I hocked his typewriter. Now the sister's 'phoned me to tip me off he's coming home at half past two. They only got word after breakfast. If I don't slip out and redeem it there'll be stinking murder. You know the set-up at home.'

Sweeney did. He was aware that the Ellis household had its complications.

'I can give it back to you at six o'clock,' Ellis prompted.

'Did you try Higgins?' Sweeney suggested hopefully.

'He hasn't got it. He told me not to ask you but I'm desperate. There's none of the others I can ask.'

'How much do you need?'

'Four quid would do me—I have two.'

Sweeney took the four pound notes from his wallet and handed them over. They were fresh and stiff. Miss Bouncing had been to the bank. Ellis took them and said:

'You'll get this back. Honest. Byrne of the Prudential is to meet me in Slattery's at six. He owes me a fiver.'

Still looking at the limp flags on the opposite roof Sweeney suggested, 'Supposing he doesn't turn up.'

'Don't worry,' Ellis answered him. 'He will. He promised me on his bended knees.'

After a pause he diffidently added, 'I'm eternally grateful. . . .'

Sweeney saw the week-end he had been aching for receding like most of his other dreams into a realm of tantalizing uncertainty.

'Forget it,' he said.

II

Sweeney, who was standing at the public counter, looked up at the clock and found it was half past two.

Behind him many of the desks were empty. Some were at lunch, others were taking advantage of the chief clerk's absence. It only meant that telephones were left to ring longer than usual. To his right, defying the grime and the odd angles of the windows, a streak of sunlight slanted across the office and lit up about two square feet of the counter. Sweeney stretched his hand towards it and saw the sandy hairs on the back leap suddenly into gleaming points. He withdrew it shyly, hoping nobody had seen him. Then he forgot the office and thought instead of the country town, the square with its patriotic statue, the trees which lined it, the girl he had met on that autumn day while he was walking along through the woods. Sweeney had very little time for romantic notions about love and women. Seven years knocking about with Ellis and Higgins had convinced him that Romance, like good luck, was on the side of the rich. It preferred to ride around in motor-cars and flourished most where the drinks were short and expensive. But meeting this strange girl among the trees had disturbed him. Groping automatically for the plausible excuse, he had walked towards her with a pleasurable feeling of alertness and wariness.

'This path,' he said to her, 'does it lead me back to the town?' and waited with anxiety for the effect. He saw her assessing him quickly. Then she smiled.

'It does,' she said, 'provided you walk in the right direction.'

He pretended surprise. Then after a moment's hesitation he asked if he might walk back with her. He was staying in the town, he explained, and was still finding his way about. As they walked together he found out she was the town librarian, and later, when they had met two or three times and accepted one another, that she was bored to death with the town. He told her about being dissatisfied too, about the office and its futility, about having too little money. One evening when they were leaning across a bridge some distance from the town, it seemed appropriate to talk rather solemnly about life. The wind rippled the brown water which reflected the fading colours of the sky. He said:

'I think I could be happy here. It's slow and quiet. You don't break your neck getting somewhere and then sit down to read the paper when you've got there. You don't have twenty or thirty people ahead of you every morning and evening—all queuing to sign a clock.'

'You can be happy anywhere or bored anywhere. It depends on knowing what you want.'

'That's it,' he said, 'but how do you find out? I never have. I only know what I don't want.'

'Money—perhaps?'

'Not money really. Although it has its points. It doesn't make life any bigger though, does it? I mean look at most of the people who have it.'

'Dignity?' she suggested quietly.

The word startled him. He looked at her and found she was quite serious. He wondered if one searched hard enough, could something be found to be dignified about. He smiled.

'Do you mean an umbrella and a bowler hat?'

He knew that was not what she meant at all, but he wanted her to say more.

'No,' she said, 'I mean to have a conviction about something. About the work you do or the life you lead.'

'Have you?' he asked.

She was gazing very solemnly at the water, the breeze now and then lifting back the hair from her face.

273

'No,' she murmured. She said it almost to herself. He slipped his arm about her. When she made no resistance he kissed her.

'I'm wondering why I didn't do that before,' he said when they were finished.

'Do you . . . usually?' she asked.

He said earnestly, 'For a moment I was afraid.'

'Of me?'

'No. Afraid of spoiling everything. Have I?'

She smiled at him and shook her head.

At five they closed their ledgers and pushed in the buttons which locked the filing cabinets. One after the other they signed the clock which automatically stamped the time when they pulled the handle. The street outside was hardly less airless than the office, the pavements threw back the dust-smelling August heat. Sweeney, waiting for Higgins and Ellis at the first corner, felt the sun drawing a circle of sweat about his shirt collar and thought wistfully of green fields and roadside pubs. By now the half past two bus would have finished its journey. The other two joined him and they walked together by the river wall, picking their way through the evening crowds. The tea-hour rush was beginning. Sweeney found the heat and the noise of buses intolerable. A girl in a light cotton frock with long hair and prominent breasts brushed close to them. Higgins whistled and said earnestly, 'Honest to God, chaps. It's not fair. Not on a hot evening.'

'They're rubber,' Ellis offered with contempt.

'Rubber bedamned.'

'It's a fact,' Ellis insisted. 'I know her. She hangs them up on the bedpost at night.'

They talked knowledgeably and argumentatively

about falsies until they reached Slattery's lounge.
Then, while Ellis began to tell them in detail how he
had smuggled the typewriter back into his father's
study, Sweeney sat back with relief and tasted his
whiskey. A drink was always welcome after a day in
the office, even to hold the glass in his hand and lie
back against his chair gave him a feeling of escape.
Hope was never quite dead if he had money enough
for that. But this evening it wasn't quite the same. He
had hoped to have his first drink in some city pub on
his way to the bus, a quick drink while he changed
one of his new pound notes and savoured the adventure of the journey before him, a long ride with money
in his pocket along green-hedged roads, broken by
pleasant half hours in occasional country pubs. When
Higgins and Ellis had bought their rounds he called
again. Whenever the door of the lounge opened he
looked up hopefully. At last he indicated the clock
and said to Ellis, 'Your friend should be here.'

'Don't worry,' Ellis assured him, 'he's all right. He'll
turn up.' Then he lifted his drink and added, 'Well—
here's to the country.'

'The country,' Higgins sighed. 'Tomorrow to fresh
fiends and pastors new.'

'I hope so,' Sweeney said. He contrived to say it as
though it didn't really matter, but watching Ellis and
Higgins he saw they were both getting uneasy. In an
effort to keep things moving Higgins asked, 'What sort
of a place is it?'

'A square with a statue in it and trees,' Sweeney
said. 'A hotel that's fairly reasonable. Free fishing if
you get on the right side of the Guards. You wouldn't
think much of it.'

'No sea—no nice girls in bathing dresses. No big
hotel with its own band.'

275

'Samuel Higgins,' Ellis commented. 'The man who broke the bank at Monte Carlo.'

'I like a holiday to be a real holiday,' Higgins said stoutly. 'Stay up all night and sleep all day. I like sophistication, nice girls and smart hotels. Soft lights and glamour and sin. Lovely sin. It's worth saving for.'

'We must write it across the doorway of the office,' Sweeney said.

'What?'

'Sin Is Worth Saving For.'

It had occurred to him that it was what half of them did. They cut down on cigarettes and scrounged a few pounds for their Post Office Savings account or Miss Bouncing's Holiday Club so that they could spend a fortnight of the year in search of what they enthusiastically looked upon as sin. For him sin abounded in the dusty places of the office, in his sweat of fear when the morning clock told him he was late again, in the obsequious answer to the official question, in the impulse which reduced him to pawing the hot and willing typist who passed him on the deserted stairs.

'I don't have to save for sin,' he commented finally.

'Oh—I know,' Higgins said, misunderstanding him. 'The tennis club is all right. So are the golf links on Bank Holiday. But it's nicer where you're not known.'

'View Three,' Ellis interjected. 'Higgins the hen butcher.'

'Last year there was a terrific woman who got soft on me because I told her I was a commercial pilot. The rest of the chaps backed me up by calling me Captain Higgins. I could have had anything I wanted.'

'Didn't you?'

'Well,' Higgins said, in a tone which suggested it was a bit early in the night for the intimate details. 'More or less.' Then they consulted the clock again.

'It doesn't look as though our friend is coming,' Sweeney said.

'We'll give him 'til seven,' Ellis said. 'Then we'll try for him in Mulligan's or round in the Stag's Head.'

III

The girl watched the arrival of the bus from the entrance to the hotel. As the first passenger stepped off she smiled and moved forward. She hovered uncertainly. Some men went past her into the bar of the Commercial, the conductor took luggage from the top, the driver stepped down from his cabin and lit a cigarette. Townspeople came forward too, some with parcels to be delivered to the next town, some to take parcels sent to them from the city. He was not among the passengers who remained. The girl, aware of her new summer frock, her long white gloves, the unnecessary handbag, stepped back against the wall and bumped into the traveller.

'No boy friend,' he said.

She noticed he had shaved. His eyes were no longer bloodshot. But the sun emphasized the grey colour of his face with its sad wrinkles and its protruding upper lip. As the crowd dispersed he leaned up against the wall beside her.

'I had a sleep,' he said. 'Nothing like sleep. It knits up the ravelled sleeve of care. Who said that, I wonder?'

'Shakespeare,' she said.

'Of course,' he said, 'I might have guessed it was Shakespeare.'

'He said a lot of things.'

'More than his prayers,' the traveller conceded. Then he looked up at the sun and winced.

'God's sunlight,' he said unhappily. 'It hurts me.'

'Why don't you go in out of it?' she suggested coldly.

'I've orders to collect. I'm two days behind. Do you like the sun?'

'It depends.'

'Depends with me too. Depends on the night before. Mostly I like the shade. It's cool and it's easy on the eyes. Sleep and the shade. Did Shakespeare say anything about that, I wonder?'

'Not anything that occurs to me.' She wished to God he would go away.

'He should then,' the traveller insisted. 'What's Shakespeare for, if he didn't say anything about sleep and the shade?'

At another time she might have been sorry for him, for his protruding lip, his ashen face, the remote landscape of sorrow which lay behind his slow eyes. But she had her own disappointment. She wanted to go into some quiet place and weep. The sun was too strong and the noise of the awakened square too unsettling. 'Let's talk about Shakespeare some other time,' she suggested. He smiled sadly at the note of dismissal.

'It's a date,' he said. She saw him shuffling away under the cool trees.

When they left Slattery's they tried Mulligan's and in the Stag's Head Higgins said he could eat a farmer's arse, so they had sandwiches. The others had ham and beef but Sweeney took egg because it was Friday. There was a dogged streak of religion in him which was scrupulous about things like that. Even in his worst bouts of despair he still could observe the prescribed forms. They were precarious footholds which he hesitated to destroy and by which he might eventually drag himself out of the pit. After the Stag's Head Ellis thought of the Oval.

'It's one of his houses,' he said. 'We should have tried it before. What's the next bus?'

'Half eight.

'Is it the last?'

'The last and ultimate bus. Aston's Quay at half past eight. Let's forget about it.'

'It's only eight o'clock. We might make it.'

'You're spoiling my drink.'

'You're spoiling mine too,' Higgins said, 'all this fluting around.'

'You see. You're spoiling Higgins' drink too.'

'But I feel a louser about this.'

'Good,' Higgins said pleasantly. 'Ellis discovers the truth about himself.'

'Shut up,' Ellis said.

He dragged them across the city again.

The evening was cooler. Over the western reaches of the Liffey barred clouds made the sky alternate with streaks of blue and gold. Steeples and tall houses staggered upwards and caught the glowing colours. There was no sign of Byrne in the Oval. They had a drink while the clock moved round until it was twenty minutes to nine.

'I shouldn't have asked you,' Ellis said with genuine remorse.

'That's what I told you,' Higgins said. 'I told you not to ask him.'

'Byrne is an arch louser,' Ellis said bitterly. 'I never thought he'd let me down.'

'You should know Byrne by now,' Higgins said. 'He has medals for it.'

'But I was in trouble. And you both know the set-up

at home. Christ, if the old man found out about the typewriter. . . .'

'Look,' Sweeney said, 'the bus is gone. If I don't mind, why should you? Go and buy me a drink.' But they found they hadn't enough money left between them, so they went around to the Scotch House where Higgins knew the manager and could borrow a pound.

IV

Near the end of his holiday he had taken her to a big hotel at a seaside resort. It was twenty miles by road from the little town, but a world away in its sophistication. They both cycled. Dinner was late and the management liked to encourage dress. A long drive led up to the imposing entrance. They came to it cool and fresh from the sea, their wet swimming togs knotted about the handlebars. It was growing twilight and he could still remember the rustle of piled leaves under the wheels of their bicycles. A long stone balustrade rose from the gravelled terrace. There was an imposing ponderousness of stone and high turrets.

'Glenawling Castle,' he said admiringly. She let her eyes travel from the large and shiny cars to the flagmast some hundreds of feet up in the dusky air.

'Comrade Sweeney,' she breathed, 'cast your sweaty nightcap in the air.'

They walked on thick carpet across a foyer which smelled of rich cigar smoke. Dinner was a long, solemn ritual. They had two half bottles of wine, white for her, red for himself. When he had poured she looked at both gleaming glasses and said happily:

'Isn't it beautiful? I mean the colours.' He found her more astoundingly beautiful than either the gleaming red or the white.

'You are,' he said. 'Good God, you are.' She laughed happily at his intensity. At tables about them young people were in the minority. Glenawling Castle catered to a notable extent for the more elevated members of the hierarchy, Monsignors and Bishops who took a little time off from the affairs of the Church to play sober games of golf and drink discreet glasses of brandy. There were elderly business men with their wives, occasional and devastatingly bored daughters.

After dinner they walked in the grounds. The light had faded from the sky above them but far out to sea an afterflow remained. From the terrace they heard the sound of breakers on the beach below and could smell the strong, autumn smell of the sea. They listened for some time. He took her hand and said: 'Happy?'

She nodded and squeezed his fingers lightly.

'Are you?'

'No,' he said. 'I'm sad.'

'Why sad?'

'For the old Bishops and the Monsignors and the business men with their bridge-playing wives.'

They both laughed. Then she shivered suddenly in the cool breeze and they went inside again to explore further. They investigated a room in which elderly men played billiards in their shirt sleeves, and another in which the elderly women sat at cards. In a large lounge old ladies knitted, while in deep chairs an occasional Bishop read somnolently from a priestly book. Feeling young and a little bit out of place, they went into the bar which adjoined the ballroom. There were younger people here. He called for drinks and asked her why she frowned.

'This is expensive for you,' she said. She took a pound note from her bag and left it on the table.

'Let's spend this on the drinks,' she suggested.

'All of it?'

She nodded gravely. He grinned suddenly and gave it to the attendant.

'Pin that on your chest,' he said, 'and clock up the damage until it's gone.'

The attendant looked hard at the note. His disapproval was silent but unmistakable.

'It's a good one,' Sweeney assured him. 'I made it myself.'

They alternated between the ballroom and the bar. In the bar she laughed a lot at the things he said, but in the ballroom they danced more or less silently. They were dancing when he first acknowledged the thought which had been hovering between them.

'I've only two days left.'

'One, darling.'

'Tomorrow and Saturday.'

'It's tomorrow already,' she said, looking at her watch. Now that it was said it was unavoidably necessary to talk about it.

'It's only about two hours by bus,' he said. 'I can get down to see you sometimes. There'll be weekends.'

'You won't though,' she said sadly.

'Who's going to stop me?'

'You think you will now but you won't. A holiday is a holiday. It comes to an end and you go home and then you forget.'

They walked through the foyer which was deserted now. The elderly ladies had retired to bed, and so had the somnolent churchmen with their priestly books.

'I won't forget,' he said when they were once again on the terrace. 'I want you too much.'

The leaves rustled again under their wheels, the autumn air raced past their faces coldly.

'That's what I mean,' she said simply. 'It's bad wanting anything too much.' Her voice came anonymously from the darkness beside him.

'Why?' he asked.

Their cycle lamps were two bars of light in a vast tunnel of darkness. Sometimes a hedge gleamed green in the light or a tree arched over them with mighty and gesticulating limbs.

'Because you never get it,' she answered solemnly.

V

Sweeney, looking through the smoke from Higgins and Ellis to the heavily built man whom he did not like, frowned and tried to remember what public house he was in. They had been in so many and had drunk so much. He was at that stage of drunkenness where his thoughts required an immense tug of his will to keep them concentrated. Whenever he succumbed to the temptation to close his eyes he saw them wandering and grazing at a remote distance from him, small white sheep in a landscape of black hills and valleys. The evening had been a pursuit of something which he felt now he would never catch up with, a succession of calls on some mysterious person who had always left a minute before. It had been of some importance, whatever he had been chasing, but for the moment he had forgotten why. Taking the heavily built man whom he didn't like as a focal point, he gradually pieced together the surroundings until they assumed first a vague familiarity and then a positive identity. It was the Crystal. He relaxed, but not too much, for fear of the woolly annihilation that might follow, and found Higgins and the heavily built man swopping stories. He remembered that they had been swopping stories for a long time. The heavily built man was a friend of Higgins. He had an advertising agency and talked about the golf club and poker and his new car. He had two daughters—clever as hell. He knew the Variety Girls and had a fund of smutty stories. He told them several times they must come and meet the boys. 'Let's leave this hole,' he said several times, 'and I'll run you out to the golf club. No bother.' But someone began a new story. And besides, Sweeney didn't want to go. Every time he looked at the man with his neat suit and his moustache, his expensively fancy waistcoat and the pin in his tie, he was tempted to get up and walk away. But for Higgins' sake he remained and listened. Higgins was telling a story about a commercial traveller who married a hotel keeper's daughter in a small country town. The traveller had a protruding upper lip while the daughter, Higgins said, had a protruding lower lip. Like this, Higgins said. Then he said look here he couldn't tell the story if they wouldn't pay attention to him.

'This'll be good boys,' the man said, 'this will be rich. I think I know this one. Go on.'

But Higgins said hell no they must look at his face. It was a story and they had to watch his face or they'd miss the point.

'Christ no,' Ellis said, 'not your face.'

Sweeney silently echoed the remark, not because he really objected to Higgins' face but because it was difficult to focus it in one piece.

Well, Higgins said, they could all sugar off, he was going to tell the story and shag the lot of them.

'Now, now,' the man said, 'we're all friends here. No unpleasantness and no bickering, what?'

'Well,' Higgins continued, 'the father of the bride had a mouth which twisted to the left and the mother's mouth, funny enough, twisted to the right. So on the bridal night the pair went to bed in the hotel which, of course, was a very small place, and when the time came to get down to certain important carry-on, the nature of which would readily suggest itself to the assembled company; no need to elaborate, the commercial traveller tried to blow out the candle. He held it level with his mouth but, of course, on account of the protruding upper lip his breath went down in the direction of his chin and the candle remained lit.' Higgins stuck out his lip and demonstrated for their benefit the traveller's peculiar difficulty. '"Alice," said the traveller to his bride, "I'll have to ask you to do this." So her nibs had a go and, of course, with the protruding lower lip, her breath went up towards her nose, and lo and behold the candle was still lighting.' Again Higgins demonstrated. '"There's nothing for it, John, but call my father," says she. So the oul' fella is summoned and he has a go. But with his lips twisted to the left the breath goes back over his shoulder and the candle is still lighting away. "Dammit, this has me bet," says the father, "I'll have to call your mother," and after a passable delay the oul' wan appears on the scene but, of course, same thing happens, her breath goes out over her right shoulder this time, and there the four of them stand in their nightshirts looking at the candle and wondering what the hell will they do next. So they send out for the schoolmaster, and the schoolmaster comes in and they explain their difficulty and ask him for his assistance and "certainly," he says, "it's a great pleasure." And with that he wets his finger and thumb and pinches the wick and, of course, the candle goes out.' Higgins wet his finger and thumb and demonstrated on an imaginary candle. 'Then the father looks at the other three and shakes his head. "Begod," says he, "did youse ever see the likes of that, isn't education a wonderful thing?"' The heavily built man guffawed and asserted immediately that he could cap that. It was a story about a commercial traveller too. But as he was about to start they began to call closing time and he said again that they must all come out to the golf club and meet the boys.

'Really,' he said, 'you'll enjoy the boys. I'll run you out in the car.'

'Who's game?' Higgins asked.

Ellis looked at Sweeney and waited. Sweeney looked at the heavily built man and decided he didn't dislike him after all. He hated him.

'Not me,' he said, 'I don't want any shagging golf clubs.'

'I don't care for your friend's tone,' the man began, his face reddening.

'And I don't like new cars,' Sweeney interrupted, rising to his feet.

'Look here,' the heavily built man said threateningly. Ellis and Higgins asked the stout man not to mind him.

'Especially new cars driven by fat bastards with fancy waistcoats,' Sweeney insisted. He saw Ellis and Higgins moving in between him and the other man. They looked surprised and that annoyed him further. But to hit him, he would have had to push his way through them and it would take so much effort that he decided it was hardly worth it after all. So he changed his mind. But he turned around as he went out.

'With fancy pins in their ties,' he concluded. People moved out of his way.

They picked him up twenty minutes later at the corner. He was gazing into the window of a tobacconist shop. He was wondering now why he had behaved like that. He had a desire to lean his forehead against the glass. It looked so cool. There was a lonely ache inside him. He barely looked round at them.

'You got back quick,' Sweeney said.

'Oh cut it out,' Ellis said, 'you know we wouldn't go without you.'

'I hate fat bastards with fancy pins,' Sweeney explained. But he was beginning to feel it was a bit inadequate.

'After all,' Higgins said, 'he was a friend of mine. You might have thought of that.'

'Sugar you and your friends.'

Higgins flushed and said, 'Thanks, I'll remember that.'

Pain gathered like a ball inside Sweeney and he said with intensity, 'You can remember what you sugaring well like.'

'Look,' Ellis said, 'cut it out—the pair of you.'

'He insulted my friend.'

'View four,' Ellis said, 'Higgins the Imperious.'

'And I'll be obliged if you'll cut out this View two View three View four stuff. . . .'

'Come on,' Ellis said wearily, 'kiss and make up. What we all need is another drink.'

It seemed a sensible suggestion. They addressed themselves to the delicate business of figuring out the most likely speak-easy.

VI

The last bus stayed for twenty minutes or so and then chugged out towards remoter hamlets and lonelier roads, leaving the square full of shadows in the August evening, dark under the trees, grey in the open spaces about the statue. The air felt thick and warm, the darkness of the sky was relieved here and there with yellow and green patches. To the girl there was a strange finality about the departure of the bus, as though all the inhabitants had boarded it on some impulse which would leave the square empty for ever. She decided to have coffee, not in the Commercial where Cissy was bound to ask questions, but in the more formal atmosphere of the Imperial. She had hoped to be alone, and frowned when she met the traveller in the hallway. He said:

'Well, well. Now we can have our chat about Shakespeare.' She noticed something she had not observed earlier—a small piece of newspaper stuck on the side of his cheek where he had cut himself shaving. For some reason it made her want to laugh. She could see too that he was quite prepared to be rebuffed and guessed his philosophy about such things. Resignation and defeat were his familiars.

'I see you've changed your location,' she said, in a voice which indicated how little it mattered.

'So have you.'

'I was going to have coffee.

'We can't talk Shakespeare over coffee,' he invited. 'Have a drink with me instead.'

'I wonder should I. I really don't know you,' she answered coolly.

'If it comes to that,' he said philosophically, 'who does?'

They went into the lounge. The lounge in the Imperial paid attention to contemporary ideas. There were tubular tables and chairs, a half moon of a bar with tube lighting which provided plenty of colour but not enough light. The drink was a little dearer, the beer, on such evenings in August, a little too warm. He raised his glass to her.

'I'm sorry about the boy friend,' he said. She put down her glass deliberately.

'I'd rather you didn't say things like that,' she said. 'It's not particularly entertaining. I'm not Cissy from the Commercial, you know.'

'Sorry,' he said repentantly, 'I meant no harm. It was just for talk's sake.'

'Then let's talk about you. Did you pick up your two days' orders?'

'No,' he said sadly, 'I'm afraid I didn't. I'm afraid I'm not much of a commercial traveller. I'm really a potter.'

'Potter?'

'Yes. I potter around from this place to that.'

She noticed the heavy upper lip quivering and gathered that he was laughing. Then he said:

'That's a little joke I've used hundreds of times. It amuses me because I made it up myself.'

'Do you often do that?'

'I try, but I'm not much good at it. I thought of that one, God knows how many years ago, when things began to slip and I was in bed in the dark in some little room in some cheap hotel. Do you ever feel frightened in a strange room?'

'I'm not often in strange rooms.'

'I am. All my life I've been. When I put out the light I can never remember where the door is. I suppose that's what makes me a pretty poor specimen of a traveller.'

'So you thought of a joke.'

'Yes.'

'But why?'

'It helps. Sometimes when you feel like that a joke has more comfort than a prayer.'

She saw what he meant and felt some surprise.

'Well,' she prompted. 'Why do you travel?'

'It was my father's profession too. He was one of the old stock. A bit stiff and ceremonious. And respected of course. In those days they didn't have to shoot a line. They had dignity. First they left their umbrella and hat in the hall stand. Then there was some polite conversation. A piece of information from the city. A glass of sherry and a biscuit. Now you've got to talk like hell and drive like hell. I suppose he trained me the wrong way.'

He indicated her glass.

'You'll have another?' he asked.

She looked again at his face and made her decision. She was not quite sure what it would involve, but she knew it was necessary to her to see it out.

'I think I will,' she said.

He asked her if she liked her work but she was not anxious to discuss herself at all. She admitted she was bored. After their third drink he asked her if she would care to drive out with him to Glenawling Castle. There were not likely to be people there who knew them and besides, there would be dancing. She hesitated.

'I know what you're thinking,' he said, 'but you needn't worry. I'm no he-man.' She thought it funny that that was not what had occurred to her at all. Then he smiled and added:

'With this lip of mine I don't get much opportunity to practice.'

They got into the car which took them up the hill

from the square and over the stone bridge with its brown stream. The traveller looked around at her.

'You're a pretty girl,' he said warmly, 'prettiest I've met.'

She said coolly, 'Prettier than your wife?'

'My wife is dead.'

She glanced involuntarily at the black tie.

'Yes,' he said, 'a month ago.' He waited. 'Does that shock you?' he asked.

'I'm afraid it does.'

'It needn't,' he said. 'We were married for eighteen years, and for fifteen of that she was in a lunatic asylum. I didn't visit her this past eight or nine years. They said it was better. I haven't danced for years either. Do you think I shouldn't?'

'No,' she said after a pause. 'I think it might do you good. You might get over being afraid of strange rooms.'

'At forty-five?' he asked quietly.

His question kept the girl silent. She looked out at the light racing along the hedges, the gleaming leaves, the arching of trees.

VII

They eventually got into Annie's place. It was one of a row of tall and tottering Georgian houses. Ellis knew the right knock and was regarded with professional affection by the ex-boxer who kept the door. They went in the dark up a rickety stairs to a room which was full of cigarette smoke. They had to drink out of cups, since the girls and not the liquor were the nominal attraction. There was some vague tradition that Annie was entitled to serve meals too, but to ask for one was to run the risk of being thrown out by the ex-boxer. The smell of the whiskey in his cup made

Sweeney shiver. He had had whiskey early in the evening and after it plenty of beer. Experience had taught him that taking whiskey at this stage was a grave mistake. But no long drinks were available and one had to drink. Ellis noted his silence.

'How are you feeling?' he asked with friendly solicitude.

'Like the Chinese maiden?' Higgins suggested amiably and tickled the plump girl who was sitting on his knee.

'No,' Sweeney said, 'like the cockle man.'

'I know,' Higgins said. 'Like the cockle man when the tide came in. We all appreciate the position of that most unfortunate gentleman.' He tickled the plump girl again. 'Don't we, Maisie?'

Maisie, who belonged to the establishment, giggled.

'You're a terrible hard root,' she said admiringly.

There were about a dozen customers in the place. One group had unearthed an old-fashioned gramophone complete with sound horn and were trying out the records. They quarrelled about whose turn it was to wind it and laughed uproariously at the thin nasal voices and the age of the records. Sweeney was noted to be morose and again Ellis had an attack of conscience.

'I feel a louser,' Ellis said.

'Look,' Sweeney said, 'I told you to forget it.'

'Only for me you could be down the country by now.'

'Only for me you could be out at the golf club,' Sweeney said, 'drinking with the best spivs in the country. You might even have got in the way of marrying one of their daughters.'

The gramophone was asking a trumpeter what he was sounding now.

'God,' Maisie said, 'my grandfather used to sing that. At a party or when he'd a few jars aboard. I can just see him.'

'My God. Where?' Higgins asked in mock alarm.

'In my head—Smarty,' Maisie said. 'I can see him as if it was yesterday. Trumpet-eer what are yew sounding now—Is it the cawl I'm seeking?'

They looked in amazement at Maisie who had burst so suddenly into song. She stopped just as suddenly and gave a sigh of warm and genuine affection. 'It has hairs on it right enough—that thing,' she commented.

'What thing?' Higgins inquired salaciously and was rewarded with another giggle and a playful slap from Maisie.

'Maisie darling,' Ellis appealed, 'will you take Higgins away to some quiet place?'

'Yes,' Sweeney said. 'Bury his head in your bosom.' Maisie laughed and said to Higgins, 'Come on, sweetheart. I want to ask them to put that thing on the gramophone again.' As they went away the thought struck Sweeney that Mary Magdalene might have looked and talked like that and he remembered something which Ellis had quoted to him earlier in the week. He waited for a lull among the gramophone-playing group and leaned forward. He said, groping vaguely:

'Last week you quoted me something, a thing about the baptism of Christ . . . I mean a poem about a painting of the baptism of Christ . . . do you remember what I mean?'

'I think I do,' Ellis said. Then quickly and without punctuation he began to rattle off a verse. 'A painter of the Umbrian School Designed upon a gesso ground The nimbus of the baptised God The wilderness is cracked and browned.'

'That's it,' Sweeney said. 'Go on.'

Ellis looked surprised. But when he found Sweeney was not trying to make a fool of him he clasped the cup tightly with both hands and leaned across the table. He moved it rhythmically in a small wet circle and repeated the previous verse. Then he continued with half-closed eyes.

> But through the waters pale and thin
> Still shine the unoffending feet . . .

'The unoffending feet,' Sweeney repeated, almost to himself. 'That's what I wanted. Christ—that's beautiful.'

But the gramophone rasped out again and the moment of quietness and awareness inside him was shattered to bits. Higgins came with three cups which he left down with a bang on the table.

'Refreshment,' he said, 'Annie's own. At much personal inconvenience.'

Sweeney looked up at him. He had been on the point of touching something and it had been knocked violently away from him. That always happened. The cups and the dirty tables, the people drunk about the gramophone, the girls and the cigarette smoke and the laughter seemed to twist and tangle themselves into a spinning globe which shot forward and shattered about him. A new record whirled raspingly on the gramophone for a moment before a tinny voice gave out the next song.

> Have you got another girl at home
> Like Susie,
> Just another little girl upon the family tree?
> If you've got another girl at home
> Like Susie . . .

But the voice suddenly lost heartiness and pitch and dwindled into a lugubrious grovelling in the bass.

'Somebody wind the bloody thing,' Ellis screamed. Somebody did so without bothering to lift off the pick-up arm. The voice was propelled into a nerve-jarring ascent from chaos to pitch and brightness. Once again the composite globe spun towards him. Sweeney held his head in his hands and groaned. When he closed his eyes he was locked in a smelling cellar with vermin and excrement on the floor, a cellar in which he groped and slithered. Nausea tautened his stomach and sent the saliva churning in his mouth. He rose unsteadily.

'What is it?' Ellis asked.

'Sick,' he mumbled. 'Filthy sick.'

They left Higgins behind and went down into the street. Tenements with wide open doors yawned a decayed and malodorous breath, and around the corner the river between grimy walls was burdened with the incoming tide. Sweeney leaned over the wall.

'Go ahead,' Ellis said.

'I can't.'

Stick your fingers down your throat.'

Sweeney did so and puked. He trembled. Another spasm gripped him. Ellis, who was holding him, saw a gull swimming over to investigate this new offering.

'It's an ill wind . . .' he said aloud.

'What's that?' Sweeney asked miserably, his elbows still on the wall, his forehead cupped in his hands.

'Nothing,' Ellis said. He smiled quietly and looked up at the moon.

VIII

'Do you mind if I ask you something?' the girl said. 'It's about your wife.'

'Fire ahead,' the traveller said gently.

They stood on the terrace in front of the hotel. Below them the sea was calm and motionless, but from behind them where the large and illuminated windows broke the blackened brick of the castle the sounds of the band came thinly.

'You haven't seen her for eight or nine years.'

'Fifteen,' the traveller corrected. 'You needn't count the few visits between.'

The girl formulated her next question carefully.

'When you married her,' the girl asked, 'did you love her?' The traveller's face was still moist after the dancing. She saw the small drops of sweat on his forehead while he frowned at the effort to recall the emotion of eighteen years before.

'I don't know,' he answered finally. 'It's funny. I can't exactly remember.'

The girl looked down at the pebbles. She poked them gently with her shoe.

'I see,' she said softly.

He took her hand. Then they both stood silently and watched the moon.

It rode in brilliance through the August sky. It glinted on the pebbled terrace. It stole through curtain chinks into the bedrooms of the sleeping Monsignors and Bishops, it lay in brilliant barrenness on the pillows of stiff elderly ladies who had no longer anything to dream about. Sweeney, recovering, found Ellis still gazing up at it, and joined him. It was high and radiant in the clear windy spaces of the sky. It was round and pure and white.

'*Corpus Domini Nostri*,' Sweeney murmured.

Ellis straightened and dropped his cigarette end into the water below.

'Like an aspirin,' he said, 'like a bloody big aspirin.'

Summer Night

ELIZABETH BOWEN

(1899–1973)

As the sun set its light slowly melted the landscape,
till everything was made of fire and glass. Released
from the glare of noon, the haycocks now seemed to
float on the aftergrass: their freshness penetrated the
air. In the not far distance hills with woods up their
flanks lay in light like hills in another world—it would
be a pleasure of heaven to stand up there, where no
foot ever seemed to have trodden, on the spaces between the woods soft as powder dusted over with gold.
Against those hills, the burning red rambler roses in
cottage gardens along the roadside looked earthy—
they were too near the eye.

The road was in Ireland. The light, the air from the
distance, the air of evening rushed transversely through
the open sides of the car. The rims of the hood flapped,
the hood's metal frame rattled as the tourer, in great
bounds of speed, held the road's darkening magnetic
centre streak. The big shabby family car was empty
but for its small driver—its emptiness seemed to levi-
tate it—on its back seat a coat slithered about, and a
dressing-case bumped against the seat. The driver did
not relax her excited touch on the wheel: now and
then while she drove she turned one wrist over, to
bring the watch worn on it into view, and she gave the
mileage marked on the yellow signposts a flying,
jealous, half-inadvertent look. She was driving parallel
with the sunset: the sun slowly went down on her right
hand.

The hills flowed round till they lay ahead. Where

the road bent for its upward course through the pass she pulled up and lighted a cigarette. With a snatch she untwisted her turban; she shook her hair free and threw the scarf behind her into the back seat. The draught of the pass combed her hair into coarse strands as the car hummed up in second gear. Behind one brilliantly-outlined crest the sun had now quite gone; on the steeps of bracken, in the electric shadow, each frond stood out and climbing goats turned their heads. The car came up on a lorry, to hang on its tail, impatient, checked by turns of the road. At the first stretch the driver smote her palm on the horn and shot past and shot on ahead again.

The small woman drove with her chin up. Her existence was in her hands on the wheel and in the sole of the foot in which she felt through the sandal, the throbbing pressure of the accelerator. Her face, enlarged by blown-back hair, was as overbearingly blank as the face of a figure-head; her black eyebrows were ruled level, and her eyes, pupils dilated, did little more than reflect the slow burn of daylight along horizons, the luminous shades of the half-dark.

Clear of the pass, approaching the county town, the road widened and straightened between stone walls and burnished, showering beech. The walls broke up into gateways and hoardings and the suburbs began. People in modern building estate gardens let the car in a hurry through their unseeing look. The raised footpaths had margins of grass. White and grey rows of cottages under the pavement level let woodsmoke over their half-doors: women and old men sat outside the doors on boxes, looking down at their knees; here and there a bird sprang in a cage tacked to a wall. Children chasing balls over the roadway shot whooping right and left of the car. The refreshed town, unfolding streets to its centre, at this hour slowly heightened, cooled; streets and stones threw off a grey-pink glare, sultry lasting ghost of the high noon. In this dayless glare the girls in bright dresses, strolling, looked like colour-photography.

Dark behind all the windows: not a light yet. The in-going perspective looked meaning, noble and wide. But everybody was elsewhere—the polished street was empty but cars packed both the kerbs under the trees. What was going on? The big tourer dribbled, slipped with animal nervousness between the static, locked cars each side of its way. The driver peered left and right with her face narrow, glanced from her wrist-watch to the clock in the tower, sucked her lip, manœuvred for somewhere to pull in. The A.A. sign of the hotel hung out from under a balcony, over the steps. She edged in to where it said *Do Not Park*.

At the end of the hotel hall one electric light from the bar shone through a high-up panel: its yellow sifted on to the dusty dusk and a moth could be seen on the glass pane. At the door end came in street daylight, to fall weakly on prints on the oiled walls, on the magenta announcement-strip of a cinema, on the mahogany bench near the receptionist's office, on the hat-stand with two forgotten hats. The woman who had come breathlessly up the steps felt in her face a wall of indifference. The impetuous click of her heeled sandals on the linoleum brought no one to the receptionist's desk, and the drone of two talkers in the bar behind the glass panel seemed, like the light, to be blotted up, word by word. The little woman attacked the desk with her knuckles. 'Is there nobody there— I say? Is there nobody *there*?'

'I am, I am. Wait now,' said the hotel woman, who came impassively through the door from the bar. She reached up a hand and fumbled the desk light on, and by this with unwondering negligence studied the customer—the childish, blown little woman with wing-like eyebrows and eyes still unfocused after the long road. The hotel woman, bust on the desk, looked down slowly at the bare legs, the crumple-hemmed linen coat. 'Can I do anything for you?' she said, when she had done.

'I want the telephone—want to put through a call!'

'You can of course,' said the unmoved hotel woman. 'Why not?' she added after consideration, handing across the keys of the telephone cabinet. The little woman made a slide for the cabinet: with her mouth to the mouthpiece, like a conspirator, she was urgently putting her number through. She came out then and ordered herself a drink.

'Is it long distance?'

'Mm-mm. . . . What's on here? What are all those cars?'

'Oh, this evening's the dog racing.

'Is it?'

'Yes, it's the dog racing. We'd a crowd in here, but they're all gone on now.'

'I wondered who they were,' said the little woman, her eyes on the cabinet, sippeting at her drink.

'Yes, they're at the dog racing. There's a wonderful crowd. But I wouldn't care for it,' said the hotel woman, fastidiously puckering up her forehead. 'I went the one time, but it didn't fascinate me.'

The other forgot to answer. She turned away with her drink, sat down, put the glass beside her on the mahogany bench and began to chafe the calves of her bare legs as though they were stiff or cold. A man clasping sheets of unfurled newspaper pushed his way with his elbow through the door from the bar. 'What it says here,' he said, shaking the paper with both hands, 'is identically what I've been telling you.'

'That proves nothing,' said the hotel woman. 'However, let it out of your hand.' She drew the sheets of the paper from him and began to fold them into a wad. Her eyes moved like beetles over a top line. 'That's an awful battle . . .'

'What battle?' exclaimed the little woman, stopping rubbing her legs but not looking up.

'An awful air battle. Destroying each other,' the woman added, with a stern and yet voluptuous sigh. 'Listen, would you like to wait in the lounge?'

'She'd be better there,' put in the man who had brought the paper. 'Better accommodation.' His eyes watered slightly in the electric light. The little woman, sitting upright abruptly, looked defiantly, as though for the first time, at the two watching her from the desk. 'Mr. Donovan has great opinions,' said the hotel woman. 'Will you move yourself out of here?' she asked Mr. Donovan. 'This is very confined—*There's* your call, now!'

But the stranger had packed herself into the telephone box like a conjuror's lady preparing to disappear. '*Hullo?*' she was saying. 'Hullo! I want to speak to—'

'—You are,' the other voice cut in. 'All right? Anything wrong?'

Her face flushed all over. 'You sound nearer already! I've got to C—.'

The easy, calm voice said: 'Then you're coming along well.'

'Glad, are you?' she said, in a quiver.

'Don't take it too fast,' he said. 'It's a treacherous light. Be easy, there's a good girl.'

'You're a fine impatient man.' His end of the line

was silent. She went on: 'I might stay here and go to the dog racing.'

'Oh, is that tonight?' He went on to say equably (having stopped, as she saw it, and shaken the ash off the tip of his cigarette), 'No, I shouldn't do that.'

'Darling. . . .'

'Emma. . . . How is the Major?'

'He's all right,' she said, rather defensively.

'I see,' he said. 'Everything quite O.K.?'

'In an hour, I'll be . . . where you live.'

'First gate on the left. Don't kill yourself, there's a good girl. Nothing's worth that. Remember we've got the night. By the way, where are you talking?'

'From the hotel.' She nursed the receiver up close to her face and made a sound into it. Cutting that off she said: 'Well, I'll hang up. I just . . .'

'Right,' he said—and hung up.

Robinson, having hung up the receiver, walked back from the hall to the living-room where his two guests were. He still wore a smile. The deaf woman at the table by the window was pouring herself out another cup of tea. 'That will be very cold!' Robinson shouted—but she only replaced the cosy with a mysterious smile. 'Let her be,' said her brother. 'Let her alone!'

The room in this uphill house was still light: through the open window came in a smell of stocks from the flower beds in the lawn. The only darkness lay in a belt of beech trees at the other side of the main road. From the grate, from the coal of an unlit fire came the fume of a cigarette burning itself out. Robinson still could not help smiling: he reclaimed his glass from the mantelpiece and slumped back with it into his leather arm-chair in one of his loose, heavy, good-natured attitudes. But Justin Cavey, in the arm-chair opposite, still looked crucified at having the talk torn. 'Beastly,' he said, 'you've a beastly telephone.' Though he was in Robinson's house for the first time, his sense of attraction to people was marked, early, by just this intransigence and this fretfulness.

'It is and it's not,' said Robinson. That was that. 'Where had we got to?' he amiably asked.

The deaf woman, turning round from the window, gave the two men, or gave the air between them, a penetrating smile. Her brother, with a sort of lurch at his pocket, pulled out a new packet of cigarettes: ignoring Robinson's held-out cigarette case he frowned and split the cellophane with his thumbnail. But, as though his sister had put a hand on his shoulder, his tension could be almost seen to relax. The impersonal, patient look of the thinker appeared in his eyes, behind the spectacles. Justin was a city man, a black-coat, down here (where his sister lived) on holiday. Other summer holidays before this he had travelled in France, Germany, Italy: he disliked the chaotic 'scenery' of his own land. He was down here with Queenie this summer only because of the war, which had locked him in: duty seemed to him better than failed pleasure. His father had been a doctor in this place; now his sister lived on in two rooms in the square—for fear Justin should not be comfortable she had taken a room for him at the hotel. His holiday with his sister, his holiday in this underwater, weedy region of memory, his holiday on which, almost every day, he had to pass the doors of their old home, threatened Justin with a pressure he could not bear. He had to share with Queenie, as he shared the dolls' house meals cooked on the oil stove behind her sitting-room screen, the solitary and almost fairylike world created by her deafness. Her deafness broke down his only defence, talk. He was exposed to the odd, immune, plumbing looks she was for ever passing over his face. He could not deflect the tilted blue of her eyes. The things she said out of nowhere, things with no surface context, were never quite off the mark. She was not all solicitude; she loved to be teasing him.

In her middle-age Queenie was very pretty: her pointed face had the colouring of an imperceptibly fading pink-and-white sweet-pea. This hot summer her artless dresses, with their little lace collars, were mottled over with flowers, mauve and blue. Up the glaring main street she carried a *poult-de-soie* parasol. Her rather dark first-floor rooms faced north, over the square with its grass and lime trees: the crests of great mountains showed above the opposite façades. She would slip in and out on her own errands, as calm as a cat, and Justin, waiting for her at one of her windows, would see her cross the square in the noon sunshine with hands laced over her forehead into a sort of porch. The little town, though strung on a through road, was an outpost under the mountains: in its quick-talking, bitter society she enjoyed, to a degree that surprised Justin, her privileged place. She was woman enough to like to take the man Justin round with her and display him; they went out to afternoon or to evening tea, and in those drawing-rooms of tinted lace and intently-staring family photographs, among octagonal tables and painted cushions, Queenie, with her cotton gloves in her lap, well knew how to contribute, while Justin talked, her airy, brilliant, secretive smiling and looking on. For his part, he was man enough to respond to being shown off—besides, he was eased by these breaks in their *tête-a-tête*. Above all, he was glad, for these hours or two of chatter, not to have to face the screen of his own mind, on which the distortion of every one of his images, the war-broken towers of Europe, constantly stood. The immolation of what had been his own intensely had been made, he could only feel, without any choice of his. In the heart of the neutral Irishman indirect suffering pulled like a crooked knife. So he acquiesced to, and devoured, society: among the doctors, the solicitors, the auctioneers, the bank people of this little town he renewed old acquaintanceships and developed new. He was content to bloom, for this settled number of weeks— so unlike was this to his monkish life in the city—in a sort of tenebrous popularity. He attempted to check his solitary arrogance. His celibacy and his studentish manner could still, although he was past forty, make him acceptable as a young man. In the mornings he read late in his hotel bed; he got up to take his solitary walks; he returned to flick at his black shoes with Queenie's duster and set off with Queenie on their tea-table rounds. They had been introduced to Robinson, factory manager, in the hall of the house of the secretary of the tennis club.

Robinson did not frequent drawing-rooms. He had come here only three years ago, and had at first been taken to be a bachelor—he was a married man living apart from his wife. The resentment occasioned by this discovery had been aggravated by Robinson's not noticing it: he worked at very high pressure in his factory office, and in his off times his high-powered car was to be seen streaking too gaily out of the town. When he was met, his imperturbable male personality stood out to the women unpleasingly, and stood out most of all in that married society in which women aspire to break the male in a man. Husbands slipped him in for a drink when they were alone, or shut themselves up with him in the dining-room. Justin had already sighted him in the hotel bar. When Robinson showed up, late, at the tennis club, his manner with women was easy and teasing, but abstract and perfectly automatic. From this had probably come the legend that he liked women 'only in one way'. From the first time Justin encountered Robinson, he had felt a sort of anxious, disturbed attraction to the big, fair, smiling, offhand, cold-minded man. He felt impelled by Robinson's unmoved physical presence into all sorts of aberrations of talk and mind; he committed, like someone waving an anxious flag, all sorts of absurdities, as though this type of creature had been a woman; his talk became exaggeratedly cerebral, and he became prone, like a perverse person in love, to expose all his own piques, crotchets, and weaknesses. One night in the hotel bar with Robinson he had talked until he burst into tears. Robinson had on him the touch of some foreign sun. The acquaintanceship —it could not be called more—was no more than an accident of this narrowed summer. For Justin it had taken the place of travel. The two men were so far off each other's beat that in a city they would certainly not have met.

Asked to drop in some evening or any evening, the Caveys had tonight taken Robinson at his word. Tonight, the night of the first visit, Justin's high, rather bleak forehead had flushed from the moment he rang the bell. With Queenie behind his shoulder, in muslin, he had flinched confronting the housekeeper. Queenie, like the rest of the town ladies, had done no more till now than go by Robinson's gate.

For her part, Queenie showed herself happy to penetrate into what she had called 'the china house'. On its knoll over the main road, just outside the town,

Bellevue did look like china up on a mantelpiece
—it was a compact, stucco house with mouldings,
recently painted a light blue. From the lawn set with
pampas and crescent-shaped flower-beds the hum of
Robinson's motor mower passed in summer over the
sleepy town. And when winter denuded the trees
round them the polished windows, glass porch, and
empty conservatory sent out, on mornings of frosty
sunshine, a rather mischievous and uncaring flash.
The almost sensuous cleanness of his dwelling was
reproduced in the person of Robinson—about his ears,
jaw, collar, and close-clipped nails. The approach the
Caveys had walked up showed the broad, decided
tyre-prints of his car.

'Where had we got to?' Robinson said again.

'I was saying we should have to find a new form.'

'Of course you were,' agreed Robinson. 'That was
it.' He nodded over the top of Justin's head.

'A new form of thinking and feeling . . .'

'But one thinks what one happens to think, or feels
what one happens to feel. That is as just so happens—
I should have thought. One either does or one doesn't?'

'One doesn't!' cried Justin. 'That's what I've been
getting at. For some time we have neither thought
nor felt. Our faculties have slowed down without our
knowing—they had stopped without our knowing!
We know now. Now that there's enough death to
challenge being alive we're facing it that, anyhow, we
don't live. We're confronted by the impossibility *of*
living—unless we can break through to something
else. There's been a stop in our senses and in our
faculties that's made everything round us so much
dead matter—and dead matter we couldn't even dis-
place. We can no longer express ourselves: what
we say doesn't even approximate to reality; it only

approximates to what's been said. I say, this war's an awful illumination; it's destroyed our dark; we have to see where we are. Immobilized, God help us, and each so far apart that we can't even try to signal each other. And our currency's worthless—our "ideas", so on, so on. We've got to mint a new one. We've got to break through to the new form—it needs genius. We're precipitated, this moment, between genius and death. I tell you, we must have genius to live at all.'

'I am certainly dished, then,' said Robinson. He got up and looked for Justin's empty glass and took it to the sideboard where the decanters were.

'We have it!' cried Justin, smiting the arm of his chair. 'I salute your genius, Robinson, but I mistrust my own.'

'That's very nice of you,' said Robinson. 'I agree with you that this war makes one think. I was in the last, but I don't remember thinking: I suppose possibly one had no time. Of course, these days in business one comes up against this war the whole way through. And to tell you the truth,' said Robinson, turning round, 'I do like my off times to *be* my off times, because with this and then that they are precious few. So I don't really think as much as I might— though I see how one might always begin. You don't think thinking gets one a bit rattled?'

'I don't think!' said Justin violently.

'Well, you should know,' said Robinson, looking at his thumbnail. 'I should have thought you did. From the way you talk.'

'I couldn't think if I wanted: I've lost my motivation. I taste the dust in the street and I smell the limes in the square and I beat round inside this beastly shell of the past among images that all the more torment me as they lose any sense that they had. As for feeling—'

'You don't think you find it a bit slow here? Mind you, I haven't a word against this place but it's not a place I'd choose for an off time—'

'—My dear Robinson,' Justin said, in a mincing, schoolmasterish tone, 'you seem blind to our exquisite sociabilities.'

'Pack of old cats,' said Robinson amiably.

'You suggest I should get away for a bit of fun?'

'Well, I did mean that.'

'I find my own fun,' said Justin, 'I'm torn, here, by every single pang of annihilation. But that's what I look for; that's what I want completed; that's the whole of what I want to embrace. On the far side of the nothing—my new form. Scrap "me"; scrap my wretched identity and you'll bring to the open some bud of life. I *not* "I"—I'd be the world. . . . You're right: what you would call thinking does get me rattled. I only what you call think to excite myself. Take myself away, and I'd *think*. I might see; I might feel purely; I might even love—'

'Fine,' agreed Robinson, not quite easy. He paused and seemed to regard what Justin had just said—at the same time, he threw a glance of perceptible calculation at the electric clock on the mantelpiece. Justin halted and said: 'You give me too much to drink.'

'You feel this war may improve us?' said Robinson.

'What's love like?' Justin said suddenly.

Robinson paused for just less than a second in the act of lighting a cigarette. He uttered a shortish, temporizing and, for him, unnaturally loud laugh.

Queenie felt the vibration and turned round, withdrawing her arm from the window-sill. She had been looking intently, between the clumps of pampas, down the lawn to the road: cyclists and walkers on their way into town kept passing Robinson's open gate. Across the road, above the demesne wall, the dark beeches let through glitters of sky, and the colour and scent of the mown lawn and the flowers seemed, by some increase of evening, lifted up to the senses as though a new current flowed underneath. Queenie saw with joy in her own mind what she could not from her place in the window see—the blue china house, with all its reflecting windows, perched on its knoll in the brilliant, fading air. They are too rare—visions of where we are.

When the shock of the laugh made her turn round, she still saw day in Robinson's picture-frames and on the chromium fingers of the clock. She looked at Robinson's head, dropped back after the laugh on the leather scroll of his chair: her eyes went from him to Justin. 'Did you two not hit it off?'

Robinson laughed again, this time much more naturally: he emitted a sound like that from inside a furnace in which something is being consumed. Letting his head fall sideways towards Queenie, he seemed to invite her into his mood. 'The way things come out is sometimes funny,' he said to Justin, 'if you know what I mean.'

'No, I don't,' Justin said stonily.

'I bet your sister does.'

'You didn't know what I meant. Anything I may have said about your genius I do absolutely retract.'

'Look here, I'm sorry,' Robinson said, 'I probably took you up all wrong.'

'On the contrary: the mistake was mine.'

'You know, it's funny about your sister: I never can realize she can't hear. She seems so much one of the party. Would she be fond of children?'

'You mean, why did she not marry?'

'Good God, no—I only had an idea. . . .'

Justin went on: 'There was some fellow once, but I

310

never heard more of him. You'd have to be very
oncoming, I daresay, to make any way with a deaf
girl.'

'No, I meant my children,' said Robinson. He had
got up, and he took from his mantelpiece two of the
photographs in silver frames. With these he walked
down the room to Queenie, who received them with
her usual eagerness and immediately turned with
them to the light. Justin saw his sister's profile bent
forward in study and saw Robinson standing above
her leaning against the window frame. When Robinson met an upward look from Queenie he nodded and
touched himself on the chest. 'I can see that—aren't
they very like you?' she said. He pointed to one picture
then held up ten fingers, then to the other and held up
eight. 'The fair little fellow's more like you, the bold
one. The dark one has more the look of a girl—but he
will grow up manly, I daresay—'. With this she went
back to the photographs: she did not seem anxious to
give them up, and Robinson made no movement to
take them from her—with Queenie the act of looking
was always reflective and slow. To Justin the two
silhouettes against the window looked wedded and
welded by the dark. 'They are both against me,' Justin
thought. 'She does not hear with her ears, he does not
hear with his mind. No wonder they can communi-
cate.'

'It's a wonder,' she said, 'that you have no little
girl.'

Robinson went back for another photograph—but
standing still with a doubtful look at Queenie, he
passed his hand, as though sadly expunging something, backwards and forwards across the glass. 'She's
quite right; we did have a girl,' he said. 'But I don't
know how to tell her the kid's dead.'

Sixty miles away, the Major was making his last round through the orchards before shutting up the house. By this time the bronze-green orchard dusk was intense; the clumped curves of the fruit were hardly to be distinguished among the leaves. The brilliance of evening, in which he had watched Emma driving away, was now gone from the sky. Now and then in the grass his foot knocked a dropped apple—he would sigh, stoop rather stiffly, pick up the apple, examine it with the pad of his thumb for bruises and slip it, tenderly as though it had been an egg, into a baggy pocket of his tweed coat. This was not a good apple year. There was something standardized, uncomplaining about the Major's movements—you saw a tall, unmilitary-looking man with a stoop and a thinnish, drooping moustache. He often wore a slight frown, of doubt or preoccupation. This frown had intensified in the last months.

As he approached the house he heard the wireless talking, and saw one lamp at the distant end of the drawing-room where his aunt sat. At once, the picture broke up—she started, switched off the wireless and ran down the room to the window. You might have thought the room had burst into flames. 'Quick!' she cried. 'Oh, gracious, quick!—I believe it's the telephone.'

The telephone was at the other side of the house—before he got there he heard the bell ringing. He put his hands in his pockets to keep the apples from bumping as he legged it rapidly down the corridor. When he unhooked on his wife's voice he could not help saying haggardly: 'You all right?'

'Of course. I just thought I'd say good night.'

'That was nice of you,' he said, puzzled. 'How is the car running?'

'Like a bird,' she said in a singing voice. 'How are you all?'

'Well, I was just coming in; Aunt Fran's in the drawing-room listening to something on the wireless, and I made the children turn in half an hour ago.'

'You'll go up to them?'

'Yes, I was just going.' For a moment they both paused on the line, then he said: 'Where have you got to now?'

'I'm at T— now, at the hotel in the square.'

'At T—? Aren't you taking it rather fast?'

'It's a lovely night; it's an empty road.'

'Don't be too hard on the car, she—'

'Oh, I know,' she said, in the singing voice again. 'At C— I did try to stop, but there was a terrible crowd there: dog racing. So I came on. Darling . . . ?'

'Yes?'

'It's a lovely night, isn't it?'

'Yes, I was really quite sorry to come in. I shall shut up the house now, then go up to the children; then I expect I'll have a word or two with Aunt Fran.'

'I see. Well, I'd better be pushing on.'

'They'll be sitting up for you, won't they?'

'Surely,' said Emma quickly.

'Thank you for ringing up, dear: it was thoughtful of you.'

'I was thinking about you.'

He did not seem to hear this. 'Well, take care of yourself. Have a nice time.'

'Good night,' she said. But the Major had hung up.

In the drawing-room Aunt Fran had not gone back to the wireless. Beside the evening fire lit for her age, she sat rigid, face turned to the door, plucking round and round the rings on her left hand. She wore a foulard dress, net jabot and boned-up collar, of the type ladies wear to dine in private hotels. In the lamp-light her waxy features appeared blurred, even effaced. The drawing-room held a crowd of chintz-covered chairs, inlaid tables, and wool-worked stools; very little in it was antique, but nothing was strikingly up to date. There were cabinets of not rare china, and more blue-and-white plates, in metal clamps, hung in lines up the walls between water-colours. A vase of pink roses arranged by the governess already dropped petals on the piano. In one corner stood a harp with two broken strings—when a door slammed or one made a sudden movement this harp gave out a faint vibration or twang. The silence for miles around this obscure country house seemed to gather inside the folds of the curtains and to dilute the indoor air like a mist. This room Emma liked too little to touch already felt the touch of decay; it threw lifeless reflections into the two mirrors—the walls were green. Aunt Fran's body was stranded here like some object on the bed of a pool that has run dry. The magazine that she had been looking at had slipped from her lap to the black fur rug.

As her nephew appeared in the drawing-room door Aunt Fran fixed him urgently with her eyes. 'Nothing wrong?'

'No, no—that was Emma.'

'What's happened?'

'Nothing. She rang up to say good night.'

'But she had said good night,' said Aunt Fran in her troubled way. 'She said good night to us when she was in the car. You remember, it was nearly night when she left. It seemed late to be starting to go so far. She had the whole afternoon, but she kept putting off, putting off. She seemed to me undecided up to the very last.'

The Major turned his back on his aunt and began to unload his pockets, carefully placing the apples, two by two, in a row along the chiffonier. 'Still, it's nice for her having this trip,' he said.

'There was a time in the afternoon,' said Aunt Fran, 'when I thought she was going to change her mind. However, she's there now—did you say?'

'Almost,' he said, 'not quite. Will you be all right if I go and shut up the house? And I said I would look in on the girls.'

'Suppose the telephone rings?'

'I don't think it will, again. The exchange will be closing, for one thing.'

'This afternoon,' said Aunt Fran, 'it rang four times.'

She heard him going from room to room, unfolding and barring the heavy shutters and barring and chaining the front door. She could begin to feel calmer now that the house was a fortress against the wakeful night. 'Hi!' she called, 'don't forget the window in here'— looking back over her shoulder into the muslin curtains that seemed to crepitate with dark air. So he came back, with his flat, unexpectant step. 'I'm not cold,' she said, 'but I don't like dark coming in.'

He shuttered the window. 'I'll be down in a minute.'

'Then we might sit together?'

'Yes, Aunt Fran: certainly.'

The children, who had been talking, dropped their voices when they heard their father's step on the stairs. Their two beds creaked as they straightened themselves and lay silent, in social, expectant attitudes. Their room smelled of toothpaste; the white presses blotted slowly into the white walls. The window was open, the blind up, so in here darkness was incomplete—obscured, the sepia picture of the Good Shepherd hung over the mantelpiece. 'It's all right,' they said, 'we are quite awake.' So the Major came round and halted between the two beds. 'Sit on mine,' said Di nonchalantly. 'It's my turn to have a person to-night.'

'Why did Mother ring up?' said Vivie, scrambling up on her pillow.

'Now how on earth did *you* know?'

'We knew by your voice—we couldn't hear what you said. We were only at the top of the stairs. Why did she?'

'To tell me to tell you to be good.'

'She's said that,' said Vivie, impatient. 'What did she say truly?'

'Just good night.'

'Oh. Is she there?'

'Where?'

'Where she said she was going to.'

'Not quite—nearly.'

'Goodness!' Di said; 'it seems years since she went.' The two children lay cryptic and still. Then Di went on: 'Do you know what Aunt Fran said because Mother went away without any stockings?'

'No,' said the Major, 'and never mind.'

'Oh, *I* don't mind,' Di said, 'I just heard.' 'And I heard,' said Vivie: she could be felt opening her eyes wide, and the Major could just see, on the pillow, an implacable miniature of his wife's face. Di went on: 'She's so frightened something will happen.'

'Aunt Fran is?'

'She's always frightened of that.'

'She is very fond of us all.'

'Oh,' burst out Vivie, 'but Mother likes things to happen. She was whistling all the time she was packing up. Can't *we* have a treat tomorrow?'

'Mother'll be back tomorrow.'

'But *can't* we have a treat?'

'We'll see; we'll ask Mother,' the Major said.

'Oh yes, but suppose she didn't come back?'

'Look, it's high time you two went to sleep.'

'We can't: we've got all sorts of ideas. . . . *You* say something, Daddy. Tell us something. Invent.'

'Say what?' said the Major.

'Oh goodness,' Vivie said; '*something*. What do you say to Mother?'

He went downstairs to Aunt Fran with their dissatisfied kisses stamped on his cheek. When he had gone Di fanned herself with the top of her sheet. 'What makes him so disappointed, do you know?'

'I know, he thinks about the war.'

But it was Di who, after the one question, unlocked all over and dropped plumb asleep. It was Vivie who, turning over and over, watched in the sky behind the cross of the window the tingling particles of the white dark, who heard the moth between the two windowsashes, who fancied she heard apples drop in the grass. One arbitrary line only divided this child from the animal: all her senses stood up, wanting to run the night. She swung her legs out of bed and pressed the soles of her feet on the cool floor. She got right up and stepped out of her nightdress and set out to walk the house in her skin. From each room she went into the human order seemed to have lapsed—discovered by sudden light, the chairs and tables seemed set round for a mouse's party on a gigantic scale. She stood for some time outside the drawing-room door and heard the unliving voices of the Major and aunt. She looked through the ajar door to the kitchen and saw a picked bone and a teapot upon the table and a maid lumped mute in a man's arms. She attempted the

317

front door, but did not dare to touch the chain: she could not get out of the house. She returned to the schoolroom, drawing her brows together, and straddled the rocking-horse they had not ridden for years. The furious bumping of the rockers woke the canaries under their cover: they set up a wiry springing in their cage. She dismounted, got out the box of chalks and began to tattoo her chest, belly, and thighs with stars and snakes, red, yellow, and blue. Then, taking the box of chalks with her, she went to her mother's room for a look in the long glass—in front of this she attempted to tattoo her behind. After this she bent right down and squinted, upside down between her legs, at the bedroom—the electric light over the dressing-table poured into the vacantly upturned mirror and on to Emma's left-behind silver things. The anarchy she felt all through the house tonight made her, when she had danced in front of the long glass, climb up to dance on the big bed. The springs bounced her higher and higher; chalk-dust flew from her body on to the fleece of the blankets, on to the two cold pillows that she was trampling out of their place. The bed-castors lunged, under her springing, over the threadbare pink bridal carpet of Emma's room.

Attacked by the castors, the chandelier in the drawing-room tinkled sharply over Aunt Fran's head.

She at once raised her eyes to the ceiling. 'Something has got in,' she said calmly—and, rising, made for the drawing-room door. By reflex, the Major rose to stop her: he sighed and put his weak whiskey down. 'Never mind,' he said, 'Aunt Fran. It's probably nothing. I'll go.'

Whereupon, his Aunt Fran wheeled round on him with her elbows up like a bird's wings. Her wax features sprang into stony prominence. 'It's never me,

never me, never me! Whatever *I* see, whatever I hear
it's "nothing", though the house might fall down. You
keep everything back from me. No one speaks the
truth to me but the man on the wireless. Always things
being said on the telephone, always things being moved
about, always Emma off at the end of the house singing, always the children hiding away. I am never told,
never told, never told. I get the one answer, "nothing".
I am expected to wait here. No one comes near the
drawing-room. I am never allowed to go and see!'

'If that's how you feel,' he said, 'do certainly go.'
He thought: it's all right, I locked the house.

So it was Aunt Fran's face, with the forehead
lowered, that came by inches round Emma's door. She
appeared to present her forehead as a sort of a buffer,
obliquely looked from below it, did not speak. Her
glance, arriving gradually at its object, took in the
child and the whole room. Vivie paused on the bed,
transfixed, breathless, her legs apart. Her heart
thumped; her ears drummed; her cheeks burned. To
break up the canny and comprehensive silence she
said loudly: 'I am all over snakes.'

'So this is what . . .' Aunt Fran said. 'So this is
what . . .

'I'll get off this bed, if you don't like.'

'The bed you were born in,' said Aunt Fran.

Vivie did not know what to do; she jumped off the
bed saying: 'No one told me not to.'

'Do you not know what is wicked?' said Aunt Fran
—but with no more than estranged curiosity. She
approached and began to try to straighten the bed,
her unused hands making useless passes over the surface, brushing chalk-dust deeper into the fleece. All of
a sudden, Vivie appeared to feel some majestic efflu-
ence from her Aunt's person: she lagged round the bed

319

to look at the stooping, set face, at the mouth held in a curve like a dead smile, at the veins in the downcast eyelids and the backs of the hands. Aunt Fran did not hurry her ceremonial fumbling; she seemed to exalt the moment that was so fully hers. She picked a pillow up by its frill and placed it high on the bolster.

'That's mother's pillow,' said Vivie.

'Did you say your prayers tonight?'

'Oh, *yes.*'

'They didn't defend you. Better say them again. Kneel down and say to Our Lord—'

'In my skin?'

Aunt Fran looked directly at, then away from, Vivie's body, as though for the first time. She drew the eiderdown from the foot of the bed and made a half-blind sweep at Vivie with it, saying: 'Wrap up, wrap up.' 'Oh, they'll come off—my snakes!' said Vivie, backing away. But Aunt Fran, as though the child were on fire, put into motion an extraordinary strength —she rolled, pressed and pounded Vivie up in the eiderdown until only the prisoner's dark eyes, so like her mother's, were left free to move wildly outside the great sausage, of padded taffeta, pink.

Aunt Fran, embracing the sausage firmly, repeated: 'Now say to Our Lord—'

Shutting the door of her own bedroom, Aunt Fran felt her heart beat. The violence of the stranger within her ribs made her sit down on the ottoman—meanwhile, her little clock on the mantelpiece loudly and, it seemed to her, slowly ticked. Her window was shut, but the pressure of night silence made itself felt behind the blind, on the glass.

Round the room, on ledges and brackets, stood the fetishes she travelled through life with. They were mementoes—photos in little warped frames, musty, round straw boxes, china kittens, palm crosses, the three Japanese monkeys, *bambini*, a Lincoln Imp, a merry-thought pen-wiper, an ivory spinning-wheel from Cologne. From these objects the original virtue had by now almost evaporated. These gifts' givers, known on her lonely journey, were by now faint as their photographs: she no longer knew, now, where anyone was. All the more, her nature clung to these objects that moved with her slowly towards the dark.

Her room, the room of a person tolerated, by now gave off the familiar smell of herself—the smell of the old. A little book wedged the mirror at the angle she liked. When she was into her ripplecloth dressing-gown she brushed and plaited her hair and took out her teeth. She wound her clock and, with hand still trembling a little, lighted her own candle on the commode, then switched off her nephew's electric light. The room contracted round the crocus of flame as she knelt down slowly beside her bed—but while she said the Lord's Prayer, she could not help listening, wondering what kept the Major so long downstairs. She never felt free to pray till she had heard the last door shut, till she could relax her watch on the house. She never could pray until they were *all* prostrate—loaned for at least some hours to innocence, sealed by the darkness over their lids.

Tonight she could not attempt to lift up her heart. She could, however, abase herself, and she abased herself for them all. The evil of the moment down in the drawing-room, the moment when she had cried, 'It is never me!' clung like a smell to her, so closely that she had been eager to get her clothes off, and did not like, even now, to put her hands to her face.

Who shall be their judge? Not I.

The blood of the world is poisoned, feels Aunt Fran, with her forehead over the eiderdown. Not a pure drop comes out at any prick—yes, even the heroes shed black blood. The solitary watcher retreats step by step from his post—who shall stem the black tide coming in? There are no more children: the children are born knowing. The shadow rises up the cathedral tower, up the side of the pure hill. There is not even the past: our memories share with us the infected zone; not a memory does not lead up to this. Each moment is everywhere, it holds the war in its crystal; there is no elsewhere, no other place. Not a benediction falls on this apart house of the Major; the enemy is within it, creeping about. Each heart here falls to the enemy.

So this is what goes on. . . .

Emma flying away—and not saying why, or where. And to wrap the burning child up did not put out the fire. You cannot look at the sky without seeing the shadow, the men destroying each other. What is the matter tonight—is there a battle? This is a threatened night.

Aunt Fran sags on her elbows; her knees push desperately in the woolly rug. She cannot even repent; she is capable of no act; she is undone. She gets up and eats a biscuit, and looks at the little painting of Mont Blanc on the little easel beside her clock. She still does not hear the Major come up to bed.

Queenie understood that the third child, the girl, was dead: she gave back the photograph rather quickly, as though unbearable sadness emanated from it. Justin, however, came down the room and looked at the photograph over Robinson's shoulder—at the

rather vulgar, frank, blonde little face. He found it
hard to believe that a child of Robinson's should have
chosen the part of death. He then went back to the
table and picked up, with a jerky effrontery, the photographs of the two little boys. 'Do they never come
here?' he said. 'You have plenty of room for them.'

'I daresay they will; I mean to fix up something. Just
now they're at Greystones,' Robinson said—he then
looked quite openly at the clock.

'With their mother?' Justin said, in a harsh imper-
tinent voice.

'Yes, with my wife.'

'So you keep up the two establishments?'

Even Robinson glanced at Justin with some surprise.
'If you call it that,' he said indifferently. 'I rather
landed myself with this place, really—as a matter of
fact, when I moved in it looked as though things might
work out differently. First I stopped where you are, at
the hotel, but I do like to have a place of my own. One
feels freer, for one thing.'

'There's a lot in that,' said Justin, with an oblique
smile. 'Our local ladies think you keep a Bluebeard's
castle up here.'

'What, corpses?' Robinson said, surprised.

'Oh yes, they think you're the devil.'

'Who, me?' replied Robinson, busy replacing photographs on the mantelpiece. 'That's really very funny:
I'd no idea. I suppose they may think I've been pretty
slack—but I'm no good at teafights, as a matter of
fact. But I can't see what else can be eating them.
What ought I to do, then? Throw a party here? I will
if your sister'll come and pour out tea—but I don't
think I've really got enough chairs. . . . I hope,' he
added, looking at Queenie, '*she* doesn't think it's not
all above board here?'

323

'You're forgetting again: she misses the talk, poor girl.'

'She doesn't look very worried.'

'I daresay she's seldom been happier. She's built up quite a romance about this house. She has a world to herself—I could envy her.'

Robinson contrived to give the impression that he did not wish to have Queenie discussed—partly because he owned her, he understood her, partly because he wished to discuss nothing: it really was time for his guests to go. Though he was back again in his armchair, regard for time appeared in his attitude. Justin could not fail to connect this with the telephone and the smile that had not completely died. It became clear, staringly clear, that throughout the evening his host had been no more than marking time. This made Justin say 'Yes' (in a loud, pertinacious voice), 'this evening's been quite an event for us. Your house has more than its legend, Robinson; it has really remarkable character. However, all good things—'. Stiff with anger, he stood up.

'Must you?' said Robinson, rising. 'I'm so sorry.'

Lighting-up time, fixed by Nature, had passed. The deaf woman, from her place in the window, had been watching lights of cars bend over the hill. Turning with the main road, that had passed the foot of the mountains, each car now drove a shaft of extreme brilliance through the dark below Robinson's pampas-grass. Slipping, dropping with a rush past the gate, illuminating the dust on the opposite wall, car after car vanished after its light—there was suddenly quite a gust of them, as though the mountain country, before sleeping, had stood up and shaken them from its folds. The release of movement excited Queenie—that and the beat of light's wings on her face. She turned round very reluctantly as Justin approached and began to make signs to her.

'Why, does Mr. Robinson want us to go?' she said.

'That's the last thing I want!' shouted Robinson.

('She can't hear you.')

'Christ . . .' said Robinson, rattled. He turned the lights on—the three, each with a different face of despair, looked at each other across the exposed room, across the tea-tray on the circular table and the superb leather backs of the chairs. 'My brother thinks we've kept you too long,' she said—and as a lady she looked a little shaken, for the first time unsure of herself. Robinson would not for worlds have had this happen; he strode over and took and nursed her elbow, which tensed then relaxed gently inside the muslin sleeve. He saw, outdoors, his window cast on the pampas, saw the whole appearance of shattered night. She looked for reassurance into his face, and he saw the delicate lines in hers.

'And look how late it's got, Mr. Robinson!'

'It's not that,' he said in his naturally low voice, 'but—'

A car pulled up at the gate. Alarmed by the lit window it cut its lights off and could be felt to crouch there, attentive, docile, cautious, waiting to turn in. 'Your friend is arriving,' Justin said.

On that last lap of her drive, the eighteen miles of flat road along the base of the mountains, the last tingling phase of darkness had settled down. Grassy sharpness passed from the mountains' outline, the patches of firs, the gleam of watery ditch. The west sky had gradually drunk its yellow and the ridged heights that towered over her right hand became immobile cataracts, sensed not seen. Animals rising out of the ditches turned to Emma's headlamps green lamp-eyes. She felt the shudder of night, the contracting bodies of things. The quick air sang in her ears; she drove very fast. At the cross-roads above Robinson's town she pulled round in a wide swerve: she saw the lemon lights of the town strung along under the black trees, the pavements and the pale, humble houses below her in a faint, mysterious glare as she slipped down the funnel of hill to Robinson's gate. (The first white gate on the left, you cannot miss it, he'd said.) From the road she peered up the lawn and saw, between pampas-tufts, three people upright in his lit room. So she pulled up and switched her lights and her engine off and sat crouching in her crouching car in the dark—night began to creep up her bare legs. Now the glass porch sprang into prominence like a lantern—she saw people stiffly saying goodbye. Down the drive came a man and woman almost in flight; not addressing each other, not looking back—putting the back of a fist to her mouth quickly Emma checked the uprush of an uncertain laugh. She marked a lag in the steps—turning their heads quickly the man and woman looked with involuntary straightness into the car, while her eyes were glued to their silhouettes. The two turned down to the town and she turned in at the gate.

Farouche, with her tentative little swagger and childish, pleading air of delinquency, Emma came to a halt in Robinson's living-room. He had pulled down the blind. She kept recoiling and blinking and drawing her fingers over her eyes, till Robinson turned off the top light. 'Is that that?' There was only the reading-lamp.

She rested her shoulder below his and grappled their enlaced fingers closer together as though trying to draw calmness from him. Standing against him, close up under his height, she held her head up and began to look round the room. 'You're whistling something,' she said, after a moment or two.

'I only mean, take your time.'

'Why, am I nervous?' she said.

'Darling, you're like a bat in out of the night. I told you not to come along too fast.'

'I see now, I came too early,' she said. 'Why didn't you tell me you had a party? Who were they? What were they doing here?'

'Oh, they're just people in this place. He's a bit screwy and she's deaf, but I like them, as a matter of fact.'

'They're mackintoshy sort of people,' she said. 'But I always thought you lived all alone. . . . Is there anyone else in the house now?'

'Not a mouse,' said Robinson, without change of expression. 'My housekeeper's gone off for the night.'

'I see,' said Emma. 'Will you give me a drink?'

She sat down where Justin had just been sitting, and, bending forward with a tremulous frown, began to brush ash from the arm of the chair. You could feel the whole of her hesitate. Robinson, without hesitation, came and sat easily on the arm of the chair from which she had brushed the ash. 'It's sometimes funny,' he said, 'when people drop in like that. "My God," I thought when I saw them, "what an evening to choose."' He slipped his hand down between the brown velvet cushion and Emma's spine, then spread the broad of his hand against the small of her back. Looking kindly down at her closed eyelids he went on: 'However, it all went off all right. Oh, and there's one thing I'd like to tell you—that chap called me a genius.'

'How would he know?' said Emma, opening her eyes.

'We never got that clear. I was rather out of my depth. His sister was deaf . . .' here Robinson paused, bent down and passed his lips absently over Emma's forehead. 'Or did I tell you that?'

'Yes, you told me that. . . . Is it true that this house is blue?'

'You'll see tomorrow.'

'There'll hardly be time, darling; I shall hardly see this house in the daylight. I must go on to—where I'm supposed to be.'

'At any rate, I'm glad that was all O.K. They're not on the telephone, where you're going?'

'No, it's all right; they're not on the telephone. . . . *You'll* have to think of something that went wrong with my car.'

'That will all keep,' said Robinson. 'Here you are.'

'Yes, here I am.' She added: 'The night was lovely,' speaking more sadly than she knew. Yes, here she was, being settled down to as calmly as he might have settled down to a meal. Her naïvety as a lover . . . She could not have said, for instance, how much the authoritative male room—the electric clock, the sideboard, the unlit grate, the cold of the leather chairs—put, at every moment when he did not touch her, a gulf between her and him. She turned her head to the window. 'I smell flowers.'

'Yes, I've got three flower-beds.'

'Darling, for a minute could we go out?'

She moved from his touch and picked up Queenie's tea-tray and asked if she could put it somewhere else. Holding the tray (and given countenance by it) she halted in front of the photographs. 'Oh . . .' she said.

'Yes. Why?' 'I wish in a way you hadn't got any children.'

'I don't see why I shouldn't have: you have.'

'Yes, I . . . But Vivie and Di are not so much *like* children—'

'If they're like you,' he said, 'those two will be having a high old time, with the cat away—'

'Oh darling, I'm not the cat.'

In the kitchen (to put the tray down) she looked round: it shone with tiling and chromium and there seemed to be switches in every place. 'What a whole lot of gadgets you have,' she said. 'Look at all those electric . . .' 'Yes, I like them.' 'They must cost a lot of money. My kitchen's all over blacklead and smoke and hooks. My cook would hate a kitchen like this.'

'I always forget that you have a cook.' He picked up an electric torch and they went out. Going along the side of the house, Robinson played a mouse of light on the wall. 'Look, really blue.' But she only looked absently. 'Yes—But have I been wrong to come?' He led her off the gravel on to the lawn, till they reached the edge of a bed of stocks. Then he firmly said: 'That's for you to say, my dear girl.'

'I know it's hardly a question—I hardly know you, do I?'

'We'll be getting to know each other,' said Robinson.

After a minute she let go of his hand and knelt down abruptly beside the flowers: she made movements like scooping the scent up and laving her face in it—he, meanwhile, lighted a cigarette and stood looking down. 'I'm glad you like my garden,' he said. 'You feel like getting fond of the place?'

'You say you forget that I have a cook.'

'Look, sweet, if you can't get that off your mind

you'd better get in your car and go straight home. . . .
But you will.'

'Aunt Fran's so old, too old; it's not nice. And the
Major keeps thinking about the war. And the children
don't think I am good; I regret that.'

'You have got a nerve,' he said, 'but I love that.
You're with me. Aren't you with me?—Come out of
that flower-bed.'

They walked to the brow of the lawn; the soft
feather-plumes of the pampas rose up a little over her
head as she stood by him overlooking the road. She
shivered. 'What are all those trees?' 'The demesne—
I know they burnt down the castle years ago. The
demesne's great for couples.' 'What's in there?'
'Nothing, I don't think; just the ruin, a lake. . . .'

'I wish—'

'Now, what?'

'I wish we had more time.'

'Yes: we don't want to stay out all night.'

So taught, she smothered the last of her little wishes
for consolation. Her shyness of further words between
them became extreme; she was becoming frightened
of Robinson's stern, experienced delicacy on the subject of love. Her adventure became the quiet practice
with him. The adventure (even, the pilgrimage) died
at its root, in the childish part of her mind. When he
had headed her off the cytherean terrain—the leaf-
drowned castle ruin, the lake—she thought for a
minute he had broken her heart, and she knew now
he had broken her fairytale. He seemed content—
having lit a new cigarette—to wait about in his garden
for a few minutes longer: not poetry but a sort of
tactile wisdom came from the firmness, lawn, under
their feet. The white gateposts, the boles of beeches
above the dust-whitened wall were just seen in re-

flected light from the town. There was no moon, but dry, tense, translucent darkness: no dew fell.

Justin went with his sister to her door in the square. Quickly, and in their necessary silence, they crossed the grass under the limes. Here a dark window reflected one of the few lamps, there a shadow crossed a lit blind, and voices of people moving under the trees made a reverberation in the box of the square. Queenie let herself in; Justin heard the heavy front door drag shut slowly across the mat. She had not expected him to come in, and he did not know if she shared his feeling of dissonance, or if she recoiled from shock, or if she were shocked at all. Quitting the square at once, he took the direct way to his hotel in the main street. He went in at the side door, past the bar in which he so often encountered Robinson.

In his small, harsh room he looked first at his bed. He looked, as though out of a pit of sickness, at his stack of books on the mantelpiece. He writhed his head round sharply, threw off his coat and began to unknot his tie. Meanwhile he beat round, in the hot light, for some crack of outlet from his constriction. It was at his dressing-table, for he had no other, that he began and ended his letter to Robinson: the mirror screwed to the dressing-table constituted a witness to this task—whenever his look charged up it met his own reared head, the flush heightening on the bridge of the nose and forehead, the neck from which as though for an execution, the collar had been taken away.

My dear Robinson: Our departure from your house (Bellevue, I think?) tonight was so awkwardly late, and at the last so hurried, that I had inadequate time in which to thank you for your hospitality to my sister and to myself. That we exacted this hospitality does not make its merit, on your part, less. Given the inconvenience we so clearly caused you, your forbearance with us was past praise. So much so that (as you may be glad to hear) my sister does not appear to realize how very greatly we were *de trop*. In my own case—which is just—the same cannot be said. I am conscious that, in spite of her disability, she did at least prove a less wearisome guest than I.

My speculations and queries must, to your mind, equally seem absurd. This evening's fiasco has been definitive: I think it better our acquaintance should close. You will find it in line with my usual awkwardness that I should choose to state this decision of mine at all. Your indifference to the matter I cannot doubt. My own lack of indifference must make its last weak exhibition in this letter—in which, if you have fine enough nostrils (which I doubt), every sentence will almost certainly stink. In attempting to know you I have attempted to enter, and to comport myself in, what might be called an area under your jurisdiction. If my inefficacies appeared to you ludicrous, my curiosities (as in one special instance tonight) appeared more—revolting. I could gauge (even before the postscript outside your gate) how profoundly I had offended you. Had we either of us been gentlemen, the incident might have passed off with less harm.

My attempts to know you I have disposed of already. My wish that you should know me has been, from the first, ill found. You showed yourself party to it in no sense, and the trick I played on myself I need not discuss. I acted and spoke (with regard to you) upon assumptions you were not prepared to warrant. You cannot fail to misunderstand what I mean when I say that a year ago this might not have happened to me. But—the assumptions on which I acted, Robinson, are becoming more general in a driven world than you yet (or may ever) know. The extremity to which we are each driven must be the warrant for what we do and say.

My extraordinary divagation towards you might be said to be, I suppose, an accident of this summer. But there are no accidents. I have the fine (yes) fine mind's love of the fine plume, and I meet no fine plumes down my own narrow street. Also, in this place (birthplace) you interposed your solidity between me and what might have been the full effects of an exacerbating return. In fact, you had come to constitute for me a very genuine holiday. As things are, my five remaining days here will have to be seen out. I shall hope not to meet you, but must fear much of the trap-like size of this town. (You need not, as I mean to, avoid the hotel bar.) Should I, however, fail to avoid you, I shall again, I suppose, have to owe much, owe any face I keep, to your never-failing imperviousness. Understand that it will be against my wish that I reopen this one-sided account.

I wish you good night. Delicacy does not deter me from adding that I feel my good wish to be super-fluous. I imagine that, incapable of being haunted, you are incapable of being added to. Tomorrow (I understand) you will feel fine, but you will not know any more about love. If the being outside your gate came with a question, it is possible that she should have come to me. If I had even seen her she might not go on rending my heart. As it is, as you are, I perhaps denounce you as much on her behalf as my own. Not trying to understand, you at least cannot misunder-stand the mood and hour in which I write. As regards my sister, please do not discontinue what has been your even kindness to her: she might be perplexed. She has nothing to fear, I think. Accept, my dear Robinson (without irony) my kind regards,

J. C.

Justin, trembling, smote a stamp on this letter. Going down as he was, in the hall he unhooked his mackintosh and put it over his shirt. It was well past midnight; the street, empty, lay in dusty reaches under the few lamps. Between the shutters his step raised an echo; the cold of the mountains had come down; two cats in his path unclinched and shot off into the dark. On his way to the letter-box he was walking towards Bellevue; on his way back he still heard the drunken woman sobbing against the telegraph pole. The box would not be cleared till tomorrow noon.

Queenie forgot Justin till next day. The house in which her rooms were was so familiar that she went upstairs without a pause in the dark. Crossing her sitting-room she smelled oil from the cooker behind the screen: she went through an arch to the cubicle where she slept. She was happy. Inside her sphere of silence that not a word clouded, the spectacle of the evening at Bellevue reigned. Contemplative, wishless, almost without an 'I', she unhooked her muslin dress at the wrists and waist, stepped from the dress and began to take down her hair. Still in the dark, with a dreaming sureness of habit, she dropped hairpins into the heart-shaped tray.

This was the night she knew she would find again. It had stayed living under a film of time. On just such a summer night, once only, she had walked with a lover in the demesne. His hand, like Robinson's, had been on her elbow, but she had guided him, not he her, because she had better eyes in the dark. They had gone down walks already deadened with moss, under the weight of July trees; they had felt the then fresh aghast ruin totter above them; there was a moonless sky. Beside the lake they sat down, and while her hand brushed the ferns in the cracks of the stone seat emanations of kindness passed from him to her. The subtle deaf girl had made the transposition of this nothing or everything into an everything—the delicate deaf girl that the man could not speak to and was afraid to touch. She who, then so deeply contented, kept in her senses each frond and breath of that night, never saw him again and had soon forgotten his face. That had been twenty years ago, till tonight when it was now. Tonight it was Robinson who, guided by Queenie down leaf tunnels, took the place on the stone seat by the lake.

The rusted gates of the castle were at the end of the square. Queenie, in her bed facing the window, lay with her face turned sideways, smiling, one hand lightly against her cheek.